Praise for
SAGA OF THE UNFATED

"*A Fate Inked in Blood* is THE must-read fantasy. . . . I could not put this book down!"
—Jennifer L. Armentrout, *USA Today* bestselling author of *From Blood and Ash*

"This book completely transports you, and I was instantly hooked! Danielle's dark fantasy world is woven together with rich history and lore, and the angst between the two main characters kept me on the edge of my seat. I am so excited to see what comes next!"
—Raven Kennedy, internationally bestselling author of *Gild*

"Captivating and sexy . . . With a fierce heroine and a smoldering hero, *A Fate Inked in Blood* is everything you want in a fantasy romance."
—Elise Kova, *New York Times* bestselling author of *Arcana Academy*

"With a forbidden romance that burns as hot as Tyr's magical fire, *A Fate Inked in Blood* will be your newest fantasy obsession. Beautifully brutal, action-packed, and full of tension, I couldn't turn the pages of this epic tale fast enough."
—Kerri Maniscalco, #1 *New York Times* bestselling author of *Throne of the Fallen*

"This is Danielle L. Jensen at her best. . . . A delicious fantasy romance that was completely unputdownable!"
—Katee Robert, *New York Times* bestselling author of *Neon Gods*

"In a rich world inspired by Norse mythology, *A Fate Inked in Blood* is an action-packed story with a fierce protagonist, an irresistible hero, and a scorching romance. Bridge Kingdom fans will love this thrilling new addition to Jensen's catalogue."

—Lexi Ryan, #1 *New York Times* bestselling author of *These Hollow Vows*

"No one does epic and sexy like Jensen. She has created a brutally sexy world filled with magic, prophecies, and Norse lore that will keep you flipping the pages well into the night."

—Olivia Wildenstein, *USA Today* bestselling author of *House of Beating Wings*

"Impossible to put down, *A Fate Inked in Blood* is a fresh take on the shield-maiden myth and the romantasy genre. This series starter is sure to enrapture fans of Sarah J. Maas and Rebecca Yarros."

—*Booklist*

"Jensen [gives] readers a glimpse into a cold, violent society, but she doesn't skimp on the heat. This reads like the love child of Genevieve Gornichec's *The Witch's Heart* and Sarah J. Maas's *A Court of Silver Flames*. Romantasy fans will be ravenous for more."

—*Library Journal*

"Heated battles and steamy interludes keep the pages turning."

—*Publishers Weekly*

"As someone who read this right after devouring book one, I can honestly say this sequel delivered everything I wanted—more action, more heartbreak, more twists, and more depth. It's a Nordic-inspired fantasy full of strong women, complicated love, and fate-defying choices. If you're into stories with Viking vibes, emotional wreckage, and a plot that keeps you guessing until the end—*A Curse Carved in Bone* is a must-read."

—*BookTrib*

"*A Curse Carved in Bone* is a fierce, feminist fantasy that embraces darkness without surrendering to it. Jensen doesn't shy away from pain, betrayal, or moral ambiguity—but she also doesn't abandon hope. This is a story about carving your own fate into the bone of the world, no matter who tries to bind you. Freya's journey will resonate with readers who want heroines forged in flame, heroes who earn redemption, and stories where love is as much about freedom as it is about fire."

—*The Bookish Elf*

BY DANIELLE L. JENSEN

THE MALEDICTION SERIES

Stolen Songbird
Hidden Huntress
Warrior Witch
The Broken Ones

DARK SHORES SERIES

Dark Shores
Dark Skies
Tarnished Empire
Gilded Serpent
Scorched Earth

THE BRIDGE KINGDOM SERIES

The Bridge Kingdom
The Traitor Queen
The Inadequate Heir
The Endless War
The Twisted Throne
The Tempest Blade

SAGA OF THE UNFATED

A Fate Inked in Blood
A Curse Carved in Bone

A CURSE CARVED IN BONE

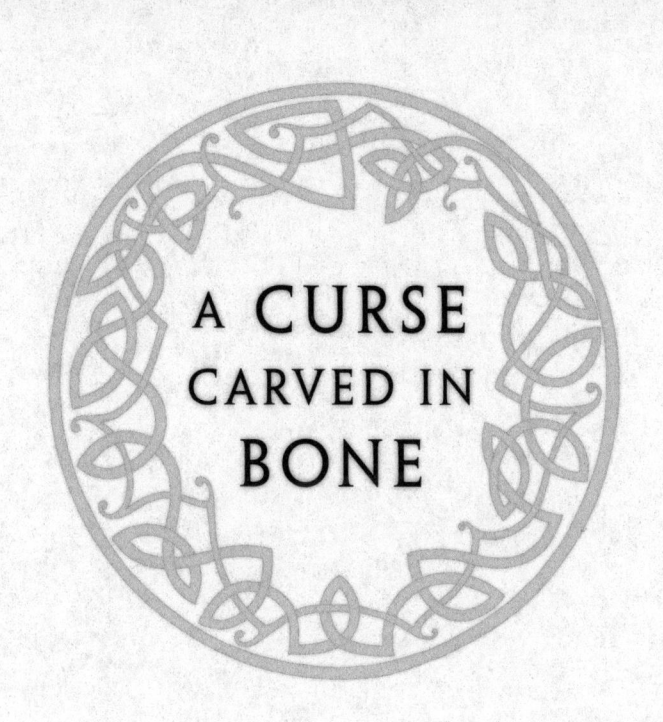

A CURSE CARVED IN BONE

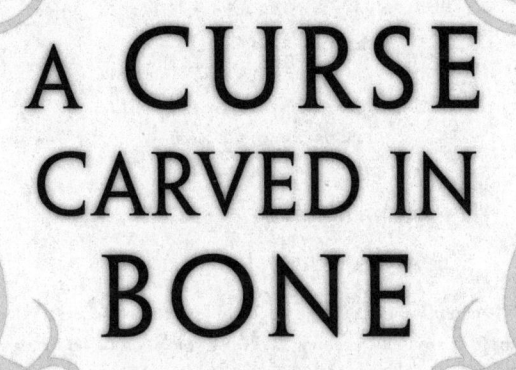

SAGA OF THE UNFATED
BOOK TWO

DANIELLE L. JENSEN

DEL REY
NEW YORK

Del Rey
An imprint of Random House
A division of Penguin Random House LLC
1745 Broadway, New York, NY 10019
randomhousebooks.com
penguinrandomhouse.com

2026 Del Rey Trade Paperback Edition

Copyright © 2025 by Danielle L. Jensen

Penguin Random House values and supports copyright. Copyright fuels creativity, encourages diverse voices, promotes free speech, and creates a vibrant culture. Thank you for buying an authorized edition of this book and for complying with copyright laws by not reproducing, scanning, or distributing any part of it in any form without permission. You are supporting writers and allowing Penguin Random House to continue to publish books for every reader. Please note that no part of this book may be used or reproduced in any manner for the purpose of training artificial intelligence technologies or systems.

Del Rey and the Circle colophon are registered trademarks of
Penguin Random House LLC.

Originally published in hardcover in the United States by Del Rey, an imprint of Random House, a division of Penguin Random House LLC, in 2025.

ISBN 978-0-593-59988-4
Ebook ISBN 978-0-593-59987-7

Printed in the United States of America on acid-free paper

1st Printing

Book Team: Production editor: Cindy Berman • Managing editor: Paul Gilbert • Production manager: Erin Korenko • Copy editor: Muriel Jorgensen

Book design by Sara Bereta

The authorized representative in the EU for product safety and compliance is Penguin Random House Ireland, Morrison Chambers,
32 Nassau Street, Dublin D02 YH68, Ireland.
https://eu-contact.penguin.ie.

For the ladies of NOFFA!

A CURSE
CARVED IN
BONE

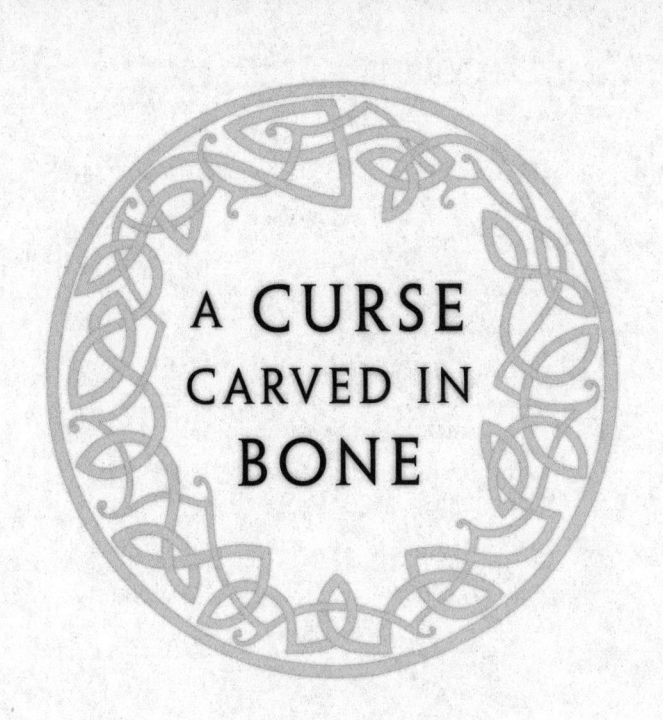

CHAPTER 1

FREYA

The storm struck without warning, attacking the drakkar and driving us away from the rocky coast with such ferocity that the gods themselves must not have wanted us to cross the strait. As the Nordelanders struggled against the violent waves, any visions I might have had about the glory of raiding across the seas were swiftly dissuaded by the cold. By the wet. But most of all, by the endless vomit.

Not mine, as my sea legs were strong, but the contents of the stomachs of nearly everyone else, including Harald's hooded thralls, was filling the hull. Better to wade through vomit than to lean over the side and risk being swept away by the angry sea.

"What a disappointment it will be," I shouted over the thunder and the raging waters, "if all your plots and all your schemes amount to nothing because we are drowned beneath the sea!"

All on board glared at me, though Tora's glare held little threat given that a stream of vomit spewed from her lips in the middle of it. I laughed and leaned against the hull where I sat beneath a seal hide coated with my magic to keep the spray from soaking through. "Or perhaps not even such a glorious death as to be claimed by Njord, but a death by turning your own innards into outtards. I have heard such grand tales of Nordelander ferocity, but this is pitiful."

"Is she ever silent?" Harald demanded of Bjorn. The king of Nordeland was not immune to the tossing waves and his temper was fraying as a result. I gave him a beaming smile and was rewarded with a scowl.

Bjorn only bent over the oar he was manning, unaffected by the waves. Which was regrettable. If anyone deserved to taste the sour burn of bile, it was him and his lying tongue.

"You'll know no peace, Father," Bjorn finally answered, the muscles of his back straining against his tunic as he put his strength into rowing. "But I'll remind you that you invited her vitriol upon yourself."

Harald's jaw tightened. Yet instead of offering a retort, he only leaned into his own oar, thin arms laboring. Not even Nordeland's king was absolved from rowing through this nightmare, everyone's strength required to keep us from floundering. The Northern Strait was notorious for claiming lives, and Njord's domain cared not for the power of kings.

Nor the children of gods.

A wave rolled over the drakkar and water slapped me in the face with such violence it hurt. Fear rose in my chest, for it was impossible to breathe in the icy deluge. The vessel tipped and slid down the trough between swells, the blackness of the depths seeming to reach for me. I clung to what handholds I could, nails scratching on the wood and my ears ringing with the shrieks of the thralls who lost their grips. To fall meant death, for there was no salvation in the crushing sea.

Yet my fear faded to longing as I stared at the dark water. It whispered words promising relief from the grief that clawed at my heart. From the rage that plagued my soul. From the loneliness that hollowed my insides, for I had lost everything that mattered to me, including my purpose.

The sea reached for me, and my fingers slackened, my broken heart yearning for the respite from the pain. To be drawn *down down down* into the darkness.

Only for my grip to tighten as Hel whispered in my head, *Why concede when you have the power to take back all that should be yours? The power to reclaim all that has been stolen from you?*

I don't have that power.

Her laughter was soft and yet as loud as thunder in my skull. *You are the mistress of death, daughter. All who draw breath fear your power.*

I don't want to be feared.

My mind's eye filled with a smile that was half curved lips and half naked bone. The sight made my heart gallop, though it was her words that made my hands turn to ice. *Fear is the weapon that will win you what you want.*

The drakkar righted itself, no longer at risk of being swamped.

I wiped the salt from my eyes, not sure if it was tears or seawater, only that the roar of my pulse had nothing to do with my near brush with death.

Fear is the weapon that will win you what you want.

What did I want?

I did not know, but the torrent of emotion in my guts needed an outlet. My eyes latched onto Steinunn vomiting up seawater, and I shouted, "Skald, will you write a song of this crossing? If you do, let it be called The Saga of the Seasick. Or perhaps Quest of the Queasy. No . . . Yarn of the Yackers!"

"Be silent!" Skade screamed at me from her oar, her crimson hair plastered across her face. "Cease your noise, you bleating bitch!"

"And if I refuse?" I laughed wildly as Skade abandoned her oar to the thrall next to her, a glowing golden bow appearing in her hands. The same weapon she'd used to kill my mother. "You'll shoot me? Cast me over the side?"

She lifted her bow, nocking the virulent green arrow that never missed.

"Do it!" The shriek tore from my throat. Not out of any desire to be shot but because I wanted her to feel the same indecision that plagued my own soul. "I dare you to do it!"

Skade only pulled the bowstring taut, glittering blue eyes filled with many things—indecision was not one of them.

My mouth went dry with the abrupt certainty that I'd gotten myself killed with my bluster. Only for her weapon to disappear as Harald snarled at her to hold her temper or suffer the consequences.

Not caring that my laughter sounded deranged, because it was surely better than sobbing, I howled, "You all sacrificed so much to steal me, so I think I can say what I please, and you all have no choice but to listen! No choice but to suffer my words. You wanted me? Now you *fucking* have all of me, so enjoy! Delight in the fruits of your labor!"

Skade dove at me, small fists swinging.

Though I'd tempted this fate, she still surprised me. Her fist struck my cheek and knocked me back. My head hit the mast, stars bursting in my eyes as Skade's hands reached for my throat.

"You need to be put down," she screamed in my face. "You are a plague, Hel-child!"

I jerked my knee up and slammed it into her cunt. The other woman rewarded me with a shriek but didn't let go, fingers implacable around my throat.

Then Bjorn grabbed Skade around the waist. He hauled her off me, but she only turned her ire on him, and all went to chaos.

Thralls recoiled as the pair collided with them. The drakkar groaned and turned sideways, dipping into the swell of a wave. Water crashed over me, heavy and relentless. Everything tipped and I rolled, my eyes filled with wood and waves and blackened sky.

And then hands had me by the wrists, Bjorn's skin hot against mine as he pinned me to the bottom of the vessel. "Are you trying to get us all killed?"

"Yes!" I screamed as the others struggled with the oars. "That is exactly what I'm trying to do!"

"If you die, you will never have answers!" He pressed down, holding me in place as I thrashed and tried to knee him in the balls. "You'll never know the truth!"

"Do not speak to me of truth!"

To avoid my knees, he forced himself between my legs, hips in the crook of my pelvis as the ship rocked. Wholly against my will, my mind filled with memories of us in the cave when happiness had felt possible. Memories of his lips on mine, hands on my body, cock buried deep inside of me as he made me his. And my traitorous desires surged in defiance of fear and logic, my lust uncaring of the fact that the man it wanted was my enemy.

Only rage had the strength to drive the *want* away, and I reached for my anger even as I unleashed all the cruelty born of the pain in my heart. Wrapping my legs around Bjorn's waist, I ground against him, my voice mocking as I said, "The truth that will regain you this?"

His grip on my wrists tightened as the drakkar rocked violently, and I dug the heel of my shoe into his back, feeling him press against me. "The truth that will get you back your pretty Freya so you can make her your wife?"

Lifting my head, I kissed him, catching his bottom lip hard enough between my teeth that he jerked away. "So that you can become a farmer with her? Have pretty daughters who look just like her? The truth that will ensure you grow old in her arms?"

I hurled the dream he'd given me in that cave back in his face, my rage relishing the flash of pain in his eyes because I wanted him to hurt as much as I did. "There is no truth that will bring me back to you, for you are a liar. A traitor. A fucking coward who does not deserve to see Valhalla!"

"You think you know everything, Freya," he said. "But you know nothing."

I spat in his face. "I know that I'll hate you until my last breath, Bjorn. And that is something."

"Hate me all you want." He let go of my wrists. "But your last breath will not be today, Born-in-Fire."

I watched him return to the oars, joining the effort to see the drakkar through the storm.

"The Allfather sees all that was and all that the Norns have said will be." Harald had ceased rowing, and his gray eyes locked on mine. "Saga is his child and knowledge is his gift. Other seers might have answers, but Saga, it seems, is bound to your fate. It may be that he'll show her the truths you so desperately desire." Without waiting for a response, Harald faced forward again, muscles bunching as he rowed.

My anger slowly faded, and its absence left me hollow. Tilting my head back, I stared at the blackened sky and swirling clouds, lightning dancing among them. What I wouldn't give to be fated. For higher powers to have already determined the course of my life, so all that I said, all that I did, and all that I ever wanted could be blamed upon them.

But the two drops of god's blood in my veins, one from Hlin and one from Hel, meant I was accountable for everything I left in my wake. Failures and successes. Nightmares and dreams. Love and hate.

What did I want?

The question sank into my soul, because I needed an answer. Needed a purpose to pull me forward. To remain where I was, as I was, would mean incinerating myself from the inside out.

I want the truth.

I wanted to hear from her lips the future that Saga had foreseen because Odin's children did not lie. Wanted the story of what had happened between her and Snorri. Wanted answers about whether Harald was as much of a villain as I'd been raised to believe.

But most of all, I needed the truth about who I was.

Climbing to my hands and knees, I crawled until I found a spot next to a thrall with heavily tattooed arms. Taking hold of the oar, I put my strength into it and looked to the rocky coast of Nordeland. The winds slackened and the seas began to ease, and if the Norns were watching, I was certain they feared for the future they had created.

Because I was Freya Born-in-Fire. Daughter of Hlin. Daughter of Hel.

And I would weave my own fate.

CHAPTER 2

BJORN

Clear skies shone overhead as we pushed the drakkar onto the beach. Every muscle in my body ached, and I felt no guilt leaving Harald's thralls to drain the vessel as I walked onto the land that was more my home than any other. We'd landed at Stormnes, the point of land that jutted into the strait on which one could see across to Skaland on a clear day. The beach was narrow and rocky, and beyond it rose mountains covered with dense forest, their tops still white with snow.

Kneeling, I took a handful of the gritty sand and squeezed it tight, relishing the feel of Nordeland even as I cursed fate for bringing me back here.

"Fate holds no claim on you, Bjorn," Harald said as he walked past me up the beach, seeming, as he often did, to know my thoughts. "You are unfated, which means you chose this path, even if you did not know where it would lead."

I'd never cared to dwell on the power of the Unfated to change the future, because it couldn't be proven. There was no way to know whether a choice had twisted the threads the Norns had woven into another pattern or whether I'd done exactly as they predicted. Everything I'd done in recent days had been with the aim of freeing Freya from those who'd kill her or use her to further their own ambitions, yet all I'd accomplished was moving her control from one king to another.

"We are here because of you, Father."

He only gave me a knowing look and continued up the beach toward the trees.

Knowing, because there was no denying that once my plans to spirit Freya away had been dashed, once she'd learned about my treachery, I'd hoped the truth would cause her to forgive my lies. The hope that the tantalizing glimpse of a future I'd so desperately wanted could be mine again once she understood why I'd done what I had done. The hopes of a man with weasel shit for brains, because no *truth* would temper the seething rage that burned in my Freya's heart.

Not yours anymore, logic whispered even as my greedy heart screamed that she'd be mine until the end of days.

Casting aside my handful of sand, I stood and followed Harald into the trees. The air was colder than it had been in Skaland, the stink of rotting seaweed mixing with the crisp scent of pine, the mossy ground spongy beneath my boots. Wind shook the boughs of the trees, the woods alive with birdsong and the scamper of small creatures. A wild place. For though the summers were mild enough, few had the mettle to survive the cruelty of Nordeland's winters.

The man who had been a father to me most of my life found a rock to his liking and sat down. Pulling off his boots, Harald shook sand from them and then tossed them aside. As I silently watched, he removed his tunic and wrung seawater from the sodden cloth, his pale skin faintly blue from the cold. Leaner than I remembered, signs of age showing in the wrinkles next to his eyes and the strands of gray in his golden-brown hair. Just a man, though there were times I'd forgotten that during my time in Skaland, as Snorri had ever painted him as a creature capable of preternatural villainy.

In Nordeland, Harald was a savior. A liberator and a champion of the weak. I'd seen with my own eyes his good deeds. Owed him my life, as did so many of those who served him. Yet he was no more a hero than he was a villain. Only a man, and no man's choices were wholly altruistic, least of all one who had clawed his way up from a small jarldom to become king.

"You sound like a Skalander again." Harald sighed and twisted the fabric of his tunic again, drops of water falling to the moss. "It reminds me of when Saga first fled to Nordeland with you delirious from the pain of the burns. Just a boy and yet you never wept, only vowed vengeance upon Snorri for what he had done. You and I would have crossed the strait together and put Snorri in his grave if not for your mother holding us back. I wanted Snorri dead more than I've ever wanted anything, and yet Saga pleaded that I stay my hand. I have ever been a slave to her wishes but now I wish I'd held firm."

"I remember." I heard Skaland in my voice but was unable to slip the accent without concerted effort. I'd adopted it to try to blend in better in Halsar, to encourage the Skalanders to forget that I'd been gone for so many years, but it hadn't worked. Always an outsider. Always a Nordelander.

Most especially in my heart.

Donning his damp garment, Harald finally looked at me. The weight of his attention was as heavy as it had always been. "Now that we are finally alone, do you care to tell me why?"

Why.

A question that needed no clarification, and I exhaled a long breath before I said, "Does it matter?"

Harald toyed with the gold ring that bound his beard, then shook his head. "Does it matter? Of course it matters why you chose to destroy plans a lifetime in the making. All that I have done was at your mother's bidding, at *your* bidding, and yet you seem content to spit in my face for doing exactly as you wished. These were your plans, Bjorn, not mine, and yet you treat me as your enemy."

"You aren't my enemy, Father. But things change."

"Oh yes. *Things.*" Harald made a face. "Things such as the shield maiden turning out to be a woman of unparalleled beauty? It is much easier to kill the ugly ones, isn't it? If Freya had been possessed of a face like a horse's arse, I've no doubt you would have done your mother's bidding without hesitation, but here we are. Snorri alive. Freya alive. The threat against Nordeland is as much a reality as it was before because our fates are unchanged. All because of a pretty face."

"Her looks had nothing to do with it." A lie because I remembered the first time I'd set eyes upon Freya. How the sunlight had illuminated the anger on her face as she'd rescued fish after fish from Vragi's fit of temper, every part of her screaming defiance. Beautiful, yes, but it had been her ferocity that had drawn me across the fjord to speak to her. Dressed in a homespun dress with no weapon but her words, she'd been fiercer than any warrior I'd ever met on the battlefield. "Killing her felt wrong," I muttered, not able to put my reasons into words that wouldn't invite his mockery. "Why should she die for Snorri's crimes?"

"Because your mother said it was the only way to save thousands of lives," Harald answered. "Though she did not understand what made Freya so dangerous, Saga knew Freya had the power to bring destruction down upon both Nordeland and Skaland. Snorri is the villain, but the shield maiden is his weapon, and killing her would castrate his ability to do any real damage. Saga set you upon this task because you, unfated as you are, had the ability to change the future the Allfather had shown her. Yet when given the opportunity, you balked. Because *it felt wrong.*" His lip curled in disgust. "Or perhaps it was because your cock was doing the thinking rather than your head."

"My mother agreed that the plan needed to change," I retorted. "When I spoke to her at Fjalltindr, she agreed that Freya might walk a different path if we liberated her from Snorri. She is not so bloodthirsty as to wish death upon an innocent woman when another solution is obvious."

Harald sighed. "Saga did not agree with you, Bjorn, she merely understood that you were enamored with Freya and would not be convinced to harm her. She asked me to do it for you, but it was the plea of a mother, not the strategy of a seer. I am but a mortal man, and I hold not the power to change the future set by the Norns, which meant I was destined to fail."

He cast a sidelong glare at me that suggested he knew my role in stymieing the attempt. Unbidden, the vision of Freya bare to the waist filled my mind's eye, her head crowned by antlers and tilted back as I tasted her for the first time. I blinked, vanquishing the vision because the same threat I had protected her from then was a threat now. "Does my mother still wish Freya dead, then? Does she still believe that is the only way to change the future?" Because the last thing I wished to do was bring Freya deeper into Nordeland if my mother was actively seeking her death.

For the thousandth time in my life, I silently screamed, *Why can't I just kill Snorri and be done with it?*

Silently, because my mother had long been adamant that killing Snorri was not an option, refusing to hear any argument to the contrary.

"I don't know what Saga now thinks on the matter or if the Allfather has given her more visions of the future." Harald rested his elbows on his knees. "I've not seen her in long weeks, for she returned to her cabin after we left Fjalltindr. Being around so many souls exhausted her."

No surprise, for my mother had always been desperate for isolation, the weight of seeing what were often tragic futures more than her heart could bear. I'd nearly fallen over from shock when I'd first seen her at Fjalltindr, but it hadn't stopped me from sneaking away later to seek her counsel.

Through the trees, I caught sight of men rushing down the beach. They bore shields painted with the blue stripes of Nordeland, along with their jarl's symbol. Warriors from Harald's fleet who'd reached the coast before us. Which meant this brief moment to discover my father's plans without others listening in was coming to a close.

"What do you intend for Freya?" A blunt question that needed an answer. Harald had sought Freya's death for a long time, yet that had changed when he'd seen her use of Hel's magic. There had been no missing the delight in his gaze upon learning what she could do. I suspected his hope was for her to join his cabal of Unfated that he used to defend Nordeland's shores. He'd not cast aside a weapon as sharp as Freya unless he had no other choice.

Or unless my mother bid him to do so, which was very much a risk.

"She's dangerous." Harald's eyes moved from the approaching warriors to Freya, who stood at the water's edge under Tora's watchful gaze. "She holds not only the power to kill but the power to send souls to her godly mother in Helheim. Warriors who laugh in the face of death will run from Freya, for she has the power to deny them Valhalla. Yet that is not what terrifies me about her." He was quiet for a long moment before he added, "It is her rage."

As though hearing our words, Freya turned, and even across the stretch of the beach and through the trees, there was no mistaking the gleam of crimson in her gaze. Her pale blond hair hung loose to her waist, tangled and matted from seawater and wind. If not for the fact she had legs rather than a fish tail, I'd have compared her to the havfrue who were said to lure the unwary sailors to their deaths. Though in truth, even disarmed as she was, Freya was far more dangerous.

"Her anger is half the reason I tried to take her and run. I didn't realize that it was Hel's influence, but I saw her changing as Snorri used her in his quest to become king. Saw her becoming the monster my mother feared and I wanted to protect her from that. I . . ."

"Wanted to change her fate?"

I gave a slow nod. "Seems foolish now given it's Hel who makes her feel like this, not Snorri. Running would have changed nothing."

Harald burst into laughter, and I scowled at him.

"Oh, to be young and stupid again," he finally said, wiping at his eyes. "Remember your stories, Bjorn, or I shall sit you down with Steinunn and have her teach you like a small child. Hel is the goddess of death and mistress of Helheim, but she is no villain set upon destruction. She is . . . *covetous,* for lack of a better word. She *wants.* Which makes me wonder what Freya wants. Makes me wonder what has been denied to her that makes rage burn so hot in her heart that her eyes turn to flame. Blame not Hel, for the anger you see is Freya's and Freya's alone."

There were countless reasons I could think of for Freya to be angry—knew I was certainly one of them—and yet my instincts told me that I could not begin to comprehend why her wrath was so fierce.

"Discover what it is Freya wants," Harald said. "That is the key to tempering her and, in doing so, changing the dark fate your mother foresees."

I frowned at his choice of word. *Tempering.* It sounded too much like *changing,* and there was nothing about Freya that I wished to change. Yet all I said was, "She wants the truth."

"Then take her to Saga so that she might know the whole of it." My father gripped my shoulder. "I forgive you, Bjorn. I forgive you because I understand that you acted out of love for Freya, not out of malice toward me or Nordeland. The gods know, I have made questionable choices for the sake of your mother, so I cannot judge you harshly. Women wield their beauty like a weapon, and none are more beautiful than Saga."

I cast my eyes skyward. "Spare me your lovesick poetry about my mother. There are things in life I'm better off not knowing, and that is one of them."

Harald laughed, but then his gaze sharpened. "Do you remember the vision your mother foresaw of Freya after you came to Nordeland?"

As though I could ever forget my mother falling to her knees before me, eyes rolled back in her head. A voice not her own whispering from her lips that the shield maiden would unite Skaland, but that thousands would be left dead in her wake. That the shield maiden would walk upon the ground like a plague, pitting friend against friend, brother against brother, and that all would fear her. "You know I remember."

Harald gave a slow nod. "Long has your life's purpose been not only to deny Snorri the fate your mother foresaw, but also to prevent the bloody toll that his rule would have upon our lands with the shield maiden as his weapon. You believed stealing Freya away would forestall that dark future, but I think it clear that she can't run from the fate Saga foresaw. She must fight it. The question you must ask is if you are willing to fight it alongside her."

That was no question. I had Freya's back to the gates of Valhalla and beyond.

Though I'd said nothing, Harald gave a small nod of approval. "Your path is as it has always been, Bjorn: to prevent Snorri from controlling Skaland. To deny him the power of destruction. How that is best achieved, I do not know. We can only hope that your mother has answers."

"If she claims that Freya's death is the only option, what will you do?" I asked, because he hadn't answered my question the first time.

Wind howled through the forest, the sound haunting and filling me with foreboding as Harald's pale gray eyes searched mine. Then he said, "Let us both pray it does not come to that."

The approaching warriors had been intercepted by Skade, and she now led them in our direction. We'd been raised by Harald as siblings, yet Skade and I had always been at each other's throats. Her mother had abandoned her, and Skade's bitterness over it had turned her against all women, most especially those she perceived as weak. She'd terrorized the servants mercilessly until Harald had punished her for it, but that had only driven her to be more clever in her pursuits. I'd never seen Skade actually kill a woman for weakness until I saw her murder Freya's mother, but in hindsight, I should have seen it coming. Kelda had embodied everything that she loathed.

Skade glared at me as though sensing my thoughts, but I ignored her as one of the warriors spoke.

"My king." He bowed low. "We are relieved to see you well. When the skies grew dark in our wake and your drakkar did not reach shore with the fleet, we feared the worst."

Harald waved a dismissive hand. "Nothing but a bit of weather."

I scoffed. "Says the man who still stinks like vomit."

"There is a difference between discomfort and danger," Harald replied. "The shield maiden was never at risk of being lost to a rogue wave, and I clung to that truth. Are all other vessels accounted for?"

"Yes, my king." The warrior adjusted the shield hanging on his back. "Most have returned to their holds and halls, as was your order. The rest have ventured to the mouth of the Rimstrom, but we waited to ensure your safe return."

"Yes, yes," Skade interrupted, then she reached into the group of warriors and tugged a small man forward. I recognized Guthrum immediately. Skinny as a spear shaft with tangled brown hair and an unkempt beard, Guthrum preferred living in the wilds as far from people as possible. He was entirely unchanged by the years we'd been apart, but the merlin perched on his shoulders was new.

"My king." Guthrum bowed low, the merlin ruffling her feathers and then mimicking the gesture. "I bring fell news. Or rather, Kaja does."

"Where is your fox?" I asked, because a small red fox had been his familiar when I'd left, and foxes couldn't cross *fucking* seas.

Guthrum's brown eyes met mine. "Wolves. Two winters past. I rescued Kaja as a fledgling and Jord saw fit to connect our minds."

My stomach sank, because that meant for almost two years, Harald had a spy in the skies of Skaland. Guthrum was a child of Jord, which meant that he was capable of speaking mind to mind with his familiar. Worse, he was capable of seeing through his familiar's eyes, and Guthrum was nothing if not loyal. He'd have relayed everything to Harald.

"What has Kaja seen?" Harald demanded. "Has she had eyes on Snorri?"

Guthrum's throat moved, his eyes skipping to me and then back over his shoulder to where Freya stood with Tora, both watching.

"The Skalanders searched the base of the falls for their bodies as soon as you departed," he said. "They also searched the Torne itself, and fishing boats now comb the coast. Snorri is convinced that the shield maiden and Bjorn yet live and has set a reward for anyone who has information of where they are."

My teeth ground together as I remembered how I'd been so certain that everyone would believe Freya and me dead, bodies caught in the endless churn of the falls. It now felt like the purest form of idiocy, and my hands fisted with anger at myself because we'd fooled no one.

Harald tugged on his beard, seeming neither surprised nor concerned. "Does he suspect Freya and Bjorn are with us in Nordeland?"

Guthrum gave a slight nod. "He believes you retreated too easily. Believes that you found them immediately after they went over the falls. He argues to Ylva that if you'd found them dead, you'd have made it known, and so they must be living."

"Snorri, my old friend, you are no fool," Harald said under his breath, but then shook his head. "It is inevitable that he'd discover you and Freya lived, Bjorn. Too many have seen your faces and while I might wish that all my warriors were loyal, all it takes is one to be tempted by the prospects of wealth and the ruse is up. We need to head inland to the safety of Hrafnheim."

My heart skipped at the mention of the fortress where I'd been raised. My home, for my mother had insisted that I remain with Harald so that I might be trained as a warrior. My friends were there, as was the family I'd forged out of bonds as strong as blood.

Freya's voice tore me from my thoughts. "I didn't agree to go to Hrafnheim, only to see Saga, whom Tora has told me resides elsewhere." She'd come up silently. Tora stood behind her, a hand resting on the hilt of her sword. My sister and friend. Or at least, she had once been. Much had changed.

"You must pass Hrafnheim to reach Saga's cabin," Harald answered. "You will need horses and supplies, all of which can be had in the town."

"The town which is your fortress." Freya crossed her arms. So beautiful and fierce that my chest ached, no part of that feeling diminishing as she cast a murderous glare my way.

"You think I'm going to willingly walk into your stronghold?" she demanded. "Even in little fishing villages in Skaland we heard about Hrafnheim, most notably that no one who is not a Nordelander has ever seen the inside of it and come out to tell the tale. Who is to say that you don't intend to lock me in a prison for the rest of my days?"

Harald wasn't the sort of man to lock people in prisons. He preferred other forms of punishment, and my eyes flicked to his thralls—his Nameless—who all knelt in the sand wearing their black hoods.

"You have my word that I have no intention of locking you in my prison." Harald adjusted the blades belted at his waist. "I don't even have a prison in Hrafnheim."

Freya snorted. "Your word is worth less to me than piss in a pot. I'm not going to Hrafnheim. Give me a guide and I will make my own way to Saga." Her eyes fixed on me again. "A guide who is not *Bjorn*."

That her words were expected did not ease the sharpness with which they cut.

"I did not volunteer." Picking a piece of seaweed off my sleeve, I cast it aside. "Walk if you must, Born-in-Fire. I shall sail up the Rimstrom to Hrafnheim, choose myself a fast horse, and make it to my mother's cabin a full fortnight before you. I'll make sure to have a cup of mead waiting, for you're sure to be thirsty from the long journey."

Freya said nothing but the ground quivered, everyone starting with alarm. I only stared her down. "Go ahead," I said. "Curse me to Helheim. Bid your godly mother to rob me of my place in Valhalla. It did not work last time, but perhaps this time will be different."

"The Allfather will thank me for sparing him your voice," she snapped. "A true punishment would be to put you somewhere alone where you'll have only yourself to annoy."

Harald sighed and rubbed at his temples. "Tell me where this place is, for it sounds peaceful in comparison to being caught between you two. Freya, the choice is yours. By ship or by foot."

Her jaw worked from side to side, but behind the stubbornness was the trace of fear. Freya was alone in a nation that was enemy to her homeland, and guilt bit at my insides for needling her. "No one will stop you from going to see my mother to seek your truths," I said. "You have my word."

The red of her eyes seemed to boil as she hissed, "Fuck your word, Bjorn. It means even less than your king's."

Turning, she strode toward the drakkar with Tora at her heels.

Harald exhaled, then waved the warriors away before giving Skade the order to make ready to sail. Then he turned to me and extracted an arm ring from his pocket. The band of silver was deeply familiar, for it had been given to me by him long ago, and then given back for safekeeping when I went to Skaland in search of the shield maiden and vengeance.

"Freya is the key to Snorri achieving his fate as king," Harald said. "He will not give her up without a fight, and the moment he has certainty that she is here, he will come in pursuit. He will go to war against Nordeland to win her back. I know you will die to defend her, but will you still fight to defend your homeland? Are you still a Nordelander, my son?"

I took the band of silver, the metal cool against my palm, remembering how much it had meant when he'd first gifted it to me. When he'd named me a defender of the people who'd taken me in and treated me with kindness when it had felt as though I'd lost everything.

"Forever a Nordelander." I slid it up my arm to its familiar place above my elbow. "It's good to be home, Father."

CHAPTER 3

FREYA

No part of me wanted to climb back in the drakkar with the Nordelanders, for beneath my anger ran a current of fear that made me sick to my stomach. I'd felt able to leave Skaland with Bjorn because I'd believed Snorri would accept that I was dead. That he'd not punish my brother or Ingrid, and what remained of my family would be able to live on. Yet the report I'd overheard indicated that Snorri had not given up on me, which meant Geir, Ingrid, and their unborn child remained at risk. Though my relationship with my brother was greatly soured, it made me ill that his innocent child might be harmed.

And I also, selfishly, feared for myself.

The men and women in the ship, as well as those who traveled in the two other vessels, were the raiders I'd grown up dreading. Every child raised on the coast of Skaland knew to fear the sight of drakkar with blue-striped sails. Knew that at the sight of the white wolf banner to run and hide in the woods with the elderly while the adults tried to fight seasoned warriors intent on taking everything of value, human life first and foremost. My uncle had died in a raid when I was a young girl, my aunt taken as a thrall and never heard of again. Distant memories but ones never forgotten, and I was under no delusion that those around me were anything less than dangerous. Especially with the white wolf snapping in the breeze above our heads.

You are far from helpless, I silently whispered, the wary distance most of the Nordelanders gave me comforting and horrifying in equal measure, because they feared me as one did a monster. I heard the whispers among them as they spoke of what I'd done to Harald's warriors when they'd tracked Bjorn and me down. How the magic gifted to me by Hel dragged their souls out of their bodies and down to Helheim, ever denied the halls of Valhalla. Whispers that said only the Unfated could defend themselves from me, Harald's life spared only because the other gods had intervened to protect Nordeland's beloved king. Which for all I knew was accurate, as Hel's magic had not so much as touched him.

They were terrified of me, and I could not blame them for that, as I was terrified of myself. I'd never understood how the catastrophic future that Saga had foreseen was possible when Hlin's magic did nothing but protect, but now it was clear how I would become the plague she'd foretold. How in a fit of anger I might kill dozens, hundreds, perhaps thousands, and imprison their souls in Hel's realm. Helheim was no place of horror, but to be sent there denied warriors the chance to sit at the Allfather's table and to fight in the last battle, the promise of which gave them the bravery to face death.

No one should have such power, least of all me, and I silently swore that I'd not use the magic again.

I would not be that monster. I refused.

You are on the path to finding out the truth about who you are, I reminded myself. *With the truth, the route forward will be clear.*

Alternatively, I was sailing toward my future prison. But that was a risk I needed to take.

Wrapping my woolen cloak more tightly around my body, I eyed Bjorn where he sat with Harald. His midnight hair was pulled back in a knot, the tattoos on the sides of his head slightly obscured from several days away from a razor. His cheeks, too, were stubbled, though it had not grown so much as to obscure the sharp line of his jaw and cheekbones. Harald said something to him, and when Bjorn answered, the sunlight illuminated the leaf-green of his eyes but also the dark circles beneath them.

No one will stop you from going to see my mother to seek your truths, Bjorn's voice repeated in my head. *You have my word.*

He'd seemed genuine, but it was not lost on me that I'd felt that way when he'd been lying through his teeth.

The twisted silver arm ring he now wore above his elbow gleamed in the sunlight, and I knew it had been given to him by Harald. A symbol of family and fealty. My brother, Geir, wore a similar one gifted to him by Snorri when he joined his war band, and my father had as well. All of Snorri's warriors wore them, and while I'd noticed that Bjorn did not, I'd thought nothing of it. Had foolishly believed that it was reflective of his penchant for discarding his shirt at every opportunity, not a small display of defiance against the man he'd apparently sworn to destroy.

Unbidden, the memory of our climb through the draug-infested tunnels to Fjalltindr filled my mind. The moment we'd rested together, the heat of his axe and arms warding away the chill of the mountain. We'd spoken of Nordeland, of how the people had treated him, and I'd asked how he felt about the idea of Snorri going to war against them. *No matter how I feel about the people, vengeance must be had against the one who hurt my mother,* he'd said. *I've sworn an oath to take everything from him, and anyone who stands in the way is nothing more than a casualty of war.*

He'd spoken the truth, and yet I'd only heard what I'd wanted to hear. That Harald was his enemy. Nordeland was his enemy. Ylva had been right in her accusations, and too easily I remembered dismissing her animosity toward him as jealousy on Leif's behalf. How wrong I'd been.

Regardless of blood, Bjorn was a Nordelander through and through, which made him my enemy.

My hands balled into fists, and I turned my head so I could no longer see him. Which unfortunately put Tora in my line of sight.

The child of Thor was a full head taller than I was and broad through her shoulders. More than capable of wielding any weapon, but what made her dangerous was the lightning she could summon from her hands. Lightning that had almost killed me but taken Bodil's life instead. Her face was covered with burn marks from when I'd rebounded her lightning bolt off my shield into the gatehouse of Grindill. The burns were still livid red though much time had passed, and I noticed that she wore her long blond hair loose to cover them. "Does Harald not have a healer in his service?" I asked.

"Volund is a child of Eir." Tora jerked her chin toward one of the drakkar that sailed in our escort. "The old fat one in the green tunic."

I squinted at the other vessel, finally picking out a rosy-cheeked older man who met the description. He appeared half asleep, head resting on one hand as the vessel slid over the waves. "Why did he not heal you, then?"

"I was denied healing." Tora's voice was toneless, but I didn't miss how she lifted her hand to touch the wounds, which appeared painful and were sure to scar.

Most of what I knew about the powers of children of Eir came from Liv, the healer who'd treated my hand after I'd been burned by Bjorn's axe. She'd told me that Eir was fickle with her magic, healing some injuries so that it appeared they'd never happened and others, such as my hand, as if time and nature had run their course. Some, Eir did not heal at all, which I'd seen after Gnut had attacked Halsar, many of the injured succumbing despite Liv trying to aid them with her magic. Liv had been a good woman, and I might have come to call her friend if she hadn't been killed when Gnut had returned to finish his attack. The thought occurred to me that Tora might have aided Gnut in that battle as well, so I said, "A fitting punishment. You killed my friend and many others besides."

Tora caught hold of my right hand and lifted it so the scars were illuminated by the sun. "Perhaps Eir saw your future and thought you deserved punishment as well. And I was not aiming for Bodil, I was aiming for you. That error was one of the greatest mistakes of my life."

I jerked my wrist from her grip.

"I met Bodil when I was very young and my uncle was seeking trade with her clan," Tora said. "She was a fierce warrior with more reputation than any woman alive, and I told her that I wanted to be like her." She drew in a breath. "I remember Bodil lifting a foot to scratch it, then smiling and saying, 'No you don't.'"

My chest hollowed. "Her feet itched when someone told a mistruth. You did not wish to be a warrior."

"Not then."

"What changed?" I met Tora's brown eyes. They were hollow with old grief.

Before she could answer, Harald rested a hand on her shoulder. "Her uncle was a bad man who did bad things. But he's long dead, isn't he, Tora?"

"Yes, my king," the child of Thor said softly. "You executed him."

"And you have been at my side ever since." Harald patted her shoulder. "A child of my heart if not my blood, and a warrior only a few have ever stood against. You are one of the few, Freya."

My skin prickled, his words sitting poorly with me though I could not quite explain why.

"Smoke!"

Skade's voice rang loud, and all in the drakkar looked onward to where the huntress pointed. Faint at first, barely more than wisps, but the plumes swiftly grew into great black columns.

Raiders.

"The Skalanders have come!" someone shouted from one of the other ships. "It is Snorri come to steal back his prize!"

My heart lurched, and I climbed to my feet. How could he be here so soon? How was it possible?

The bird I'd seen riding on a man's shoulder earlier shot down from the sky, crying loud as it circled its master, who rode in the other vessel. He roared, "Not Skalanders! Islunders!"

My hands turned clammy at mention of the island nation, for they occasionally raided Skaland's shores. When they did, none were left alive. Yet every Nordelander on all three ships was now on his or her feet, voices roaring in fury, not fear.

"It seems the Islunders noted our absence and took advantage," Skade said. "Our villages were left undefended."

Harald's jaw tightened and his eyes flicked to the columns of smoke. "They shall pay the price, because the white wolf is here now." Then he roared, "Ready your weapons, my friends, for we sail to bathe in Islund's blood!"

CHAPTER 4

FREYA

The smoke had seemed distant. Yet as we flew along the coast of rocky beaches and verdant forest, it felt only a matter of heartbeats before the black and yellow painted ships came into sight. Islunders, there was no doubt. There were three drakkar dragged onto the beach with a handful of warriors standing guard. And though we had the same number of vessels, the Nordelanders were outnumbered because all the warriors who'd normally sail in Harald's vessel were in Helheim thanks to me. The only warriors in our drakkar were Bjorn, Tora, and Skade.

And me.

From the flickers of lightning coming from the village, the Islunders had Unfated of their own.

Bjorn moved past me to the fore, and our elbows brushed. I shifted to the side to put space between us, hating how my body seemed to draw closer to him against my will. If Bjorn noticed, he didn't show it, for his attention was on Tora.

"You vowed to kill Arkyn before I left for Skaland, Tora," Bjorn said, axe already burning in his hand. "Yet from the show of light, it seems he is very much alive."

Their familiarity turned my mouth sour. Though he'd not denied knowing Tora, he'd also allowed me to believe he saw her as an enemy when she was clearly anything but.

Tora scowled. "Arkyn has been hiding from me, so I've not had the chance."

"He's not hiding now." Bjorn gave her a smirk that made me want to push him overboard. "Best to make good on your vow lest people start to worry your threats are more bark than bite."

"Says the man who vowed every day of his life to kill the shield maiden and ended up fucking her instead."

I scowled at the barb but Bjorn only shrugged. "If you envy my course, you are welcome to find a secluded spot to discover whether Arkyn's fingers tickle as well as his lightning. I will not judge you poorly for it. Even if he is old and ugly and smells of goat."

"How do you know what he smells like, Bjorn?" Skade gave him a sly smile.

"He fell on me during a skirmish and I nearly perished from the stink, though perhaps he has found a bath since then. Tora, you may let me know what you discover during your sojourn."

"Enough chatter, children," Harald interrupted, and I found myself grateful for it. I was aware that Bjorn knew these people, but I had believed it was knowledge gained as a prisoner. Not knowledge gained because they were comrades. Because they were . . . *family*.

"What do you wish to do, Freya?" Harald turned his gray eyes on me. "Will you fight for me to protect the village, or do you wish to remain in the drakkar?"

Every part of me tensed at the request, because I sensed what he desired. For me to call upon Hel to take the Islunders' lives and souls, ending this fight with my curse so that it cost him nothing. "Fight your own battle," I hissed. "I do not serve Nordeland, nor will I ever."

"Islund is no friend to Skaland," he answered. "They raid your coasts as well."

"The enemy of my enemy is my friend."

He only shrugged. "As you like." Raising his voice, Harald shouted, "Make ready!"

My heart raced as the Nordelander ships sped toward the beach, and the Islunders standing guard over their drakkar finally noticed our approach. Runners raced up the beach toward the burning village to warn the main war band while the others hefted their weapons, preparing to fight. Their shields were painted black and yellow, bodies clad in mail and fur, and their heads bore the elaborate helms they were known for.

"Skade," Harald said softly. "End them."

"Gladly, my king." Skade's glowing bow appearing in her hands. Drawing the string, she let the arrow loose and it shot through the air to punch through a man's chest. Bile burned up my throat as visions of her doing the same to my mother filled my mind's eye, but then Bjorn shouted, "Beware! The sand is wet!"

I had no understanding of why that was cause for concern, but everyone cried out in alarm and caught what handholds they could.

"Freya!" Bjorn roared. "Hold on! There's a child of—"

Whatever he'd been about to say was drowned out by a loud moan beneath our drakkar, and then the stern of the vessel lifted out of the water. Steinunn screamed, clinging to the mast even as Skade risked another shot before flinging herself at the edge to hold on. Fear clawed my insides as we rose higher and the drakkar tipped sideways. I saw the flash of a gray shape.

Child of Njord.

There was a child of Njord among the Islunders and they'd called a *whale*.

I had only a heartbeat to wonder what such a person could accomplish in battle before the whale flung the drakkar over. I sucked in a mouthful of air just before I was cast into the water.

I plunged deep and could not see anything but froth and darkness, my body flipping end over end as a wave rolled. It was impossible to tell which way was up. Which way was air.

Water surged, instinct screaming at me to move just before a massive fin swept before me. Then lashed back again, barely missing me a second time.

I kicked hard and broke the surface in time to watch the massive gray whale overturn another of the drakkar. Warriors spilled into the sea, and the whale disappeared into the depths.

It was chaos, made worse by the third drakkar having reached the beach only to encounter dozens of Islunders waiting, including the infamous Arkyn. Lightning flew from his fingers, blasting holes clean through Nordelander warriors and spraying smoking blood across the beach. At his side stood a man whose gaze was fixed in concentration, whatever plans he had for those of us in the water far from finished.

Something bumped my arm and I thrashed only to find Tora floating limp in the water next to me.

"Freya!" Bjorn shouted. "Swim!"

His eyes were on something farther out to sea.

Turning in the water, my stomach lurched at the sight of a black fin shooting through the water toward Tora and me.

Many black fins, and unlike the gray whale, these whales had teeth.

Terror filled me but as I turned to swim for shore, Tora jerked and coughed. Still alive but clearly addled from a blow to the head, blood streaming down her cheek.

Leave her, my anger whispered. *She killed Bodil.*

The fins were closer now. Bigger than I'd realized.

There is no honor to be had in this death, my conscience answered, the first I'd heard from it in a very long time. But it had power over me still, and I reached for Tora even as I called Hlin's name. Magic bloomed from my fingers to cover Tora's body and my own.

A black-and-white shape attacked, mouth opened wide to reveal sharp white teeth, and I screamed.

Yet it was magic the teeth bit down upon, not Tora's body, and the whale was flung back with incredible violence.

But more came on.

An entire pod of whales attacking one after another, from all sides. Teeth flashing and biting. Water from their thrashing fins sending Tora and me twisting and spiraling, all of my strength needed to keep hold of her. They couldn't break through my magic but neither could I escape.

Tora was half again my size and I struggled to keep our heads above water as the whales came on and on. Drowning us in water and fear. Through it, my fury blazed hot because these creatures were being used in a way that was against their nature. The child of Njord on the beach was no better than Vragi. No better than my dead husband who had used the lives of innocent creatures to torment me.

A wave washed over me, and though my magic flung it back in a burst of spray, we still sank in the water. I gasped for breath and twisted, trying to see over the attacking whales to the beach where the monster who controlled them lurked.

My heart lurched. We'd drifted far out to sea, the figures fighting on the beach now tiny in the distance. The whales didn't need to kill us, because the water would do the work for them.

"Tora!" I choked on a mouth of salty water. "Wake up! Swim!"

She blinked at me. Then her eyes sharpened and a shriek tore from her lips as a whale struck.

It had a mouth large enough to cut a grown man in half and swallow one of those halves whole, with teeth longer than my fingers.

Teeth that clamped down on her outstretched arm—only for the whale to be flung through the air to land with an explosion of water that set the ocean to rolling.

Tora thrashed, lost in fear and trying to get away. I clung to her like a barnacle, fingers latched around her chest and my legs around her waist.

Unable to swim, we sank beneath the surface.

Desperate to breathe, I caught hold of her face and met her eyes. Willed her to understand what was happening as we slipped deeper.

Fins and bubbles roared around us. But Tora was a warrior and before my eyes, she mastered her fear and nodded once.

I released my legs from around her waist, and holding hands to keep my magic in place, we kicked our way to the surface.

To discover we'd been pushed even farther from the shore.

"They're going to drown us," Tora gasped, flinching as another whale attempted to close its jaws around my legs only to be cast aside, waves surging. "We have to kill them!"

"No!" I choked on a mouthful of water. "It's not their fault! He's making them do this!"

"Then we're going to die!"

Tora jerked her hand free, and the glow of my magic disappeared. I grabbed her shoulder, and in a heartbeat she was once again aglow. She pressed her palms together and then cursed. "I need your magic off my hands!"

I shook my head. "You can't. You can't kill them."

"We've no choice!"

She was right. It was the whales' lives or ours.

Tears ran down my cheeks, and knowing I'd never forgive myself for this moment, I withdrew my magic from Tora's hands.

CHAPTER 5

BJORN

The pod of orcas closed in, drawn by the magic of Njord's blood. "Freya!" I screamed, but a hand closed on the back of my tunic, preventing me from swimming to her.

I shoved Harald away, but he lunged at me again. "Look!" he shouted. "Look!"

A familiar silver glow flared as Freya caught hold of Tora's still form and covered her with magic just before one of the whales struck. My heart stuttered with certainty they were both lost, then the whale flipped through the air. The rest of the pod closed in, but the glow didn't diminish. I couldn't see her through the spray of water and flash of fins, but with each passing second, she drifted farther out to sea. And the whales would continue attacking until she was drowned. Not because they wanted to but because the child of Njord bid them.

Fury boiled in my chest, and I turned to look past the battle on the beach to the two men standing behind the line of driftwood. One had copper hair and a beard that stretched nearly down to his large belly. The other was as tall as me and uglier than a cat's arsehole. Both unfated. Both pointing at Freya and Tora, and I saw the words their mouths formed.

Shield maiden.

The child of Njord nodded and lifted his hands, his long beard blowing on the wind. His gaze focused on Freya and he drove the whales at her again. Willing to harm as many of the creatures as necessary to see her dead, because even in Islund, they knew of my mother's prophecy.

"You are going to die," I whispered. "And die badly."

I swam for the beach, the waves flinging me toward shore as though Njord himself saw fit to end the abuse of the creatures of the sea. Skade lay still on the sand with Steinunn next to her, trying to rouse her. I ignored both and raced up the beach, picking up a fallen shield as I ran.

The roar of the sea mixed with the clash of steel and cries of warriors locked in merciless combat. The beach stretched wide before me, the sands slick with blood from the dead and dying. An Islunder swung an axe at me, but I only blocked it and ran on, weaving between comrades and foes caught in a deadly dance, my eyes on the child of Njord.

He paid me no mind, focused on the whales while Arkyn called lightning down upon those still in the water, both secure behind their guard of warriors. They believed me in Skaland, which meant they thought Skade and Tora the only weapons in Harald's war band who could stand against their magic.

They thought wrong.

"Tyr." I leaped over a still body, its guts mixing with the drying seaweed. The warriors guarding the pair finally took notice of me, but it was too late. "Grant me your flame."

My axe manifested in my hand. It was cool to my flesh, but I did not miss the way the Islunders recoiled from the heat. Or the way their eyes widened, lips parting to shout, "The Firehand!"

I attacked, screams filling my ears even as the sizzle of burning blood attacked my nose. I hated the smell. It haunted my dreams, a nightmare I couldn't escape, but in this moment, I relished it. Warriors fell beneath my blows, clutching severed limbs that did not bleed, the stink of charred flesh intensifying.

Arkyn lifted his hands and lightning crackled between them. The bolt lanced out and exploded against my axe, god against god. The impact drove me a step back, the noise deafening. The glare so brilliant it left spots in my eyes.

A helmed warrior ran screaming at my left and I backhanded him with my shield. The rim sank into his skull, the man dead before he hit the ground. Lightning flared, and I ducked instinctively even as I swung.

Arkyn screamed as my axe sank into his arm. He staggered, but I didn't pause for the kill because the man trying to kill my Freya was running up the beach.

He should've run faster.

I threw my axe. The blade spun through the air and took off one of his legs. As he fell, it reappeared in my hand. I strode after him, his screams faint in my deafened ears. The child of Njord rolled on his back, a knife in his hand. He threw it at me, but I batted the blade away and planted one foot upon his chest. "Call the whales off," I said. "Let their minds go free from your shackles."

"Only if you let me go!" he pleaded. "Let me go and I'll call them away."

"Call them off!" I rested the blade of my axe against his throat. Flesh sizzled and smoked. He shrieked, loud and piercing as he gestured wildly toward the sea. "They are gone! They are gone! Stop!"

I glanced over my shoulder to discover the orca pod speeding away from Freya and Tora. Then I turned my gaze back upon the man on the ground below me. "You dishonor your blood." I leaned on my axe, the blade glowing bright as it burned straight down to his spine.

His howl turned into a gurgle as his blood boiled under Tyr's flame, smoke rising from his blackening, bubbling flesh. A bad way to die but fitting for this bastard, and I kicked the knife in his hand away from him. His eyes went dark, and I muttered a curse that the gods condemn his soul to the cold depths of Niflheim.

Freya.

Turning from the corpse, I took a quick step back at the sight of Arkyn only a dozen paces away. Blood oozed from the blackened wound on his arm, but lightning crackled between his palms. "You should not have come back, Firehand."

He abruptly staggered but his lightning still shot from his hands to explode into the sand at my feet. I leaped backward and barely kept my balance. *Kill him,* my fury snarled, and I lifted my axe to send the ugly bastard to his death. Only to discover a blackened hole had appeared in Arkyn's chest.

Arkyn took one step toward me. Then two. He dragged his foot up for a third step, but life vanished from his eyes and he fell, landing face down in the sand.

I immediately looked to the sea, hunting for Freya's face. She was treading water far from shore, but next to her, Tora lowered her hands and the lightning between them disappeared. I nodded once at the woman who'd fought at my back more times than I could count—the woman I'd once named as my sister. Tora inclined her head, then began swimming alongside Freya. I allowed myself a moment to gain certainty they were safe, then I raced toward the smoke and screams coming from the village.

CHAPTER 6

FREYA

Tora and I struggled through the surf toward shore and my body trembled with exhaustion when my feet finally struck sand. The battle had shifted to the village, and the beach was now empty of warriors. The thralls who'd survived all knelt unmoving in the sand, hooded heads lowered. The strangeness of their behavior might have held my attention if it hadn't been drawn to Steinunn and Volund, who knelt on the beach next to Skade.

The huntress was retching blood. Her right arm hung limp, the awkward angle suggesting it was broken.

Steinunn eyed me nervously as Tora and I stumbled out of the water. "The drakkar struck Skade when it overturned," she said. "She can't fight."

"Yes, I can." Skade spat more blood, then slowly climbed to her feet. In her hand was her glowing green arrow with its murderously sharp tip.

"Get down, you idiot," Volund snapped. "Half your ribs are cracked."

Skade only pushed wet strands of red hair off her face. "I'm fine. I can fight."

The idea of it would have been laughable if not for the desperate fear in the woman's eyes as she stared at the flashes of combat visible through the trees. I knew the desire to push past the limits of my body to war against those trying to harm me and mine.

Tora appeared less moved, for she only shook her head. "I'll go, Skade. You stay with Freya."

"You don't tell me what to do," Skade hissed. "I can fight."

The child of Thor only gave the huntress a small shove backward. "You know how Harald feels about foolish choices, Skade. You might survive the fight only to wish you had not. Take cover in the trees until this is over."

Skade's already pale face blanched colorless and she gave a tight nod. "Fine. Go. Volund, help me now so that I might join them."

Tora broke into a sprint up the beach to the village, and it was all I could do not to follow her. Battle sang in my blood, the clash of steel coming from just out of sight calling my name. Yet I could not move.

Harald's voice filled my head: *Will you fight for me to protect the village?*

My heart stuttered and unease rose in my chest because my feet felt fixed to the sand.

I vow to serve no man not of this blood. I silently repeated the oath I'd sworn to Ylva. Words bound by blood magic. My teeth clenched together so hard they risked breaking. To fight would be to serve Harald, and Ylva's magic kept me from doing that.

Steinunn and Volund were helping Skade up the beach to the tree line to take cover. I took a deep breath, worried that my oath would anchor me in place until the battle was finished, but my feet moved. I stooped to retrieve a fallen shield, as well as a small axe. Neither of the trio ahead of me made any move to prevent me from arming myself, though Steinunn kept casting glances over her shoulder as though convinced I'd put the axe between her shoulders.

I bared my teeth; she might have stabbed me in the back, but I was not such a coward as to do the same.

You could run.

The thought reared in my head, tempting me with its logic. Neither the skald nor the healer had the capacity to stop me, and with her arm broken, Skade wouldn't be able to draw her bow. Wouldn't be able to pursue me at all given she could barely walk. Nordeland was a wild place, which meant a person could get lost in it and never be found.

If I disappeared into the wilderness to live in solitude, I wouldn't be able to curse anyone. Would be hidden from all of the men desperate to use me to gain power.

But running meant never speaking to Saga and never learning the full truth of what she'd seen. Meant losing the only opportunity I had to learn more about the magic gifted to me by Hel with her one drop of blood.

Was that knowledge worth my freedom? Was I an idiot not to take this chance?

My steps faltered, the distance between me and the trio growing without their noticing.

Run.

My body tensed, ready to burst into a sprint. Only for my eyes to catch sight of the familiar glow of Bjorn's axe in the distance. Fighting on Nordeland's behalf, yet my bitterness over that fact was tempered by the bodies on the beach. Fishermen who'd died so that raiders might take the few meager possessions they had. Through the trees, I could now see the cowering row of bound prisoners the Islunders intended to take as thralls. Mostly young women. Nordelanders, and yet if not for the magic in my veins, I'd be no different than they were. The wife of a fisherman trying to survive in a harsh world.

Run.

I had no supplies. No knowledge of the land. And with Skade at Harald's disposal, the chances of being hunted down would be high. A failed escape might mean Harald choosing to have me bound where I currently walked free, making another attempt a far greater challenge.

Better to bide my time.

Better to learn what I could.

Better to . . .

My thoughts trailed off as a group of warriors burst from the trees, their elaborate helms and yellow-painted shields telling me that they were Islunders. They did not see us because their focus was on their ships. With them, they dragged a group of crying children.

My stomach dropped.

Children were taught at a young age to take the babies and run into the woods to hide during a raid. We were also taught not to clump together. Yet I remembered how fear drove us to one another, clutching hands and holding our breath in our hiding spots. This group had been found.

"No!" Skade stumbled past me only to fall to her knees, blood running down her chin. She staggered upright only to fall again, and then tried to crawl toward the children, glowing arrow clutched in her hand.

Harald had ordered me to protect the village for him. He'd said nothing about defending children on the beach. If Skade reacted, I could not have said, for I was already running.

"Hlin," I snarled, "lend me your strength."

Magic exploded over my shield and obscured the Islund colors painted on the wood with its glow. The Islunders were shouting at Harald's thralls to aid them, to get in the drakkar, but none moved. With their black hoods covering most of their faces—and their expressions—they seemed like statues set in the sand.

I made it halfway down the beach before the warriors heard my steps and turned, but a few strides later, I was on them. The axe was not my weapon of choice, but by the gods I'd chopped enough wood in my life to know how to swing one.

Screaming, I dodged around one warrior and slammed the small axe down on another's shoulder. Blood sprayed me in the face as I wrenched it out, whirling to take the impact of the first warrior's sword upon my shield. My magic smashed it away, and as he staggered, I fell upon him and hacked like a woman possessed.

"Behind you!" Skade shouted, and I rolled. An axe came down on my shield, flinging the female warrior to one side. I stumbled to my feet and barely managed to block a blow from another. The children screamed and clung to one another, and rage burned in my chest that they had to experience this. Had to suffer because those in power always wanted *more more more* with no care for what it cost others.

With a shriek, I took off a warrior's leg at the knee, my feet sliding in sand made slimy by gore. Yet beyond, more Islunders were fleeing the carnage in the village. Retreating to live and fight another day, and they'd take the children from me.

You can stop them, Hel whispered in my head. *Condemn these slavers of children to my keeping.*

No. My stomach twisted even as I slammed my shield into the face of a warrior, finally getting between the Islunders and the children. But there were too many of them.

I could not stop them all.

They'd kill me and take the children.

Curse them, Freya, Hel whispered. *Give these wicked men to me and save these children.*

"Get back," I screamed at the warriors, the sourness of desperation rising in my chest. "You leave them be!"

The Islunders circled warily, glancing toward the village and then back to me. Afraid Bjorn and Tora would pursue, but unable to let go of the profit they'd make off these children without a fight.

"Back away, Skalander," one of them snarled, a large man with a helm carved like the maw of a bear. "This is not your fight."

"I am the daughter of Hlin." I lifted my shield. "This fight is in my blood."

"So be it." The bear helm glittered as he charged, a powerful down strike aimed at my shield.

Which he reversed at the last moment.

He sliced at my thighs instead, and though I fell back, the tip of his blade still opened a shallow wound. I landed on my arse and barely managed to shove myself out of range as his blade fell. He cut at me again, then withdrew when I raised my shield and circled for a better angle. Like he had trained to fight against someone with Hlin's magic.

"Get them on the ship!" he bellowed. "This one is mine!"

A howl of fury tore from me as they grabbed the crying children and hurled them into the ship. Pushed the vessel into deeper water while I fought to get around the man in the bear helm.

"Freya!"

Bjorn's distant shout reached my ears, but he wasn't close enough to help. Wasn't close enough to stop the Islunders as they readied to row.

I stumbled as Bear Helm attacked without mercy, avoiding my shield and pulling back to keep from striking it even as he wore me down.

"You fight well," he said between panted breaths. "We will take you with us, if you wish. Our last shield maiden went to Valhalla many seasons ago."

"I want nothing to do with slavers!"

He gestured to the still-kneeling thralls. "Says the woman fighting for Harald of Nordeland." He abruptly backed away and waded into the waves.

His fellows caught hold of his arms and lifted him. Fury and fear boiling in my blood, I threw my axe, but it only glanced off the pauldron on his shoulder to fall in the water. He turned to look at me and he laughed. "Come to Islund if you change your mind, Shield Maiden."

The Islunders began to row, the drakkar slipping over the waves as Bjorn and Tora slid to a stop next to me. Harald arrived next, face splattered in blood as he watched his young subjects stolen away. "Tora," he asked softly. "Can you stop them?"

"Not without risking the children." She pushed bloodied hair off her face. "What would you have me do?"

Harald waded into the water, waves rising to his thighs as his gaze went from the drakkar smoldering from a lightning strike to the two overturned vessels floating on the waves amidst corpses of the fallen. No time to right them and pursue, for the Islunders would soon be out of sight. Villagers were stumbling down the beach and screaming for the children who'd been taken. Begging for someone, anyone, to help them. Harald's shoulders slumped and he said nothing.

"What would you have me do?" Tora's voice was frantic. "My king, I must act now if you wish them sunk. The children who survive might swim well enough to reach shore."

Or be swept away by the current to drown.

Nordeland's king remained silent, and I fell to my knees. Blood splatter dripped down my face, the taste of it not half so awful as that of the failure I felt, because this was not right. Not right that these children should be stolen from their families for a life of servitude. A life destined to be short and miserable. "Hel, grant me your power."

Though part of me screamed warning, though Bjorn shouted, "Freya, no!," it was not enough to silence the words that rose to my lips. "I curse you."

The ground shuddered as power flooded my veins, driving me to my feet. "I curse every warrior on your ship," I screamed at Bear Helm, whose smile had fallen away beneath the fangs of his helmet. "You will never see Valhalla, for Hel now claims your souls!"

The waves churned and roots exploded from the depths. Water surged up the beach so that I was drenched to the hip. The roots reached like the tentacles of a great sea monster, snatching up the screaming Islunders and yanking them under the water one by one, but leaving the children untouched. Bear Helm fought the hardest and the longest, wrenching the roots off his body until one wrapped around his waist and dragged him under.

As one, the lifeless bodies, their souls now in Helheim, floated to the surface. It was over.

The only sound to break the silence was the roar of the sea and the weeping of the children in the listing boat. Every breath I took brought the stink of gore, and rivulets of blood trickled down the sand to stain the waves pink as they rolled in and out.

Finally, Harald spoke. "Fetch the children back."

I sat down heavily in the sand.

A hand closed on my shoulder, and even before I turned my head, I knew it was Bjorn. His face was covered with blood and bits of ash. "Are you all right?"

"I'm fine."

"You're not."

Logically, I knew he was right. My thighs stung from the slice across them and blood dripped down my legs. Yet the pain felt distant. "Why did you try to stop me?"

He dropped to his knees next to me. In a voice so low that only I could hear, he said, "Freya, you just won a battle with a few words."

A tremor ran through me, because this was but a taste of the future that stretched out before me. Bodies everywhere and their souls bound to my godly mother's domain.

I clambered to my feet and strode down the beach, walking until there were no more bodies. Until there was no more blood and each breath brought nothing to my nose but the scent of the sea. Then I fell to my knees and pressed my forehead to the clean wet sand.

Weep for what you have done, I screamed at myself. *Weep for what you are!*

But no tears would come.

CHAPTER 7

BJORN

This was precisely what I'd hoped to protect Freya from. Violence that drove her to dark places. The best parts of her forced to use the worst parts of her to do what needed to be done. And though she'd surely saved the lives of all those children, as I watched her sit on the sand farther down the beach, I knew that no part of her felt good about it.

I felt compelled to go to her. To say something, anything, that would ease the burden pressing her down and down. To fall into the careless banter between us that had always felt so easy. A war of retorts that meant nothing and everything. Except the skill seemed lost to me. My tongue frozen with the certainty that everything I said drove Freya farther away from me, because our words were no longer moves in a game but blows on the battlefield, cutting and cruel.

"Does Volund need to see to her?" Harald asked, watching as Tora and Guthrum swam out to the drifting drakkar to secure it with a rope.

"She won't accept help." All too well, I knew how Freya lived with pain as a form of self-punishment for her perceived transgressions.

Vragi had been a piece of weasel shit, abusive to her and all around him. An insult to the god who'd fathered him. He'd deserved death, and yet Freya had always acted as though the burns she'd inflicted upon herself to kill him were a fair punishment. Pain that would sit with her the rest of her life so that she might never forget what she'd done. There was little doubt in my mind that the bleeding wounds on her thighs would serve the same purpose. She'd heal, but the scars would ever remind her of this moment. Though I thought the Islunder raiders deserved their fate, my heart told me that Freya felt no such certainty.

"She fought well," Harald said. "Saved innocent lives."

Even from this distance, the horror they'd witnessed was visible on the faces of the children. Innocent no longer, if they ever had been. Nordeland was a hard place, and those who did not have it in their hearts to rage against land, weather, and violence were not long for the mortal realm. "Of course Freya fought well," I answered. "What is of more surprise is that you also fought well, Father. I had half wondered if you were still capable of swinging a sword in your advanced age, but you acquitted yourself like a man still in his prime."

He cast me a sidelong look. "Have I mentioned that your wit has been missed?"

"No, it strikes me that you haven't. An oversight, I'm sure."

A soft snort exited his lips, then he handed me the end of the rope now bound to the drakkar. "As my strength is spent, I'll leave it to the young bucks such as yourself to pull them in. Beach it farther down where there is less . . ." Harald trailed off, looking at the beach soaked in blood and littered with the dead. "Less horror."

I debated which direction to go before walking down the sand until I stood in Freya's line of sight. Then I began to pull. Survivors from the village lent their strength and we drew the large vessel onto the beach. Weeping women waded into the water to lift out their sons and daughters, but many children stood unclaimed, teary eyes searching for mothers and fathers who would never sweep them into their arms again. A fact I well knew, for I'd stepped over many bodies of villagers as I'd fought the Islunders. Men and women who'd fought to the last to give their children a chance to escape.

Which was not how it should be. Skade and I rarely saw eye to eye but there was no denying that Nordeland had been left nearly undefended while Harald supported my ambition. An ambition I'd torn to shreds. Which meant the lives lost today had been sacrificed for nothing.

Freya was not alone in feeling sick with guilt, but unlike her, I deserved much of the blame here.

I fastened the end of the rope to a heavy piece of driftwood and then stooped in the waves to wash away the worst of the blood on my skin. Heaving myself into the drakkar, I sat down with the remaining children and then called to the sky, "Kaja!"

The bird was circling above, but at my call, she descended to land on my outstretched arm. Kaja and I had never properly met, but Guthrum knew me well, which meant so did she. Her talons dug into the leather of my bracer as she ruffled her feathers, yellow eyes watching me with a predator's focus. Yet it was the eyes of the children around me that commanded my attention. Flickers of interest filtered through the haze of shock that held them in its grasp. I stroked the back of Kaja's head, and she leaned into the pressure.

"Do you wish to touch her?" I asked them. "She is very vain and appreciates the attention."

Kaja cocked her head and gave me a reproachful glare that suggested she understood my words. Yet she preened beneath the small hands that reached out to tentatively touch her feathers. A small distraction to pull their minds from what they had seen, and though it changed nothing, it would create a different memory to fill the moment when no one had come for them. In my periphery, Harald spoke to the survivors. Those who had a connection to these children were dispatched to claim them until I finally sat alone with the bird.

Bending my head to Kaja's ear, I murmured instructions. She took flight and I climbed out of the drakkar to join Harald, who stood in the company of Tora and Skade. The latter was bare to the waist but for the leafy branches Volund had woven around her torso and arm. It seemed Eir had deigned to heal, at least in part, whatever injuries Skade had suffered for she moved with relative ease.

"Some of the Islunders will have escaped," Harald said. "Most will not have seen Freya's battle on the beach, but all saw Bjorn. If given the chance, they will spread the word that he is returned to Nordeland and it will reach Snorri and confirm his suspicions." His eyes fell on Skade. "You will hunt them down and ensure they are silenced."

"Guthrum and Kaja can deal with a few scampering rats," Skade protested, her eyes flicking to me and then away again. "As your right hand, I should be with you, my king."

A role I had served until I'd returned to Skaland, and though I had little interest in reclaiming it, I did find it curious that Harald had filled my place with Skade. She had value to him, there was no denying that, but though no one was more loyal to Harald than she was, it had always struck me that he was put off by her sycophancy.

A thought confirmed in the flatness of his eyes as he said, "You are my huntress and none will escape your arrow."

Typically such flattery would make Skade preen but she instead frowned. "The shield maiden has been on Nordeland's shores less than a day and already death follows. Saga had the right of it that she should be put down lest all of Nordeland suffer."

"This raid was not Freya's doing." I fought the urge to call my axe as Skade's bow appeared in her hand. "The Islunders were here for wealth and thralls, not Freya."

"But they risked coming because we were consumed by her." Skade spat on the ground at our feet. "If we were here to defend our shores, this would never have happened. It is an ill omen."

"We are here now." Harald rubbed at his temples. "And Islund has paid a heavy price for their boldness. See the rest of them dead so that they might know the cost of attacking my lands when none of their drakkar or warriors return. Go."

Skade wavered, and though my concern was the threat she posed to Freya, this defiance was not something I'd ever seen from her before.

"Bjorn is returned," Harald said softly. "I do not need you at my right hand any longer."

Skade blanched, her eyes widening with hurt only for Harald to reach out to cup her cheek. "Islund struck a blow against me, my sweet Skade. They killed our people and that hurts me. You are the only one I trust to deliver appropriate vengeance. Islund must taste the ash of defeat."

Silence stretched and my skin prickled with the certainty that more was being communicated than just the words Harald had spoken aloud, for a slight smile formed on Skade's face. As always, she saw praise where I saw manipulation, inclining her head and murmuring, "I shall see it done, my king."

Twisting on her heel, Skade strode up the beach toward the trees, pausing only to retrieve her tunic and mail before disappearing.

"Skade's fear makes her a threat," Harald murmured. As I followed his line of sight, it was to discover him staring at Freya. She still sat in the sand, though now she was tentatively petting Kaja. "Better for her to go somewhere she can do no damage."

Unease pooled in my stomach. For though it should be a relief that Harald was taking steps to protect Freya's life, there was something off in the method he was doing it. He didn't trust Skade the way he once had, and the way Tora stared dead-eyed at the sand spoke to yet more conflict. Much had changed during the time I'd spent in Skaland, and I did not think it was for the better. When I'd left, it had felt as though we were all united in our goals. But now I could feel tension and divides between everyone.

Harald stepped away to give orders to his Nameless. Most of the thralls were Islunders, though some were from Skaland and others still from parts of Nordeland. All big and strong, arms tattooed with knotwork and ravens and wolves, yet I knew what unified them were their crimes. The darkest and worst sort of men who delighted in the ugliest of behavior, all tamed by magic and made to wear hoods that obscured their faces for the rest of their lives as punishment. Men without names. They were the only sort of thralls Harald ever took, and though they deserved punishment, I'd always thought death would be more merciful than what they endured.

Shaking my head, I gripped Tora's arm. "Thank you for keeping Arkyn from blowing a hole through my chest. Inkwork is costly, and I'd not be best pleased if I had to pay to have it done again."

The faintest glimmer of her usual spirit filled her eyes and Tora said, "I did not do it for you, arsehole. I vowed to kill Arkyn, and if I'd let you do it, I'd never have heard the end of it."

"Unfortunate you didn't get to test out his fingers before you put him down, but I suppose some sacrifices must be made to win the war."

Tora punched me in the shoulder with enough force that I staggered. "You are such an arse. But I'm glad to have you back, brother."

My stomach twisted, because Tora and I had been nearly inseparable as children. Siblings of blade, not blood, and all the stronger for it, but the gulf between us was wide because of the things we had done. We had stood on opposite sides of the battlefield twice and lost comrades to each other both times. Bodil had earned a place in Valhalla, but I'd never forget how Tora had broken Freya on the walls of Grindill, Thor's lightning rebounding off Hlin's shield into dozens of civilians, the smell of burned flesh thick in the air. Never forgive how Freya had been driven to the point she believed her own death was the only way to protect those she cared about. Though it was not lost on me that Tora had been acting under orders, which made me question whether Harald deserved forgiveness.

Harald had sought Freya's death right until the moment he'd learned just how dangerous she was, and what she'd done today would only have affirmed in his mind what a weapon she might be.

Tora's lips parted as though she had more to say, but nothing came out. She swallowed hard, then squeezed her eyes shut, and I could see the artery in her throat fluttering from what must be a rapidly beating heart.

"What is it?" I asked softly, my hackles rising because some heavy thought clearly preyed upon her. "Tell me."

She drew breath as though to speak.

But Harald had finished giving the Nameless their orders, and he shouted at her, "Tora, enough chatter! Get my drakkar set to rights!"

In years past, Tora would have retorted with softhearted defiance but instead she lurched toward the listing vessel, the awkwardness of her motion catching my attention. Tripping and stumbling until she finally righted herself and began giving commands for others to help her overturn the large vessel. The strangeness of it had me watching her with narrowed eyes, wondering if the blow she'd taken when the whale had struck had rattled her skull badly enough that she needed care.

"We leave for Hrafnheim without delay." Harald's voice drew my attention back to him. "Only my drakkar and the Nameless necessary to row up the Rimstrom. Volund and the rest shall remain here to help with the injured and see to the dead."

I frowned, and some strange instinct drew my gaze out to sea. Just in time to catch the flicker of sun catching on metal. Lifting my hand to shade my eyes, I saw the faint outline of a sail. Impossible to tell what sort of vessel it was or how close it had come, but it was heading across the strait toward Skaland.

"The fate your mother foresaw has not been altered." Harald surveyed the bodies his warriors were dragging up the beach to be burned. "A dark cloud looms over Nordeland, and I think Freya needs to speak to Saga before the storm descends." He exhaled a breath. "And pray to all the gods that it is not already here."

CHAPTER 8

FREYA

I felt the shift as Harald berated his warriors and hooded thralls to make his drakkar seaworthy. A growing sense of urgency that infected everyone with a tension that sang through the air. And though the result was us soon continuing down the coast to the mouth of the river Rimstrom, the desperate need for the answers Saga might have for me far outweighed the fear I felt at sailing toward the king of Nordeland's stronghold.

The beaches we passed were barren but for the occasional village eking out a living from the sea. Villages little different from my own childhood home of Selvegr. A dozen small homes. A market. A handful of rough wooden docks. A few fishing boats. The villagers came out when they recognized the blue-striped sails and Harald's white wolf banner, lifting their hands in greeting to their king as he passed. The land beyond these villages was dense with conifers. Endless green that covered the sides of mountains, which had white tips despite it being the end of summer. Fjords ran between them, and it was up one of them we sailed. The entrance to the great river Rimstrom, the waters icy cold from the glaciers that fed it.

I kept to the front of the drakkar, away from Harald and Bjorn, who stood at the rear, Steinunn with them. The silent thralls worked the oars, leaving me only Tora for companionship.

The child of Thor touched the burns on the side of her face, then sighed. "Thank you, Freya. For saving my life. You had plenty of reasons to leave me to die, and instead, you risked your own life to save me. I owe you a debt."

"You don't owe me anything." I watched a school of fish swim beneath us. "If I'd let the whale eat you, I'd have lost the chance to kill you myself, so it was worth the fight."

Tora stared at me for a minute, then a loud guffaw burst from her lips. "For such a small woman, you have a great deal of spirit, shield maiden."

"But not much sense, I'm afraid." I gave her a lopsided smile. "But we all have our flaws."

"It's a good thing you are pretty, then." Tora's laughter slowly faded, and I noticed her glance to where Harald stood talking with Steinunn. "I'm sorry for what happened in Grindill, Freya. I . . ." Her throat moved as she swallowed hard. "I don't like to hurt people. Thor chose poorly when he gave me his blood, because I don't relish battle the way one of his children should."

"Harald ordered you to do it, then?"

Tora didn't answer, but the merriment was fully vanquished from her face now. "War is war," she finally said. "But I will try to repay my debt to you as best I can, Freya Born-in-Fire."

Harald's eyes moved to us, and beneath his scrutiny, the other woman fell wholly silent. Minutes passed, then longer, but Tora only watched the passing trees as she incessantly touched the scars on her face. Haunted, I thought, but while it made sense that it had been Harald who'd ordered her to turn my shields against my own people with her lightning, my gut told me it was something deeper. It made me wonder if Thor influenced Tora the way Hel often tried to influence me.

Darkness fell on Nordeland, and I pulled a sealskin around my shoulders as wind bit into my skin. It moaned through the trees, smelling of frost and pine, and on the far side of the river, I watched a brown bear come down to the water. It stared at me, two cubs behind it. One was injured and walking on three legs. The fourth leg was mangled with wounds that would never heal, the cub already skinny and mangy compared to its sibling. Not long for this world.

As I watched, the mother waded into the water and began to swim. The healthy cub followed while the other cried from the bank, knowing its fate. A slow death. I prayed it would be ended by a merciful predator.

It was as Bjorn had said: Nordeland was the same as Skaland, only colder. Harder.

Motion caught my attention at the rear of the vessel. Bjorn had retrieved a bow and was nocking an arrow. I'd never seen him use the weapon, but he lifted it in a way that spoke to some expertise. He let the arrow fly.

A merciful predator.

My heart ached as the river fell silent again, but my eyes remained dry as stones.

Feathers rustled. Kaja landed on the bow, which was carved in the snarling visage of the wolf Fenrir. She stared at me with her too-canny eyes, but it was a splash alongside the vessel that caught my attention. Tora sighed and reached over the edge, hauling a dripping Guthrum onto the ship.

"Any sign of pursuit?" Harald called. Guthrum shook his head, sitting next to me and eating a piece of jerky that Tora handed him before she retreated to join the others at the rear.

I had gathered that he was a child of Jord, which made him at one with the land, most especially the bird that was his familiar. Yet that was the extent of what I knew. I'd never met one of his blood before, nor heard many stories, but he was the only person on this ship besides the thralls who had not caused the death of someone I loved. "You see what Kaja sees, then? Hear what she hears?"

"If she's of a mind to share," he answered. "Kaja takes what is confided to her seriously, so she'll not betray words intended for just her."

My cheeks warmed, for I had spoken to the bird after the battle and confessed my misery before realizing the extent of their connection.

Guthrum pulled the tunic he'd abandoned earlier over his head. His hair stood up in all directions and made him appear rather feral, for his beard was also unkempt. A man who belonged in the wilds, who belonged to the land, and I sensed that being around so many people was uncomfortable to him. And while I was not uncomfortable around people, the discomfort I felt in this vessel full of enemies made me reach for the small piece of solidarity, so I said to Kaja, "Thank you."

She only ruffled her feathers and turned her head to watch the passing trees as dusk settled further.

"How did you come to be in Harald's service?" I asked so as to steer the conversation away from myself. And to possibly learn more about the man who now held me as a pseudo prisoner.

"As a boy," Guthrum answered, breaking off a piece of the jerky to offer it to Kaja. The bird turned her beak up at it, and he laughed. "Before Harald was king, he was jarl of Hrafnheim. The village I lived in with my mother was on the edge of his territories and deep in the wilds where beliefs in the older ways are strong. My father had left years prior for he held resentment toward my mother. She held desire only for women, which he witnessed when she invited a woman to couple with them."

"The goddess Jord?"

He nodded, chewing. "We knew not of the nature of Jord's children, for skalds never ventured to our village and stories of the Unfated were few. My father believed me to be a foundling. A fae child left to stir trouble. A boy more beast than human.

"My mother cared for me on her own and the village paid little mind for my feral nature or my father's parting words. My familiar then was a dog, so no one thought twice when I spoke to him. A big mastiff whom I loved with all my heart."

My chest tightened, for I knew the tone of a story about to turn to tragedy.

"My father came back when I was perhaps ten," Guthrum said. "He demanded that I go to serve the jarl so that I might honor him. When my mother refused, he set to convincing her with methods other than words." His throat moved. "The next day he was found mauled to death by a beast of tooth and claw. The village blamed me. They believed that I had set my dog on him, and all those accusations he'd once cast upon me reared to life. They came for blood, and when my dog defended me, they killed him. And when my mother barred their path, they killed her, too."

"I'm sorry," I breathed, horrified at his tale.

"Jarl Harald, as he was called then, came to the village as it was the season of collecting tithes. He and his warriors intervened and heard my story. It was Harald who told me the truth of what I was. The son of a goddess and bound to the land. He berated my village for their ignorance and executed those who'd killed my mother, then offered me an opportunity. A home in Hrafnheim when I wished it in exchange for a promise that I watch for others such as me who were mistreated by those who were ignorant of the gods and their children. He believed it his destiny to raise the Unfated up high, as their blood deserves. I accepted his offer and have often brought word of others who suffered as I once did, so that he might aid them. Bjorn included."

I tensed, it taking all of my willpower not to look to where Bjorn stood at the far end of the ship, out of earshot. Curiosity rose in my chest because this was at least part of the explanation for Bjorn's loyalty to Harald. For all I claimed that I didn't care and that his story didn't matter, the quickening in my heart spoke a different truth.

"The burns Bjorn suffered were severe and had fouled. He was near death when he arrived on Nordeland's shores and Saga had to leave him to search for aid. She found my familiar, who told me what had happened. I was able to bring Volund down the Rimstrom to heal him. Saga then found Harald, and he came immediately. He was the first person Bjorn saw when he finally awoke."

"Why are you telling me this?" I whispered, hating the feelings twisting inside me.

"Because it is the truth," Guthrum answered. "And I do not think you would hear it from Bjorn."

"I do not wish to hear it at all." I turned away from him, pulling the sealskin up higher because I felt so painfully cold.

"Why is that, Freya?" Guthrum asked. "It is the truth, seen with my own two eyes. Why do you not wish to know it?"

"Because I am not stupid," I hissed. "If I forgive Bjorn for his betrayal, it will be easier to make me do what you all want. Your truths are wielded to turn me into a monster."

"We all have a monster within us." As I turned to meet his gaze, it was to find his eyes had gone as yellow as Kaja's in the fading light, wholly inhuman.

He rose to his feet and cast aside his tunic, obviously intending to jump back into the water to again blend into the forest. But as he slung his leg over the edge of the drakkar, I said, "It was your dog who killed your father, wasn't it?"

The corner of his mouth turned up. "Yes, because I asked him to do it. The monster was let loose but the monster wasn't the dog."

Guthrum dove into the depths of the Rimstrom and disappeared into the darkness, Kaja along with him.

We are all monsters, I thought, then Harald's voice broke the silence. "We camp here tonight."

CHAPTER 9

FREYA

Though Harald's thralls had rowed through the day and were no doubt exhausted, not one of them said a word when he ordered them to set up camp in a clearing surrounded by dense woods. After the tents were pitched and the fires crackled brightly, they lay down in rows and immediately fell to sleep, hoods still firmly in place. Though I'd spent time around Snorri's thralls in Halsar, I found the behavior of these men to be strange and myself deeply uncomfortable around them for reasons beyond their enforced servitude. The leather hoods they wore concealed most of their faces and they never spoke, only obeyed Harald's commands without question. They were dressed identically, so the only way to tell them apart was through their size and the myriad of tattoos on their arms. Not one of them carried a weapon but every time one of them stepped near me, I reached for my sword. Only to remember that it had been left behind in Skaland. Steinunn appeared equally uneasy around them, for she volunteered to cook rather than accepting Harald's offer to wake a thrall to do the task.

Yet after examining the meal, I couldn't help but wonder if waking one of the strange thralls would have been the better option.

"Do spice merchants not travel to Nordeland?" I muttered after one mouthful of the watery soup, which tasted like river mud and boiled rabbit. "Or is blandness a Nordelander preference?"

"Our supplies were lost," Steinunn answered. "Eat it or starve, your choice."

Dumping the soup back in the pot, I lit a branch to serve as a torch and started down to the riverbank. Bjorn followed and I glowered at him. "I don't need an escort. I'm only foraging."

"As will be many predators in the woods at this time," he replied. "Predators foraging for spicy shield maidens. If you are eaten, I'll have nothing for dinner but Steinunn's disgusting soup, so I am invested in seeing you back to the fire in one piece."

"What you should invest in is a bath."

"I had one when I was dumped into the sea."

"With soap." I pulled up a thick pepperrot plant, then moved into the trees where I spotted some fine mushrooms. "There is not a soup good enough to give me an appetite with your stink wafting over the fire."

Bjorn didn't answer. Wondering if I'd pushed him too far with my insults, I paused in my mushroom foraging to look over my shoulder. But Bjorn's face held no irritation, only concern.

"Are you well, Born-in-Fire?" he asked quietly.

I knew he didn't mean my injury, yet I said, "It was not a deep cut." My fingers moved swiftly to pluck up the small mushrooms so as to escape the conversation. "It has already scabbed."

"I wasn't speaking of the cut." He hesitated. "I ask because you killed many men today."

My stomach plummeted. The hollowness it left behind made me feel oddly short of breath. "As did you. Are you well, Bjorn? Or do you wish some privacy to weep over the Islunders you hacked apart on the beach and in the village?"

"I am not well."

"I do not actually care." I bit the insides of my cheeks until I tasted blood, hating how I reached for the nastiest possible thing to say only to regret the words the moment they passed my lips. "No one made me kill those men. I made the choice myself and I do not regret it. Now leave me be."

Pine needles crunched beneath my shoes as I walked past him, but Bjorn caught hold of my wrist. His hand felt like fire against my cold skin and all the world fell away. I stared up into his eyes, the shadows of the torch dancing across his face as I waited for him to say whatever it was that had driven him to follow me. My mind suggested several ideas for what might be going on in his head, including that he might fall to his knees and beg my forgiveness. But Bjorn only gave a tight nod and let go of my wrist, the echoes of heat on my skin making me feel colder as I hurried back to camp.

The others had all dumped their soup back into the pot and watched me with interest as I washed and chopped the plants I'd foraged and allowed them to simmer until it was to my satisfaction. Spooning it into the bowls, I set to eating though I had no appetite.

"It's good," Steinunn said. "You've skill."

I gave a noncommittal grunt. She'd said little on our journey, and if not for the fact that the skald had been the one to drug me as I tried to escape Harald, I might have thought her as much a prisoner as I was.

Yet as my eyes fell on her shoes, the leather dyed a brilliant red, I was reminded that she'd been Harald's spy all along. When she'd sung the song of our journey through the tunnels beneath Fjalltindr, Steinunn had accidentally revealed that she'd indeed followed us rather than returning to Snorri's camp, for the cup I'd knocked down the stairs had bounced past those very shoes. She'd negotiated her survival in the tunnels with the draug jarl by promising to compose a song about his fame, spied on Bjorn and me, and then conspired with Harald once she'd reached the top. It had been Steinunn, not Ylva, who'd tried to come into the hall only to be repelled by Ylva's wards. It had been Steinunn who'd left the message of Snorri's plans for Grindill carved in runic magic on the tree, shown to me by the specter.

And it had been Steinunn who'd passed word to Skade that I'd gone to see my mother, which meant it had been Steinunn who'd caused my mother's death.

It was all I could do not to fall upon her and beat her bloody, but I forced myself to keep eating.

"Would you grace us with a song?" Harald asked the skald after we'd eaten. "A story about the gods?"

"Yes, my king."

As Steinunn climbed to her feet, Bjorn gave a soft snort of annoyance. "I'm going for a bath."

I glared at the fire, but my traitorous eyes followed him. Watched as he pulled off his tunic and the naked muscles of his back were illuminated, as well as the old burn scars. Guthrum's tale had begun only after Saga had brought Bjorn to Nordeland, so the exact details of what had happened before were still unclear. I'd been led to believe it was Harald who had attacked Saga and kidnapped Bjorn, only to be told that Harald had saved them. Logically I should just ask for the truth and be done with it, but deep in my heart, I feared that his story would make all the lies he'd told reasonable and just. That I'd lose my grounds to be angry with him, and if I could not be angry, all that would be left was grief.

As though she played for a large group in a great hall, the skald removed her cloak and straightened her red dress. Though the curves of her full breasts strained against the bodice, I noted that her face had gained hollows, the skin beneath her eyes dark with exhaustion. She ran her fingers through her light brown ringlets, which spilled down to her waist and gleamed in the firelight. Steinunn picked up her small drum as Bjorn moved out of the fire's illumination, and then clucked her tongue in irritation for the instrument was still wet from having been immersed in the sea.

Bjorn had surely known Steinunn was a spy and yet had done little to dissuade me from blaming Ylva for all my woes. So many lies. So many cursed lies, and I was such a naive fool who'd been played by everyone.

Steinunn began to sing, and I tensed, my eyes fixed on the crimson tattoo on her neck that pulsed with the beat of her heart. No part of me wanted her visions playing in my head. But the words were an old poem written about the death of Baldur by way of Loki's trickery. How Hel had refused to release the most beautiful of gods from Helheim unless all the world wept for his loss. All had but one, the giantess Thokk, and in Helheim, Baldur had remained.

The song trailed away on the wind through the trees, and I lay down to sleep, rolling so that my back was to the fire. The moss beneath me was thick and soft, and every time I moved, it released an earthen scent. The fire crackled, the pine sap making loud *pops,* but I scarcely noticed. My focus was on the sounds of the others readying their bedrolls for rest. On the soft tread of Bjorn returning to the camp, though I refused to look at him.

Sleep, I ordered myself. *You must rest.*

But Steinunn's song had filled my head with thoughts of Helheim and the souls I had sent there. For many, it would be no curse to go to Hel's realm, but for a warrior, it was worse than death itself to be denied Valhalla.

The Islunders had deserved death. They'd raided an innocent village, killed many, and had intended to steal those children to make them into thralls. But it should be the gods who decided which realm their souls went to after death, not mine. Not in a split-second decision driven by desperation and fear. It was too great a power and the consequences of using it were far too high.

Never again, I promised myself.

Then a branch snapped.

I lifted my head to discover Steinunn creeping away from the fire. I'd vaguely heard her volunteer to take the first watch but instead of doing so, the skald disappeared into the forest. A quick survey of those around me revealed all were asleep, so I silently rose to my feet and followed.

It was the darkest sort of night, neither moon nor stars visible in the sky. To follow her would have been nearly impossible except that

Steinunn carried a lamp. It allowed me to keep enough distance that she did not hear the errant crackle of needle and branch beneath my own shoes, and as a pair, we made our way farther into the woods.

What precise reason drove me to follow the skald, I didn't know, but with each step, I silently repeated her lies. Her betrayals. The names of those I loved whom her actions had cost me. So by the time Steinunn stopped moving, my fists were balled tight and my anger seethed. I wouldn't kill her. But by the gods, I fully intended to make her hurt for what she'd done.

As I readied myself to give the skald a pummeling she would not soon forget, my eyes picked up familiar shapes in the shadows around me. Not just trees, but the remains of burned structures. The charred bones of what had once been a village. Steinunn dropped to her knees, and my anger faltered as I took in the row of cairns she knelt before. As I watched, the skald bent her head over a smaller one and her body shook with sobs.

The memory of a conversation she and I had had after the taking of Grindill filled my head. *I endured a tragedy that cost me nearly everything I held dear.*

A family, it seemed. A child, judging from the small cairn. And from violence, if the remains of the village around me spoke true. A pang of sympathy struck me in the heart, her sobs so thick with grief that it made the air around me unbreathable.

That Steinunn had suffered did not absolve her of the harm she'd caused me, but I would not sink so low as to attack her in the depths of her grief. Exhaling a breath to find some measure of calm, I stepped back with the intent to return to camp.

Only for my shoulders to slam into something solid and warm.

A hand clamped over my mouth to smother my shout even as an arm wrapped around my waist and lifted me off my feet. Panic rose only to burst into aggravation as I inhaled Bjorn's familiar scent of pine, as well as the soap he seemed to have used while bathing. Only respect for the dead kept me from lashing out as he backed away from the village and carried me deeper into the forest. But once we were far enough distant that Steinunn would not hear, I slammed my heels against his shins as hard as I could.

He hissed in pain, muttering curses about my parentage that I did not appreciate as he dropped me to the forest floor. Spinning, I slammed my palms against his chest. His *bare* chest.

My hands jerked away from his skin as though he'd burned me. To cover my reaction, I glared at him in the darkness. "Did your clothes wash away while you were bathing or is it Nordelander custom to wander the woods in the nude?"

"You know it is my preferred attire for fighting," he replied. "And given I followed you, I needed all the advantages I could muster."

"Nudity does not serve so well in the dark."

"I beg to differ." He leaned closer, the heat of him warming my skin. "Now lower your voice. I bribed Kaja with a rabbit, but she may yet follow and her ears are keen."

It was tempting to be contrary, but I had enough pragmatism left in my soul to drop my voice to a whisper as I said, "Why? So that she does not hear you brag about your good looks and report back to your master about your excessive vanity?"

"It is only you who comments on my looks, Born-in-Fire," he retorted. "Unlike yours, my mind is on more serious matters."

It was a struggle not to grind my teeth. "Something equally self-serving, I'm sure."

He exhaled a long breath of frustration. "Freya, I know you are angry with me, but could you please set aside your emotions and listen to what I have to say?"

"No," I snapped. "But as luck would have it, my *emotions* have no impact on the functionality of my ears, so say what you wish to say and be done with it."

He kicked at the underbrush. "There are no words that you'll not take issue with."

Triumph filled me at having bested him. "Perhaps, but it does not help that you choose the worst of them. Or that half of them are lies."

Silence stretched between us, the tension so thick I could barely breathe.

"I do not trust Harald's intentions." His voice was soft, barely audible over the wind in the forest around us. "He was driven by my mother's visions of the future and my desire for revenge against Snorri to see you dead. Over and over, he tried to kill you, Freya, and I can't fault him for that. What worries me is that upon seeing that you have Hel's blood, he has turned away from the path my mother set him on. My concern is why he wants you alive."

I scoffed. "What concerns you is that he is no longer trying to kill me? This feels like backward thinking."

In truth, I had considered Harald's motivations as well, but I was curious what Bjorn might say in the face of my willful denseness.

"Don't," he growled, not fooled. "You know what a weapon your magic is, Born-in-Fire. If you'd wanted to, you could have fought that battle on your own. Put every Islunder on the ground with a few words."

"I'll never do it again." My nails dug into my palms. "To decide where a soul should go is not a power any mortal should have. I refuse to wield it again."

"You say that, but desperate moments drive desperate actions. If you think that thought has not lighted upon Harald's mind, you are wrong. I think he balances the risk of what my mother has foreseen with the reward of having you defend his shores because the moment anyone you perceive as innocent is in danger and your back is against the wall, I think you'll call Hel's name."

Even if I desired to serve Harald, it was impossible with the oath I'd sworn to Snorri, but instead I said, "You name him Father and wear his arm ring as a sign of fealty, but it seems you do not trust your king."

"I trust him to do right by Nordeland," Bjorn replied. "But I fear what that means for you. He believes you cannot run from your fate as it has been foreseen—that you must change it or succumb to it. I think he aims to help you change it."

My eyes narrowed, uncertainty filling my chest because that was not something I'd considered. Harald was the enemy and no part of me was inclined to see him as otherwise. Yet perhaps even enemies could have common goals. "Given the dark future your mother sees for me, I fail to see how Harald aiding me to change it is a bad thing."

"You assume it will change for the better. What if it changes to something worse?"

For reasons I could not explain, his words struck like a punch to the stomach. "What would you have me do?" My eyes burned but no tears fell. "Do something. Do nothing. Either way, it seems I am cursed."

"No!" Though we stood in the deepest dark, he caught hold of my hands with unerring precision. The feel of his palms against mine, large and calloused and so painfully familiar, made my body shake. "That is not what I mean, Freya. I know you don't trust me. That you believe everything I've ever said is a lie and that you hate me for it. That you have no reason to listen to me now. But I will beg one thing from you, and that is that you do not serve him."

"In that you have nothing to fear, for even if I desired to serve Harald, I cannot." I pulled my hands away. "I'm bound by Ylva's blood magic with a vow to serve no man not of Snorri's blood, which unless there are yet more secrets I'm unaware of, does not include Harald."

Bjorn didn't answer, and his silence conveyed his shock even if the darkness hid his face. Finally, he said, "When did you make this oath?"

"The night I was wed to him."

"Why would you swear such a thing?" he demanded.

"Because the alternative was far worse." The words came out choked, and I swallowed hard to steady my voice. "I made the choice I could live with."

"I wish you'd told me." His shadow shifted restlessly. "I'd have . . ."

"You'd have what?" No matter how many times I swallowed, the emotion strangling me would not clear my throat. "Killed him? Because that's a lie. You apparently have had just cause to kill Snorri all these long years and have not, so do not pretend my oaths to him would have moved your hand."

We stood inches from each other, though I'd not remembered either of us closing the distance. So close that I could feel the heat of him. The brush of his breath against my face. My heart fluttered in my chest like a wounded bird, emotion choking me, drowning me. I wanted to be away from it and from him. So I said, "There was a moment I believed that I stood strong because you were always at my back, Bjorn. Now I know better. I stood alone then, and I'll stand alone now."

Not allowing him the chance to respond, I strode back in the direction of camp without making any effort to be silent. The forest was alive with the sounds of nocturnal creatures, or those who were hunted by them, and my ears filled with the bark of a fox and the hoots of an owl. But it wasn't enough to drown out the flap of heavy wings overhead. I froze and looked skyward, searching for a shadow. But I could see nothing through the branches of the trees.

Was it Kaja?

Whatever it was had sounded larger than the merlin but sound behaved strangely in the night. Gooseflesh broke across my skin at the idea that she'd been spying on us, but there was nothing to be done about it now. I continued on until I reached the camp. Steinunn was still gone, everyone else sound asleep, including Guthrum. But just outside of the firelight, Kaja picked at a dead rabbit.

Circling around, I knelt before her. "If it was you," I whispered, "please don't tell."

And then before Bjorn or Steinunn could return and force me to acknowledge them, I crawled into my bedroll and squeezed my eyes shut, willing myself to sleep.

CHAPTER 10

FREYA

Though our absence had surely been noticed, no one said anything about it as we continued our progress up the Rimstrom at dawn the next morning. Yet neither was I left to my own devices, for Steinunn joined me an hour into our journey. Together, we watched the banks of the river slip past, nothing beyond the rocky shore but endless trees and dense foliage.

"You followed me last night," she asked, "didn't you?"

"What of it?"

Steinunn's lips pursed, and she appeared ready to retreat to the other end of the ship, but instead said, "I do not owe you an explanation but I will give you one so that you will understand that my actions against you in Skaland were just. That village was my home. I was wed to the love of my life, and together we had a son. I lost both in a raid." Her voice shook ever so slightly. "A raid led by Snorri and his warriors."

I said nothing, part of me having known this must have been the motivation for all she'd done.

"In Snorri's pursuit of his destiny as king of Skaland, he believed he needed Bjorn's magic to reveal the shield maiden and was willing to stop at nothing to take him back from Harald. His raid on my village was one of many that occurred as he fought his way up the Rimstrom to Hrafnheim." Her chin trembled. "I was away when it occurred but those who survived told me how Snorri killed my husband, who was jarl, with his own hand. My young son as well."

My stomach tightened. Logically I'd known that Snorri had pursued Bjorn using violence but had never once considered what that had cost the people of Nordeland. In truth, even if I had considered it, I might not have cared, for they were the faceless enemy. Yet faceless no longer.

"I wanted to die," Steinunn whispered. "Wanted to stab my seax into my broken heart, because I had no reason left to live. But Harald arrived in time to stop me. Told me everything, including the plan for Bjorn to return to Skaland to change the future Saga had foreseen so that Snorri would never wear a crown. He asked me to seek vengeance by aiding in the plan, and, in doing so, gave me a reason to live."

"I wish it had been any other way," Harald said, having come to the fore of the vessel without me noticing, so caught up had I been in Steinunn's story. "A good man, Jarl Dag. A loyal jarl. It is Odin's good fortune to have him in Valhalla."

"But my son is not with him," Steinunn answered. "Not only was he robbed of life, he was robbed of the chance to join the Allfather. I will not rest until he is avenged, and then I will join him in Helheim."

Harald rested a hand on her shoulder. "You will have your vengeance, Steinunn. Yet I hope you will reconsider leaving us and instead compose a ballad of our victory, including your family's part in it, so that their legacy might live."

"I cannot sing of their loss." She wiped away tears. "Because to sing it would mean witnessing their end. My broken heart cannot bear that pain."

"Perhaps if you did, then you'd understand how the rest of us feel when you sing our horrors for entertainment," I said. "You told me once that no one cares to hear your stories, but the truth is that you are too much of a coward to sing of them."

Steinunn's face darkened with anger. "You hateful bitch!"

"Perhaps. But I have done nothing to you, skald. Whereas your actions cost the lives of those I cared for deeply. Be glad that all I give to you is contempt because I assure you, I am capable of far worse."

Steinunn hissed a stream of curses as I turned my back on her, but stuck on the drakkar as we were, there was nowhere to go. We were all trapped together, enemies who had caused harm to each other. Who would continue to cause harm, and I wished desperately to be away from them. Bjorn most of all.

From the corner of my eye, I watched him at the rear of the ship staring at the passing trees. Silent, though he'd surely heard much of our conversation. I wondered how he felt learning that it wasn't only his desire for revenge against Snorri that had driven Harald, but Steinunn's as well.

"Vengeance is a circle without end." Harald rested his hands to either side of one of the shields mounted on the vessel's rail. "But Steinunn is a good woman, Freya."

"No one on this ship is good." I thought of Guthrum's words, though I'd not seen any sign of him since the prior night. "Did she and Bjorn know they both served you?"

"Neither of them *served me*. It was their own vengeance they sought."

I snorted. "Just answer the question, Harald."

"Steinunn knew Bjorn's goal." He sighed. "Bjorn was unaware that Steinunn sought her own vengeance or even that she was Nordeland born."

Surprise filled me. "Why? You didn't trust him?"

"Bjorn was under a great deal of scrutiny." Harald toyed with the rim of the shield. "If he'd known Steinunn was like-minded in goal, a connection would have formed between them that might have caused the same scrutiny to fall upon her. And she was our best source of information on everything that was happening."

So I couldn't hold Bjorn culpable for Steinunn's actions. That didn't mean he was absolved. Far from it. Changing the subject, I asked, "How much longer must we travel?"

"We near the Skjoldfjell." Harald gestured upstream. "So not much longer now." My eyes traveled to the twin peaks of a mountain that reared higher than any other in the range. Between them rested a glacier that formed the Rimstrom, and at the base of the mighty mountain was Harald's stronghold of Hrafnheim. The seat of his power, and the next step on the journey toward the answers I sought.

True to Harald's word, within a few hours I had my first look at the center of Nordeland's rule. The rushing water of Rimstrom divided into two around a large island, which held the fabled fortress. Rising out of the water were walls I guessed to be at least fifty feet tall, made of blocks of stone covered with runes. Towers were equally spaced around the wall, and bridges jutted out over both branches of the river. It seemed to me that the bridges could be raised, for thick chains stretched between them and the walls. I wondered what sorts of giants of men were required to lift them.

The downstream end of the island had a gap in the wall flanked by towers, a thick chain stretched between them to block passage. As Harald's banner was spotted by those on the watchtower, a horn bellowed and the chain began to rise. We drew closer, and my heart thundered in my chest, because the fortress of Grindill seemed a hovel by comparison. It made me wonder if what I'd seen of Nordelander strength in the raids was but the tip of the iceberg of the force Harald could muster.

Ropes were floated out to the drakkar. Tora and Bjorn caught hold of them and fixed them to the front of the vessel as the thralls drew in the oars. Then the drakkar was slowly pulled through the narrow gap between the towers, revealing a stone harbor that was large enough to hold perhaps two such vessels, though it would fit many smaller ones. Men and women hurried along the quay, tossing ropes to the thralls.

"In my youth before I became jarl, I traveled a great deal to other nations," Harald said. "Saw fortresses and cities of a scope beyond my wildest dreams, and I studied the art of their construction. When I became jarl of Hrafnheim, it was made of wood and rushes. With years of labor, it has become what you see now."

"Labor and wealth stolen in raids on Skaland." I gave him a saccharine smile. "I am surprised the stone is not red."

Rather than taking offense, Harald only shrugged. "Raids on Islund, to be accurate. They have made themselves wealthy plundering lands to the west, and so we take only what they took from others." He gestured to his thralls, whose eyes glittered behind their hoods. "Most of my Nameless were warriors of Islund who attacked Nordeland's shores. They discovered that we are far from defenseless and paid a heavy price for their hubris."

"Was the price their tongues?" I remembered what Bjorn had told me about Ragnhild after he'd cut off her head. She'd been able to speak directly with Harald because he held her token—her tongue. "I've never known thralls to be this silent."

"The price they paid for their crimes was losing their names and their reputations, but yes, also their voices. Open your mouth." Harald snapped his fingers at one of the thralls—a man with thick arms, the snarling teeth of a wolf visible beneath his pushed-up sleeve. He obediently opened his mouth and held out his tongue. On it was a brand of a rune I did not recognize.

"Magic," I murmured, horrified that it could be used in such a way.

"I did not just learn about building fortresses in my travels." Harald nodded once at the thrall, and the man obediently closed his mouth. But he still watched me, and his unblinking eyes made my skin crawl. "In other places, there are other gods. And other powers. Perhaps one day you'll have the chance to see for yourself."

If this was the sort of magic in these other places, I was happy enough never seeing them but I kept my own mouth shut as the drakkar was pulled against the quay.

Hrafnheim buzzed with excitement. From all directions, civilians and warriors alike flowed toward the harbor, all waiting in obvious anticipation. My skin prickled, and to my left I found Bjorn had an expression on his face I'd not ever seen before. I hadn't the words to describe the precise emotion, but it was the look of a man who has returned to the place of his heart after too long away.

Yearning.

That was the word.

As I realized it, anger filled me. "You told everyone this was your prison. But this is your home, isn't it?"

"You are my home, Freya," he answered. "Everywhere else is just a place to lay my head."

I bared my teeth, not caring if I looked feral because his words made me remember all the promises he'd made that were now lies. Made me remember how, for a heartbeat, I'd thought I'd had everything only to realize it had no more substance than smoke on the wind. I willed my anger to rise and drive away the hurt, but it was as though my rage had consumed all its fuel, leaving behind nothing but glowing coals.

Harald leaped out of the drakkar onto the quay to the cheers of those watching. "We have returned victorious!" he shouted. "We have liberated the shield maiden from Snorri, and she will change the fate of all who cross her path, for she is the child of two bloods! Daughter of Hlin and of Hel!"

Shock stole my voice, because I didn't understand why he had chosen to announce my presence. It might well be true that Snorri would discover I was here eventually, but this was akin to Harald inviting Skaland to his doorstep.

Shouts of astonishment filled the air, and Tora nudged me in the ribs with one elbow. "Get out," she muttered. "And don't make a scene."

I climbed out of the ship and onto the quay and stood with my arms crossed while everyone gaped at me. Someone pushed a shield into my hands, and I stared at it, knowing they wanted a demonstration of my power. Proof that the lives lost in my taking had achieved something. Memory of black roots exploding out of the ground to drag warriors down into Hel's domain filled my mind's eye. Her power. And mine. The darker half of me that I'd always known existed: harsh, greedy, and indifferent to the plight of others.

The part of me that had enticed Harald into allowing me to live, but the truth was, *she* terrified me.

So I whispered Hlin's name and reached for the magic that was my old friend, and a brilliant glow flowed over the wood of the shield. The king of Nordeland gave me a slight smile, as though he understood my choice, and then he shouted, "And greater news still, my people! For my son and heir, Bjorn, has returned to us!"

There was no mistaking the delight in the eyes of these strangers. Dozens of them called out Bjorn's name as Harald slung an arm around his shoulders. Not a prisoner. Never a prisoner.

They ventured into the crowd and the people touched Bjorn's arm. Clapped him on the back and gave him well wishes. The smile on his face was a knife to my gut. Never once had he behaved this way in Halsar, always distant and aloof even when he'd been eating, drinking, and laughing with my people. Because they had never been *his* people.

Biting my lip, I handed off the shield and gave no protest as Tora guided me onward. We followed Bjorn and Harald deeper into Hrafnheim, and I drank in everything around me. While the walls and exterior of the fortress had been of foreign construction, the buildings inside were familiar in style. Yet what struck me was the incredible number of wards carved into every wall and door. I had no notion of what they meant, but from time to time, one would flare bright. "What are the wards for?"

"Protection," Tora answered.

I flexed the fingers of my right hand, which were painfully stiff from neglect, and asked, "Protection from what?"

"Fire. Pestilence. Flood. Islund." Tora looked down at me. "Skaland."

The idea of attacking this fortress seemed like the sort of madness that no jarl would consider, but that had been Snorri's goal when he became king. To rally the clans all across Skaland into a unified force capable of taking on these defenses. Yet looking around at the endless wards, part of me wondered if even that would have been destined to fail.

Harald's great hall was at the center of the town, and though it was large, it was not half as large as what I'd expected. It was formed of thick timbers with a steeply pitched roof formed of wooden shingles. The walls were carved with runes larger than I was tall, as were the twin doors, though they were also carved with elaborate knotwork that must have taken the woodworker half a year to create. Large statues of wolves guarded the entrance. The work was remarkably realistic, eyes formed of glass so flawless that I swore they must be alive.

Then the white one moved.

It stretched, nose to the ground and arse in the air, then trotted with long strides to Harald. He dropped to his knees to pet the wolf with enthusiasm, and the black one trotted over to share in the attention.

"Skoll and Hati," Tora said. I stared at the massive wolves, which had to weigh as much or more than most men. Were these the sons of Fenrir in truth or just their namesakes? Both animals had designs painted on their furry foreheads and collars of silver around their necks.

"Do they chase the sun and moon?" I watched as Skoll licked Bjorn's hand, seeming to know him.

"No," a familiar voice said.

Skade stepped next to me, the mocking tone of her voice identical to the one that she'd used toward my mother right before she'd killed her. "But run, and they will join me in the hunt for you."

Both wolves chose that precise moment to turn their heads to regard me, the intelligence in their eyes far beyond what I'd ever seen an animal possess. A shiver passed over me. "Did you find your quarry?"

"Within the hour," she replied. "And then I found a fast horse. No one ever eludes my hunt, Freya. Remember that." Lengthening her stride, Skade disappeared into the hall.

"Beware her," Tora said beneath her breath. "In Bjorn's absence, she has been our king's right hand and she has a jealous nature."

"Shouldn't you be warning him?" I muttered back.

"No." With that cryptic response, Tora stepped through the doors and I was forced to hurry to catch up.

Inside, a wave of warmth and the scent of woodsmoke washed over me. The feasting space was full of large tables and benches that were overlooked by a dais with two thrones. The upper level was supported by thick pillars carved with depictions of the gods, and in the center, a large stone hearth burned, smoke rising to the opening above.

Servants were already at work loading the tables with casks of mead and wine. The smell of grilling meat caused my stomach to rumble. Moving away from Tora and Skade, I stopped before the dais and stared at the thrones formed of antlers, the seats cushioned with thick white pelts. One was larger than the other, the smaller of the two somehow . . . *feminine.* Turning to Harald, I asked, "Who is your queen?"

The king of Nordeland rocked on his heels and cast a sideways glance at Bjorn, then he said, "Saga is my wife, but not my queen. She has no wish to rule, but I keep the seat for her should she change her mind."

I blew out a slow breath from between my teeth, because the answer seemed so obvious now. The way Harald spoke about Saga. The way he had named her son as his son and heir. "I would like to go to speak to her now."

"It is nearly a two-day journey to her cabin," Bjorn said. "To be around people is a burden for her, as she sees their futures, good and bad, and it weighs upon her. So just as in Skaland, she lives in isolation."

My eyes narrowed, suspicion filling my chest that all of this was more lies. That Saga was dead in truth, all of this a fabrication to manipulate me. But then Harald said, "Bjorn will take you to Saga. But first we have planned a feast for you."

I didn't want food. I wanted answers. "I wish to go to Saga now," I said. "But I wish for you to take me, not Bjorn."

"As much as I desire to see the woman of my heart, it is not possible for me to leave Hrafnheim right now. There is much requiring my attention after my long absence, none the least making plans to deal with Islund's raids." Harald tilted his head. "If you wish to wait a fortnight, I would gladly accompany you."

"I don't wish to wait." I lifted my chin. "Anyone may guide me but him. I do not wish to be in his presence."

"And I do not wish to deny the love of my life a visit from her son, from whom she has been long absent." Harald's tone was flat. "My goodwill stretches only so far, Freya. Be careful of testing its limits, especially when it comes to Saga's happiness. She has endured enough hardship, and I won't allow you to cause more."

I bit my lower lip, torn for many reasons, including some I was unwilling to admit to myself.

"Bjorn is leaving at dawn to visit his mother," Harald said. "Go with him or wait a fortnight and travel with me. Your choice."

I closed my eyes because I didn't want to be alone with Bjorn. Didn't want to sit across a fire from him, or walk by his side, or sleep near him under the stars, because it hurt too much. Every time I looked at his face, I was reminded of how happy I'd been for that singular moment, and then the sensation of being gutted when the truth had been revealed. "Aren't you worried he'll try to steal me again?"

Bjorn gave a soft snort that sounded a great deal like '*I don't have a death wish,*' but Harald only shook his head. "No. But I do worry that you might take revenge on my son in his sleep, so I will send Skoll and Hati to protect him."

"I don't need your pets to protect me from Freya, Father," Bjorn said.

Harald burst into laughter as though Bjorn's words had been the greatest of comedy, then he wiped his cheeks and said, "The wolves will come with you, my son, and you will leave at dawn."

"Seems unnecessarily early."

All amusement vanished from Harald's face. "Your absence these long years has taken a toll on your mother, boy. While Freya has a choice of whether to go with you or not, *you* will ride to see your mother at dawn without argument."

Everyone in the hall fell silent. For my part, it was because of the weight of authority in Harald's voice. A tone I'd not heard him use but which reminded me that he was king of all of Nordeland for a reason. Bjorn alone appeared uncowed as he stared Harald down in a battle of wills, though whether it was over the request itself or the fact it had been delivered as an order, I didn't know. Bjorn's gaze moved from Harald to me for a heartbeat, green eyes dark with some inner debate, and then he said, "As you say, Father. I'll leave at dawn."

The tension dissipated in a rush and everyone, including me, took a breath.

Guthrum chose that moment to enter the hall with Kaja flying overhead to perch upon the rafters. He inclined his head. "No signs of pursuit up the Rimstrom, my king," he said. "By your leave, I would return to the coast so that Kaja might journey across the strait to see what plans our enemy makes against us."

Harald held up an arm and the bird flapped down to land upon his wrist, claws digging deep enough that it must have hurt. Yet he showed no reaction. Only stroked a gentle finger over her feathers. "Keep a wary eye, Kaja. And show care, for Snorri is no fool and his archers have skill."

Kaja ruffled her feathers as though the very thought of being caught was foolishness, then took to the air and soared out the open doors. "You show care as well, my friend," Harald said to Guthrum. Digging into his pocket, he extracted a chain festooned with tiny silver medallions, which he tossed to the man. "The southern merchants bring unbiased gossip, most especially when their cups are kept full."

Guthrum touched the silver armband above his elbow and nodded. "Yes, my king. I'll send a message the moment Kaja returns to me."

He left without another word and Harald moved to sit at a table, pouring himself a cup from the pitcher that sat at its center. "It's only a matter of time until Snorri confirms you're here, Freya."

Sweat broke out on my palms at the reminder. Not just because of the consequences for me or for Nordeland but because Geir and Ingrid were under Snorri's control. Would he harm them out of spite or attempt to use them against me once again? The clamminess of my palms intensified, icy sweat dripping down my spine because if Snorri sent a direct order for me to return, would I be able to refuse him? Or would my oath bind me to obey him and force me back across the strait whether I wanted to go or not?

I desperately tried to remember the exact words that I'd sworn that night, but my mind was a chaos of anxiety and the phrasing kept mixing up in my head. Dismay was rising on the faces of the Nordelanders as though they, too, had thought we'd have more time. Steinunn's hands twisted the fabric of her skirts, Skade touched the seax belted at her waist, and Tora stared blankly at the floorboards, tension growing with every passing moment.

Then Steinunn blurted out, "It will be as it was when he was desperate to claim Bjorn. As long as he can muster the men or afford mercenaries, Snorri will never cease trying to claim his destiny, which means doing whatever it takes to get his shield maiden back. How many Nordelanders will die in his attacks as he attempts to reach her?" Steinunn's voice broke and she coughed to clear it. "Saga, who has seen visions of the future granted to her by the Allfather, said Freya must die to prevent Nordeland from falling to darkness and we have all suffered to achieve that end. Yet Freya stands here as a favored guest. I say we kill her and send Snorri her head so that we might have a chance at a better future."

"I agree with Steinunn." Skade's bow appeared in her hands. "The risks that come with keeping Freya alive are obvious. The advantages much less so. Especially given she has made it clear she will not fight for Nordeland. She is a liability, my king. Put her down."

"Put her down!" Steinunn cried out.

Bjorn stepped in front of me with his axe in hand, and it reminded me that I was unarmed. Steinunn was no warrior but she had a seax at her belt and unfated as she was, Hel's magic was no threat to her.

"And you!" Tears flowed down Steinunn's cheeks, a lock of her light brown hair sticking to the dampness. "You betray us all by defending her. And why? Freya hates you, Bjorn. She has made that clear, yet you trail after her as though you believe that time will make her forgive you. But I assure you, it will not. So you betray us for *nothing*. How much more must I lose because of you?"

"It was Snorri who killed your family." Bjorn took a step in Steinunn's direction only to shift his stance as Skade made to circle around him. My eyes jumped wildly around the hall to fix on a shield mounted on the wall. If I could get to it before Skade shot her arrow, I might have a chance.

"For years you lived in Snorri's house," Bjorn continued. "For *fucking years,* Steinunn, and I know for a fact he showed no caution or care around you. You could have killed him a hundred times over and did not." He gestured to me. "You could have put a knife in Freya's back just as easily but did not. Your tears ring hollow given that you could have achieved all that I *failed to do* but chose not to because you're too much of a coward."

"Then I will do it now!" Tearing her seax free of her belt, Steinunn lunged. My heart lurched. Not out of fear for myself but fear that this burst of bravery would cost the skald her life.

But then Harald was between her and Bjorn. How he'd moved so swiftly, I couldn't have said. Only that one moment he was seated and the next he had Steinunn by the wrists. Her blade dropped from her hand as he spoke soft words that I couldn't hear, and then she rested her forehead on his shoulder, sobbing.

"Saga told you herself that death was no revenge on Snorri for he would only find glory in Valhalla," Harald said, this time loud enough that I could hear. "True revenge can only come from denying him the fate that was foreseen, as then he will fall into a spiral of obscurity and despair that will end in an inglorious death that earns no place at the Allfather's side. Is this not the revenge you seek, Steinunn?"

"It is," she choked out. "But Saga said that the only way it would be achieved is with the shield maiden's death, so why do you protect her?"

"Saga said the only way it could be achieved is if Snorri *lost control of* the shield maiden." Harald hooked his thumb on his belt, expression thoughtful. "We've always interpreted her words as demanding the certainty of death. But what if there is another path?"

My heart galloped in my chest and my body warred between whether it should fight or flee, for my life felt very much in the balance.

Steinunn lifted her head, brow furrowed as she stared into Harald's eyes. "Are you certain?"

"No," he answered. "And I will not deny that I am motivated by the thinnest thread of hope in suggesting it, for my son loves this woman and I'll risk much for his sake."

Squeezing Steinunn's shoulders, Harald stepped away from her. "There is but one person who can confirm whether my hope is a strategy to be pursued or a fool's dream, and that is Saga. If she says the only choice is to kill Freya, then in the name of Odin himself, I swear that I will see it done. But if Saga says there is another path, then I swear that I will stand in the way of any who attempt to do Freya harm. Does this content you, Steinunn?"

The skald wiped at her eyes, then gave a tight nod. "Yes, my king."

I exhaled the breath I was holding, this exchange not at all what I'd been expecting. Nor did I know what to make of it, only that a spark of hope had bloomed in my heart and it was not dimmed by the knowledge that it hung upon a nuance of phrasing. On there being another way for Snorri to lose control over me other than death. Nor was the spark dimmed by the very real threat to my life if Saga dashed my hopes to dust.

Yet despite the promises that Harald had just given, Bjorn's axe still burned bright in his hand. "You understand that if my mother demands that Freya must die, you'll have to kill me first?"

Before my eyes, Harald's face seemed to grow older and more haggard, as though this admission were draining the very life from him. "I understand, my son."

Bjorn's axe flickered out. "I don't think I should wait for dawn." His head turned, our eyes locking. "If you are in agreement, Freya, I think we ride out now."

The tightness in my throat that had been troubling me so long eased and I drew in a breath. "Agreed. But I want my own horse."

CHAPTER 11

BJORN

Harald clapped his hands together sharply, and servants appeared. "See that they have everything they need to journey to Saga's cabin," he said. "Arrange for my two fastest horses to be saddled."

"Steadiest horses," I corrected, because Freya was not an experienced rider and the terrain was rough.

She only crossed her arms, eyes mercifully amber in hue, but that only made the defiance in them more obvious. "Fastest."

Harald cast his eyes toward the rafters. "I'm sure a happy medium can be accommodated. If you'll excuse me, I have other matters to attend to." He left the hall, Skade following at his heels.

The servants led Freya into the rear of the great hall and I moved to follow her, unwilling to chance anyone who felt like-minded to Steinunn and Skade stabbing her in the back, but Tora gripped my shoulder. "I'll keep an eye on her. You two will have enough time to bicker on the road to Saga's, so save your energy."

A fair point, so I nodded. Tora followed Freya, leaving me alone with Steinunn.

We stared each other down. I'd known her for years as Snorri's skald, and we'd never gotten along particularly well. She'd always been lurking in the shadows, often watching me, and I'd believed her to be Snorri's spy as much as his skald. Even if I hadn't been living a lie, the behavior would have irritated me. But with the stakes as high as they'd been, Steinunn's spying had made me avoid her at all cost. That she'd been Harald's informant didn't change the way I felt about her constant lurking, but her motivations for working for him did. "I'm sorry."

"For what?" Her head tilted, gaze full of venom. "Being an unrepentant prick?"

"For being a prick, I remain unrepentant." Hooking my thumbs in my belt, I considered what I wished to say. "But I am sorry for what happened to your family, and for being the cause of it. Snorri's pursuit of Tyr's fire cost many Nordelanders their lives, which is why I allowed him to *rescue* me when he did. In hindsight, I should have arranged it sooner."

Steinunn's chin trembled but then she clenched her teeth, swiftly regaining her composure. "I wished you dead more times than I can count and considered killing you more than once. I, too, am unfated, and if you were dead, Snorri would have lost his method of finding the shield maiden."

"Why didn't you just cut my throat while I slept?"

"Because I'm a coward." Her tone was bitter but not directed at me. I knew self-loathing when I heard it.

Given she'd just threatened Freya, there was a part of me that was happy to allow Steinunn to wallow in contempt for herself, but instead I said, "A coward wouldn't have followed us into draug-infested tunnels."

I recalled my conversation with the draug jarl. *I shall win great fame and honor for your death, Firehand. A song sung by the skalds for generations to come.* "You negotiated with the draug jarl, didn't you? Promised to compose a song about him if he let you live?"

Steinunn shook her head. "I promised to compose a song about him if he killed you and Freya. But for that to be possible, it necessitated allowing me to live."

Though she'd conspired against us, I couldn't help but smile. "Clever."

"Not clever enough. Freya was . . . more capable than I'd anticipated."

As I blinked, visions of Freya reaching for my axe filled my mind. Her hand had been covered with Hlin's magic, but with the burn scars fresh, it had still taken incredible courage to risk Tyr's fire. Freya was impetuous and rash and meaner than a cornered minx when she was angry, but never in my life had I met anyone half so brave or half so selfless. There was no one who I'd rather have fighting at my back than Born-in-Fire.

Focusing again on Steinunn, I said, "You two have exchanged harsh words, but Freya isn't the threat. Snorri is."

"You only think that because you're in love with her." Steinunn lifted her chin. "The rest of us see more clearly."

She left the great hall, closing the doors with heavy thuds.

"Bjorn?"

I turned to find one of Harald's servants standing a few paces behind me, a woman I recognized from before I'd left for Skaland. "Remind me of your name."

"It's Una."

I recalled that my friend Troels had been quite taken with her before I left, but that was the extent of my memory of her.

"We saved your things because we knew you'd return to us." She looked up at me through thick lashes. "We brought the chest out for you."

I had nothing but the clothes on my back, which all needed mending. "Thank you."

Una gestured to the upper level of the great hall. "This way."

I followed her up the wooden steps, which shifted beneath her swaying stride, my mind all for the conversation I'd had with Freya the night prior. Most especially the oath she'd sworn to save herself from having to endure Snorri. Gods, but every man in her life was a weight around her neck. Her father and brother. Vragi and Snorri.

Me.

There was a moment I believed that I stood strong because you were always at my back, Bjorn. Now I know better. I stood alone then, and I'll stand alone now.

Her words repeated in my head, and it took me far too long to realize Una had stopped next to a dusty chest and was watching me expectantly.

"Thank you," I muttered, recognizing the look she was giving me and wanting no part of it.

"Is there anything else you need?" She leaned against the wall and twisted a lock of her hair around one finger.

I silently cursed my much younger self, because his behaviors were what had invited this flirtation. "No. Thank you."

She pushed away from the wall, then gave me a slow smile. "Let me know if you change your mind."

I'd chosen Freya, and she'd remain my choice until the end of days, even if I suffered for it. "I won't change my mind."

Kneeling before the chest, I opened it and stared at the clothing and weapons. All mine, yet they seemed foreign and strange, as though they'd belonged to a different version of myself. I pulled off my tunic and tossed it aside. Digging in the chest, I extracted a similar garment and held it up, swiftly determining that it would not fit. Years of good eating and nothing to do but fight had put more bulk on me than I'd realized. These looked like the clothes of a boy.

They'd fit Leif.

The thought was a punch to the gut, my younger brother the one person I'd refused to allow myself to think about. Leif's grinning face filled my mind, his smile falling away as he learned what I'd done. That I was not his brother but his enemy.

Time and again, I'd told myself that my actions would benefit Leif in the long run, but it had all been hollow platitudes. Necessary, so that I could live day after day in the deception that I was loyal to Snorri. Loyal to Skaland.

Before I'd met Freya, the only thing that hadn't been deception were my feelings about my brother.

Lowering the garment to the chest, I allowed myself to remember when Snorri had first brought me back to Halsar. I hardly knew the town given I'd been raised in my mother's remote cabin, and most of the faces were strange to me. As was mine to them.

Leif had been so very young. Skinny as a rail where he stood at Ylva's side, and though his mother's blue eyes had been frost on the coldest of winter mornings, Leif had been smiling. He'd come down the dock with no hesitation and said, "You are Bjorn?"

At my nod, he'd taken my wrist and lifted it as high as he could, shouting, "My brother has returned!"

His acceptance had changed everything, and every one of those strangers had cheered. From there after, he'd been my shadow, wanting me to teach him everything I knew. Wanting me to take him everywhere I went. Not once did he begrudge the nature of my birth or the fact I'd taken his place as heir, only loved me as his elder brother.

And the gods strike me down, but I'd loved him back.

Yet I couldn't help but curse myself for allowing it, because the moment he learned of my betrayal, Leif would know that he'd been the one who'd made it possible because he'd been the one who'd opened the gates of Halsar and let the enemy in.

"You aren't weeping over your old clothes, are you?"

I twisted on my knees to find Troels setting a bucket of steaming water on the floor. The passing years had not changed his ferret-like face, though his lank brown hair had grown longer. He looked me up and down and said, "You always were such a mother's boy, Firehand. Weeping over pretty sunsets and sad songs. Never understood why the girls always chased after you."

"Because the alternative was your ugly face."

"It's not so bad in the dark."

"Troels, your face is the sort that sears itself into memory. Not even the darkness can spare you." I wrinkled my nose. "And it certainly does nothing about your stink."

Troels grinned, his hazel eyes bright. "Gods, but it's good to have you back!"

Then he tackled me to the floor. All the wind rushed from my lungs and my ribs groaned beneath his embrace, no amount of flailing on my part enough to break his hold. Troels was a child of Magni and possessed of such strength that he could fling me about like a rag doll if he was of a mind to do so. More than once, I'd seen him rip enemy warriors clean in half. "You're going to kill me, you ugly fuck. Let go!"

He laughed and sat back on his heels, pounding me on the back with such vigor that I was going to have bruises.

"All the girls are placing bets on which of them you'll take for a tumble first," my friend said. "But I told them they'd have to be content with me, because that shield maiden needs only to crook a finger and you'll come running."

"So that she can stab me in the gut," I grumbled, still struggling to catch my breath.

Troels shrugged. "To have that face be the last thing you see before you go to Valhalla would not be a terrible thing. And if you're dead, I might have a chance."

I gave him a flat glare but he only laughed. "You're right. She and all the rest would probably prefer your pretty corpse to me. I take it back, I didn't miss you at all."

There was something off in his tone that caught my attention. As though my friend's ever-present humor hid a very different emotion. "Troubles?"

He reached for the bucket of steaming water and set it in front of me. "Your stink. It wasn't me you were smelling, Firehand."

"Besides that." I wrung out the cloth and set to washing, waiting to see what he'd say.

He shrugged, then shoved a pile of clothes toward me. "Una sent these up with me. Put them on so I don't need to look at your stomach. It makes me want to give up mead."

"Start talking, and I'll put on clothes *and* put in a good word for you with Una."

My friend huffed out a laugh, but then his face turned serious. "It was as though Harald's focus went with you to Skaland. He was obsessed with every piece of information that could be gleaned and left everything else to Skade." He made a face. "You know how she is."

I grunted in agreement, digging a razor out of the chest and testing the edge. "What has my mother said on the matter?"

"Couldn't tell you. I haven't seen Saga once since you left."

I lowered the razor. "Truly?"

"Not once. I heard that Skade brought her over to Skaland to see you at Fjalltindr but not until after the fact. Saga's been even more reclusive than usual. I don't even think she allows Harald to visit, because I don't recall the last time he traveled to see her."

The metal of the razor reflected my frown, no part of me liking that Harald hadn't mentioned this. "Does he still heed her council?"

Troels hesitated, then said, "I believe her council serves primarily as justification for his obsession with Snorri. Islund has taken advantage, but he cannot see past your mother's prophecy. Snorri. The shield maiden. Skaland. There is nothing else."

Troels's words added fuel to the fire of doubt in my chest over my father's intentions for Freya.

"But perhaps he's in the right." My friend unfastened the wineskin at his belt and took a swig before handing it to me, the smell of strong drink filling my nose. "Everyone knows that the only thing I'm good for is knocking over the threat right in front of me. Harald always sees the long strategy and he's never led us astray. Has led me *away* from astray, for which he will always have my loyalty. But suffice it to say, Bjorn, I'm glad you're back."

"It's good to be back." But as I took a mouthful of the liquor, it struck me that every time I said those words, they felt more and more like a lie.

CHAPTER 12

FREYA

Though my body was exhausted, the glimmer of hope that Harald had put in my chest infused me with more energy than a night's rest. Servants hurried about to provide me with supplies. I was given fresh clothes and leathers, as well as a glittering set of mail. A servant named Una wove my swiftly washed hair into tight war braids while another added to the bag small comforts, such as soap and rags for my courses, that only another woman would know I'd want on the journey.

Harald's servants seemed strong and healthy, and they were all men and women who resided in Hrafnheim rather than thralls captured in raids. They were dressed well, and though their nervousness was betrayed by the way they watched me as though I might bite, they did their duties without complaint. I made a half-hearted effort to learn more about Harald, but in truth my mind was all for whether Saga would fuel the spark Harald had ignited or whether she'd crush it.

Stepping out from behind a woven hanging depicting Freyja and Freyr, I walked back to the main room of the great hall. Though such places were usually bustling with activity, Bjorn sat alone at a table, absently flipping a knife in his hands while he stared at the glowing hearth fire. I paused and took a moment to watch him, for he was so deep in thought he'd not heard my approach.

He had taken time to wash, and the sides of his head were freshly shaved so that the inkwork was clearly visible, the long black lengths twisted into a knot with a piece of braided cord. In flagrant disregard of the customs of our people, his face was also freshly shaven, the scruff of dark beard no longer hiding the sharp line of his jaw. The muscles in his arms flexed above his bracers as he flipped the knife. The motion made the chain mail that ended just above his biceps jingle softly. He'd changed clothes, and I wondered if they were garments he'd packed away before going to Skaland. Another reminder that this had been his home, not a prison. That these people were to him a family, not his enemies. That Bjorn was a Nordelander through and through.

"Have you gotten your eyeful, Born-in-Fire, or do you wish me to sit still a moment longer?"

I scowled, annoyed to be caught staring at him. "Merely considering the best places to stick a knife, though I think ridding myself of your tongue is where I should start."

Bjorn turned his head to look at me, green eyes drifting up and down. "You'd regret that choice."

My insides flipped but all I said was, "I doubt that."

I hefted my bag across my shoulder and crossed to his table. "Are you brave enough to allow me a weapon?"

He handed me the knife he'd been flipping. "I'd find you a shield, but you'd do just as well with a cooking pot."

"If that is a not-so-subtle hint that I should cook for you on this journey, consider yourself warned that I will spit in every meal I make for you."

Bjorn only shrugged. "Won't be the first time I've tasted your spit, Born-in-Fire, and I think not the last."

I stared at him, my cheeks burning hot. "You think I wish to hear jokes from you?"

"Was not a joke." Heaving a pack over his shoulder, he gestured to the door. "Do you wish to go, or do you wish to stand here arguing with me?"

"Arsehole," I growled, then I shoved his knife into my belt. A sword would have been better, but my father's weapon had not only been ruined when Bjorn had hit it with his axe in Grindill, it was now likely turning to rust in the hot springs where I'd left it. Though it was impossible to mend a warped blade, a pang of sadness hit me, as it was the last thing I had of my father. The last thing I had of my family at all, and its loss made me feel even more alone.

Skoll and Hati trotted beside us as Bjorn led me through Hrafnheim's narrow streets, walls rising high on all sides so my only view was occasional glimpses of the sky. Laughter emanated from buildings, drowned out from time to time by the heavy clanking of blacksmiths at work, far more in number than I'd expect for a town this size. We walked through the market square, which was full of merchants, most local, but many with the darker skin of those from the distant south. More than a few southerners were traders that I recognized from Halsar's market, so I pulled the hood of my cloak forward. Harald might be content to share my identity with the entire fortress, but any steps that I could take to delay Snorri's discovery of where I was seemed wise to me.

We reached the fortified gates leading to the bridge that stretched to the eastern bank of the Rimstrom. A tremendously tall and broad woman with thick red braids stood waiting. She wore the garments of a blacksmith. And the sword in her hands was mine.

At the sight of Bjorn, her face broke into a smile. "I could scarcely believe the news when I heard that you had returned to us, you little shit." She pounded him on the back with such force that Bjorn staggered. "You finally put on some muscle, so you must have been eating well in the south. This is her?"

"This is Freya." Bjorn nodded to the muscular woman and said, "Gyda is the finest smith in Nordeland by virtue of being a child of Brokkr."

Gyda made a face. "Your silver tongue doesn't work on me, boy." Then she looked me up and down. "She was certainly the runt of the litter."

I crossed my arms and scowled up at her. "Would you like to fight me?"

Gyda laughed, then reached down to stroke Hati's back, the wolf leaning against her leg. "She is like a small dog who thinks it is a wolf. All bark."

"She bites, too," Bjorn said, and my face burned.

"Then let's give her back her teeth." Gyda handed me my sheathed sword. "See if this suits, shield maiden. Harald sent it ahead to have me mend the blade, and I had time to do a bit more than straighten it."

I frowned at learning Harald had facilitated the repair, but all thought of Nordeland's king vanished as I took hold of the weapon. A lump formed in my throat as I unsheathed my father's sword, the blade no longer warped from Bjorn's axe but reforged straight and true with her magic. As I ran my fingers over the blade, I felt etchings in the metal that I could not see with my eyes. Etchings that felt to me like runes. "What do these markings mean?"

"What they mean is my business," Gyda answered. "What they do is ensure your blade will hold true against magic and steel alike. Unbreakable, so your only limitation is your own strength." She reached over and pinched my bicep. "Though that seems a significant limitation, you scrawny little bird."

Bjorn laughed, but I barely noticed as my eyes fell on the cloth-wrapped object that Gyda had retrieved from where it rested against the wall. Pulling off the cloth, she revealed a shield made of a silvery metal that had been hammered thin, more designs etched into its surface. She handed it to me. "Empowered to be light as a feather."

My jaw dropped as I held the shield, which indeed seemed to have no weight at all.

"I can only give an object one power," Gyda said. "So it is not strong. But with your magic . . ."

"Hlin," I murmured, and magic illuminated the silver surface. It felt as though I could hold it up high forever. "Thank you."

"Ain't interested in thanks." She held out a hand. "You want it, you need to pay for it. I'll bleed Harald for the sword."

My heart sank because I had nothing to give beyond the clothes on my back. Then next to me, Bjorn dug into his pocket and extracted a handful of golden chains that I could only imagine had been waiting for him in the same chest as his clothes. Plunder from raids in the service of Nordeland, which meant there was every chance it had been stolen from Skaland.

"No," I snapped. "I'll pay."

"With what?" Bjorn demanded.

"Don't be a fool, girl." Gyda tugged on one of her crimson braids and looked me over as though I was the purest form of stupid. "If he's idiot enough to spend his wealth on you, then take it."

"No." I looked down at the beautiful shield in my hands, trying to ignore how badly I wanted it to be mine. "If I let him pay, then every time I look at it, I'll be reminded that he's a lying traitor and I might be tempted to cast it aside in the middle of battle."

"You're being ridiculous," Bjorn said between his teeth. "Be mad at me all you want, but don't make bad decisions just to spite me."

Gyda looked between us and then whistled between her teeth. "You little shit. You were supposed to kill her and instead you cuckolded Snorri, didn't you? I'd heard rumors you were bedding her but I didn't think you were that stupid . . ."

"Not your business, Gyda." Bjorn stepped closer to me, but I stepped back. "Freya . . ."

"I don't want your gifts, Bjorn. I don't want anything from you. If it were possible to erase you from my memories, I would do so." Not giving him a chance to respond, I said to Gyda, "This is truly beautiful work, but you will have to sell it to someone else. He's right that I have no way to pay."

The smith tilted her head sideways. "It's good for nothing but a decoration without your magic, shield maiden."

Guilt pooled in my stomach that her effort, time, and magic had been wasted. Then from behind me, Harald said, "You are not without means, Freya."

Stepping alongside us, he nodded at Gyda before plucking up the handful of gold chains Bjorn still held and handing them to her. "He damaged the sword, so it is fitting he pay for it."

Then Harald held out a leather sack to me. "This is yours. Spoils collected from the Islunders you defeated. The mail you wear was taken off one of the female warriors you sent to Helheim."

My mouth went dry because I felt no honor in those deaths. Yet I still took the sack and looked inside. Precious metals and jewels shone in the fading light of the sun. Armbands, bracelets, and rings cut out of the dead men's beards. It made me want to vomit and I closed the sack.

"This is how it is done, Freya," Harald said. "They'd have done the same to us, had they been the victors."

Why had I ever wanted this life? Why had I ever believed I'd feel good picking the valuables off the people I killed to line my own pockets?

I shoved the entire sack at Gyda. "Take this as compensation."

The smith opened the sack and examined the contents before turning a discerning eye on me. Silently, she unfastened her belt and pulled off a sheath that held a beautiful seax, which she handed to me. "Never loses its edge. I'll include it along with the shield to make this a fair trade. Are you content?"

She could have given me a crust of stale bread instead of steel and I'd have called it even just to get the spoils of the dead out of my hands. "Yes."

The smith gave a satisfied nod, then looked to Bjorn. "It is good to have you back. Less good to find out you've been something of an idiot, but hopefully you'll grovel your way back into her good graces." Gyda buckled her belt. "May your steel serve you well, shield maiden. My king." She nodded at Harald, and turned on her heels and rounded the bend.

"The hour grows late," Harald said. "Show care in your ride into the wilds, both of you. Nordeland is *not* Skaland, and she gnaws the bones of any who forget it." Inclining his head to me, he said, "I will pray to the Allfather to give my wife the answers you seek and for you to return to Hrafnheim armed with the knowledge needed to change all our fates, Freya."

Bjorn had a strange look on his face.

"I pray for this as well." I touched the hilt of my sword, every part of me feeling better with it back in my possession. "Thank you for not leaving it to rust. It was my father's."

"Family is important." The king of Nordeland clasped my shoulder. "Please find a way that I don't have to lose mine."

I gave a tight nod as I watched him walk away, then turned to find Bjorn crossing the bridge to where a man waited with two horses. The wolves sat with their tongues lolling and I said, "Come!" and hurried across the bridge. I swiftly fastened my bag and shield to the saddle of one of the horses. Bjorn was already astride by the time I'd finished.

"Keep up, Born-in-Fire," he said. "And keep your eyes on your surroundings, not on my backside."

Before I could retort, Bjorn dug in his heels, leading me into Nordeland's wilds at a gallop.

CHAPTER 13

FREYA

The pace Bjorn set forced me to concentrate on guiding my horse and staying in the saddle, for once we left the main road, it grew rough indeed. The path was narrow and rocky, and it frequently crossed deep streams with treacherous footing. Branches of birch and pine stretched over it, threatening to take the unwary rider out of the saddle at every turn. The air was heavy with the scent of earthy moisture, and it was hard to see very far into the forest courtesy of the thick foliage. Deer and rabbits frequently darted through the underbrush, and the canopy overhead was full of chorusing birds that fell silent as we rode beneath. It would have been a challenging ride on a calm horse, but the mount I'd been given spooked at every shadow, its nerves made all the worse by the wolves that haunted our heels.

Bjorn didn't stop for an evening meal, only slowed his horse, and dug through the supplies he'd been given, eating while his horse trotted calmly up the path. My own foolish mount nearly caused me to inhale a piece of dried meat when it shied away from Hati for the hundredth time. I was painfully tired, but I'd happily ride through the night in pursuit of the glimmer of hope burning inside me.

Saga was a seer. A child of the Allfather, which ranked her above all other Unfated. He allowed her glimpses of the future as the Norns had woven it, and seers were sworn to reveal the truth of his words lest they face his wrath in the next life. In a world of liars, Saga might well be the only soul I could trust to tell me the truth. Yet it was not lost on me that seers spoke in riddles and prophecy, so truth was not the same as clarity. I would have to glean useful information from what she told me in order to understand Hel's magic and exactly what she foresaw me doing, because only by understanding the steps the Norns saw me as taking could I confidently walk a different path. Or, at least, not ignorantly stumble off a cliff.

Ahead, Bjorn drew his horse to a sliding stop, the light breeze carrying with it his loud curse. I increased my pace even as I watched Bjorn dismount and leave his horse to wander over to a patch of grass. As the animal moved out of the way, it revealed a woman sprawled on the ground. Bjorn bent to help her sit, and I swiftly dismounted and approached.

Perhaps my age, she had long honey-blond hair woven into a thick braid. She was also shockingly pretty. "Are you hurt?" I asked.

The woman's eyes moved to me, and her head cocked slightly as she took me in. "No," she finally answered. "Your husband's horse startled me, and I fell. But my mushrooms . . ." Lifting her hand, she pointed down the shadowed slope to where a basket had rolled until it came to rest against a bush, the mushrooms she'd been gathering spilled.

"He's not my husband," I muttered. "Go fetch her things, Bjorn. You shouldn't have been riding so fast on a narrow trail."

He made no argument, only growled, "Stay with her," at the wolves, then headed down the slope to retrieve the basket and mushrooms.

Once he was out of earshot, the woman said, "I've never seen a man so beautiful."

"Baldur incarnate," I said. "But he's also a lying traitorous arsehole, so don't let his looks fool you."

"I see." She straightened her skirts, and I noticed a piece of hide tufted with fur hanging below the hemline. Not a garment I'd ever seen worn, but who knew what was common to Nordelander women. "I think your underskirt has come unfastened."

She gave an embarrassed chuckle and reached down to tuck it under her skirts. "Thank you."

We watched Bjorn gather the mushrooms, and the woman said, "You're angry with him?"

"That's an understatement."

"Was he unfaithful with another woman?"

It was such a pointed question that my whole body twitched. Yet the woman did not seem to notice, her eyes all for Bjorn as he hunted in the shadows for the rest of the mushrooms. "Not that it's any of your business, but no."

"Do you desire him?"

"No!"

Her eyes flicked to me, and at my side, Hati gave a soft growl as she said, "So you don't love him?"

I loved him so much that the emotion set my body ablaze. But I also hated him in equal measure. "You should not ask strangers these questions. It is not right."

The woman sighed. "I am sorry. I do not spend much time in conversation."

Bjorn chose that moment to return with the basket, once again full of mushrooms, and he handed it to the woman. "You shouldn't be out here alone this late," he said. "It's not safe."

"You are thoughtful." She gave him a beaming smile that made me want to punch her in the face. "But set aside your fears. I will not be alone when darkness falls." Then she stepped off the path. "Safe travels."

Shaking my head at the strange forwardness of the woman, I mounted my horse. Bjorn drew alongside me. "There's a camp not far from here. We'll stay the night and head out at dawn." Nodding at the woman, he dug in his heels and cantered down the road.

I followed, noting that both wolves pressed between me and the woman, Hati biting at my horse's heels to make him go faster.

Bjorn didn't stop until the darkness was fully upon us and he had to use his axe to light the way. The camp was a small clearing with a firepit that showed signs of use, although not recently given the thick carpet of grass and wildflowers. There was also a worn rope tied between birch trees to serve for picketing horses, and in the distance, water gurgled. Tension thickened the air as we saw to our mounts, then began the task of setting up camp. Neither of us spoke a word, but I saw everything Bjorn did. Heard every breath he took. It was as though the woman's strange questions had brought to the forefront of my heart the magnetism between us, for jealousy was a fierce emotion and I had ever been victim to it.

In his typical haphazard manner, Bjorn lit the fire by dumping an armload of wood on top of his axe, while I extracted from the bags the supplies we'd been sent with. He took the pot I handed him and disappeared into the trees without comment, and my lip quivered at the silent rhythm because the comfort of it did more to fill the gulf between us than the groveling Gyda had suggested ever would.

Except I didn't want that gulf filled. I didn't want to forgive. Didn't want to step onto that slippery slope that would only see me hurt again. Or worse, used again.

Bjorn returned and handed me the pot. As he did, our fingers brushed together and the feel of his skin against mine sent a shiver through me. Jerking away, I began filling the pot with ingredients to make a stew.

"You need to take care of your hand, Freya," Bjorn said softly, watching me work. "Gyda repairing your sword won't matter if your fingers won't bend enough to grip it."

"My hand is fine." My eyes stung, but I blamed it on the smoke as I put the pot over the fire to cook.

"Freya, you hurting yourself doesn't change—"

"Fine!" I interrupted him because I didn't want a lecture on my irrationality. Going to my bag, I retrieved a pot of lanolin that had been included and began rubbing it onto my scarred hand. Not half as good as my old salve made with Liv's recipe, and it smelled like sheep, but it eased the tightness of the skin. And forestalled the need for Bjorn to tend to my scars, as he so often had. I could not bear his touch. But above all, I could not risk it.

Bjorn said nothing, only silently watched the flames while I returned to stirring the stew. A sliver of moon rose slowly in the sky and Hati tipped back his head and howled mournfully.

"Is it really them?" I asked, needing to break the silence. "In his endless collection of the divine, has Harald found Fenrir's children?"

"No," Bjorn answered. "Just orphaned wolf pups that he adopted. He has a fondness for rescuing damaged or unwanted things."

"Like you, apparently." I tasted my stew and deemed it ready. "Guthrum told me."

"Like me." Bjorn hesitated. "Guthrum doesn't know the full truth. Do you wish to hear it?"

Yes.

"I'll hear it from your mother," I muttered. "Odin's children don't lie, so I'll know her words are the truth. I can't say the same for you."

"I have no reason to lie to you now."

"But you had reason to lie to me before?"

He exhaled slowly. "I wish it were otherwise, but yes. My reasons for lying to you were honorable. But my reasons for making you mine while telling you lies had not a measure of honor to them. I wanted you from the first moment I set eyes on you, Born-in-Fire, so I took you. Now I pay the price for my greed because I have lost the woman I love more than life itself."

My teeth clenched so hard that I swore they would crack, but it was better than allowing the words rising in my throat to fill the air. Though my stew was cooked through, I stirred it again. Stirring and stirring until I was finally able to swallow my maelstrom of emotions.

I ladled our dinner into two bowls, then tasted a mouthful. It was quite good, but I reached for the salt bag and added a handful to one bowl. Stirring the contents, I handed it to Bjorn. "Enjoy."

Looking me straight in the eye, he took a large mouthful, then smiled. "Delicious. Thank you, Freya."

Arsehole.

He ate the entire bowl, then seconds, to which he added another handful of salt of his own accord, eating with gusto.

I ate with no appetite despite the fact my stew was excellent. Nor did I argue when Bjorn took my bowl and the pot down to the stream to wash. He returned with clean dishes and a pot full of water, which he set on the fire to boil.

"I'm going for a swim." He extracted a chunk of soap from his supplies. "The wolves will stay with you, and I'll take my time so you can do what you wish to do in privacy."

I watched him disappear into the darkness, the idea of needing privacy from him feeling so foolish given that he'd seen every inch of me. Touched and tasted every inch of me. Just as I had him.

Every part of him is yours, Hel whispered, and I made a face and muttered, "I do not know if it is truly you or if I am talking to myself. But if it is you, perhaps you might tell me something I don't already know. Preferably something helpful."

Whoever it was speaking in my head, they did not give me clarity. So I removed my clothes to wash away the sweat I'd accumulated during the ride. Using a cloth, I cleaned myself with the water warmed in the pot. A welcome comfort given the chill of the night air, all while the wolves sat with their backs to me, watching the darkness.

Yet still Bjorn did not return.

Feeling ill at ease for reasons I couldn't identify, I tidied up the camp. Checked the horses. Laid out my bedroll. Added more wood to the fire. Examined the etchings Gyda had made in my father's sword.

Still no Bjorn.

"One of you go look to make sure he hasn't drowned himself," I said to the wolves, but while they both turned their heads to regard me with intelligent eyes, neither moved.

My skin was crawling and, unable to sit still, I walked to the edge of the firelight and shouted, "Bjorn! I've been decent for over an hour! Get your arse back here!"

No answer.

Unease turned swiftly to fear, for while Bjorn seemed keen to test my patience, this was not how he'd do it. What if he had fallen and drowned? What if he'd been dying while I trimmed my fingernails and cleaned the camp?

I drew my sword and picked up my shield, the silver metal gleaming in the firelight. "Hlin, grant me your strength."

Silver magic flowed over my featherlight shield, illuminating my path as I trotted toward the sound of running water.

The stream was nearly large enough to be called a river, black water running fast and frothy, the far side of the bank hidden by darkness. I found Bjorn's haphazard pile of clothes, boots discarded next to it, but looking up and down the banks, I saw no sign of him.

"Do you hear him?" I asked the wolves, who had not left my side. No sooner did the words leave my mouth did I hear a woman singing. Hati growled, and as I glanced down at him, it was to see his hackles were up, teeth bared.

Tightening my grip on my sword, I started in the direction of the singer. Whoever it was had a voice to rival Steinunn's, the wordless song seeming to curl around me, beckoning me closer. The wolves circled around my legs, trying to drive me back, but I pushed past them until I saw two figures.

Bjorn's distinct broad shape.

And a woman, who swayed and danced.

Bjorn stood waist-deep in the running water, staring up at the woman on the bank. The clouds covering the moon abruptly shifted, light illuminating the face of the beautiful woman we'd met earlier.

And her entirely naked body.

Vicious anger flooded my veins and, extinguishing my magic, I prowled closer to listen, for the song had turned to conversation.

"I want you to take me," the woman crooned. "I want to feel you inside of me."

Bjorn took a step closer to her.

"I'm the only woman for you, am I?" I growled under my breath. "You love me more than life, do you?"

That I'd told Bjorn I was through with him didn't matter, and I cared not whether that was hypocrisy.

"I'm going to kill you," I muttered, ignoring the hollowness growing in my belly. "I'm going to kill you very slowly."

The woman stepped into the water, taking Bjorn's hand in hers and trying to guide it to her full breast, but he pulled away.

"No." His voice sounded strange. Like it was a struggle for him to speak. "I love her."

Next to me, the wolves growled, and my own hackles rose. Something about this wasn't right.

The woman pulled insistently on his hand, and while I couldn't hear her words, I could hear the invitation in them. An invitation made clear as the woman lay back on the bank, spreading her thighs wide and stroking her sex with her fingers.

Bjorn only shook his head, pulling from her grip. "No." He pressed his hand to his temple. "I . . . I don't want you. I only want her. Only Freya."

I gave myself no time to think about what his words meant to me, because he was shaking his head as though disoriented.

What was wrong with him?

What magic was at work here?

"Bjorn!" I shouted his name, but he didn't so much as twitch.

But the woman's eyes shot in my direction, and she scrambled to her feet with a hiss. "You said you didn't want him!"

"That doesn't mean you get him!" I shouted. "Hlin!"

My magic poured once again over my shield and turned the night bright as day, allowing me to see clearly.

My stomach flipped.

Because the woman had a tail.

Long and fleshy with a tuft of hair on the end, it twitched angrily as she rounded on me. As she did, Bjorn jerked as if slapped, his eyes going wide.

Fury filled the woman's gaze, and she whirled around to face him, revealing to me a back that belonged to no woman. Instead, it looked for all the world like a hollowed-out tree, the tail below it twitching angrily.

Huldra.

The name rose from my memory, a barely forgotten myth heard in stories of my youth. Creatures that seduced men. Bedded them.

And then killed them.

"You saw," the huldra shrieked at Bjorn, then, to my horror, began to grow. Taller and taller, her body twisting into a monstrous creature with skin like tree bark, the hooves and tail of a cow, and the teeth . . .

The teeth were unlike any creature born of this world. Long as my hand and curved into needlelike points.

"Freya, run!" Bjorn shouted, axe appearing in his hand. But a heartbeat later, the huldra's tail lashed out with swift violence. Bjorn tried to move but the deep water slowed him down. The tail struck him, knocking him back into the deep flowing current.

I can't lose him.

My anger rose, wild and vengeful and half at myself for still caring, and then I dug deep and screamed, "Hel take your cursed soul, you foul creature!" because if anything deserved to be cursed, it was this beast.

The ground beneath my feet quivered, my divine mother hearing my call, but no black roots rose to drag the huldra down.

No soul, I realized a second before the creature attacked.

I barely managed to lift my arm in time, but its mammoth arms slammed into my shield rather than my body. Hlin's magic sent it staggering away, but I also lost my grip on my sword, the glowing runes winking out. Skoll and Hati attacked its legs, and the huldra screamed, lashing out at them and driving the wolves back.

Howling, I drew the seax, slicing at the creature. Gyda's knife was as sharp as she had claimed, and the blade cut deep into barklike skin. The huldra tried to strike me, but its hooves rebounded off the magic on my shield.

My next blow took off its wrist, the huldra screaming in pain, but before my eyes its wooden flesh knitted together, hoof re-forming. It attacked, hoof slashing through the air and forcing me to duck. I swung at its legs, but it was too quick and dodged effortlessly, striking again. Its hoof struck my arm, agony spiking up to my shoulder. I bit back a cry, nearly losing my grip on the seax.

I needed my sword. Where was my sword?

The huldra's eyes glittered with triumph as it pressed its advantage. My right hand was growing numb, and I struggled to keep on the offensive, my movements growing sluggish.

The huldra lunged, its maw reaching for my throat. I dropped to the ground and rolled away just in time. Before I could get to my feet, its tail wrapped around my leg and dragged me to my stomach.

I kicked desperately, managing to free myself, but my shield slipped from my grasp.

The huldra loomed over me, eyes glowing with a deadly light. I reached desperately and caught hold of my shield, gasping Hlin's name just before its hooves slammed against the glowing surface.

The huldra exploded backward and landed heavily in the brush. If the beast was injured, it didn't show it as it clambered upright. But I'd gained enough time to snatch up my sword from where it had fallen in the water.

Back and forth we warred, and for all my magic, my strength faltered.

The wolves kept up their attacks, biting and tripping the creature.

Knock it down, I willed them, and as though they could hear my thoughts, they flung themselves at the huldra's legs.

It stumbled and fell. Blocking a swipe from its tail, I let go of my shield to lift my sword. With two hands, I brought the blade down as hard as I could.

Severing the neck.

The head rolled toward me to stop near my feet. Teeth gnashed and an awful scream exited from between its fangs. The headless body staggered upright, lashing out at me as though it could yet see out of its awful eyes.

I did not know how to kill it. Didn't know how to put down something that grew back all its parts. That could fight on even with its head severed.

Snatching up my shield, I braced for an attack, wondering if it might be better to run. Better to race downstream and pull Bjorn from the water before he was lost to me.

Knock it down, then run.

Bracing, I stepped into the huldra's wild swings. The impact of it striking my magic caused it to soar backward—

And a flaming axe exploded through its chest.

Like the driest of tinder, the huldra burst into flame, dancing and screaming. A macabre parody of how it had tried to seduce Bjorn.

Then it dropped to the ground and exploded into ash.

Bjorn stood on the far side of the stream, breathing hard, his hair loose and dripping river water. He was also naked as the day he was born, every inch of hard muscle and tattooed skin illuminated by the light of my shield.

I love her.

His words to the huldra filled my head, and with a curse, I vanquished my magic.

Darkness fell, rendering Bjorn and his muscles just a solid shadow in the night. "You're an idiot!" I shouted. "You're the one who is supposed to know the ways of these wilds, but you allowed yourself to almost be seduced by a monster that was half cow and half tree!"

Almost.

"In my defense, she did not look like that at first," he said, and though I couldn't see his face in the dark, I could *feel* his grin.

"She had a cow's tail, you arse!" I shrieked. "Or could you not see beyond her massive breasts?"

"There is only one woman I cannot see beyond, and it is not the huldra."

I only want her. Only Freya.

I made a rude noise because I didn't trust what I might say. Spinning on my heel, I stumbled up the riverbank. Not wanting to risk another look at his bare skin, I did not use magic to light my way and only found the path leading back up to camp when I tripped over Bjorn's boots and nearly fell face-first into the dirt.

I followed the faint glow of the dying campfire, adding more wood to it immediately and holding my hands over the flames, as they were icy despite my exertion. My heart hammered, my stomach a twist of panic and anger, but when Bjorn appeared, he had a faint smile on his face.

"What have you to be happy about?" I demanded.

"You saved my life, Born-in-Fire," he said. "Which was only possible because you were worried enough about me to come looking."

"Do not flatter yourself." I fussed with my bedroll knowing that the rush of blood in my veins would give me little sleep tonight. "I saved you because I do not know the way to your mother's home. If you had died, I would have had to go back to tell Harald that his beloved son was killed because he let his cock do his thinking. Then I'd have to wait for him to bring me to your mother, to whom I'd have to relay the same story. I was merely sparing myself."

"Of course." He hooked his thumbs on his belt. "How foolish of me to think it might be residual sentiment."

"Very foolish."

I rested my head on my rolled-up cloak, pulling the blanket over my shoulders. One of the wolves lay down at my back, his weight pressing against me. Welcome heat against the cool mountain air, but rather than bringing me comfort, I only felt the sorrow of loss for the time when it had been Bjorn at my back. A time when I had absolute trust in him, with my heart and my life.

I knew he cared for me. Loved me. Wanted me. Knew that for all my rage and grief, I felt the same for him. All those feelings refused to be extinguished even though logic demanded that I vanquish them from my heart. But his betrayal hadn't just harmed me—his lies had resulted in those I cared about losing their lives, and I couldn't forgive that. Couldn't ever trust that he wouldn't withhold truths from me again that might cause more of the same sort of hurt.

Through the flickering flames of the fire, I watched Bjorn lie down on his own blankets, his face cast in dancing light and shadows. Watching me even as I watched him.

I'd never feel the way I felt about him with another man, that I knew. Would never slip the hold he had on my soul no matter how many years I lived.

But it was over between us. It had to be.

Rolling over, I buried my face in the wolf's fur. And for the first time in far too long, I wept.

CHAPTER 14

FREYA

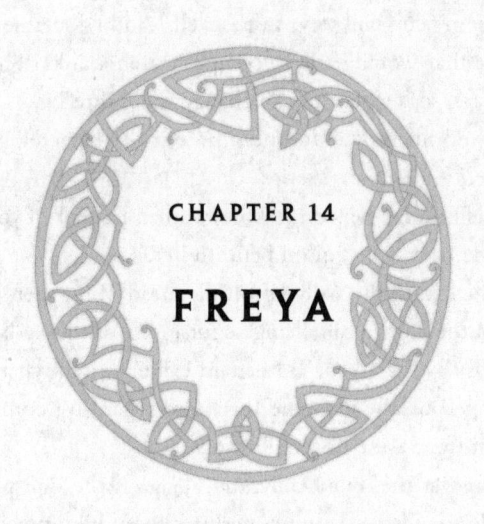

I woke at dawn to Hati licking my face and frost on the ground surrounding camp. Bjorn was already seeing to the horses, so I swiftly made porridge and then packed my things. The pair of us were on the road before the sun had fully crested the sky, sleep having done much to repair my composure.

But with composure came logic and reason, and trepidation marched along with them. It was because of Saga that Bjorn and Harald had pursued my death. She'd seemingly dedicated much of her life to destroying the future she feared. Even if Harald was correct in his interpretation that there was nuance in how that might be accomplished, it was not lost on me that the path Saga pursued might put me in the grave. That she might still want me dead, and I was riding directly toward her.

Bjorn and I had not exchanged so much as a single word, but clinging to silence when he might offer some insight seemed like willful stupidity. "Will your mother try to kill me herself?"

Bjorn's horse sidled into the brush, which drew muttered curses from his lips. "No," he answered. "She has no stomach for violence."

"Poison in my cup will serve just as well." And I'd seen several plants in our travels that would easily accomplish such a task. "She is as unfated as you are, so her actions can change the future."

He furrowed his brow. "It would be out of character. She's never killed anyone."

"Given she ordered her son to kill a woman neither of you had ever met, I struggle to believe poison beneath her."

His eyes flicked to the wolves trotting ahead of us, then he met my gaze and mouthed, "We can change course. We can leave Nordeland."

"What was that?" I asked. "I'm afraid I didn't catch what you said."

Skoll stopped on the path and turned to regard us, confirming my suspicion that these were no simple wolves.

Bjorn glared at me, but I only said, "Saga is the one person who might be able to aid me. I simply wish to know how much caution I need to show around her."

Silence stretched and my discomfort grew. Bjorn finally said, "I've been away from my mother for long years, Freya. Much could have changed. So I would suggest you take every caution."

"Understood." My answer was toneless, but unease turned my mouth dry as sand.

The path became more overgrown as we climbed. Rocky enough that our horses could go no faster than a trot, often forced to walk slowly around obstacles that had fallen. Bjorn always dismounted and took the time to move away debris, and from his muttering, it was clear he was displeased that this trail had not been cared for in his absence. I was less surprised given that we saw no signs of habitation—it seemed that if Saga desired isolation, she'd chosen this location well. It was just before midday when I spotted signs of human life in a pair of posts flanking the path, both heavily decorated with carvings.

"There is a perimeter of runes around her home," Bjorn said. "They warn her of arrivals and dissuade those who might wish her harm."

"She knows runic magic?" I asked, my discomfort growing because that made her significantly more dangerous. Ylva had taught me that.

"No." He slowed his horse alongside mine, our knees bumping when his horse tripped on a rock. "Harald carved them. He's very cautious with her safety."

"How do you feel about them being together?" Knowing it would annoy him, I added, "Were they fucking before you came to Nordeland or did that only happen after?"

Bjorn gave me a flat glare. "It is not my business. Ask her what you wish to know. It isn't as if you believe a word I say."

Digging in his heels, he cantered down the path ahead of me, a cabin with two outbuildings appearing through the trees. Smoke rose from the opening in the roof, and my nose picked up the faint scent of baking bread.

As we reined in our horses in front of the cabin, a woman wearing a green dress trimmed with fur stepped out of the doorway. The shawl draped over her head in combination with the shadows cast by the trees made it hard to see her face, but as I dismounted, she came closer.

My shock nearly caused me to drop the reins of my horse, because Bjorn's mother was *beautiful*.

Rather than showing surprise at our presence, Saga smiled happily and declared, "My son has returned!" then skipped to Bjorn. Reaching up, she cupped her hands around his cheeks, tiny before Bjorn's impressive bulk. "Foolish boy. You know better than to fall for a huldra's song. They love your pretty face and always come for you. Didn't Troels save you from the previous one?"

Though I knew her to be a seer, her knowledge of what had befallen us was still unnerving.

"I was distracted."

Saga made a humming noise but pulled him into an embrace before kissing both his cheeks. "It is your good fortune that you have proven to have excellent taste in women."

I twitched, because those were not words one said about someone you had dedicated your life to killing.

"Freya is not mine, Mother."

"Because you did not listen." Saga shook her finger at him. "I told you, my darling. I told you to steal her that night at Fjalltindr. That you should tie her up and put her over your shoulder, never once looking back. Instead, you made her love you while lying to her, and now she will not forgive you." She gave him a gentle cuff. "How is a boy of my blood so stupid?"

Bjorn crossed his arms. "You only told me that Harald might kill her outside the confines of the temple. He has been honest with me since, so you can let go of the deception."

Saga shrugged. "My assessment of your behavior stands."

Before he could answer, she turned away from him and strode to me. As I stared into her green eyes, the color identical to Bjorn's, I found it hard to breathe. It should have been no shock that she was lovely given how beautiful Bjorn was. But face-to-face, it was striking. Her blue-black hair hung in long silken lengths to her waist, skin as suntanned as her son's, and entirely unmarked by age despite her having to be nearly twenty years my senior. She was slender in the waist but curved in both breast and hip, and her face possessed the sort of perfection that seemed almost divine. High cheekbones and wide eyes, with full lips curved into a bow that any man, and many women, would be desperate to kiss.

And I realized I'd seen her before.

"You were at Fjalltindr," I breathed. "You passed us while we were walking to the ritual. You wore a headdress of raven's feathers."

"I was there," Saga answered. "The Allfather warned me that my son would struggle to keep to his path, so I journeyed back to my homeland to guide him." She turned her head to give Bjorn a sour look. "Not that he listened. Even so, with that many Unfated present at Fjalltindr, I was hopeful that threads would twist and my visions would change."

"How often does that happen?" I was desperate for her wisdom and comforted by the certainty that Odin would demand she speak the truth. "How often do the Unfated change the future you have foreseen?"

"More rarely than you might think." Her green eyes searched mine, long black lashes sweeping down. I wondered what she saw. "The Norns know our hearts and minds as well as we do ourselves, and their ability to predict what we will do is rarely faulty. It is only when the Unfated go against their nature that the threads must be rewoven. It was why I hoped that Bjorn killing you would change things, for it is not in his nature to murder pretty young women. He had to do something entirely at odds with who he is."

"I see." Though she was bluntly explaining plans for my death, my thoughts were all for the times I'd tried to change fate. My failures now made sense. Then my skin prickled and our eyes locked. "Is it out of *your* character to murder pretty young women, Saga? Will you attempt to rectify Bjorn's failures now that I am within reach? A knife in the back? Poison in my cup?"

Bjorn tensed, but I ignored him as I tried and failed to read Saga's expression.

Tension mounted, breath and wind the only sounds to break the silence.

"If you try to harm Freya, Mother, I will stop you," Bjorn said softly. "If I fail to stop you, I will follow her to Valhalla. I swear it on Tyr's name."

My chest clenched so painfully I could barely breathe, his words eliciting a twist of emotion in my core.

Saga only rolled her eyes. "You inherited Snorri's penchant for dramatics, Bjorn. Rest easy, no one will die today. I swear it on Odin's name."

Linking arms with me, she gave Bjorn a pointed stare. "Horses. Wood. Then go hunting for something to put in the cooking pot, for your appetite will do my larder no favors."

Bjorn hesitated, then took my reins and led the horses away. "Take the wolves with you," Saga called. "They eat even more than you."

At his whistle, Skoll and Hati broke into a loping run, my foolish horse squealing and trying to bolt, ever afraid of the large predators.

"Come." Saga tugged on my arm with surprising strength. "It's easier to talk about him when he's not around."

Her behavior was not at all what I'd anticipated. I'd expected one of Odin's children to have a level of gravitas, yet Saga acted and spoke more like a village gossip. "I don't wish to speak about Bjorn."

Saga hummed softly, then said, "I'll not press you to forgive my son, Freya, for I understand the hurt of lies and the pain men inflict better than most. But as his mother, I must tell you that what he feels for you is no deception. All of Nordeland desired your death, for we knew you were destined to be our curse, but Bjorn fought for your life at Fjalltindr. Fought to change your fate."

"Has it changed?" It was hard to ask the question, but I forced it past my lips.

Saga stopped in her tracks, looking at me for a long time. "Yes. And no."

"What does that mean?" My legs started moving as she pulled on my arm.

"The path you walk has been altered, but you will arrive at the same destination."

My hands turned cold because Bjorn had described that destination to me, and his words echoed through my thoughts. *She told me that the shield maiden would unite Skaland, but that tens of thousands would be left dead in your wake. That you'd walk upon the ground like a plague, pitting friend against friend, brother against brother, and that all would fear you.*

"It's not a place I wish to go," I whispered as we stepped into the dim confines of the cabin. Saga didn't answer, and I took the opportunity the silence presented to examine the interior. As was common in Skaland, it was only one room, though there were touches of wealth that spoke to Harald's influence on her life, from the multitude of thick pelts to the quality of the pots hanging near the hearth, to the richly colored hangings on the walls that I recognized as craft from the distant south.

The cabin itself was made of thick logs with a thatched roof, the smoke from the hearth minimal for it was well constructed. A well-made table with two benches dominated the space, and to one side, a curtain hung from the ceiling to hide away the sleeping area. Dried herbs covered one wall, though the dust on them suggested that Saga was no better cook than her son. Indeed, I'd seen no sign of livestock, so either she was an excellent hunter or Harald arranged for her to be well provided.

"Sit." Saga gestured to one of the benches. She then went to the fire and lifted off a steaming pot that smelled of red wine, cinnamon, and cloves. I revised my opinion of her skills as she ladled a cup for me before sitting on the other bench.

"It's a relief speaking with you." I curled my hands around the cup to warm them. "It has been so long since I spoke with anyone I could trust to answer honestly."

Saga took a sip of her drink. "I can lie just as easily as you, Freya. But not about the visions that the Allfather has gifted me."

"That's something." I drank, wincing as the liquid scalded my tongue. "It makes me feel at ease around you, even though we don't know each other." Shaking my head, I added, "It feels as though I know you because your words have impacted my life so greatly."

"The Allfather's words, not mine." Saga smiled, revealing perfect white teeth. "I wish I could say the sentiment is shared, Freya, but in truth, you terrify me. In my weaker moments, I weep that my son did not kill you the moment he set eyes on you, but he has drawn a line in the sand and I will not cross it. I will not kill the woman he loves so dearly for it would mean losing him, and that is not a loss I can bear. I am selfish, and it seems the Norns know that well."

I hesitated, then said, "Harald questions whether your foretelling has other interpretations. You believed that for Snorri to lose control over me, I had to die. What if there is another way?"

"Harald does love to chase even the smallest embers in the darkness," she replied. "I do not share his hope, but I cannot say with certainty that it's not possible."

I swallowed the lump forming in my throat, forcing myself to press onward. "Did you witness when the gods stepped onto the mortal plane at Fjalltindr?"

"Yes. I watched from afar. They called you a child of two bloods and said that they were watching you."

"They did not mean mortal and divine," I said. "They meant that I had the blood of two goddesses in my veins. Hlin. And Hel."

Saga sat up straight.

"I can curse people." My words were no more than a whisper. "I can tear their souls from their bodies and send them to Helheim, leaving behind only an empty corpse."

"In my vision, your eyes burned red."

"They do that now when my emotions run high. Especially when I'm angry. It feels as though she's taking control. She . . ." I trailed off, not wanting to admit the truth lest Bjorn's mother believe me mad.

"What does she do?" Saga pressed.

Perhaps I was wrong to think she'd judge me for hearing Hel's voice, for did not Odin show his children visions? "Hel speaks to me inside my head."

Saga's head tilted, and the faint wariness in her eyes made my face burn. Yet all she said was, "You communicate with Hel?"

"Yes," I whispered. "At least, I think I do."

"And Hlin?"

I shook my head. "Not in the same way."

"What does Hel tell you?"

"She is covetous. She pushes me to take what I want and fuels my anger when I am denied. She . . . she encouraged me to send the souls of Islunder raiders to her."

Saga shivered, then took a long sip of her wine. "When I saw you in my second vision, you stood in a field of countless dead, your eyes burning like coals. It was not clear how they'd died, and I assumed that it was in a great battle, but this makes a great deal more sense. In the future I have foreseen, you use Hel's magic to send thousands to your godly mother in Helheim." She let out a shaky breath. "You are a mistress of death, Freya. Even the bravest of warriors will flee before you lest you steal their chance to journey to Valhalla. In Snorri's hands, you truly would be a plague upon Nordeland."

I could feel her fear and it turned my belly sour. "I'm not in his hands. I'm here, with you."

"And yet I cannot shirk the sense that you remain under his control." She pressed fingers to her temples. "As though he has a leash upon you."

I could not speak on the matter. My oath to keep silent held my tongue still. Instead, I asked, "Saga, I do not want this future, but neither do I wish to die. Tell me how I might change my fate."

The seer gave a slow shake of her head. "I see only one future, Freya. One dark and horrible future. If you came here seeking answers to how you might change your fate, I fear your journey was for nothing."

Despair carved out my insides, that fleeting spark of hope extinguished and leaving me in darkness. She'd been my one chance for answers and now I had no notion of where I might turn. My eyes welled with unshed tears, and needing to come out of this moment with something, I said, "Then let it not be for nothing. Bjorn told me that it was not Harald who tried to murder you, but Snorri. From your lips, I would hear all that happened that night."

Saga took a long drink, then refilled both our cups. "I will give you the truth."

CHAPTER 15

FREYA

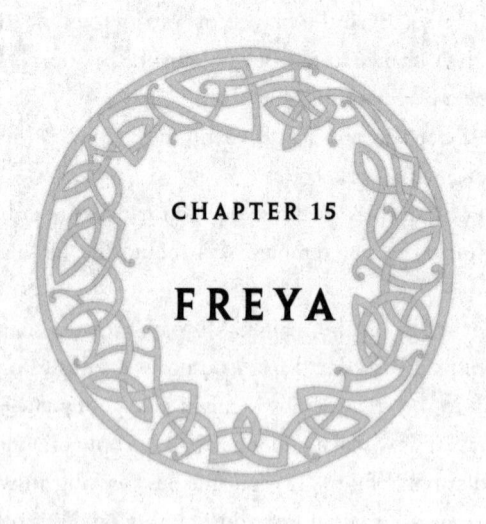

The fire in the hearth crackled and popped, and the walls of the cabin felt as though they pressed in on us as I waited for Saga to begin.

"From the moment my magic appeared in my youth, I was sought after by jarls and fishwives alike who were eager to know their futures," Saga said, staring into the depths of her cup. "I would tell them they were fools to wish to know their fates, because with the exception of the Unfated, what will come to pass is certain and unchangeable. To know your own death accomplishes nothing but haunting your living years with an inescapable certainty. It is better not to know."

"I don't want to know," I swiftly said. "I'm already haunted by what you've seen of my future."

Saga's mouth curved into a smile. "Wise."

I sighed. "I've been accused of many things, but wisdom is not one of them."

"To know one's limitations is a form of wisdom." She was quiet for a long moment, then continued. "To see the futures of everyone I cross paths with is a burden few can understand. To see that a child will die by drowning or that a hunter will run afoul of a bear or that a mother will risk one last pregnancy only to die in childbirth, but have no ability to save them, isn't a gift. It's a curse. So when I was fifteen, I left my family's home and the village where I had been raised in order to live apart. To hide from all the futures I possibly could, though many people still sought me out."

"Including Snorri and Harald?"

Saga nodded. "The Allfather showed me little of Snorri's future other than that he would have sons, but each time Snorri visited me, he asked if I'd seen more. Of Harald, my godly father showed me nothing at all, but Harald did not care about the uncertainty of his future. Instead, he desired to know the futures of others, and it vexed him greatly when I refused to reveal what I knew. He'd bring me the most beautiful gifts to entice me into revealing fates, knowing full well that I never would. Both men were handsome beyond compare in their youth, so I took both as lovers. My appetite for sex was great in those years, and one man could not hope to satisfy me."

"Both?" My cheeks flushed at her frankness. "Did that not spark jealousy between them?"

"For a long time, neither knew the other shared my bed." Saga laughed. "Though once they discovered I was entertaining other cocks, neither was pleased. Which I always believed unfair given that Snorri was betrothed to Ylva and Harald always did as he pleased, but such is the way of powerful men. They believe the rules that bind women do not apply to them. Their friendship was always fraught, but discovering they shared me drove a wedge between them that escalated the tensions between Nordeland and Skaland."

From most women, this would seem an unlikely tale. But Saga was both beautiful and powerful, so it was easy to understand men fighting wars to possess her.

"Always, there is conflict between jarls, endless raids and battles, but in making the conflict between two such powerful men personal, the animosity became so much worse. Especially after the Allfather graced me with visions of you and what you would achieve, though that comes later in my tale."

"Do you regret your choice to take both as lovers?" I asked, curious. "Given the consequences?"

"I do not believe in regret."

I wished I could feel the same. The idea of accepting the mistakes I had made rather than allowing them to consume me with guilt felt so much easier.

"Not long after they discovered they were both my lovers, I fell pregnant with Bjorn."

"Did you know he had Tyr's blood?" I asked. "Did . . ." It was too awkward for me to ask.

"I did not get to experience lovemaking with a god," Saga clarified. "Tyr was surely there in the moment but clearly took his pleasure from watching Snorri and me together rather than participating. So I did not know at the time that my child had a god's blood."

My face felt aflame. "I see."

"When my stomach began to swell, Snorri demanded that I break off my relationship with Harald." Saga took a sip of her wine, then shook her head. "That made me very angry because he was to wed Ylva. It would be Ylva who would rule alongside him. Ylva's children who would inherit the jarldom. I was naught to Snorri but a lover, a seer, and the soon to be mother of a child he voiced no interest in claiming. I was young, and it enraged me that he'd make demands when he gave me nothing in return. Yet I also feared for the child in my belly, for men can be cruel. So I conceded and told Harald that the friendship between us could not continue."

Her lip quivered. "Though it hurt Harald's heart as much as mine, he accepted my request even as he made me promise to come to him if ever my circumstances changed. He said his love for me would endure beyond this lifetime."

I took several mouthfuls of my wine because I knew what it felt like to hear words like that. Knew what it felt like to have it not come to pass. "Did you love him?"

"Yes. But for all his faults, I also loved Snorri. He had a magnetism about him. An ability to convince me of anything. And young women are easy to fool with sweet words."

Truer words I had never heard spoken.

"Seers cannot see their own fate." Saga rose to add a piece of wood to the fire, though the cabin was already warm. "But the moment Bjorn was born, I saw his." A tear trickled down her cheek. "I saw him call flame. I saw him burn. I heard him scream."

"He told me that you instructed him never to say Tyr's name."

"Yes." Saga wiped away the tear. "He was four. Perhaps five years old, and Snorri had come to see me. We quarreled, and in the midst, I was overtaken by a vision more powerful than any I'd ever experienced. I fell into a trance, words spilling from my lips in a tide of a shield maiden who would unite the clans of Skaland beneath the one who controlled her fate."

"Saga, what exactly did you see?" I pressed. "Did you see Snorri? Was it he for certain who was destined to rule? Was it he who was meant to control my fate?"

"I did not see Snorri." Her expression was distant, as though she were watching something that was not there. "I saw your face, Freya. With eyes like fire and a crown of blood."

I drew in a steadying breath. "So not Snorri?"

Saga lifted a shoulder. "I do not see all that is fated. Only the pieces that Odin chooses to reveal to me. Snorri believed that the Allfather had chosen to give me the vision while he was present because it was his fate, so he immediately began to hunt for you. There is no denying that his power has risen considerably since he brought you under his control, as he is now the uncontested king." She hesitated. "He has used you to unite Skaland, Freya, and in my heart, I fear he still uses you. For the future I saw still burns bright in my mind's eye."

I didn't answer. Couldn't answer, because of my blood oath.

Sitting back, I stared into the depths of the fire, uncertain how I felt about what she'd told me given that all I'd gained from it was more uncertainty.

"Finding children born under the blood moon became his obsession," Saga said. "I told him often that if it was his destiny to find you that he would, but my words only enraged him. My unwillingness to confirm that he would be king was a rot on the love between us, and I began to fear him. One night he came to my cabin alone. I knew he wanted answers I could not give, and that he'd punish me for my failure. I made Bjorn hide, but as the violence I feared came to pass, my son tried to protect me. Called upon his magic for the first time and set our home ablaze. And so the fate I'd foreseen for him became reality."

She lifted her cup, hand trembling. "All around was fire, Bjorn screaming from the burns on his back, but I managed to lift him out of the flames and carry him. Snorri tried to pursue us, but I cracked him over the head with a rock and fled. Fled to the love that had never betrayed me. To my sanctuary."

"Harald."

She nodded. "I would have been content to let things be. To live a quiet life in Nordeland. But Odin gifted me another vision of you. I saw thousands of dead beneath your feet with the Skjoldfjell beyond. I could not let my love and savior's kingdom fall to ruin because I did nothing. So I vowed to change the future. I had no certainty that it was Snorri who would control your fate, but I did know your power would be the tool for Nordeland's destruction. Snorri had stronger means for finding you, so I ordered that we use him to find you and then send you to the gods. That way the future I saw would be rewoven. And yes," she gave a soft laugh, "to have vengeance upon him for what he did to me and Bjorn."

"So you sent Bjorn to watch for me."

"That was my plan. To arrange for Snorri to finally succeed in *rescuing* Bjorn, who would then feign love and gratitude until you were discovered, when he would strike the blow that would save Nordeland. But my son could not kill you, Freya, and he has sought to protect you every step of the way. He has been his true self."

"He lied to me." I drew in a ragged breath. "Over and over, he lied."

"The only way he could have risked the truth was to steal you," Saga explained. "To take you to Nordeland, where you could do no harm with the truth. For to have revealed his goals while you shared a house with Snorri risked you turning on him and, in doing so, cursing Nordeland to the fate he'd sacrificed so much to prevent."

I found myself on my feet, though I didn't remember standing. "So you believe what Bjorn did was right? That I should forgive him for lying to me?"

Silence stretched between us, and between the tension and the heat of the air, it was hard to breathe.

Finally, Bjorn's mother said, "*Right* depends on perspective, Freya. From Nordeland's perspective, *right* would have been killing you or taking you somewhere you could do no damage. So no, I do not think what my son did was right because he risked many lives. But I think that is not the same reason you believe his actions were *not right*. You care only about your hurt feelings. About the damage to your trust in him. You think only of yourself, and knowing that you are Hel's child, your callousness to others makes a great deal of sense."

My own anger flared, because I wanted to blame Bjorn. Except Saga's words forced me to accept that he'd had no good choice. No choice that was right for all involved. I wanted to tell myself that, if he'd have been truthful, I would have heard him out and considered my actions, except I knew otherwise. Nordeland was a known foe, and to have learned that Bjorn fought loyally for them would have turned me against him. Would have caused me to reveal the truth to Snorri in order to protect my people.

"Shit," I hissed, pacing back and forth across the small space, trying to logically sort through what I had learned while my emotions raged in every direction. Trying to put the good of the many ahead of the hurt in my heart. But it was as though my heart had put her fingers in her ears, refusing to listen to anything that countered how she felt.

"You do not have to forgive him," Saga said. "I might not forgive him, for I hate being lied to. But do not think that holding on to your anger makes you good and righteous, Freya. It only makes you like every other woman."

I felt suddenly sick to my stomach, doubt twisting my guts like I'd eaten something rotten.

Was I wrong to be angry with him?

Was I only trying to use Bjorn as a scapegoat when the real problem was me?

Saga rose, circling the table to wrap a slender arm around me. "I've upset you. I'm sorry. Isolation may be a blessing to me, but I think it is a curse to anyone who is forced to bear my company, for I say what I think without thought for how it might hurt."

"You haven't said anything that isn't true," I answered. "I . . . I don't know what to do. I don't want to die but neither do I want thousands of people to die because of what Hel's power can do."

Reaching up, she tucked behind my ear a lock of hair that had come loose from my braid. "Be kind to yourself, Freya. You are but a few years out of girlhood, and you were not raised to cope with the expectations placed upon you. Wisdom comes from years of experience and from learning from one's past mistakes. Your situation has been made worse as those around you have given poor guidance."

I bit the insides of my cheeks, an ache at Bodil's loss rising fresh in my chest, for it felt as though she was the only one who had guided me true.

"You must take a breath." Saga gestured for me to sit back down. "Take time to consider all that has happened and all that you hope will happen before you decide on a path forward."

This seemed like reasonable advice, so I sat.

Bjorn chose that moment to return, stepping inside holding a rabbit who'd clearly met a swift end courtesy of a magic axe. I'd normally have made a comment about overkill but I felt suddenly without the energy to say much of anything at all.

"Is rabbit acceptable to you?" he asked, lifting it up.

"It is fine," Saga replied. "Clean and dress it, and then I think you can do the cooking."

"I'll do it," I mumbled.

Bjorn huffed out a breath. "Are you that afraid of my cooking, Born-in-Fire?"

I shook my head, then crossed the room and took the rabbit from his hand. "Are Skoll and Hati outside?"

"Yes." He caught my wrist, and I looked up at him as he said, "Are you all right?"

I forced a smile on my face. "I'm fine."

A lie. Because I'd believed that hearing Saga's truth would make me feel better. Stronger. Ready to do what needed to be done.

Instead, all I felt was worse.

CHAPTER 16

FREYA

I said little as I cooked, feeling Bjorn's scrutiny as I worked even as he made conversation with his mother, who filled every heartbeat with chatter.

When I handed him a bowl, he asked, "Should I prepare myself?"

I shook my head, because the thought of tampering with his food hadn't even occurred to me. All of my thoughts were too twisted up with what step I should take next.

"Do either of you intend to tell me what you discussed?" he asked, then took a mouthful and swallowed. "Or am I to be kept in the dark?"

Saga didn't answer. Staring at the contents of my bowl, I said, "Your mother does not know if there is a way forward for me that will not end in many deaths. She has seen nothing that offers a solution." Putting my bowl aside, I forced myself to meet Bjorn's eyes. "She also told me how you came to be in Skaland. Of Snorri's actions. I understand now why you have turned against him."

Bjorn only stared at his stew as he chewed and then swallowed. Pushing his bowl away, he asked, "What do you wish to do, Born-in-

Fire? Because my mother's inability to see a better path does not mean one does not exist. You just need to choose what direction you wish to go."

To run seemed the right choice. But could one outrun fate?

I didn't know, so I didn't answer, only finished the meal in silence.

"Bjorn will clean up," Saga announced. "Freya, come. Let us rediscover your cheer."

Pushing cups into my hand, she tucked a small cask under her arm and led me outside, where it had started snowing.

"It comes early up here," she remarked. "And stays for longer. Though this will melt before midday tomorrow, I should think."

One of the outbuildings was a sauna not dissimilar from the style we used in Skaland. Constructed with rough-hewn logs and a turf roof, it blended into the forest almost as though it had grown out of the earth. Saga entered to stoke the fire while I retrieved a bucket of water from the well, both wolves tracking me everywhere I went.

"The heat will help you think clearly." Saga removed her garments and hung them on a hook outside the door. I did the same. It was hard not to look at her, for it seemed time had no more touched her body than her face, every inch of her taut and smooth. On the right side of her rib cage was Odin's mark, a large crimson tattoo of a raven that throbbed to the beat of her heart. Just as did the tattoos that graced my hands. Tattoos given to me by Hlin. And by Hel.

Saga was so incredibly beautiful that it was easy to understand the actions of Snorri and Harald. Their desire to possess her. Yet here she was, free and living alone in the wilds with no one troubling her, which clearly suited her just fine.

I envied her.

Filling my cup and her own, Saga sat on a stool and leaned back against the wooden walls, steam rising as I poured water on the heated stones. "You feel hopeless, don't you, Freya?"

I took a mouthful of the wine, then paused to look into the cup, for it had a finer taste than anything I'd had before.

"Harald keeps me well supplied." Saga smiled. "Southern vintage made from grapes that grow in places winter never touches. It is my one vice."

"I would like this to be my one vice." I took another sip. "Though I expect it takes a king's coffers to afford such a thing."

Saga only took a small sip, watching me over the rim of her cup.

Sighing, I said, "Harald gave me little choice as to whether I would come to Nordeland or not."

"I think you should be grateful it was my husband who captured you, not me, because I'd have instructed Skade to do what my son could not. But please, continue to complain about the choices made."

The corner of my mouth turned up. It seemed Bjorn's wit had come by way of his mother, for I'd never heard Snorri speak so. "After I learned you were alive, I became convinced that you would not only be a source of truth in a sea of lies, but also that you might help me understand the magic Hel's blood has given me. I also hoped you could guide me as to how I might evade the future you have seen. Yet now I've spoken with you and know no more than before. So yes, I do feel hopeless."

"What does Bjorn believe you should do? He's not one to withhold his opinion, even if it is not asked for."

"He believes I should run," I responded.

"His suggestion holds a great deal of merit. It is difficult to be a plague upon a nation you are half a world away from. But I sense you aren't inclined to walk that path. Why?"

"Every time I try to escape, something happens to stop me," I said. "When I tried to jump off the cliff at Grindill to end the battle, the specter stopped me. When I tried to leave Skaland with Bjorn, Harald found us. I can't seem to evade my fate, either through death or a different life."

Saga fell still. "Specter?"

Taking another mouthful of wine, I nodded. "She has appeared to me many times and guided me on several occasions. A woman burned down to the bone, embers and ashes floating in her wake. Snorri believed that she was you, but obviously that is not the case, so I have no idea who she might be."

Saga made a face. "He would believe that. No doubt he fears that I will reveal the truth of his murderous ways."

I considered how Snorri had reacted in the ashes of Halsar after I'd met with the specter. He'd been overwhelmed, to be sure, but not afraid. If anything, he'd taken strength from the idea that Saga might be guiding me from another realm. Yet I kept that to myself and asked, "Do you know who she might be?"

"Perhaps someone sent by Hlin. A puzzle, to be sure. Have you seen her since Grindill?"

I shook my head, and Saga asked, "So you feel that if you try to run, you will be turned back?" Not waiting for me to answer, she added, "Is there some other reason you feel your freedom limited?"

My lips parted to tell her about the blood oath I'd sworn, only for my jaw to lock in place.

"Freya?" Saga leaned forward, green eyes full of concern. "What is wrong?"

All I could do was stare at her.

Saga sucked in an abrupt breath. "Gods, he's bound you." Her eyes narrowed. "*Ylva* has bound you."

I could do nothing but stare at her.

"I wish Harald had traveled with you," she said. "This is his expertise, not mine, and he might understand better what has been done to you. For I can only speculate."

Catching hold of my wrist, she lifted my cup to my mouth. "I'll not ask you to answer questions, for I think that you cannot. But I would prefer you do something other than gape at me like a fish tossed upon a beach."

As I took several long swallows, Saga sat back and tapped her lips with her index finger. "From your behavior, it is my belief that Snorri, via Ylva's expertise with magic, has bound you to them with an oath that forces you to keep silent on the matter." She tapped her lips again. "Yet you were able to at least attempt to pursue escape with Bjorn, which causes me to believe that you were bound not only to Harald but to his son." She dropped her hand to rest it on her bare thigh. "To his blood, is my guess. Clever of Ylva, for it assured you were also bound to her son, Leif. That Bjorn was also included is likely something she could not easily figure her way around."

Shock that she'd landed so close to the truth caused me to drain my cup, Saga absently refilling it as she thought.

"Bjorn might be the key to your escape," she murmured, staring at the fire. "If you've been sworn to the blood, then Snorri's hold over you is no stronger than Bjorn's, nor indeed, Leif's." She turned her head so that our eyes were once again locked. "Though this might not be a welcome revelation given that you are at odds with my son."

I could feel the wine buzzing in my skull, yet I still took another swig as I watched her think.

Excitement rose to Saga's face and her eyes brightened. "Bjorn could order you to travel to the distant south. He could order you to never use Hel's gift." She dropped to her knees before me. "This could be the answer, Freya!"

My whole body began to tremble, and it suddenly felt very hard to breathe.

"Let my son take you away." Saga's eyes searched mine. "I will explain to Harald why it is necessary, and he will abide by my wishes."

"It didn't work before." My skin felt like ice despite the heat radiating from the stove. "Why will it work now?"

"Perhaps you were not fully committed." She rose and poured water on the hot stones, steam rising from them to haze the space between us. "Perhaps you sensed that you did not know the full truth. Felt something holding you back. Now that I've told you everything, that is no longer the case."

It was true that I'd felt doubts when Bjorn and I had planned to run away, but the truth hadn't vanquished them. If anything, they'd made them worse.

Saga made a noise of irritation and refilled her cup. "I feel your resistance, Freya, and I cannot help but shake my head at it. I understand your feelings were injured at learning of Bjorn's lies, but are you really willing to risk thousands of lives because you are unwilling to forgive a handful of mistruths?"

My cheeks flushed and I looked away, shame flushing my skin.

"And not just the lives of others! Your stubbornness causes you to risk your own chance at happiness, and for what? What do you gain by digging in your heels and refusing to forgive?" Not giving me a chance to argue, Saga said, "You have the opportunity to travel somewhere warm and wed a man who loves you so much, he'd risk everything for you. To have beautiful babies and never again know the touch of violence. This life could be yours, and though you sit in silence, it is as though you scream in my face, 'I refuse to forgive him for not being perfect.'"

My eyes welled and I blinked rapidly to keep tears from falling. Said like that, all my actions seemed so terribly foolish. The actions of a girl, not a woman grown. I hunted for my anger, for my reasons for refusing to forgive, but all I felt were embarrassment and shame. "He should have waited until I knew the full truth before allowing us to be intimate."

"Was it Bjorn who pushed you for intimacy, Freya?" Saga asked. "Or was it you who pushed him?"

My whole body was burning, although my hands still felt like ice as my mind replayed all those moments when I'd sought his touch. "Me."

"He's but a young man," Saga said. "Hot-blooded and in his prime of life, and you are a beautiful woman. There was no hope of him resisting what you offered, so is it fair to blame him? He was only giving you what you wanted."

It was all I could do not to cry, I felt like such a fool. "Perhaps you're right."

"Oh, sweet girl, do not weep." Saga abandoned her cup and came to my side, pulling me against her. "It is a mistake of youth and inexperience to base your decisions on the emotions in your heart. All you can do is learn from your errors and press forward in such a manner that you do not make the same mistakes again. Let us abandon this topic for now. You've much to think on and you need to let it sit in your mind before making any decisions. You have time, sweet Freya, for you are safe here in the wilds."

Breathe, I silently whispered. *Just breathe until you find composure.*

Except every breath felt too short, as though no air reached my lungs. Saga was right to chastise me. All the nasty things I'd said and done to Bjorn repeated in my head. Yet despite all of that, he was here at my side. I did not deserve his loyalty.

"You already have his forgiveness," Saga murmured, filling my cup again. "You never needed it, because he is consumed by guilt at having wronged you. Let this strife between you two go. You are both unfated, and together, I have faith that the Norns will bend and the future will be yours to choose."

Blinking, I drank again. "Thank you for your wisdom, Saga."

"I am not always so wise," she said with a shrug. "And my calm temper has come with age. Let me tell you the story of the first time I learned that Harald was sleeping with other women back in Nordeland."

It was a relief to set aside my own failings and listen to Saga regale me with stories of her youth, including an instance where she chased Harald while throwing eggs at the back of his head. Story after story, until I was so deep in my cups I could barely sit straight on my stool and my whole body ached from too much laughter.

"I must find my bed," Saga finally declared. "For I will surely regret my indulgence come morning."

Arm in arm with our dresses held against our chests, we staggered through the ankle-deep snow back to the cabin where Bjorn sat out front.

"Are you both drunk?" he demanded. "You are supposed to be here for wisdom, Freya, and you, Mother, to impart it, and this is how you behave?"

"There is much truth to be found in wine," Saga snickered, then stumbled over the threshold, weaving her way to her bed. Flopping onto a pile of furs, she pulled one over the top of her. "Sleep where you will," she slurred. "I have no more wisdom left in me tonight."

Bjorn had set out my bedroll and pack, and I extracted a nightdress and pulled it over my head. My eyes kept going to the door, waiting for Bjorn to come inside, but the latch never stirred.

Saga was snoring softly now, and in the absence of her stories, the more serious aspects of our conversation moved back to fill my head. Most especially my growing sense that I was in the wrong for being angry with Bjorn and that I needed to make things right. I silently rehearsed an apology over and over as I waited for him to return, but he never came. So I picked up a lamp and stepped outside, marking his larger tracks heading to the sauna we'd just abandoned, his clothing hanging on a hook outside.

"Go to bed, Freya," I muttered. "You are drunk."

But not *that* drunk.

And if I didn't get my apology out of my mouth tonight, I feared that with morning and sobriety, I'd lose my nerve.

Not allowing logic any more chance to talk me out of it, I scampered barefoot through the snow. I flung open the door, stumbled inside, then slammed it behind me.

Bjorn sat on the stool I'd vacated, shoulders resting against the wall, the heavy steam not enough to conceal his nakedness. My heart skipped as I took in the hard lines of his body, the tattoos and scars I had traced my fingers over what now felt like a lifetime ago.

"Forget your cup?" He nudged the cup I'd used earlier, which lay on its side against the wall.

"No. I want to talk to you."

"It can't wait until morning?"

I shook my head. "Your mother told me everything."

"Wonderful." Bjorn shifted his weight on the stool, the tattoos on his body seeming to move in the steamy light. "Unfortunately, you are so drunk that you'll likely have forgotten half of it come morning and still won't believe anything that comes from my lips."

"Maybe. But right now, I have been made to understand why you lied to me. That you had no choice."

"I had a choice."

"Not a good one," I replied, ignoring the part of me, deep down, that screamed in defiance. "You didn't make me do anything I didn't want to do, so I have no right to be so angry. Especially given you are potentially the only person who can help me."

Bjorn's brow furrowed. "Exactly what did my mother say to you, Born-in-Fire? Because you do not sound like yourself."

I believed that, because for many long days, every word that I'd said had been nasty, selfish, and spiteful. And what had it earned me besides more misery? The chance at a good life was hanging before me and instead of reaching for it, I'd spat on it for the sake of my pride. My eyes prickled because I felt so empty. So alone.

"I didn't just swear an oath to serve Snorri," I confessed. "I swore to his blood, which means I also swore to you. That's why I can speak to you about it, because I also swore to silence."

"What all did you promise?" he asked. "When we were in Grindill, after Steinunn's performance, you said that you and Ylva had made a deal that Snorri would never touch you."

"Not to serve anyone else." I frowned. "Allegiance. Protection. Silence."

"What was the exact phrasing?" When I didn't answer, he added, "Well?"

"I'm thinking." But I'd been nearly as drunk when I'd sworn the oaths as I was now.

Bjorn exhaled an aggrieved breath. "Freya, a blood oath is something you should remember the details of!"

My cheeks burned. "I do remember the details. Give me a moment to recall the phrasing."

Staring at the floorboards of the sauna, I dragged myself back into that awful moment in Snorri's bedroom. The basin with our blood smeared into runes around the edge. "I vow to serve no man not of this blood. I vow allegiance to him who is of this blood," I whispered softly. "I vow to protect, at all cost, him who is of this blood. I vow to speak no word of this bargain except to him who is of this blood."

Bjorn drew in a shaky breath.

I bit my bottom lip but then forced myself to finish. "Snorri thought that a child would create the same form of loyalty, and I would have promised anything to avoid that." Laughing because the alternative was to cry, I added, "I also really did not want to have sex with Snorri."

"I'm sorry." Bjorn leaned forward and rested his elbows on his knees, pressing his fingers to his temples. "I didn't want you to go with him. Wanted so desperately just to kill him that night and be done with it, but I had promised my mother I wouldn't. Still, I hated myself for letting him take you. Was so angry I could barely see straight, which was why I left the great hall."

I wondered if everything would have changed if he'd decided differently. If he'd flipped me over his shoulder and stolen me away.

Except that I knew I wouldn't have gone easily. That I'd have fought him out of fear for what would happen to my family. Bjorn hadn't *allowed* me to walk into that room with Snorri and Ylva. I'd chosen to do so myself.

I crossed the small space between us. I didn't want to feel this way, miserable and angry. What I wanted was to go back to the moment when Bjorn had held me in his arms and I'd been so happy. And the only thing preventing that was *me*.

Bjorn looked up, the light from the fire casting shadows across his face, but I could see the want in his gaze, and it stirred the embers of my own desire. I trailed a finger down the side of his face, the scrape of stubble against my skin making my core tighten as I cupped my hand around his cheek.

He leaned into my touch, eyes closing. "I want you so badly." His voice was quiet, and I wasn't certain whether he spoke to me or himself. "There is nothing I wouldn't do to win you back."

I felt unsteady, wanting this but also not ready to want this. Not ready to let go of my hurt. *What do you gain by digging in your heels and refusing to forgive?* Saga's voice whispered in my head, and wanting to drive away the shame her words made me feel, I lifted my nightdress and cast it aside.

Bjorn's eyes drifted over my naked form, but instead of claiming me, he whispered, "Freya, this isn't what you want."

I straddled his legs, silencing his protests with a kiss. The touch of his lips to mine was a bolt of lightning through my body. My bare toes curled against the wooden floor and a flood of desire filled my core. I slid my hands over the slick skin of his shoulders, tasting him even as I unknotted the tie holding back his hair, burying my fingers in the silken strands.

He was already hard, his cock pressed against my sex, and a whimper tore from my lips. Every part of my body wanted him. Needed him. But my heart felt like it was trembling inside my chest as I whispered, "I want you to fuck me."

"Because you're drunk." His teeth caught my bottom lip, even as his hands gripped my hips, moving me along his length. "You're still angry with me."

I was. But my justification for my rage was so badly eroded that it was ready to collapse. And I was so desperately afraid of how I'd feel without it. "I don't want to feel like this." Moisture dripped down my cheeks. Not steam but tears. "Make me not feel like this."

Instead of driving into me and filling the void, Bjorn's lips pulled away from my throat, his hands stilling. "No. Not like this."

The hurt of his rejection was a battering ram to my stomach. Rather than allowing it to drown me, I fed it to my rage. "You've taken away so much from me and you won't even give me this?"

The ground trembled.

Hissing softly between his teeth, Bjorn slid his hand up my throat and caught hold of my chin. He forced my face sideways until the lamp illuminated my eyes. With a snarl, he flipped me over his shoulder and carried me out of the sauna.

"What are you doing?" I got my answer a heartbeat later when he set me down, arse first, into the snow.

I shrieked as the cold pressed against my overheated core and tried to get to my feet, but he held me down.

"I love you, Freya." His knees were on either side of my body, the cold not seeming to touch him. "And there is little I want more than to fuck you until you forget everything but my name. But not like this. Not while you're so angry it turns your eyes to flame."

"My anger is a part of me!" I shouted. "You can't love only half of me, Bjorn, because that means you don't love me at all!"

"I love the whole of you!" he shouted back. "Even when you are as mean as a feral cat and say things that break my heart, I still love you! But no matter what my mother has convinced you of, you don't want this right now. So neither do I."

He let go of me and climbed to his feet.

The truth of his words rushed through me, but it only caused me to snarl, "You brought me here because you thought the truth would erase the damage and that I'd forgive you. You got what you wanted, because it has become clear to me that my anger isn't just. Yet when I try to give you my forgiveness, you throw it in my face!"

"I brought you here because you wanted to learn the truth about yourself, not because I thought it would change the way you feel. And right now, it feels like a mistake bringing you here at all." He gave a sharp shake of his head, nothing more than a shadow in the night. "As for your forgiveness, Freya, you haven't given it because I don't deserve it. The only way I will ever have it is by earning it."

Without another word, he strode through the snow and back into the sauna, slamming the door behind him.

CHAPTER 17

BJORN

I gave up on sleep as dawn painted the eastern sky, and silently rose to my feet. Freya was curled in a ball beneath a blanket, just as she'd been when I'd come back hours ago. It was the heavy sleep of too much to drink that never contributed to rest, and she'd pay for it when she woke. Yet I was careful not to disturb her as I crossed to where my mother slept, easing aside the curtain and poking her in the shoulder.

One green eye opened and gave me a dark glare.

"Get up," I muttered. "We need to have words."

She sighed but then dragged herself out of the furs and wrapped a heavy cloak around herself before putting on her worn shoes. I held open the door until she was outside, then shut it firmly. Skoll and Hati sat in the snow, and I said to them, "Watch over her."

Not that Freya was likely to wake for several more hours.

The early light filtered through the frost-laced branches of the trees and a thin layer of snow crunched beneath our feet as we walked. This high in the mountains, it already smelled of coming winter, and it would not be long until the lush vegetation turned brown under the onslaught of bitter winds. I said nothing until we were far enough away from the cabin that Freya wouldn't be woken by what would be a heated conversation. "What the fuck did you say to her, Mother?"

She crossed her arms and glared up at me. "Mind your tongue, boy. I'll not tolerate such language from one whose arse I wiped as a babe."

I cast my eyes skyward, beseeching the gods to grant me patience.

Yet rather than continuing to berate me for my language, my mother's voice turned cold and serious. "The stakes are high, Bjorn. Once Snorri determines that Freya is in Nordeland, he will stop at nothing to get her back. You know this, for he once did the same for you. The cost was great and many people died, but when he comes for Freya, it will be far worse."

I exhaled. "I know."

"Are you aware that she is bound by a blood oath to Snorri?" she asked. "To secrecy as well, although I was able to discern much."

"I'm aware, though it was only last night she told me the entirety of what she swore." When she glared at me askance, I repeated Freya's oath, "'I vow allegiance to him who is of this blood. I vow to protect, at all cost, him who is of this blood. I vow to speak no word of this bargain except to him who is of this blood.'"

My mother's jaw tightened. "Better and worse than I thought. I only suspected the allegiance and the silence. Ylva is as thorough as always, though. She knows even a leashed hound can turn on its master."

"She can't harm him." Memory abruptly filled my head of those final moments we spent in Grindill. How Freya clearly wished harm upon Snorri but had not acted, and he'd laughed at her and said, *You swore your own oaths, Freya, so it seems both my fate and life are safe from you.*

Why hadn't I killed him when I'd had a chance? Challenged him. Put a knife in his back. Cut his throat when he was sleeping. Why had I done none of those things? Why had I been so obsessed with keeping my promise to my mother? "How is it better than you thought?"

"I know little of blood oaths." My mother's expression was grim.

"But allegiance and protection . . . They are both words open to interpretation. How Freya is bound by them is determined by what she felt the words meant when she swore them. The magic may have been Ylva's, but the limits of the oath were determined by Freya herself."

"She probably doesn't remember," I said, hating how fear had driven Freya to such a desperate bargain. "She was desperate."

"Yet another reason to hate the creature who sired you," my mother growled, then gave her head a sharp shake. "Even so, we can glean her limitations by her actions. Allegiance does not demand she remain at Snorri's side, nor does it seem to command her loyalty." Her eyes grew distant and thoughtful. "She was raised to believe that allegiance to one's jarl meant obeying a call to arms and fighting on his behalf."

"So she's obligated to fight for him if he can call her to arms."

"A call which he'd have to communicate to her in some fashion, and we can prevent that." My mother gave a nod of approval. "As to protection . . ."

"It does not extend to protecting his feelings," I muttered. "Of that, I can attest."

My mother laughed, slapping her hand against her thigh. "I have no sympathy for you on that count, Bjorn, so do not weep to me about your wounded heart."

I glared at her. "She cursed me to Helheim after she discovered my lies. Hel's magic manifests as roots that drag the souls of the living down into the earth. They took all of Harald's warriors but me, Harald, Tora, and Skade, but only because we were able to fight them off." Even now, I remembered the strength of those roots wrapping around my legs, the tug from within as they attempted to extract my soul for Hel. "If she can curse me, then she can curse Snorri."

"So she is not bound to protect your feelings or your soul," my mother said. "But I think it safe to assume she is bound to protect you from physical harm, even at the cost of her own life."

I gave a tight nod knowing no oath was required on that front. Freya risked her life for others without question. It was who she was at her core.

"The solution is obvious," my mother continued, interrupting my thoughts. "You must take Freya and lead Snorri in a direction other than Nordeland. Keep her far enough ahead of him that he cannot communicate with her himself, or through others. Once you are far enough away, disappear entirely and never come back. Live a beautiful life together that is wholly different from what I envisioned." Her bottom lip quivered. "I'll know you have succeeded when the vision I have seen fades from my mind's eye, and I will be content."

It seemed far too easy, and I remembered Harald's caution about trying to outrun fate. "This is what you and Freya discussed? She agreed?"

My mother looked away. "*Agreed* is a strong assessment, although I think her reticence has more to do with her conflict with you than disagreement over the validity of the plan. I aimed to grease the path to forgiveness for you, but I suspect that you bungled my efforts entirely."

However she'd *greased the path to forgiveness* had made more of a mess of Freya's heart than before. "She's not forgiven me, Mother. Not really. Nor should she, after what I did."

"The pair of you will be the death of me." She kicked at a tree root with the toe of her shoe. "You were in the right, Bjorn. Freya is being selfish and childish if she doesn't see that, so you ought to work to put her mind on the right path."

I took a step back, disliking that sentiment, but then my mother pressed her hands to her face. "Forgive me. Fear poisons my tongue because every time I close my eyes, I see Freya standing in the shadow of the Skjoldfjell and gazing out with red eyes over a sea of dead. Nowhere do I see you." Tears leaked out from behind fingers, and she let out a soft sob. "You say you would die rather than allow her to come to harm. If she is allowed to live, I think you will also perish. Yet when I offer a solution, you both dig in your heels and refuse to consider it."

I opened my mouth to argue that it was not the solution but her methods of communicating it that I took issue with, but then Freya's voice filled my ears. "She's right, Bjorn. We need to go."

I turned to find her a dozen paces away, flanked by the wolves. Her face was pale and somewhat green but her voice was steady. "It's a good plan. Together, we will lead Snorri away from both Nordeland and Skaland. Leave a trail that anyone could follow so that there is no doubt where we have gone, and draw him to the deep south. Allow him to chase us until the jarls of Skaland grow weary of his antics, his warriors give back their armbands, and he has impoverished himself beyond the capacity to hire mercenaries. Then we will disappear."

"And then?"

Freya looked away. "And then we go our separate ways."

CHAPTER 18

FREYA

I didn't know if I meant it. Only that after what had occurred the prior night, it seemed the safer path to walk toward. There was no future where I could envision fully trusting Bjorn again, but also no future where I trusted myself around him.

"We should go now," I said. "Saga, you will make Harald understand? We won't need to worry about him trying to stop us?"

"He will argue," she replied. "But he will abide by my judgment." A sharp whistle drew the wolves to her side, where they sat with their tongues lolling. "As will his pets."

"Do you wish for more time?" I felt cruel because this plan necessitated Bjorn being gone from Nordeland for years upon years. Perhaps even forever, lest dark fates weave themselves back into existence. "We could delay—"

"Any delay might cost us everything," Saga interrupted. "Take what you need and ride hard and fast. Begin setting the trail before Snorri has the chance to set sail to Nordeland."

I heard the unspoken words. *If he hasn't set sail already.*

Twin tears trickled down Saga's face. "I will miss you, my son. Miss you more than you'll ever know, but this sacrifice is small compared to the alternatives. Go now and go with my—"

She cut off, her chin snapping upward and her eyes rolling back in her head, her body twitching.

Oh gods. "Bjorn, what's happening to her?"

"It's a vision." He caught hold of his mother's arms, holding her steady. "There's nothing to do but wait to hear what Odin chose to show her."

I held my breath, my heart thundering with anticipation.

Then Saga spoke, her voice hollow and strange. "A son of Skaland, a false king, sails forth on a wave of darkness. Lies unite the clans, their banners a harbinger of death, their battle cries heard in the realms of gods and men. All tangled in the shield maiden's thread. All drawn by her call. And in their wake, they will leave weeping widows, orphaned children, and a feast for the carrion crows, their fates certain unless the shield maiden cuts her thread free of the false king's control and weaves her new destiny."

"Snorri," I breathed even as Saga collapsed into her son's arms.

Saga pressed fingers to her head, tears running down her cheeks. "So much death. So much loss." A sob tore from her lips. "He is coming. He is coming for her."

Cold certainty filled my veins, my mouth tasting sour. It didn't matter that I was no longer within Snorri's reach, because he had still used me to unite the clans of Skaland beneath his rule. The only thing that had changed was that I was no longer sailing to war alongside him but was now the justification for an invasion. "Snorri still controls my fate."

Bjorn's eyes snapped to me. "There is no reason to believe this has come to pass. This could be the distant future, we do not know."

"Saga?" I dropped to my knees before her. "Has Snorri already set sail? How much time do we have?"

"I do not know. It could be tomorrow. A year from now. Or a decade." Bjorn's mother wiped tears from her face. "All I know is that in your name, Nordeland will suffer."

And seers could not lie.

I sat down heavily, melted snow and mud soaking into my trousers. No matter how I felt about Nordeland, this was not a future I wanted. Not a war I wanted.

I couldn't escape it by running—that was growing clearer to me by the second.

"Whatever you are thinking, push it from your thoughts." Bjorn grasped my shoulders. "Gathering an army and the ships needed to transport it takes time. There is no reason to believe he's already set sail, because that borders on impossibility. We head to the coast and ensure that we are seen by merchants boarding a ship sailing south. Leave a trail that he cannot deny or, at least, the jarls who are sworn to him cannot deny." His grip tightened. "Snorri doesn't know you have Hel's magic. He doesn't know what you can do. There is only so much Skaland will risk for the sake of a magic shield."

"I wouldn't be so sure." Snorri's face consumed my thoughts, his expression filled with fanatical self-certainty. "It's not just me he wants—it's revenge against Harald. And in my name, he now has an army capable of achieving it."

Disappearing south would change nothing. Hiding in the wilds like Saga would change nothing. *Dying* would change nothing. All Snorri needed was my name, his zealotry, and the bad blood between the nations to unite Skaland's clans against Nordeland. War was coming. Could be sailing this way right now.

How could I stop it?

Saga had said that the only way to change fate was to do something the Norns had never considered I might do. Which meant something *I'd* never considered doing.

Or . . . did it mean something I *couldn't* do?

The answer rose in my chest. The one path I'd yet to take a step down because I'd sworn a blood oath forbidding it.

Taking a deep breath, I said, "I have to cut Snorri's thread."

CHAPTER 19

BJORN

It was the determination in Freya's eyes more than the words she spoke that sent a jolt of trepidation through my guts. "Excellent," I grumbled. "Our plan is for you to do the one thing that you cannot do. As always, Born-in-Fire, your plans fill me with the utmost confidence of our certain success."

Instead of rising to my bait, Freya only fixed me with an emotionless stare. "Call me to arms."

"What?" I demanded, even as I heard my mother suck in a breath of air.

"The tendency to shout must run in the family," Freya said, "because both of you argued at top volume and I heard every word. If *allegiance* means that I must answer a call to arms, you can do so just as easily as Snorri. So call me to arms and name him your enemy."

Everything felt suddenly distant, as though I watched myself from afar.

"And once you do that, I will call upon Hel to take his soul to Helheim." Her chin trembled slightly, betraying that she wasn't as calm as she was pretending.

"You said you refused to use Hel's gift again," I said. "You said that you did not believe it a power a mortal should wield."

"I did say that." Freya inclined her head in acknowledgment. "And I feel the same way, which is why I believe this is the right path."

There was no denying the logic but every part of me recoiled at the idea of using the oath my piece-of-weasel-shit of a sire had forced upon her. At compelling her to do something, even at her request. "No. If this is the path you wish to walk, then walk it. But it will not be on my orders."

Freya made a noise of disgust. "You will have my back until the gates of Valhalla, will you? Except only on your terms."

"Having your back doesn't mean agreeing to every wild scheme you come up with."

She scowled at me. "I can't look at you anymore." Nodding at my mother, Freya strode back to the cabin, wolves at her heels.

"I understand your concerns, my son. But by standing on morality, you put her at greater risk."

My mother had risen to her feet, her cloak wrapped tightly around her despite the heat of the sun now fully risen in the sky.

"If you harness her oath first, there is a good chance that Snorri will hold no power over her," my mother said. "Or at least, much less power. If you allow her to go on her own, all it will take is one word of command naming Nordeland her enemy and Freya will turn on us. The horror I just witnessed will become reality."

"Or perhaps this is how it becomes reality," I snapped. "By compelling her to march straight toward him. Who is to say if she remembered the words correctly or if there is some nuance of magic Ylva used that will grant Snorri more control? It's better for Freya to run. To get as far away from Nordeland as she can."

"Do you truly believe that?" my mother asked. "Or do you see that path as holding a higher hope for you reclaiming Freya's heart?"

My jaw clenched, anger burning in my chest. "Do you truly believe I'm that selfish?"

"I know you love her and will do anything to get her back." She looked away. "It is not lost on me how you prioritized your own desires over her well-being while you were in Skaland. Freya is young and has been conditioned all her life to give the men around her what they want, and you took advantage of that."

Her words were a punch to the stomach, driving the air from my lungs. "I . . ."

"Banish that word from your lips." Her eyes shot to mine, green irises bright with anger. "And replace it with Freya's name. If you truly love her, then you will do what is right for her, even if it costs you what you want."

"I am trying to do what is right for her!" Yet doubt crept into my mind, despite my protests. "There is a simple solution, Mother. I'll kill Snorri. I should've fucking killed him half a lifetime ago, but you wouldn't let me. You were so set on your own vengeance and needing to deny him Valhalla that you never stopped to question whether it was *your* actions that secured Freya's dark fate. So do not speak to me of selfishness."

Her expression was unmoved. "Selfishness must be in the blood." Her face tilted. "Doubt my judgment all you wish, Bjorn. But remember the Allfather did not reveal to me Bjorn Firehand cutting his thread free of the false king's control to weave a new destiny. He showed me Freya."

Then she twisted on her heel and strode toward the cabin.

Turning my face to the sky, I fought for calm. Fought to reclaim logic and reason. All my life, I'd been driven by prophecy and destiny and fate, accepting the Allfather's guidance given through my mother's lips without question.

But I questioned it now.

Questioned why the woman I loved more than life needed to embrace the darkest parts of her soul to achieve a brighter future. Why I had to be the one to order her to do it. Why the weave of fate seemed like a cruel trick played upon the living, no one ever coming out victorious because this life always ended in death.

But I'd sworn to be at her back until the gates of Valhalla, and not even doubt in the Allfather himself was enough for me to break that vow.

CHAPTER 20

FREYA

The speed at which we traveled did not allow for conversation, our attention all for keeping our horses upright on the rough trail while the wolves raced through the trees on either side. Though the weight of too much wine and too little sleep should have rendered me exhausted, I practically trembled with anticipation.

I'd traveled to see Saga in the hope of finding answers, and though there had been dark moments when it had felt like a fool's hope, I now had what I'd come for.

I had a goal. Something I could relentlessly drive toward knowing I was on the correct course. It gave me a sense of validation for the uncertainty I'd felt about fleeing with Bjorn. Because I felt no uncertainty now.

We stopped long after the sun had set to rest the horses and eat. While our dinner cooked, I warmed my hands over the fire and stared at Bjorn's axe beneath the pile of smoldering wood. Waited for him to start arguing against my plan, all my counterarguments ready to deploy. Yet he was silent and entirely focused on digging through his bag, perhaps because he had the wisdom to realize that my arguments were the strongest.

Extracting his hand from the bag, he reached over the fire and handed me a jar.

I opened it and inhaled a familiar scent.

"I made it while you two were drinking Harald's wine. The herbs I found were old, for it seems my mother has been lax in her gathering, but it's better than lanolin. You smelled like a sheep. That's probably why the wolves are so taken with following you about."

I rolled my eyes, but there was no denying that the heady scent of cloves was much superior to the salve Harald's servants provided me. Yet the smell reminded me of past moments. There was a part of me that desperately wanted Bjorn to take care of my scars so that I could feel his skin against mine. Feel the strength of his fingers working the tension out of the old injury. Yet even though wine cast a haze over my memories of last night, I still felt the flush of shame at his rejection. Especially given that he'd been in the right.

My anger toward Bjorn was fading, but all of my distrust remained. Maybe that did make me selfish and childish, but after a lifetime of being used by men, I was not sure I had any forgiveness left in my heart for the choices they made that harmed me. To be with someone I couldn't forgive would be like living with a curse hanging over my head, constantly reminding me of past transgressions and never giving me any peace. Perhaps my destiny was to be alone. To be my own rock in the storm. To take care of myself until the end of my days.

Digging out a glob of the salve, I set to working on my own scars. The relief to my stiffness was almost instantaneous, and yet I kept rubbing at my skin until the friction created a different sort of pain. "I was expecting an argument. For you to tell me what a foolish plan this is and that it is destined to fail."

"It's not a foolish plan." His axe disappeared from beneath the firewood, and the forest grew darker with only natural fire to illuminate our surroundings. "It is a dangerous plan."

"It's only dangerous if you refuse to help."

Bjorn rested his elbows on his knees. "Taking your leash from Snorri only to hold it myself sits poorly with me. I don't want . . ." He broke off and shook his head.

"It's out of necessity," I said. "Surely you see that?"

"Necessity according to whom?"

I stared at him. "According to the Allfather. You . . . you aren't questioning his wisdom, are you?"

"When my mother spoke of the vision he showed her, no mention was made of me. This is a solution that you and my mother have come up with, so yes, I do question whether it is *necessity*."

Closing the jar of salve, I set it aside. "Offer an alternative, then."

"Maybe you are more capable of resisting Snorri's orders than you realize. When Harald brought his army to Grindill, you refused the order to fight. I heard you with my own ears."

"An order given by Ylva, not Snorri." I sighed. "The moment that Snorri began giving me orders on the battlements, I did what he asked."

Bjorn lifted his head, green eyes appearing black in the dim light. "Fine. Then kill the volva whose magic binds your oath. With it broken, you'll be free and can stick your enchanted sword through Snorri's heart and let the gods decide who will take his soul."

I blinked, horror rising in my chest. "Murder Ylva?"

Bjorn shrugged. "She's far from innocent, I assure you of that. Much of my mother's plight at Snorri's hands was driven by her jealousy, so I would not weep over her death. I'll do it, if you wish."

The callousness with which he suggested murdering a woman who might not be innocent but certainly didn't deserve to die caused me to draw back. To look at him in a different light.

"Or perhaps I just order you to leave Nordeland with me," Bjorn said. "You are bound to serve me, yes? Your allegiance is to me, correct?" He rose to his feet. "Then I call you to arms against Islund. Those bastards have been a thorn in my arse for long years, and I wish for you to fight at my side to kill as many of them as possible. We leave now."

I felt the sudden urge to get to my feet. To reach for my sword and shield. Only to realize my hand was already closed around the pommel of my weapon. And that I was already standing.

Nausea coursed through me because how many times had I obeyed Snorri's directive believing myself acting of my own free will when it had only been the oath driving my actions? Looking back, it was impossible for me to tell.

"I changed my mind." Bjorn sat back down across the fire, brow creased with a scowl.

"You arsehole." I sucked in breath after breath, hating the sense of powerlessness that I felt.

"However you feel, know that it feels worse to me," he snapped. "Because now I can't help but wonder how much you've done because you wanted to and how much was influenced by the oath."

Bile burned in my throat as comprehension reared in my mind. "No . . ." I whispered. "It was me. I swear, it was my choice."

"How can you know?"

I crossed my arms, trying to ward away the chill.

"I'll follow you down this path, Born-in-Fire," he said. "I'll fight at your side to see this through. But you've spent your life serving at the whims of men, allowing them to control you, and despite knowing that suffering, hating that suffering, your solution is to serve yet again."

I flinched, feeling like I'd been slapped.

"I refuse to control you." Bjorn picked up a stick and jabbed at the fire, sending an explosion of embers skyward. "And that order I just gave you? Consider it the last that will ever pass my lips."

"Even if it costs the lives of thousands of Nordelanders?" I asked.

"If it comes to that, I'll already be dead." Taking the pot off the fire, he ladled portions into two bowls, then handed me one.

I stared at the contents. "I'm not hungry."

"Neither am I." Bjorn dumped out the contents of his bowl. "If there is news to be had of Snorri setting sail, Harald will be the first to know."

I dumped out my own bowl, the wolves rushing to eat the steaming meat. "Then let's ride."

CHAPTER 21

FREYA

The rising sun glowed over Hrafnheim as we came within sight of the fortress, which was silent and imposing. Both of the drawbridges were raised and I noted that the battlements were heavily patrolled. Light gleamed off the warriors' weapons, their breath visible in the cool morning air.

"How much do you want to tell him?" Bjorn asked, the first words we'd shared since our argument the prior night.

"Everything he needs to mount a defense," I said. "Getting close enough to Snorri to take his soul will be no easy thing, and I've no desire to give Hel any more souls than his. Which means the defense of Nordeland's shores needs to fall upon Harald's shoulders. Besides, I can only assume your mother will somehow tell him everything she's learned."

"Maybe," Bjorn grumbled. "I'm not sure they are communicating as much as they used to. But either way, he'll want you to be part of the defense, Born-in-Fire."

"Explain to him that I cannot serve him." I rolled my shoulders, my back stiff from being so long in the saddle. "You say he is an expert in runic magic, so he may have answers. He has been accommodating so far, and . . . we have a common enemy in Snorri."

"Be wary of setting Harald on a pedestal," Bjorn muttered. "He likes to have his way, and those who deny him what he wishes usually regret the choice."

I turned my head, something about his tone making my hackles rise. "You call him Father and yet all I've seen from you since we stepped onto Nordeland's shores is the most reluctant of loyalty. Why? Did he do something to you in the past that caused a breach between you?"

"No," Bjorn answered. "But it's been years since I left, and things have changed. He's withheld information from me. And I don't like the way he looks at you."

Gooseflesh rose on my skin. "How does he look at me?"

"Like a child looking at a new plaything." Bjorn lifted his chin, eyes on the battlements. "Last chance to run, Freya. After we enter those walls, I think it will be a fight for you to ever escape."

I bit the insides of my cheeks, no part of me disregarding the threat. Yet the threat of Snorri to thousands of innocents was also very real, and I wouldn't turn back now. "I'm not running."

Bjorn made an aggrieved noise but then muttered Tyr's name. His axe flamed into being, and the sight of it caused shouts of recognition. More shouts still as the sun reflected off the silvery metal of my shield. Soon after, the chains clanked and the thick wooden bridge began to descend, fully flush with the shore by the time we reached the river's banks. Handing off our horses to a waiting man, we shouldered our bags and crossed the frothing river.

Hrafnheim was already awake as we weaved through the narrow streets. A blacksmith's hammer rang out and women retrieved water from rain barrels. It smelled of hearth smoke and porridge and humanity—a familiar scene of families breaking their fasts just as they would be in Skaland. Pots clanging and people talking, children squabbling and babies crying. Part of me hated that. How similar it was. I wanted them to be different and strange and off-putting, but instead all I could think of was that an army intent on their blood was potentially crossing the strait. An army that sailed in my name, and Hrafnheim was far from the first place that Snorri would strike. Visions of all the villages and hamlets we passed sailing up the Rimstrom filled my head, only to be replaced with the remains of Steinunn's home. Nothing but the charred debris of lives that had been reclaimed by the earth.

Servants had already begun their days in Harald's great hall as we entered, and so, I swiftly discovered, had the king himself. He sat at a table with significant company, including Tora, Skade, and Steinunn.

Skade called out, "The favored son returns so soon. Did your mother have no time for your venom-tongued woman, Bjorn?"

Bjorn didn't respond, but Harald said, "Be silent, Skade." He rose, and I noticed dark shadows beneath his eyes, as though he'd slept as little as Bjorn and me.

"The gate guards sent word you'd been spotted, but your return is unexpected." He pulled Bjorn close and pounded him on the back. Then he held him at arm's length, shadowed eyes scrutinizing him. "What has happened? Is Saga well?"

"She's fine," Bjorn answered, then gestured to me. "This is your plan. Lead the way."

I bit back sharp words and took a deep breath. "Odin gave her a vision of the future," I said as Harald's eyes fixed on me. "'A son of Skaland, a false king, sails forth on a wave of darkness. Lies unite the clans, their banners a harbinger of death, their battle cries heard in the realms of gods and men. All tangled in the shield maiden's thread. All drawn by her call. And in their wake, they will leave weeping widows, orphaned children, and a feast for the carrion crows, their fates certain unless the shield maiden cuts her thread free of the false king's control and weaves her new destiny.'"

Harald grimaced and tucked a lock of hair behind his ear. "Kaja may have reached Skaland by now, but she won't have had time to return to Guthrum with news. Did Saga indicate when this is set to occur?"

Bjorn shook his head. "You know she never does. Tomorrow. Ten years from now. Who can say?"

Irritation flashed across Harald's face, and he cursed under his breath.

"Even if she did, it would not matter. I've not the power to change the future she foresaw. I'm nothing but a thread the rest of you manipulate."

As he spoke, he gestured at the table behind him. My skin prickled, and I looked more closely at the table full of men and women. Some I knew—Tora, Skade, Steinunn—but most were strangers. Seemingly from all walks of life, warriors, craftsmen, farmers, and others whose vocations were unclear from their garments. And yet some instinctual part of me *knew* what I was looking at even before I picked out the edges of crimson tattoos. Children of the gods. Every last person at the table was unfated.

I'd known he had many in his service. Known Guthrum had been instrumental in bringing many of them to Harald. Yet not in my wildest imagination had I envisioned so many.

It was as though he'd collected all the Unfated in Nordeland and brought them to one place.

"Might we speak to you alone, Father?" Bjorn asked, and I set aside the question of how he'd collected so many Unfated for later contemplation as I followed them behind the dais.

"Is there a way to break a blood oath?" Bjorn began without preamble.

Harald shrugged. "Of course. Kill the volva whose magic bound the words." His brow furrowed. "Why? What did you promise?"

"Not me." Bjorn jerked his chin in my direction. "She can't speak of it to anyone not of Snorri's bloodline, so my explanation will have to suffice." In terse words, he swiftly laid out my oaths, though I noted that he left out our speculation of the oath's limitations, as well as my desire for him to call me to arms against Snorri.

"Ylva knows her runes." Harald looked me up and down before turning back to Bjorn. "Yet this is precisely why I forbid such oaths in my company. They never bind individuals entirely but do force them to seek creative ways around them. It is better to earn the loyalty of those in your service because then they are bound by their own hearts."

There was undeniable logic to that, and I found myself nodding in agreement.

Harald began to pace, expression grave and pale gray eyes seeming to see nothing around him, so lost was he in thought. Finally, he stopped before me. "What do you wish to do, Freya? For it is clear to me that you must lead us through this ordeal if there is to be any chance of success."

Shock rippled through me, freezing my tongue as surely as my oath ever had. Bjorn seemed equally stunned, though he recovered more swiftly. "Have you been struck on the head, Father? The jarls will not follow a Skalander."

"They followed you," Harald said. "Bent the knee to you in this very room as my son and heir."

"That's different," Bjorn snapped. "I'd been here most of my life. And I'm a—"

"Man?" Harald interjected, then shot me an amused smile as though we shared some inside joke. "You were but a boy of seventeen at the time, as I recall. Whereas Freya is a woman grown and possessed of the blood of two goddesses, making her the most powerful Unfated to ever live. As close to a god as a mortal can be."

My mouth turned sour, no part of me feeling good at being so elevated, for I already felt less than human.

"Father—"

Harald waved him to silence. "It makes sense. Ylva's runes ensure that Freya cannot serve any man not of Snorri's blood: *I vow to serve no man not of this blood.*"

He laughed and clapped his hands, and I tensed with the expectation that he'd point out that Bjorn could control me. Instead, Harald said, "But Freya is no man, so she can serve herself, correct?"

Not waiting for a response, he added, "And Saga's words were: 'Their fates certain unless the shield maiden cuts her thread free of the false king's control and weaves her new destiny.' To me this says that the dark future is unchangeable unless Freya acts, unless Freya *leads*. It must be she who frees herself of the false king's control. And the only way for her to do that is to kill Snorri."

"Or Ylva."

Harald made a face and shook his head. "I do not believe that killing Ylva will change anything. Freya has already made Snorri king and he uses her name to hold the allegiance of all of Skaland. But you and I arguing will achieve nothing. Freya must lead, and you and I must bite our tongues and listen."

This reaction was so distant from what I'd expected that I didn't know quite what to say. I'd been prepared to buck against Harald's control, not for him to hand me all the might of Nordeland to achieve my ends. "You would willingly give up to me, a woman who was until recently a fishwife who'd never been more than a few hours from her village, control over your warriors, your jarls, your people?"

"If that is what it takes to save them."

My hands balled into fists. "But I don't know anything about leading."

"You know what you wish to achieve," Harald answered. "And I am a tool in your arsenal. My knowledge is yours, Freya."

"Doesn't it bother you to be reduced to a tool?" I asked. "To be so . . . so . . . powerless?"

"I'm not powerless," Harald countered. "It is only that what I will do with my power is already known. Except that I am surrounded by Unfated. Which means you can cause me to act differently. You can snip my thread early or weave it into another pattern, and I relish that uncertainty. That chaos!"

Both his wild grin and his words struck me as strange but I only said, "Is that why you collect the children of the gods around you? Why you created a cabal of people with magic?"

"This is no collection, Freya. No cabal. This"—he gestured to the distant table full of people—"is my family. To have a child of one's own blood is a blessing from the goddess Freyja, but it has been my privilege to provide a home for so many children of the gods."

"Which you do entirely out of the goodness of your heart?" I tried to keep the scowl from my face because I did not truly believe he was willing to give me total control. "Not at all because it allowed you to use their powers to rise to rule. To control a kingdom. To make yourself wealthy above anyone else."

"Nearly all that I do is try to aid my family in achieving their own goals," Harald said. "Or to protect them. Power allows me to do both these things, which is where I gain my true joy. Ask Bjorn." Harald abruptly laughed. "Actually, do not. You'll believe not a word he says, nor, I think, a word that comes from my lips. So ask others. Ask whoever you like, Freya. I can't force you to trust me. That is something to be earned, not demanded. But while I earn it, have faith in the certainty that our goals are the same: to tear asunder the dark future my wife so deeply fears."

I didn't trust him. But what was less clear was whether my distrust was because I refused to see him as anything other than the villain I'd been raised to think him or because he was a villain in truth.

"What is to be our first course of action?" he asked. "Saga has given us some insight, but we are woefully lacking in facts."

The insides of my cheeks were raw from how often I had bitten them, my mouth tasting of blood as I forced myself to think. "We need to hear from Guthrum. Discover what Snorri is doing. Right now, we hold the advantage Saga's vision has given us, for Snorri believes us ignorant to his intent. But if we begin to marshal our defenses too obviously, we will give ourselves away to his spies."

"Agreed," Harald said. "I will send a messenger to seek out Guthrum."

"How swiftly can the jarls come to your call?" I asked.

"They will have the advantage of having just set sail on the prospects of war. They can sail within a day or two of receiving word. Astrid can be dispatched to deliver messages at speed."

"She's a child of Hermod," Bjorn muttered. "She's fleet of foot."

It struck me how dangerous Nordeland was for no reason other than that they were united. But Skaland was larger and more populous, which meant if Snorri had achieved such a union, my people were now also a force to be reckoned with.

"I'll arrange for Astrid to find Guthrum first, then?" At my nod, Harald walked swiftly from the great hall, leaving me alone with Bjorn.

Who stood with his arms crossed and a glare on his face, clearly displeased.

"What?" I demanded. "Do you take issue with my plan?"

"It is not *your* plan, Born-in-Fire." He gave an angry shake of his head. "Don't you see? You only repeated back to him the very ideas he supplied. You are not leading anyone—you are being led."

My cheeks warmed, half in embarrassment and half in anger. "I'd be a fool not to take advice from him. What do I know of rule? What do I know of his resources? Or how quickly he can gather his jarls? To pretend as though I know more about leading Nordeland into battle than the king of fucking Nordeland would make me an idiot."

"You're a puppet being used by two men who have desired to make war against each other for nearly as long as you've been alive," Bjorn snapped. "Harald *hates* Snorri for what he did to my mother. Do not let the veneer of civility he wears fool you otherwise. Death is not enough. He wants Snorri destroyed in such a way that the stain of it follows him into the next realm. Until now, he believed killing you would achieve that end, but now I think he sees that he can use you to truly destroy Snorri's chances at Valhalla, because you can send him to Helheim and deny him the last battle."

A chill ran through me, because though I'd not been unaware of Harald's fixations, Bjorn's words made them feel so much darker. "What would you have me do? What solution do you have to my circumstances that has not been voiced?"

"Run," he said softly. "Leave all of this behind. That is my solution."

"Except it is no solution." My hands balled into fists. "Whether I am here or not, war is coming in my *name*. Running will not stop it. Falling on my own *fucking* sword will not stop it. And I refuse to leave thousands to die just to save my own skin."

"It may not come to that," he said between clenched teeth. "Nordeland and Skaland have always warred. Just as both have always warred with Islund, and with the nations beyond. The north *wars*. Nothing you do will change that."

"Not wars like your mother has foreseen." I felt sick, my own imagination supplying visions of the carnage. "You heard her. Unless you do not believe visions gifted by Odin to a seer who is your own mother, you have to know the threat is greater than ever before."

Bjorn looked away, jaw tight.

"It was not so very long ago that my days were spent gutting fish," I said quietly, an ache forming in my chest. "I knew everything about keeping a home and living a quiet life. Knew the gossip of Selvegr and the stories of our people. Then in a single moment, I was cast into circumstances I had not prepared for. Surrounded by others with more skill and knowledge, all of whom desired to use the magic in my blood to achieve their own ambitions. I know my limitations, Bjorn. I know that I'm out of my depth. But I am *trying* to do the right thing."

My voice broke and I took a steadying breath, knowing I was on the verge of tears. "All my life I dreamed of being a warrior. Of sailing on a jarl's drakkar and making a reputation for myself. Now I've seen what such a life brings. The stink of open bowels and beaches full of flies crawling on corpses. Sacks of bloodstained gold and rings cut from dead men's beards. Children with empty eyes, their whole worlds torn away from them in a moment. Who dreams of being the cause of such things? Why did I dream of it?" Tears started to pour down my cheeks no matter how rapidly I blinked. "I don't care if the whole world calls me naive. An idiot. A fool. At least I know in my heart that I am doing all that I can to prevent that nightmare from becoming an even worse reality."

"Freya—"

I held up a hand to silence him. "You say you will fight at my side through all of this. Yet the truth is that I am surrounded by warriors who will do the same. Unfated such as Skade and Tora, who are just as deadly as you. Yet the one thing you can do to ensure my victory and see this nightmare averted is the one thing you refuse to do. So who is the real fool here?"

Wiping tears from my cheeks, I walked away from him and sat down blindly at the table full of Harald's cabal.

A few glanced my way, but most carried on in their conversations, eating and drinking from the excesses piled on the tables. Only Steinunn sat apart, sipping from a cup and listening, just as she had in Snorri's hall. She had not quite belonged in Halsar, and did not belong here, either. She'd come into Harald's service only after the death of her family, and in fairly short order had traveled to Skaland to aid in the efforts of finding me.

"How is your sword treating you?"

I twitched, then realized that I'd sat next to the smith, Gyda. "Very well. I killed a huldra with it."

"Oh ho!" She slammed her hand down on the table with a laugh, and all the others turned their heads. "A huldra! Lured by our Bjorn, no doubt." Resting her elbow on the table, she leaned closer and said in a loud whisper, "That is the third time they've tried to take him. I told him to grow a proper beard to hide his good looks, but he's either too vain or too stupid to listen."

I wiped at my cheeks, remembering how he'd resisted the creature's power. *I only want her. Only Freya.*

A sudden wave of guilt caused me to look over my shoulder, but Bjorn had left the great hall. Sighing, I broke off a piece of bread from a loaf on the table, eating more for something to keep my mouth busy than out of hunger. "How long have you known Harald?"

"Since we were children," Gyda answered around a mouth of stew. "His father was jarl. He and Harald never saw eye to eye, and the old man had a heavy hand that he used often and regularly. I suspect it was because of him that Harald abandoned Nordeland to travel in the south for many years. He'd become a man by the time he returned and challenged his father. Killed him in the square and, with his face splattered with his father's blood, swore to rule in a different way."

"Has he?"

Gyda shrugged. "Mostly."

"So he didn't save you?"

She made a face, then refilled her cup from a large pitcher. "I was a woman grown when he became jarl, and I had no need of saving. Harald pays me, and whenever I threaten to take my skills elsewhere, he bends and pays me more. You want to hear of salvation, talk to the young pups surrounding you."

I scanned the Unfated seated at the table and saw what she meant about young. None appeared older than thirty and a handful were years younger than I was. "Why does he save them if not for power?"

A question I'd intended for myself, but Gyda shrugged. "Perhaps because no one saved him." Then she pounded the table again. "Shut your gobs, the lot of you. Freya here wishes to hear how you all came to serve Harald so that she might judge his worth."

Then she winked at me. "That is the reason, isn't it?"

My cheeks burned. "Yes."

"Fair enough." She slammed the table one more time. "Troels, you go first. Tell Freya about what your brother Aksel did to you. Steinunn, pay attention, because these stories would be much more entertaining as a song."

CHAPTER 22

BJORN

I wasted the balance of the day away but as the sun set, I found myself on Hrafnheim's walls. I leaned my elbows on the edge of the battlements and watched the drawbridges slowly lift skyward for the night, the chains rattling loudly. When I'd been a boy, Harald had filled my ears with stories about his adventures in the south. Of cities so large that they sprawled farther than the eye could see, towers touching the sky, and bridges spanning massive rivers. Palaces with great domed ceilings made of copper and castles with layers of ring walls that had never been breached. But I'd always held a fascination for the drawbridges. The mechanisms in the guard towers that raised and lowered them, as well as the sheets of paper with the designs drawn upon them that he'd used to replicate the structures. They had writing on them in strange foreign tongues, many of which Harald spoke. He told me that the southerners wrote everything down and that they had buildings full of bound pieces of paper that held all that had ever been.

It seemed strange to me to put that which could be told with speech onto paper and lock it in a room, but I still wished to see the places from his stories. To discover more about those who lived in lands of endless summer, their languages, and their customs. To walk in the domain of different gods and see the different magics. When I'd held Freya in my arms next to the hot springs in Skaland and everything had felt possible, I'd dreamed of taking her to the places in the stories. She'd never been given the chance to travel, and it had seemed a gift she'd value more than jewels and gold.

It made me want to scream that I'd chosen to linger that night. That I hadn't immediately found a merchant ship and sailed out of reach. Built a life for her away from prophecy and violence in a world where I'd heard all people were masters of their own futures.

But it seemed that not even the Unfated could outrun destiny.

The drawbridges thudded into place, and with a last glance at the setting sun, I headed down the steps in the direction of the music. Hrafnheim never fell dark in the way other places did, lanterns hanging from posts on every intersection. Laughter and chatter spilled out of the homes, some making ready for bed while more still headed toward the great hall for revels.

Harald loved revels, and I knew he'd be sitting and watching his people sing and laugh and dance, all drunk on mead that he never allowed to run dry. He didn't like to be alone and always wanted a press of people, though often he only watched them from his throne on the dais. I'd found it overwhelming when I'd first come to Nordeland, used to the isolation that my mother preferred, and I'd asked why he invited the noise night after night. "That is how I understand them," he'd said. "Like the drawbridge mechanism: I had to understand it before I could make it work."

It had made little sense to me then, but now I knew that the key to the strength of his rule was that Harald understood people. Their hopes and dreams and desires.

Their fears.

I'd once admired it, for it had made him so very good at getting people to do as he wished, but I hated watching Freya succumb to his charm. Hated how she was beginning to see him as the one who'd help her to change her fate.

The great hall doors were flung wide, the heat of the hearth and what had to be at least a hundred people rolling over me. It smelled of smoke and meat. Sweat and mead. And the noise of drums and pipes and stomping feet was deafening.

Someone shoved a horn of mead into my hand, but I only took a small sip as I searched the crowd. Harald sat on his throne with one booted heel on the opposite knee, holding a delicate glass from one of his travels that was filled with wine I suspected also to be of foreign origin. Someone threw more wood on the hearth and sparks exploded into the air, floating up to the rafters and turning to ash before disappearing out the smoke hole in the ceiling. It reminded me of how Freya had scaled the rafters in the hall in Halsar when Gnut had attacked. How she'd escaped out the smoke hole and then leaped onto the neighboring building, falling through the roof into a pigpen.

Blinking, my eyes filled with a vision of her scowling at the angry pigs, her hair covered in shit. Unwilling to run then as she was now. Half my size but possessed of twice my bravery.

Gods but I loved her.

It was Tora who I spotted first, for she towered over men and women alike. Yet as the crowd shifted, it revealed Freya standing next to her. She wore a red dress with gold embroidery on the neckline and cuffs, the color like blood against her pale skin, the garment fitted to the lean length of her body and accentuating her breasts. Her long hair hung in loose waves to her waist, a blond so pale that in some lights it appeared almost white. She held a cup but did not drink, instead surveying those around her as though she did not quite wish to believe what she was seeing, her brow furrowed in a crease. Her eyes were mercifully amber, light from hearth and torch turning them into molten suns.

So beautiful. So painfully beautiful that I'd never had a hope.

"Quiet! Quiet!" Harald's voice cut through the noise, and everyone fell still. Steinunn rose onto the dais next to him, her golden-brown hair woven into a coronet around her head.

"Nordeland's most beautiful skald has returned home after too long away," Harald shouted. "But tonight, she will grace us with the song of our victorious return and the battle that greeted us upon arrival. Lift your cups!"

"*Skol!*" the crowd shouted, cups clacking together and mead spilling to join the puddles already pooling on the floor.

I set aside my mead, half expecting Freya to leave the hall given she had no fondness for Steinunn's magic. Instead, her chest moved as though she were taking a steadying breath, and she sat on one of the benches.

Harald stepped off the dais, watching as Steinunn lifted her drum and began to pound a beat, her voice rising in wordless song. Deep and resonant tones that seemed to draw from the earth itself, vibrating with the raw power of the magic of her blood, and stirring something deep and primal in my veins.

Like I was being called to war.

When her voice turned to words, visions of stormy seas exploded across my eyes. The taste of the surf and the violent echo of thunder, as though the gods themselves sought to keep us from Nordeland's shores. Drawing in a deep breath, I focused on the beat of my own heart until the visions faded.

All around me, the people of Hrafnheim stared with rapt wonder at visions I could no longer see, Steinunn's magic transporting them into the story she told so that it was as though they were there. Gasps tore from their lips, women clutching their skirts from fear and excitement, and a few of the men instinctively reached for the weapons at their belts. Freya listened with her head down, the muscles of her jaw standing out against her skin, and I knew that she was watching herself.

I listened only to my own heart, not allowing Steinunn's magic any hold.

Which was why I saw Harald slowly slip away from the dais and out through the great hall doors.

Confirming that Tora remained on guard at Freya's side, I eased between those watching the performance, knowing they saw nothing but the visions created by Steinunn's song. The night air was cool after the stifling heat of the hall, smelling of pine and the wind coming off the glacier between the Skjoldfjell's peaks. I caught a flash of Harald disappearing around a corner. Knowing that it would be easy to lose him in the tangled web of paths and streets forming Hrafnheim, I broke into a trot.

The fortress had grown quieter, everyone either asleep or at the revel in the great hall to see Steinunn's performance. Every impact of my boots against the ground seemed to echo between the walls of the buildings and though I had no reason to hide my presence, I softened my step. In my periphery, the runes on the towering walls surrounding Hrafnheim occasionally flared. Vanquishing disease that had found its way in during the day, most likely, though they did the same thing when the waters of the Rimstrom rose too high, every etching in the stone designed to protect those who lived here.

I ignored them, listening to the sound of Harald's steps and drawing to a swift stop when he fell silent. Glancing around to ensure no eyes watched me, I peered around the corner to find Harald with Skade, their heads close together. The wind howled through the streets and obscured their words, but Skade was nodding as though receiving instruction. My palms prickled, the intensity of their expressions telling me this was no idle conversation, and then the wind ceased its gusting.

"Double the guard on the battlements," Harald said. "No harm must come to Freya, am I understood? She is precious to me and if you allow your petty jealousy to allow her to come to harm—"

"I won't," Skade interrupted. "I swear it on Ullr's name that I will allow no harm to come to her."

Harald's face softened, and he bent to kiss her forehead. "I trust you, my sweet Skade. Now go."

She touched the silver armband above her elbow and smiled up at him once before breaking into a run toward the wall.

Stepping around the corner, I walked toward Harald. He appeared deep in thought, his eyes fixed on the night sky, so I was nearly upon him before he noticed my presence.

He started in surprise and took a quick step away from me as though to flee an attack before regaining his composure. "Bjorn! What are you doing out here?"

"I have no patience for Steinunn's caterwauling," I said.

"You should be kinder to her." He frowned at me. "I know she came into our family after you left for Skaland, but she's a good woman who has suffered much."

I crossed my arms. "She spied on me."

"On my orders, so if you wish to be angry at anyone, be angry at me." He tilted his head. "Though perhaps you are. I have noticed a gulf between us, my son, and I don't think it can be blamed on our time apart."

Instead of answering his silent question, I asked, "Why are you skulking around in the dark?"

Harald was silent, his eyes again on the stars overhead. Then he sighed. "Your mother's vision has me more concerned than I allowed myself to reveal before Freya. For long years, we have fought to prevent your mother's foretelling from coming to pass. Yet for all our efforts, your sire is now king of Skaland and his eyes are set upon us, all the jarls at his back. I fear we will not be able to stop him and that thousands of innocents will fall in his pursuit of his destiny. I've posted more guards tonight, but in truth, there is nothing I can do to stop him. The only person capable of saving us is the one woman who can just as easily destroy us all."

His voice seethed with uncharacteristic frustration and helplessness.

"You have the greatest gathering of the Unfated in the north, Father," I said. "Each with the capacity to change the Norns' plans. Do not place the weight of this solely on Freya's shoulders."

"But your mother—"

"You put too much weight on her words," I interrupted. "When I was small, she told me time and again that one should not live life with the weight of prophecy guiding one's every step. It was not until she came to Nordeland and you took her every word as certain truth that she stopped saying that."

His eyes narrowed. "You don't just disrespect your mother, Bjorn. You disrespect Odin. Not wise given you dream of Valhalla."

I'd once dreamed of Valhalla. About the glory of fighting for the Allfather during the end of days. Now I dreamed of something else entirely. "I don't disrespect them. I—"

My tongue froze as a flash of light exploded overhead. Then another and another. Flaming arrows exploded against the net of protection cast by Hrafnheim's wards, the symbols carved on the walls flaring as the defenses were tested.

Hrafnheim was under attack.

CHAPTER 23

FREYA

It hadn't been perhaps the best use of my time to spend the day listening to stories, but it had been better than hours of dwelling on my own situation. Each of the members of Harald's so-called family had shared how they'd come to be in his service. Not all of them were as dramatic as what had happened to Bjorn and Saga, but all of them had been delivered from the misuse of others by Nordeland's king. Most were from Nordeland itself, but some hailed from Skaland and Islund, as well as the smaller island nations of the north. Children born of all different members of our pantheon, their magics more often than not unclear to me.

Their stories were all different, but there was no denying the loyalty they shared for their king. It made me remember how Harald had told me that the sentiment could not be forced by an oath—that it had to be earned. He had surely done that, for I had every confidence that everyone in his cabal would fight to the bitter end for the man who'd liberated them from their darkest moments.

It also made me wonder if I might one day feel the same way.

After the cabal had finished their stories, they'd dispersed and the servants had begun preparations for a feast in the great hall. I was given a dress to wear, over which I belted my father's sword and Gyda's seax, though I left my shield in the room given to me. Then I let myself drift through the great hall under Tora's watchful eye, meeting more Nordelanders and learning of their lives and customs.

Not once did I see Bjorn, and unease clawed at my insides that perhaps I'd pushed him too far. That I'd stepped over the line and he'd left Hrafnheim without me.

So it was relief that filled my chest when he arrived in the great hall, Harald's words of introduction for Steinunn barely reaching my ears, my focus all for watching Bjorn in my periphery.

"Do you wish to hear her sing?" Tora asked me. "I've never cared for skald magic, myself."

"Yes."

I wasn't certain of my precise reasons for remaining in the hall to listen to Steinunn's song. My prior experiences with her magic had not been moments I'd enjoyed. I told myself it was because Harald would, much as Snorri had, use the skald to manipulate his people, and it was important for me to understand the information he wished them to know. Yet in my heart, I knew that it was because I desired to see myself in the throes of using Hel's magic. To see if I could identify some good in it to ease the dread in my heart of using it against Snorri.

If I even could.

With Bjorn's refusal to take control of my oaths, I had doubts whether I could face Snorri and not be forced to bend to his will. Frustration burned in my chest at Bjorn's reticence, for while I could understand it, this rare lack of pragmatism was not helpful. To do this one thing might allow me to change all our fates to something better, yet Bjorn showed no signs that he might bend.

It was not that I desired his control. I didn't desire to be under *any* man's control. But I did not see another way to go to war against Snorri and destroy him. Or at least, not another way that I was willing to pursue. Ylva and I had our conflicts, but it was not lost on me that I had willingly accepted my oaths over the alternative. She did not deserve to die for my choices.

I was drawn from my thoughts as Steinunn lifted her drum. Next to me, Tora had pulled pieces of wool from a pocket and was in the process of stuffing her ears.

"I cannot watch over you if I am caught in Steinunn's visions," she explained. It was strange to accept protection from one who'd once tried to kill me, but there was a quiet sadness about Tora that made me inclined to trust her at her word. She absently touched the scars on her face, a soft sigh exiting her lips as though part of her hoped to find the burn marks miraculously healed and endured disappointment each time she discovered they were not.

Steinunn began to sing, wordless at first and then the story unfolded, beginning with a vision of the walls of Grindill. I drew in a steadying breath as I stared upon my own miserable face, Snorri shrieking defiance, and then it shifted to me leaping over the wall and racing toward the cliff. I blinked, pulled from the moment, because Steinunn had skipped over the part where Tora had shot bolts of lightning at the walls that had rebounded off my magic and into the villagers outside. Skipped over the smoking corpses and Harald's demands, so it appeared as though I'd fled because I'd wanted to.

I stuck my fingers in my ears to muffle Steinunn's singing and the visions disappeared. As they did, I elbowed Tora so that she looked at me. "She's skipping pieces," I mouthed, and the child of Thor's mouth twisted into a bitter smile suggesting that omissions did not surprise her.

Unplugging my ears, I watched and listened, my discomfort building because Steinunn made it seem as though I had wanted to come to Nordeland. As though Harald had aided me rather than kidnapped me. And when it came to the battle against the Islunders, she showed none of my defiance, only me fighting alone on the beach against the helmeted warrior. Me, falling to my knees and cursing the Islunders, and then the bodies floating on the sea. Not the hollow expressions of terror on the children as the drakkar had been dragged back to the beach but of them being folded into the arms of the villagers.

I had always been told that a skald's song showed only the truth, but now it was clear to me that partial truths could amount to a significant lie.

The last notes of her voice drifted into the rafters, taking with them the visions. A cheer broke out in the hall, the people clapping their hands and shouting toasts. Not to Steinunn.

But to me.

I tensed at the reaction, and a tightness bound my chest as they turned to give me thanks for saving the children. They came forward in twos and threes to clasp my shoulder and praise me. My responses were reflex, the words merely noise in my ears as I came to terms with the fact that they did not see me as something to be feared but as a hero and protector.

Someone who did good.

It was so at odds with how my own people had seen me. Logically, I knew that it was a manipulation of Steinunn's art but I could not deny that their response made me feel better about what I had done.

All of that fell away as horns blared outside and everyone around me tensed.

"The gods have mercy!" Una shrieked, the servant almost falling as she climbed out of Troels's lap. "The Skalanders have come for her!"

CHAPTER 24

BJORN

"He's here!" Harald shouted, and the terror in his voice made me want to slap him. "We need Freya!"

"It's impossible for Snorri to be here," I snarled. "Mustering an army takes time, and it would take days for them to travel to Hrafnheim from the coast on foot!"

Yet there was no denying the fortress was under attack. "Get Tora and the others!" I shoved him toward the great hall. "But leave Freya be! She can't fight for you anyway!"

Harald took off at a sprint that belied his age, and though every instinct told me to go to Freya's side, my feet took me to the wall. I was a Nordelander and my promise to defend my people meant something.

Horns blared warning from the watchtowers and Hrafnheim filled with shouts of alarm that turned to screams of terror as civilians stepped out their doors and saw the arrows flying overhead. But the net of wards kept them from coming through, everyone in the streets safe unless the runes were damaged.

No sooner had the thought rolled through my head did I hear a cry of alarm from the wall that the wards had been breached. A heartbeat later, arrows tipped with flame began to fall upon the buildings, catching them ablaze. Panicked people exploded out of their homes and raced to the wells for water, desperate to put out the fires before they spread.

A crying boy crouched in the path before me and I put on a burst of speed, catching him up just before a falling arrow struck. It sliced along my arm instead, the pitch catching my tunic alight until I rolled into a puddle. "Run to the great hall," I shouted to the boy. "Go! Quickly!"

He obeyed without hesitation. Nordelander children always did.

I ran in the opposite direction, taking the steps rising to the battlements three at a time. Skade was in the thick of things, shouting orders at warriors to fetch water even as she released arrow after glowing arrow into the darkness.

"They covered the runes," she roared over the noise. "We need to wash away the blood or they'll set the entire fortress ablaze!"

Leaning over the battlements, a curse tore from my lips at the sight of blood and gore dripping down the wall. It concealed one of the wards, and I knew that it only took damaging one to erase the net of protection they cast over the city. An arrow flew past my shoulder and I ducked behind the wall.

"Shoot them!" I shouted at her.

"I can't see them!" Skade shouted back. "It's too dark and they move each time they loose an arrow!"

"Tyr!" I growled the god's name and my axe appeared in my hand. Immediately two arrows flew in my direction, but I batted them out of the air.

Taking a few steps back, I ran forward and hurled my axe. It flipped end over end, soaring over the dark current of the Rimstrom to sink into the ground a dozen feet up the river's banks.

Brighter, I silently willed the fire and the flames flared. Illuminating the shadows of the men attacking the fortress. "Skade!"

She'd already lifted her bow. The green arrow arced through the night and punched through the chest of one of the shadows only to reappear in her hand. But the attackers were already running. Fleeing into the darkness where they were out of reach.

Tora exploded up the steps behind me, lightning crackling between her palms. I pointed, and with no hesitation she released a bolt. A scream of agony split the night, and then there was silence outside the walls.

Not so behind us.

Several roofs were engulfed with flame, and smoke hung in a choking cloud over Hrafnheim. If it spread, the bridges would have to be lowered to allow people to escape the fire. Except that meant facing whatever force lurked in the darkness.

"Go!" Skade shouted at the warriors. "Get water! Put out the flames!"

I hesitated, then broke into a run, Tora alongside me.

"Is it Snorri?" she demanded as we raced to collect water from rain barrels. "Did you see him?"

I shook my head, unease that had nothing to do with the fire souring my stomach. Something about this didn't feel right.

Taking two buckets of water each, we ran back to where the flames were the thickest. The smoke was choking but Harald stood on the roof of the home nearest to the fire, a pot of paint and a brush in his hands. Painting wards on the rushes to keep them from catching ablaze, coughing and choking, tears streaming down his face.

Guilt pooled in my stomach as I threw the water onto the worst of the fire. If this was indeed an attack by Snorri, every loss that Hrafnheim took tonight was on my shoulders because my decisions had brought him here.

All the people of Hrafnheim worked together to extinguish the flames. Six homes were reduced to sodden ashes, and their former owners stared miserably at what remained of their belongings. Harald waved away Volund when the healer attempted to treat his cough, demanding the man see to individuals with burns.

All around was misery and darkness and fear, but with the attack over and the wards back in place, I headed to the great hall.

Only to find it nearly empty.

"Where is everyone?" I asked a passing warrior.

"Harbor," he responded. "They fled for fear the hall would be lost to the fire."

An intelligent choice, but I still felt a prickling of dread as I headed in that direction. The air was heavy with the stink of ash and the streets loud with coughing and crying, the darkness feeling as though it pressed down from above. The quay was packed and the harbor chain lowered during preparations to flee the fire. I searched the crowd for Freya's pale blond hair but she was nowhere in sight.

"Freya!" I shouted, fear swiftly turning to panic. "Freya!"

Tora appeared.

"Where is Freya?" I demanded. "I can't find her."

"I left her in the great hall." She wiped sweat from her forehead. "She has to be in Hrafnheim somewhere. The bridges are raised."

The efforts put toward the fires now turned to hunting for Freya. Her name echoed through the town and Harald put the wolves to the search, but with each passing minute, my hope we'd find her helping in some corner of the fortress diminished.

"Skoll and Hati say she came to the harbor," Harald said, then doubled over coughing.

"Well, she's not here now!" I scanned the dark waters, gaze moving out to the rapids of the Rimstrom.

"Would she hide?" Harald asked.

"Born-in-Fire does not hide." What if she'd fallen in the water? Or been pushed? "Freya!"

Then Skade pushed through the crowd, dragging an old man by the arm. "He says his boat is missing. She must have taken the opportunity to escape."

"She would do no such thing." I was deeply conscious of my last conversation with Freya. Escape was the last thing on her mind. Yet there was no denying that both wolves stood on the edge of the quay, their yellow eyes fixed on the Rimstrom.

"I saw who took your boat," a small voice called out. It was the boy I'd rescued during the attack, then sent to the great hall. "It was a stranger carrying his sick wife. He said the smoke was killing her."

No.

"It wasn't an attack," Harald snarled. "It was a diversion."

Dread pooled in my stomach, along with vicious rage at myself because I could have prevented this. "He's taken her back."

CHAPTER 25

FREYA

"What is it?" I demanded of Tora, because Una had swooned to the floor. "What is happening?"

"Those manning the walls have signaled an attack."

My pulse escalated, dread slowly pooling in my stomach. "Snorri?"

"It is too soon for him to have brought an army across the strait," Tora said with a frown.

"Then who?" Sweat slicked my palms and I closed my hand over the hilt of my sword. "Islund? Have they come for vengeance?"

Tora only shook her head, not in denial but in bewilderment. "No one attacks Hrafnheim."

My lips parted to argue that was clearly not the case, only for Harald to explode into the hall at a run. I'd not even known he was absent.

"We are under attack!" The edges of panic shone in his eyes. "The wards over Hrafnheim have been breached. Warriors to the walls!"

There was no hesitation in the Nordelander ranks. Those who could fight raced out of the great hall and those who remained, mostly children and the very old, silently drew together.

"Tora, go find Bjorn on the wall," Harald ordered as he approached. "They attack with fire and will set all of Hrafnheim aflame if they are not stopped."

Tora left the hall at a run.

"Harald, who is attacking?" I caught hold of his arm and pulled to keep him from leaving. "Is it Snorri?"

"I don't know." His expression was grim. "But you should stay away from the walls, Freya. If Snorri is outside, all it could take is one command from him and you would be forced to turn on everyone in Hrafnheim."

My hands felt like ice. How was this happening? How was Snorri already here?

Questions I had no chance to ask, for Harald was already racing out of the great hall to defend his people.

No one stopped me as I walked to the doors and took in the sight of distant roofs engulfed in flame. Arrows tipped with burning pitch fell from the sky to land on the buildings closest to the walls and fear throbbed in my heart because I knew how quickly they'd spread over the thatched roofs. It would only be a matter of time until it drove Harald to lower the drawbridges for the people to flee smoke and fire. Whether it was Skaland, Islund, or someone unknown waiting in the woods, they were here for violence.

Already a choking haze filled the night air and I coughed as the wind blew it in my face.

"They attack only from the west," a voice said from next to me, and I turned to discover a man standing but a pace away. He was bearded and heavily muscled, his bare arms covered with inkwork depicting Fenrir. Once a warrior, but no longer, it seemed, for he held a well-worn crutch and limped heavily as he moved for a better vantage of the flames.

"We should move to the eastern side of the fortress," he muttered. "Away from the fires."

"What if they attack from that side as well?" My skin crawled with the sense that a strategy was in play. "Better to go to the harbor where there is a chance that people can escape by boat."

"There are not enough boats."

"Then we can swim," I said, then winced as I remembered his crippled leg. "Save the boats for those who cannot."

He nodded, watching the growing flames. "We should go now." As he turned to go back into the hall to spread the word, the man stumbled and nearly fell. It was only my quick reflexes that kept him from sprawling.

"I'll tell them," I said. "You start toward the harbor."

Hurrying into the hall, I shouted, "The flames are spreading across the rooftops. We should travel to the harbor. Those who cannot swim will board the boats and be ready to take to the Rimstrom if the flames cannot be contained."

Cries broke out as the composure of the Nordelanders began to fracture. Children clung to their grandparents, faces slick with tears. All of them stood to lose everything, even their lives.

If it was Snorri and his men out there, I'd brought this down upon them.

Perhaps Saga's vision had already begun.

"There is sense in what she says!" Steinunn's voice carried over the noise. "Head to the harbor!"

A tide of people moved out of the great hall and I felt validation in my choice because many of them moved with painful slowness. If we'd waited for the flames to grow they would not have made it, including the man with the limp.

"I am sorry," he said to me between coughs. "I cannot go faster, shield maiden. You should go ahead with the children to protect them."

I was coughing now as well, smoke searing my lungs and eyes. Just as it had in Halsar the night Gnut had attacked. "Let me help you."

I pulled his arm over my shoulder, my back groaning beneath his weight. Yet with my help he was able to move faster, and he guided me through the twisting paths toward the harbor.

We were nearly there when he drew to a stop. "I must rest," he said between coughs. Unfastening the waterskin at his belt, he took a mouthful and then handed it to me. "Water."

I gratefully took several gulps. At first I tasted only ash and smoke but on my fourth swallow, I registered something else in the water. Something bitter and foul.

My body stiffened.

The man's smile slowly changed from kind to cruel, and he shoved away the crutch and stood straight. "Your king has come for you, Freya," he said, his accent now that of a Skalander. "Sleep well."

My lips parted to call Hlin. To call Hel. Yet my tongue would not answer the screaming panic of my thoughts.

Slowly, my knees buckled, and as the warrior's arms caught me, all faded to darkness.

CHAPTER 26

BJORN

"Skoll!" Harald shouted as he leaped into his drakkar. "Hati! To me!"

The Nameless who'd been aiding in the search were already climbing into Harald's drakkar and readying the oars. I leaped into the vessel, Skade alongside me. The ropes mooring us were unfastened, and within moments we were in the Rimstrom's swift current.

Yet for all our speed, it still felt too slow.

They'd taken her. They'd taken Freya.

"They can't have much of a head start," Harald shouted. "Row!"

The Nameless bent their weight into the oars, the black hoods they wore causing them to blend into the darkness as we passed out of Hrafnheim's harbor.

The drummer pounded a rapid beat for them, but over the noise, I couldn't hear. Wouldn't know if Freya cried out for help.

"Silence!" I barked at him, and the hooded man's hand stilled over his drum.

As the Rimstrom's current tore us away from the fortress, silence fell. The only sounds were the rush of the river, the moan of the wind, and the faint splashes of the oars striking the surface of the water.

I moved to the fore of the vessel, muttering Tyr's name to call my axe so that I might light the way. The Rimstrom was wide and deep, yet still treacherous if one did not know it well. Sharp rocks jutted out from the depths, but the navigator wove around the hazards with ease.

My eyes roved the darkness ahead, hunting for any sign of her.

Harald joined me at the fore. "If Snorri himself is here, he may already have rendered Freya a threat against us," he said softly. "Stolen her will from her by exerting the control of the oath."

I clenched my teeth. If I'd called her to arms and ensured she served me, this might not be happening. "Freya's will is her own."

"We can hope." Harald lifted his fingers and whistled softly. Skoll and Hati wove through the Nameless and rested their large paws on the edge of the drakkar, tongues lolling.

"Our enemies have taken Freya from us," Harald said to the wolves, and both stiffened. The runes painted on their fur allowed them to understand in some strange capacity, but it was to my father that they were bound.

Skoll's lips peeled back and he snarled, massive teeth glimmering in the light of my axe. Hati tilted back his head and howled, the rage in the wolf's voice echoing my own.

"Find her," Harald ordered.

Both wolves leaped off the side of the ship and swam with ease to opposite shores. Within moments, they were racing parallel to us with their noses to the wind.

"What will you do if he has her under his control?" Harald murmured.

"Kill him." The words came out as a growl. "Kill them all."

He gave the slightest of nods, but I did not miss how he glanced back toward Hrafnheim. Knew he feared that if Snorri had Freya under his control that our people could be at risk.

"He doesn't know what she can do," I muttered. "He doesn't know about Hel's blood."

"I wouldn't be so sure." Harald rested his hands to either side of the ship's figurehead. "Prepare for the worst."

I would not prepare for the worst. Could not. Because it meant she was lost to me forever.

From the banks, one of the wolves howled. I lifted my axe to cast its light farther and it illuminated Skoll's white fur. He stood next to a small vessel that had been dragged up the riverbank. Its hull was smashed, likely from an encounter with a rock. Without hesitation, I jumped into the water. It was frigid but the cold barely touched me as I swam to shore. Scrambling onto the bank, I flung myself at the vessel and turned it over.

Empty.

No, not empty. Freya's sword and seax rested in the mud next to the vessel. I picked them up, fear boiling in my stomach, because if she'd been disarmed here, it meant they'd incapacitated her in some way.

Skoll yipped at me, then ran several paces into the woods before stopping.

"Is she alive?" I demanded, but the wolf only stared at me. Hati exploded out of the water, pausing to shake it from his black fur.

"Find her!" I commanded them and, ignoring Harald's shout from the drakkar, I followed the wolves into the blackness of the forest.

CHAPTER 27

FREYA

My mind spun through strange dreams. Darkness and flame. The stink of male sweat and voices full of fear.

"Wake up," a voice twisted with agony whispered.

I reached for consciousness, but it eluded me, and I descended once more into blackness. Only for the scent of burning flesh to fill my nose.

"Wake up!"

My eyes snapped open to find the specter's green eyes staring into mine, her face a ruin of charred flesh.

"Your name was born in fire." Embers drifted behind the specter. "Skaland will be united beneath the rule of the one who controls your fate." Then she exploded into ash.

I blinked, uncertain if I was dreaming or awake. My body was bouncing up and down, the impact against my stomach painful. My mouth tasted foul, and with a violent heave, my stomach emptied its contents. Vomit burned in my mouth and nose, sharp coughs wracking me. Whoever had hold of me tossed me sideways with a muttered curse.

I yelped in pain as I landed on my side in some brush and the branches scratched my face.

"She's awake," one of them hissed, the accent that of a Skalander. "Silence her! Silence her!"

Terror pulsed through my veins, and I rolled away in a tangle of my skirts. Managed to get onto my hands and knees, though nausea still roiled in my guts. The darkness spun around me and I grasped for my sword, only to find the scabbard empty.

"Hlin," I croaked, and magic coated my fingers, illuminating the darkness.

As well as the faces of my kidnappers.

I immediately recognized the man who'd feigned the limp, but his three companions were strangers to me. All were muscular and heavily armed, warriors through and through.

But so was I.

Climbing to my feet, I said, "You've made a significant mistake."

In the light of my magic, their fear was obvious but the men held their ground. "You are to be returned to your king," the one who'd tricked me said. "Show your loyalty to your nation and come without quarrel."

Final confirmation that Snorri had sent them. Any hope that lingered in my heart vanished. The future Saga had foreseen was arriving faster than any of us had believed possible.

I shook my head. "I'm not going anywhere with you. My allegiance is to Skaland but Snorri is not my king. Leave now, and I'll let you live."

A seemingly empty threat given I was unarmed.

But not all weapons were steel. It was not lost on me how swiftly I questioned my own vows not to use my magic when put to threat. Hel's name and her power were already climbing my throat on the back of my fear.

I could smell their sweat. See the way their throats moved as they swallowed. Yet instead of running, they exchanged glances and then began to circle me. I bent and fumbled in the brush until my hands closed around a stick. It was so thin that on its own it would have snapped on a single blow, but I covered it with my magic.

Unarmed no longer, and I had the advantage in that they'd no doubt been ordered not to harm me.

I wouldn't hesitate.

It was their souls I had no wish to condemn, but I had no compunctions against killing them and allowing the gods to decide their final fate.

Swaying on my feet so they'd believe me still incapacitated by whatever they'd dosed me with, I struck without warning. My glowing stick descended to crack against one man's neck.

He cried out and stumbled back, but I was already twisting to meet the hands reaching toward me.

Fingers collided with my magic with a crunch of breaking bones as Hlin's power flung him away.

The air was abruptly driven from my lungs as the weight of the third man slammed into me. I fell face-first into the dirt, the stick spinning out of my grip.

I writhed, trying to get out from beneath him even as I fought to get a breath of air into my lungs, but he was twice my size. His thick hands pinned my wrists and his knee dug into my back.

"Get the waterskin," he snarled. "Dose her again."

I tried to scream but one of the other men pushed my face into the mud.

Condemn them.

No, I silently screamed. *I won't do it!*

But I couldn't breathe. Couldn't escape as they pulled my arms behind my back and rough ropes scored the skin of my wrists.

Give them to me.

No!

The world was spinning with darkness and fear, Hel's name rising to my lips as the men's rough hands handled my body.

Take back control.

I didn't want to do this. Didn't want to use her power. But I couldn't fight them off any other way and if they returned me to Snorri, any chance of changing my fate would be lost.

One of them reached into the mud and pinched my nose, then the others rolled me. I tried to suck in a breath but choked instead as they poured water in my open mouth.

Curse them.

Tears rolled down my cheeks, and I could taste Hel's name on my tongue.

Only for blood to spray across my face.

My body shook as I stared at the blazing axe blade protruding from between my captor's eyes, his skull split nearly in half.

Bjorn. His name drove Hel's from my lips and I screamed, "Bjorn, I'm here!"

The dying man stared down at me, eyes full of shock, and then he swayed forward and collapsed.

I shrieked as the burning blade descended, the heat familiar and terrifying.

It disappeared just before it struck my face. The man's split skull fell to either side of me, the dead weight of his body holding me in place.

Boots pounded the ground and my ears filled with the snarl of wolves. The screams of men.

I squirmed, trying to get out from under the dead man, but with my wrists bound, it was impossible to get leverage. Finally I got my heels beneath me and bucked him off.

Rolling onto my knees, I spat out the taste of blood even as I took in the moving shadows.

The wolves were ravaging two of the men, their screams shrill and awful.

And Bjorn's familiar shape was crouched over the final shadow, fists striking downward over and over, bone crunching beneath his blows.

"Bjorn." It came out as barely a whisper. Swallowing hard, I shouted, "Bjorn, stop! He's dead!"

He went still, head turning in my direction. Though it was too dark to see his face, I felt his fury.

"Freya?" His voice was hoarse.

"It's me."

In a heartbeat, Bjorn had his arms around me and pulled me close. His hands found my bound wrists, untying the ropes. "Are you hurt?"

My gut twisted with unspent adrenaline over how close Snorri had come to taking me back. At how close I'd come to calling Hel's name. "No."

It felt like a lie.

I buried my face in his throat, my hands clutching at his clothes before finding the bare skin of his arms. It was hot against my chilled palms and I clung to the hard curve of his biceps, unwilling to put to words how close I'd come to breaking my promise to myself.

"The attack was a ruse to take you." One of his hands moved up my back to tangle in my hair. "If they'd managed to get you to him, then he'd—" Bjorn's voice cracked. "I'm sorry, Born-in-Fire."

His apology felt like a weight around my neck, pulling me down and down, because it spoke of the places we'd have to go to see this through. Of the things we'd have to do. And I could not help but wonder what both of us would be like on the other side of it.

Skade burst into the clearing, her bow casting eerie light over the forest floor. Harald appeared a heartbeat later, breathing hard. "Freya? Is she hurt?"

"I'm fine." I pulled out of Bjorn's arms and got to my feet, hoping they couldn't see the shake in my knees. "That one tricked me." I gestured to the man whose skull was split in half. "Put something in the water I drank that caused me to lose consciousness. I didn't rouse until we were well away from Hrafnheim. They said . . ." My voice turned gravelly and I swallowed hard, remembering the specter's face but not sure if it had been a dream or reality. "They said I was to be returned to my king. I didn't recognize any of their faces."

"Did they say if Snorri is already in Nordeland?" Harald demanded.

I shook my head. "But they called me a traitor to Skaland."

"Then it's only a matter of time." Harald kicked a rock, cursing. "Skade, do you recognize any of their faces?"

"What faces?" The huntress's tone was sour. "This one is split in two and this one is so much meat. Those two," she gestured in the distance where the sound of rending flesh was audible, "are in the stomach of your pets."

Bjorn stood, wiping at his face with the back of his hand and leaving behind smears of blood. "His inkwork is Skalander." Reaching down, he lifted the arm of the man who'd tricked me and then held it against his own tattooed arm for comparison. "You can see it in the knotwork patterns."

I agreed, but again my eyes were drawn to the tattoos of Fenrir, something about them familiar. As Hati approached and began licking blood off my hand, I said, "I feel as though I've seen them before."

"You likely have." Skade spat on the dead man. "Men always choose the same things. Bjorn likely has Fenrir inked on his arse and that's where you saw it."

My jaw tightened.

"You are only jealous," Bjorn said, wiping his face again, though there'd be no ridding himself of the blood without water. "I recall very clearly how you fainted when the artist got out his needles, your skin cursed to remain as interesting as spilled cow's milk, Skade."

She glared at him, the golden light of her bow reflecting in her eyes.

"What they said to Freya is proof enough that they fight beneath Snorri's banners," Harald said. "He knows she is here, and it won't be long until he learns that the kidnapping attempt failed. Snorri is no fool. He won't try to use the same ruse twice, so I expect next time, he'll come in force. Guthrum and Kaja should bring news soon, but I don't think it will be long until Skaland sails across the strait."

His eyes locked with mine, waiting. Giving me control of everything, risking everything, all on the belief that I could be a savior rather than a plague.

I gripped fistfuls of my skirt. "I'm tired of waiting for the axe blade to fall. At dawn, we sail down the Rimstrom and bring the fight to him. It's time to send Snorri to Hel."

CHAPTER 28

FREYA

The balance of the night was consumed with preparations made all the more frantic by the arrival of Kaja. Clutched in her claws was a red glass bead, and at the sight of it, Harald sat down heavily upon a bench.

"What does it mean?" I asked, though in my heart, I already knew. What opportunity we might have had to sneak across the strait and quietly cut Snorri's thread had come to an end.

War was here.

Which Bjorn confirmed as he picked up the bead. "Skaland's fleet is gathering. The red bead means an attack is coming."

I drew in a breath, none of the air seeming to reach my lungs. I'd desperately hoped that we'd be able to enact our primary plan, which had been to sail across the strait in secret and get me close enough to send Snorri to Hel with my magic. To end this with no loss of life. A hollow hope, yet one that I'd clung to all through the night.

"I have no choice but to take his soul on the battlefield." I stared down at the table full of figurines that outlined the plan Harald and I had devised. "Send word to your jarls, and make ready to sail."

"It shall be done," the king of Nordeland answered, then left Bjorn and me alone in the great hall.

It was the first time we'd been alone since those few moments in the woods. Though he'd been present through all the planning between Harald and me, Bjorn had remained broadly silent. I knew it was because he was debating my words to him. Debating what he should do. And as the air thickened with tension around us, I allowed hope to once again fill my chest that Bjorn would take the one step that would nearly guarantee our success. That he'd set aside his compunctions and have my back the way he'd once promised.

Yet as I met his gaze, his green eyes told me this hope was equally hollow.

"I know you were forced to choose between two terrible options, Freya," he said. "I regret that I did not act then to spare you, but the past cannot be undone. Snorri and Ylva have put a leash on you, and whether I like it or not, it is within my power to rip it from their hands. To take control of your will to protect you from him using you to achieve his ends."

"But you will not," I said, unwilling to draw out the explanation when all that mattered was the decision.

"I will not." He blew a breath out between his teeth. "I manipulated you with lies before, Freya, and it is my greatest regret. This feels the same, but worse, and I will not do it to you."

"You mean *for me*?" My nails dug into my palms. "Do not stand there pretending this is the righteous choice, Bjorn, because it is the purest form of selfishness."

Twisting on my heel, I strode from the great hall only to meet Harald outside. He took one look at my face, then said, "He still refuses, then?" At my behest, Bjorn had explained to Harald how he might be able to control me via the oath, just as Snorri did. Yet though Harald had pressed him to exercise that power, Bjorn was no more swayed by him than he'd been by me.

"Yes." And Bjorn's refusal to do this for me felt like the greatest betrayal.

Harald gave a grim shake of his head. "We cannot force him. He has to want to control you. Needs for it to burn in his heart with a greater ferocity than what burns in Snorri, for make no mistake, it *will* be a contest of wills between them if it comes to it." He hesitated, then added, "All those times you resisted Snorri? It was not your will that allowed you to do so, but Bjorn's. It will be difficult for you to resist Snorri without him."

"But not impossible." I accepted my bags from the servants and waited for them to move out of earshot before I continued. "We will do this as I planned, Harald. We will meet his fleet on the strait, and once Snorri is in my sights, I'll curse his soul to my mother's domain. With luck, his demise will break the union of the jarls sailing in his fleet, but if not, your warriors will fight. I will not use Hel's magic against them, is that clear?"

"I understand." Harald clapped his hands at Skoll and Hati, but the wolves bypassed him to come to my side, Hati licking my hand. Harald frowned but said, "I have faith in you, Freya, and when it comes to it, Nordeland will have your back, even if my son does not."

The journey down the Rimstrom was swift, the river's current speeding us to the coast, where the ships of Nordeland's jarls were gathering to defend against Snorri's attack. We slept on the ship and only stopped on a handful of occasions so that Harald could take reports from riders or messengers traveling upstream. All believed Harald was in command, but every order was mine. Harald was my puppet, but he seemed comfortable with the role.

There was no mistaking the fear in the eyes of the Nordelander civilians because it was so painfully familiar to me. I'd seen that fear in the eyes of Skalanders, felt it in myself when word would race up the fjord to Selvegr that raiders were on the horizon. Before my magic had been revealed and I'd started down this path, I had never thought there was a reason the raiders came beyond the desire to *take*. Take wealth, take thralls, take lives—I believed that was all there was to it. Yet now I understood that those were only the tools that jarls and kings and warlords used to motivate their warriors. Incentives to make them fight, because victory gave those leaders that which they coveted most: power. With enough power, you could have anything you wanted.

"Warning has spread up and down the coast," Astrid said to Harald, the pair standing on the riverbank next to a small village, its people gathered around. "At first sight of Skalander ships they know to flee inland."

"Yet they won't." Skade yawned and picked at her nails with her magical arrow. "They'll send the children and the old inland; the rest will stand their ground and fight to protect their halls and holdings. Fight and die. And the children and the old will follow when winter comes and there are none to care for them."

I hated how she was right.

Harald shot Skade a dark glare. "It will not come to that." Lifting his voice, he shouted, "We will protect Nordeland from attack! We will meet the Skalander army in force on the Northern Strait and drive them to fall back or drown beneath the waves!"

The crowd cheered, all of them gazing at Harald with utter certainty that he would hold to his promise to protect them. This was the type of loyalty that could only be earned with deeds, not words. I still didn't wholly trust him, but less and less was I able to deny that Harald was a good king. He walked through the crowd, clapping men on the shoulder, complimenting the women, grinning at the children, and admiring the babies.

Steinunn watched him, her eyes gleaming with unshed tears.

"It must be hard to listen to him say those things given your own family was not so protected," I said softly.

"The opposite." The corner of the skald's mouth turned up. "Harald took what happened to me to heart, and since then has done all he can to protect every soul under his rule. He is not infallible, of course, and Nordeland still suffers the occasional attack, but I think there is nowhere else that one can live and feel so protected. Every day I feel the pain of what I lost to Snorri and his raiders, but it is a comfort to know that the deaths of my husband, son, and the rest of those in my village have done some good. That I have done some good, because the fact that Harald cares for me as family ensures he never forgets the pain I felt at losing mine."

"I'm sorry, Steinunn," I said, knowing that my words were long overdue. "What I said when you told me of your family's death was cruel. I regret my words."

"You'd been used, Freya, and in hindsight, I see that your anger was less for me and more for your circumstances. I've been unduly harsh to you in my words as well." Steinunn reached down to trail her fingers in the water of the Rimstrom. "Harald is imperfect, as are all men, but the bad blood between Nordeland and Skaland is older than us all. Two peoples who have taken so very much from each other. Yet Snorri's goals go beyond raids and petty quarrels between clans. He seeks war, seeks revenge against Harald for trying to deny his destiny, and I will do whatever it takes to prevent him from bringing that pain to my people."

I toyed with the edge of my silver shield, which was fixed to the side of the drakkar. Out of necessity, we'd kept my plan a secret, and that, as much as my oaths, kept me silent. From the corner of my eye, I could see Bjorn sitting at the far end of the vessel. We'd not spoken, and if not for the fact that leaving him would be akin to leaving my sword behind, I'd have done so just to be away from him. Because every time I looked at Bjorn, all I felt was anger.

Harald said his farewells to the villagers and climbed back in the drakkar.

"We will stop Snorri," he said to Steinunn and me. "And when we do, I believe that there will be a true chance at peace between our nations. A chance for Nordeland and Skaland to be united in a way they never have before."

A cause worth fighting for. If my destiny was to twist the fates of two nations, then peace was the tapestry I hoped to weave. "How long until we reach the coast?"

"A few hours," he answered. "But I suggest we don't linger. As you have said, Freya, if we can keep the battle to the sea, then the only cost will be to those who have come to fight."

Anxiety pooled like poison in my stomach; for all this was my strategy, the thought of a battle on the strait terrified me. To face not only the threat of arrows and blades and fists, but also the threat of falling overboard or the ship sinking. The idea of being lost at sea, clinging to shattered boards with no chance of rescue, made my skin crawl. Though in truth, with the chain mail I wore to protect me from arrows and blades, I'd likely just sink beneath the waves and drown.

"How do you fight at sea?" I asked Harald, for though our plan was to avoid battle at all costs, it could still come to it.

"Depends on the goal." He scratched Skoll's neck, but the wolf moved to put his big head in my lap. Since the night of my kidnapping, the wolves stuck close to me at all times. "Typically, the desire is to capture as many vessels as possible, so we'd board the enemy ships and fight to kill all on board or at least get them in the water. Taking Skalander ships gives me the advantage in the future. But in this case, I think we'll try to sink the vessels with fire and lightning, and then let the sea do much of the work for us. With any luck, once they suffer enough losses they'll retreat."

"With luck, there will be almost no fighting at all," I said quietly. "Once Kaja shows me where Snorri is, I'll call Hel's magic."

"Snorri must know that he is our goal, because he surely understands your desire to be rid of the oath you swore," Harald said after glancing to ensure that Steinunn was distracted by conversation with Skade. "What's more, Snorri is no fool. He'll ensure he's surrounded by his fleet."

"If we have to fight to get close to them, I'll call Hlin's magic to protect our ship." I spoke with confidence despite remembering how difficult it had been to protect everyone when we attacked Grindill. How one stumble had pulled my protection away from my comrades and cost them their lives. "They won't be able to board and we'll need only to maneuver close enough for me to see him."

"Is it necessary to see him? Or only be in proximity?"

"You've witnessed what happens when I unleash Hel's magic without focus. Everyone in proximity is taken by the roots. I need Snorri in my sights so that I can ensure he's the only one Hel takes."

"I suggest Bjorn stay close to you." Harald kept a careful eye on Steinunn to ensure she wasn't listening. "If you find yourself unable to fight through the bonds of your oaths, he will be the only one you can warn that you aren't in control."

Bjorn was also the only one who could do anything about it, but I kept those words in my chest as Harald continued.

"If your plan falls apart, we'll have the option to retreat and take you out of the battle," Harald said. "My warriors and Unfated will fight them until they retreat."

In a bloody battle that would turn the strait red.

"I have faith in you, Freya," Harald said. "We both desire to spare lives. Let us win with clever strategy rather than bloodletting."

Harald's voice was filled with confidence, but my skin crawled with the certainty that no matter what we did, how we fought, many would die. The drakkar fell into silence as we carried on downstream, the only sound the strike of oars against water as the Nameless rowed to aid our speed.

I drifted into sleep with my head resting on the side of the vessel, woken by the scent of the sea, the cries of gulls, and the roar of waves washing onto Nordeland's coast. My heart clenched as we rounded a river bend and the merciless gray of the Northern Strait was revealed. On it floated vessels of every size. I'd known Nordeland was prepared, but it was still shocking how large a force Harald had rallied so swiftly. How the nation must constantly be ready to be called to arms.

Our drakkar landed as we reached the mouth of the river, and Harald leaped out and started toward a group of men and women who waited in a camp that had been formed. Tora and Skade went with him, but Bjorn remained at my side as we climbed out.

"The Nordelander jarls," he said. "All have bent the knee and sworn loyalty to Harald."

"So many," I breathed, for there were at least a dozen of them, all listening to Harald's urgent explanation of what was to come. Then all eyes shifted to me, and I knew my role in the battle had finally been explained.

I wondered if Harald had revealed my limitations. Wondered if he had told them there was the chance Snorri would be able to compel me to turn on them and kill them all. Given the confidence on their faces, I thought not.

Wings fluttered above me, and I smiled as I recognized Kaja. She descended to land on my raised forearm, talons digging into the leather of my bracer. Guthrum approached from down the beach and lifted a hand in greeting.

Harald gave a few final instructions to the jarls, many moving to vessels drawn up on the beach. He spotted Guthrum and strode swiftly so as to reach us at the same time as his spy.

"Snorri has set sail," Guthrum said. "All the jarls of Skaland who could reach Grindill in time are with him. They believe they sail to rescue Freya. Snorri has convinced them that you have kidnapped her and Bjorn both, and that you will use her to make yourself king of Skaland. The idea of it has them in a frenzy and they come for blood."

"My old friend always had a way with words," Harald muttered under his breath. "How long until they reach our coast?"

"By tonight with these winds." Guthrum tilted his head to meet Kaja's yellow gaze. "Snorri sails in his drakkar beneath his black and green banner."

"What about Ylva?" Bjorn demanded.

Guthrum tilted his head, in silent conversation with his familiar. "Kaja said she remained in Skaland with a heavy guard."

"Not that heavy given he'll need his best for the battle," Bjorn said. "Send a vessel around the main fleet and take Ylva, Father. We might never have another opportunity like this to free Freya."

One of Guthrum's eyebrows rose askance, but he did not press for an explanation as Harald looked to me. "Do you wish this?"

"Yes," I said. "But Ylva is not to be harmed unless we have no choice."

Unless my plan fails.

"I'll relay the orders to a jarl I trust," Harald said. "On your command, Freya, we set sail. As planned, Tora, Skade, Guthrum, and Bjorn will sail with you and me under the power of my Nameless on the oars. We will disperse the rest of the Unfated among the jarls to aid if it comes to battle."

"See it done." My throat was painfully dry.

Harald adjusted his sword belt, then said, "By dusk, it will be over." Then he headed into the trees where many of the jarls still gathered, Skade and Tora shadowing him.

I toyed with the hilt of my sword, feeling as though I should be doing something more as warriors and Nameless moved to make sure our vessels had the supplies we needed. *How many of them will die if this plan doesn't work?* I couldn't help but wonder. *How many Skalanders will die in Snorri's pursuit of power?*

"I think it's a mistake to not try to kill Ylva before we do this," Bjorn said.

I turned to find him sitting in the sand. He held a small piece of driftwood, which he flipped over and over again in his hands. "Put Skade in sight of her, and Ylva will die swiftly. Cleanly. Then you can kill Snorri with a blade, no need to use Hel's powers."

"Harald is sending someone to take her," I muttered. "You heard the conversation."

"*Take* her, not *kill* her." Bjorn threw the piece of wood down on the sand. "I understand you don't wish to kill her. That you don't think Ylva deserves death. But this is the wrong time for allowing morality to guide your decisions. Hundreds might die if this goes wrong and your oath prevents you from cursing Snorri. If she's dead, there is no uncertainty."

"Kill her or don't kill her, it doesn't much matter," I snapped. "Snorri will be halfway across the strait by now. What do you propose we do? Ask him to sit and wait while we murder his beloved wife so it will be easier for us to defeat him?"

"We could attempt to negotiate. Buy time on the open seas for

Skade to do what she does best." He climbed to his feet. "Snorri is not so fanatical that he'll throw away countless lives when there is a chance he can get what he wants with negotiation. It is worth putting a white flag on a mast and trying to stall while we get rid of Ylva."

"Negotiate in bad faith?"

"Yes. Don't allow honor to make decisions for you—it will only put you in a grave."

When I didn't answer, he said, "If you won't kill her, then at least let Skade or Tora make an attempt at killing Snorri from afar."

"Your mother said it has to be me. You may not trust the Allfather, but I do. And so does Harald."

Bjorn made a face of disgust. "This plan is madness and I do not understand why Harald has agreed to it. There are easier ways to kill Snorri. Cleaner ways."

"It must be Freya."

With a start, I whirled around to find Saga approaching. She was dressed in trousers and a tunic rather than her usual flowing dresses. Her black hair was in a plait, and a seax was sheathed at her waist.

"The Allfather says it must be Freya," Saga said. "I've seen it, Bjorn. Why do you insist on arguing?"

"Because it doesn't make any sense!" he shouted, and the vehemence caused me to take a step back.

"There are countless better ways to rid ourselves of Snorri, but because of a vision you had in your mind, we pursue the most illogical!" He kicked at the sand. "I should have ignored you and killed him myself, because the gods know, it would have been *fucking easy*! Yet I listened and now I find myself going along with a wild strategy that makes sense to no one!"

"Exactly what are you saying, Bjorn?" Saga demanded. "Are you accusing the Allfather of *lying*? Or do you merely deny his wisdom?"

"I am saying that this does not feel like wisdom." The muscles in his jaw stood out against his suntanned skin. "It feels like we are pieces in a game played for amusement. That everything we are doing is a great joke. Make of that what you will."

"Sacrilege!" Saga hissed and lifted her hand as though to slap him. "I cannot believe my own son is speaking against Odin himself. Not only do you jeopardize your place in Valhalla, you risk the lives of everyone by trying to turn Freya away from the Allfather's guidance."

"I'm trying to turn her away from lunacy. I'm trying to turn *all of you* away from lunacy!"

"Perhaps Bjorn is partially right." I stepped between them before the argument escalated. "Perhaps this is a game devised by the gods. A way to make us all dance for their amusement. It only means that we *must* dance or else we risk displeasing them."

"Who can say for sure." Saga crossed her arms. "All I know is that the Allfather has never led me false before."

"Do what you will." Bjorn crossed his own arms, meeting her glower with his own. "I have said my piece."

The tension was awful and to ease it, I asked, "Saga, why are you here?"

"I have decided to sail with you."

"I don't think that is wise," Bjorn muttered, and I was inclined to agree. "You are no warrior and all it would take is one stray arrow and Snorri would finish what he started all those years ago."

"My thread is bound to Freya's," she replied. "I must see this through."

"Harald will never agree to it," Bjorn said, eyes searching the beach full of warriors for Nordeland's king. "He values you too much to risk you."

Saga's eyes narrowed. "Harald does *not* decide what I do or where I go. He will abide by my choice to sail with him. And I think you will find that I am not as helpless as you seem to believe, my son."

Bjorn cast his eyes skyward, but I sensed his irritation hid fear that he wouldn't be able to protect her. That she'd lose her life to a plan he very clearly did not support.

"Have you seen more?" I asked. "Anything that might help us win this fight?"

"No," Saga said. "Which tells me nothing has changed. But if we are victorious today, I believe that the Allfather will show me a glimpse of the future we fought for." Her lip curled. "Even if it is nothing more than a reward for playing his game. Now if you will excuse me, I intend to find my husband and tell him how this will go."

Saga strode off in the direction Harald had gone.

Warriors were pulling longships and the larger drakkar off the beach and rowing out to deeper water where yet more vessels waited. Sunlight gleamed on the sea, casting a golden glow on the curved prows of the ships, many carved with fierce figureheads. Weapons of every sort sent flashes of light with each rise and fall of a ship over a wave, and every shield mounted to the side was painted in Nordeland's blue. A fleet of incredible size, hundreds upon hundreds of Nordelanders ready to fight. My eyes went beyond them to the strait, and though I knew it was impossible, I imagined I could see Skaland's fleet, just as large and dangerous, flying toward us. I blinked, and the waves turned crimson with blood, bodies floating in the froth and foam while weapons slowly sank to the sea floor.

"You can still stop this," Bjorn said. "You can—"

"Just get me close enough to him to finish this," I interrupted. "Let's not pretend you have any other role in this."

Bjorn shook his head and looked away, both of us standing in angry silence until Harald appeared. He stormed toward us, a scowl on his face, and I said, "It seems Saga got what she wanted."

"Your mother has made it clear how this will go," Harald said to Bjorn as though it was all his fault. "I don't like it, but never has Saga led me astray."

He closed his eyes, seemingly seeking calm, then he added, "I will sail on another of our drakkar with Skade and my wolves. Tora will remain with you and Bjorn, for her lightning will be of great advantage against the other ships. I—" Harald broke off, shaking his head. "It is my instinct to give you a strategy, but Saga believes every decision must be yours, Freya. So instead, I say this: Know that Nordeland is at your back. We will not abandon you. Now I will leave lest I influence your course and ruin everything. Bjorn, keep your mother safe."

He left, leaving me with Bjorn and Tora. The latter's expression was grim as she stared out to sea, but she offered no insight into what she was thinking. We made our way to Harald's drakkar, which was surrounded by his thralls. The Nameless were dressed in their typical black attire with hoods concealing most of their faces. None were armed, but if they feared what was to come, they did not show it. They took down Harald's banner, blue with the white wolf, a boy running off with it, though I did not see which ship it went to. The Nameless then began pushing the vessel out into the gentle waves.

Saga joined us, now wearing a mail vest over her clothes. I recognized it as Harald's; Nordeland's king obviously cared enough about her safety that he was willing to risk his own. "The longer we tarry, the closer Snorri comes. If he lands on these beaches, it will be the moment in which all that I foresaw will come to pass."

"We leave now." I pushed as much confidence as I could into my voice, and then waded out into the water and climbed into the drakkar. The Nameless rowed us through the surf into deeper water, then we lifted the blue-striped sail. The rest of the fleet did the same, and soon we were all heading across the strait toward Skaland, Kaja leading the way.

Silence stretched for minutes, then hours as we sailed farther into open waters. There came a point when I believed I'd been misled. That Skaland was not on the verge of attacking us and that this had all been a ruse to get me to fight for Nordeland.

Then Saga called out, "I see the fleet."

Heart in my throat, I joined her. What I saw took my breath away. All across the horizon were ships. Dozens of them, the sails a rainbow of colors reflecting all the clans who'd sworn allegiance to Snorri as king. But at the center was a grouping of Snorri's ships, their black and green banners raised high.

"We are outnumbered," Bjorn said. "If it comes to a fight, there is a chance that Nordeland will lose."

Turning, I stared behind us at Harald's fleet. It was large, but Skaland was substantially more populous than Nordeland, and that meant something. Yet there was determination on the faces of the Nordelanders. These warriors would fight to the bitter end, and unlike Snorri, Harald had many Unfated in his service with weapons of magic. All the years he'd spent gathering them from across various nations had the potential to be Nordeland's salvation if I failed them. But if it came to that, it would be the bloodiest of victories.

"Guthrum," I said, "we need to find Snorri's ship."

"Kaja is looking," he answered, and I shivered as his eyes changed to the same shade of yellow as the bird's. "There. She has found it."

His eyes changed back to brown and he lifted a hand to shade them before pointing. "In the middle."

It took me a minute, but eventually I saw Kaja's small shadow circling above one of the Skalander vessels. It flew Snorri's green and black banner, and as we drew closer, the details of the familiar carved figurehead came into view.

"He's here," I whispered, swallowing the fear that rose. It had all felt so distant until now, but with Snorri almost in my sights, the weight of what I needed to do threatened to drag me down.

"Get me close enough to see him." I cast a backward glance, noting that the fleet had lowered their sails, allowing us to press ahead, just as we had planned. "I need to be able to see him."

The Nameless at the helm did not acknowledge me, but the drakkar turned, heading directly toward Snorri's vessel. Saga moved from the fore to sit near the mast. She pulled the hood of her cloak up to obscure her face, then gave me an encouraging nod.

Sails were dropping now, the Skalanders running out oars and moving closer together. The Nameless did the same, the drummer hammering a vigorous beat, and behind us, Harald's fleet fell farther behind. I moved to the front of the vessel and stood on a sea chest to ensure I was in full sight of the Skalanders, with Bjorn at my elbow. My hope was that, in his desire to possess me, Snorri would have relayed orders to every warrior that I wasn't to be harmed. But in case I was wrong, I held my silver shield in my left hand, magic already blazing across it.

"Where is he?" I searched the faces, hunting for Snorri's even as the Skalander fleet slipped around us. "Guthrum, where is he?"

He lifted a hand to shadow his eyes. "He's wearing a helm with a face piece."

My eyes finally latched onto a bearded man, the top of his face obscured by a helm. He was shouting orders and pointing in our direction. Bjorn muttered Tyr's name, and his axe burned to life.

"Steady." I wasn't certain whether I spoke to him or to myself. "We don't want to raise alarm."

"We're surrounded, Born-in-Fire," he replied. "No matter what happens here, we are in for a fight if you wish to get out of this alive."

Snorri was waving his arms, motioning for the warriors in his drakkar to lower their weapons.

"What does he think is happening here?" Sudden anger filled me because Snorri was acting as though he was rescuing me. "Does he really think he's going to take me alive? That I'll be content to live under his control? That Harald is just . . . just handing me over?"

"That is exactly what he thinks, Freya," Saga said, her tone frigid. "End this!"

"I curse you, Snorri!" I screamed, feeling Hel's power fill my body as I pointed at him. "I curse your soul to Helheim!"

The sea quivered and shook, but no roots exploded from its depths. Nothing happened.

Why wasn't it working?

"Get closer!" Saga shouted. "He needs to know it was you who sent him to Hel's realm!"

Something felt wrong here. Fear pooled in my stomach because we were entirely surrounded. The Skalander vessels were close enough to see the grim determination on the warriors' faces. Their weapons were in hand but none lifted their bows, all watching.

"Bjorn, if we get closer, I'll be able to hear Snorri as well. He'll be able to take control of me," I said. "Something isn't right. Why isn't my curse working?"

"Maybe it's the oath." He gave a sharp shake of his head. "We need to retreat."

My stomach plummeted. I'd failed, and now it would be a battle to the bitter end.

Bjorn lifted his voice to the Nameless. "Row back! Reverse course!"

But before Harald's thralls could obey, a familiar voice shouted from one of the vessels approaching on our port side. "Freya, stand down! I am here!"

My heart lurched at Snorri's familiar voice, and my head snapped sideways to the approaching drakkar that held no banner. One of the warriors pulled off his helm to reveal dark brown hair laced with gray and a familiar face. Sickness pooled in my stomach as my eyes locked with Snorri's. The other vessel—and the warrior pretending to be him—had been a diversion to allow Snorri to get close.

"Stand down!" he repeated, the order reverberating through my body.

And in a heartbeat, my entire plan disintegrated.

CHAPTER 29

BJORN

My father's voice filled my ears, and I whirled, ready to throw my axe.

But I was too late.

"Stand down!"

Freya doubled over as though she'd been punched, and then fell to her knees on the bottom of the ship.

"He's got control over her," I shouted. "Tora, sink them!"

Tora lifted her hands and lightning crackled between them, but before she could send a bolt into Snorri's ship, Freya moved.

Quicker than I'd believed possible, she threw herself at Tora, a cry of pain tearing from her lips as she hit the charge of lightning.

"Freya!" I fell to my knees next to her. She was curled up in a pool of water, teeth clenched in pain but alive. Tora lay stunned next to her.

"Don't hurt him," she choked out. "Don't hurt him!"

"Bjorn, they're going to board us!" Guthrum shouted. "What do we do?"

Freya caught hold of one of Tora's wrists, covering her hands with Hlin's magic so that Tora could not call her lightning. "No!"

Tora struggled to get out of her grip. "Bjorn, what do we do!"

"Stay down," I shouted at Tora, then caught hold of the side of the drakkar and pulled myself up. Three vessels were almost near enough to board. Near enough for me to hear Snorri scream, "Sink his fleet! Let Nordeland pay the price for its actions, but bring me Harald alive!"

Word spread across the fleet like wildfire, and with a roar, they began to row. I knew that even with Skade, Troels, Astrid, and the other Unfated among them, my people might not win this fight. My eyes filled with my mother's vision of thousands of dead. Not in fields but floating on the waves while the Skalanders carried on to inflict carnage across all of Nordeland.

"Bjorn, stop him!" my mother screamed, on her knees next to Freya. "Stop Snorri!"

"Tyr," I snarled, my axe manifesting in my palm as Snorri's drakkar bumped against ours.

"Freya!" Snorri shouted, clambering to the edge. "Freya, we are here! You are liberated!"

"Get back!" I shouted at him and our eyes locked.

"What are you doing, Bjorn?" he demanded. "Stand down! You are saved, and all of Nordeland will burn for taking you!"

I lifted my axe to throw. Ready to silence him once and for all, to Hel with my mother's prophecy. But Freya slammed into me right as the vessel rolled over a swell.

I staggered and nearly went down, vanquishing my axe so that I could catch Freya without burning her.

My mother was still on her knees in the bottom of the drakkar, cowering out of Snorri's sight. "Stop him," she repeated. "You must wield her to stop him."

"No!" I regained my balance. The Skalanders were converging on the Nordelander fleet, Skade's arrow flickering over and over. "I will not!"

"Freya!" Snorri shouted. "Come to me! Climb over!"

Freya's arms wrapped around my waist and her whole body shook with the effort of resisting his command. "Do not let him take me!"

Lightning burst from Tora's hands into one of the other drakkar but the vessel only glowed a bright blue, the runes carved into the wood flaring brightest of all.

"It's warded!" Tora's eyes locked on mine. "Ylva's put protection wards on them!"

"Tyr!" I growled the god's name, then threw my axe. It embedded into the wood of a ship, but the flames didn't take hold. Cursing, I recalled it and threw it at a man.

It sank deep into his chest, his scream cutting short.

In an instant, Tora was sending bolt after bolt of lightning into the Skalanders, the stink of burned flesh filling the air even as they poured onto our vessel.

"Freya, stop the child of Thor!" Snorri howled. "Kill her!"

Freya drew her sword, but I caught her wrist. Held it tight as I fought back the seemingly endless warriors trying to climb aboard from all sides.

"Bjorn!" Guthrum screamed, his eyes brilliant yellow. "They are sinking our ships! Astrid's ship is sinking!"

"Bjorn, control Freya!" my mother screamed. "Don't let Snorri take her back!"

"Fight, Freya!" Snorri roared over the tumult. "Fight for Skaland!"

It was all I could do to keep a grip on Freya. Blood dripped from her nose and tears from her eyes, misery written across her face as she tried to combat Snorri's will.

"Bjorn, help them!" Guthrum screamed. "Freya, help—"

His pleas were cut short as he was knocked overboard and disappeared beneath the hull of Snorri's ship. Freya screamed, the grief in her voice tearing at my heart as I cut down yet another Skalander. Thunder boomed and lightning flashed, but my eyes kept drawing back to the fleets.

To the smoke rising.

To the masts sinking beneath the waves.

"Bjorn, wield her!" my mother screamed. "Protect Nordeland! Control the shield maiden!"

Freya abruptly ripped from my grip, leaving her bracer clutched in my hand. She snatched up her shield and advanced on Tora.

"Kill the child of Thor, Freya!" Snorri screamed from where he still stood on his drakkar. "Have vengeance for Skaland!"

"Bjorn!" my mother howled. "It's happening! My vision is becoming reality!"

"Freya, stop!" The order slipped from my lips almost without thought, and yet she fell still. Lowering her shield, she met my gaze. "Don't hurt him."

My axe burned in my hand, every part of me wanting to take off Snorri's head. But if I tried, Freya might act. And beyond, Nordeland's fleet was losing the battle.

"You promised." My mother clutched at my ankles, face drenched with tears. "You swore to protect them. Swore to help her change her fate."

Killing Snorri would not stop the carnage. It was beyond his control.

"Bjorn, no!" Freya screamed. "Bjorn, don't do it!"

The terror in her voice made me sick, but our plans were in tatters and the sea already red with blood.

I had to change our fate.

Looking into her amber eyes, I said, "Freya, I call on you to fight for Nordeland. I call upon you to send all who attack her to Hel."

CHAPTER 30

FREYA

It was like having my skull crushed between the palms of a giant, the weight of Bjorn's will crashing over me with such intensity that it drove all thought of anything else from my mind.

"Hel," I whispered. "Give me your power."

"Destroy the Skalander fleet!" Saga shouted, but all the noise and chaos slipped into the background as I stared at the distant battle.

I did not want to hurt my people.

I did not want to use my power.

But I had sworn an oath to obey, and so I had no choice but to heed Bjorn's order.

Magic surged through my veins, wild and fierce and hot, but my voice was nothing more than a whisper as I said, "I curse every Skalander warrior before me to Hel's realm."

The ships all rocked violently, the large vessels flung about like a child's toys in a bath. Waves washed over the decks, knocking warriors into the water, and the air filled with screams.

Then black roots exploded from the sea.

They coiled around the waists of the Skalanders, ripping them down into the depths. Dozens upon dozens of them, lashing out with unerring aim to capture those who would harm Nordeland and bring them down to my divine mother's realm.

The seas boiled, our drakkar spinning wildly. Bjorn caught hold of me and pushed me down against the hull. Tora did the same, and to my shock, Snorri leaped into our drakkar to catch hold of my wrist. "What have you done, Freya?" he pleaded. "What have you become?"

Above us was a twist of roots and shrieking warriors wrapped in their lengths, so thick it cast us in shadow, and I screamed and screamed at the horror that I had caused as they wrapped around the waists of the Skalanders and yanked them down. But not Snorri. I covered him with my magic and repelled every root that reached for him.

The waves flung our vessel this way and that, threatening to overturn us in swells as deep as canyons.

Then, as suddenly as they had appeared, the roots withdrew, and the seas went still. Silent. As though the whole world was holding its breath.

I pulled out of Snorri's grip and pushed onto my hands and knees. Bjorn did the same, blood dripping from a cut on his cheek and his green eyes wide. We both twitched as the drakkar jerked, but as I looked over the edge, it was to discover that we'd run up on the beach of a small island.

All around us were empty ships listing on the waves. Every one of them was empty.

Because I'd sent the soul of every Skalander on the horizon to Helheim.

All, except for Snorri. The one I'd wanted most to send to Hel and yet he still lived and breathed.

Jerking out of Bjorn's grip, I stumbled onto the beach and then fell to my knees, retching. Vaguely I heard the thud of boots and the crunch of feet against sand. The thump of someone being flung onto the beach accompanied by a grunt of pain.

Then Snorri demanded, "What have you done?"

I wiped my mouth and looked sideways to find Snorri on his back, Bjorn's boot pressed against his chest. Tora stood behind him, bleeding from a wound on her temple, and the Nameless stood blank-faced in the vessel. Where Saga was, whether she lived, I could not have said.

"What have you done?" he screamed at me.

What *had* I done?

Bodies not weighed down by mail or weapons drifted to the surface of the sea, dozens upon dozens. Hundreds.

It had come true.

I had not changed fate. Everything Saga had foreseen had come to pass, and I wept.

CHAPTER 31

BJORN

I turned my back on the sea of dead, not ready to come to terms with what I'd done.

With what I'd forced Freya to do.

To protect my people, I'd used the love of my life as a weapon and condemned countless souls that deserved Valhalla instead to Helheim, all because of the man before me. All because he cared more for his destiny than for anything else.

"You did this," I screamed at Snorri. "You brought this upon all of us with your endless pursuit of a crown. Every dead warrior should be piled at the foot of your endless fucking ambition!"

Snorri pushed his way out from under my boot and crawled up past the tide line of the small island, dragging seaweed with him. I followed, knocking him down when he tried to get to his feet. On his hands and knees, he passed through the few scraggly trees that eked out an existence on this bar of mud and sand in the middle of the strait, but there was no escape for him.

Once we were well away from Freya, I slammed my boot into his ribs, flipping him over. Then I rested my boot on his chest and leaned.

"You may have achieved the destiny you dreamed of, but it will be short-lived."

"Why?" Snorri demanded, tears flooding down his face. "Why have you turned on your family? On your clan? What lies has Harald filled your ears with to cause you to do this?"

"It is you who lies, Snorri!" I screamed. "Who continues to lie. You tried to kill my mother for not doing your bidding. I saw you with my own fucking eyes!"

"I did no such thing!" Snorri grabbed at his hair, wrenching at it in despair. "I found your mother's cabin burned. I found her body but not yours, and I hunted for who had taken you. Went to war with Harald to get you back, only to discover now that your loyalty is to him. You are his weapon against me. I do not know what sorcery he has wielded to cause you to believe it was me who harmed your mother, but I vow on all that I hold dear, it was not me! I grieved her death more than you can know."

"Lies!" I leaned my weight down, my heel grinding into the mail across his chest. "Not killing you years ago is a mistake I intend to remedy."

"Bjorn, no!"

Freya had run up the beach and through the trees. "Stop!"

"Stay out of this, Freya!" Already, I'd hurt her enough with what I'd done. This would be all me, and no blame would fall down on her. "Go back to the beach."

She caught hold of my arm. "Bjorn, don't do this. Please!"

It was the oath that made her plead for his life, and my rage burned hotter.

Tora approached, and out of desperation I said, "Restrain Freya. Keep her out of this."

"Bjorn, no!" She dragged on my arm, but Tora caught hold of her wrists and knocked her to the ground.

"Stop!" Freya struggled, but Tora was stronger and heavier, easily holding her wrists to the ground. I hated having her restrained, but soon she'd be free.

I could only pray that it would be worth it.

"Whatever Harald has told you is a lie," Snorri pleaded, then groaned in pain as I kicked him in the ribs. "I loved your mother. Loved you. Still love you, despite all of this, for I know it is nothing but Nordelander trickery!"

I called my axe, ready to end this. Ready to silence him for good.

But my mother's voice stilled my hand. "No more lies, Snorri. The truth is out. Bjorn, let him go."

Reluctantly, I lifted my foot, but I kept my axe burning as Snorri forced himself to his knees.

"Saga?" he whispered. "How . . . How is this possible? I saw your body."

Saga's mouth twisted with scorn. "I do not know what hapless soul you burned to give evidence to your lies, but it was not me. I escaped the flames with my son and fled to my only true friend. And during all the long years since, Harald has fought to give me the vengeance I deserved."

Snorri stared at her with bewildered eyes. "Saga . . . you know it was not me. You . . ."

"Stop!" Saga barked the word, her hands balling into fists. "I know what I saw with my own eyes. Bjorn knows who he saw with his own eyes."

"Bjorn!" Freya begged, but Tora pushed her face into the mud to silence her.

"It is time for you to die for your crimes, Snorri," Saga said. "Time for me to have justice for all that I have suffered."

Snorri stared at her in horror. "This is not the fate you foresaw for me."

Her head tilted, green eyes glittering and cruel in a way I'd never before seen. "I said that the one who controlled the shield maiden's fate would unite Skaland. And it has come to pass, Snorri. For you have united the clans with Freya's name and made yourself king. But my words never said anything about how long you would keep your crown. Bjorn, challenge him."

CHAPTER 32

FREYA

I turned my face out of the mud and drew in a breath right as Snorri's eyes moved from Saga to me. "Freya, help me. You must help me. You must save me from her lies. She is lying!" Bjorn caught hold of his arm, dragging him to the square of runes Saga was marking. "She is lying!"

The urge to stop this was no longer a prickle but a fire across my skin, burning with such ferocity that I screamed. I flung my body from side to side, my hair ripping from my scalp as I pulled from Tora's grip. I lunged to my feet only to be struck in the back, a jolt that had to be lightning coursing through my body.

Stunned, I lay in the dirt, watching Saga close the square, binding Snorri and Bjorn within. "Stop," I whispered as Tora knelt on my back and took hold of my wrists. "Stop this."

I could not get loose. Could not use Hlin's magic with my hands pressed to the earth. But Hel's magic was not so easily contained, and though her roots would not pull those with god's blood to Helheim, it would distract them enough that I might be able to escape. "I curse you, Saga," I screamed at her. "I curse you to Helheim!"

Power surged through me, calling to my divine mother for her aid, but the ground did not stir. No roots exploded from its surface.

And in my failure, my body burned and burned.

"Get up!" Bjorn kicked Snorri, who had prostrated himself to the ground. "At least die with honor, you lying prick."

Snorri raised his head. "I will not lift a weapon against my son. I know not why, but your mother has deceived you. Kill me if you must, but there is no honor for you in this. The gods know the truth even if you do not."

"Bjorn, do not listen to him." Saga stood outside the wards, hands fisted and tears slickening her cheeks. "Kill him. End our horror once and for all!"

"Bjorn, no!" I tried to scream, but Tora shoved a glove into my mouth, garbling my voice.

"I'm sorry," she whispered. "I'm sorry, Freya, but this is how it has to be."

"She's lying to you!" Snorri said. "Odin knows her lies and will not welcome her! She is cursed!"

"Get up!" Bjorn kicked Snorri's sword in front of him. "Fight like a man!"

Snorri ignored the weapon but climbed to his feet, expression resolute. "I will not fight you, my son. You are deceived by one who you have every reason to trust, and I'll not harm you for that. Kill me if you must but know that this is not justice."

"No!" I howled around the glove, trying to force it out with my tongue, but Tora's hand was clamped over my mouth, my body the purest form of agony.

"Kill him." Saga spat the words. "Silence him."

"Fight!" Bjorn's axe flared with the ferocity of his emotions. "Fight me, Father!"

"No." Snorri lifted his chin, arms relaxed at his sides. "There is no honor in this fight. I refuse it."

I felt Bjorn snap, and it was like a stab to my own heart. His arm swung in a wide arc, and his flaming axe sank deep into Snorri's chest.

Snorri stumbled backward, pulling himself free and revealing a blackened and bubbling hole in his chest. He dropped to his knees, and Bjorn lifted his weapon to deliver the killing blow.

"No," Saga snarled. "Let him die slowly."

Tora released me.

I didn't stop to question why, only staggered to my feet and snatched up my fallen shield. Springing across the distance, I threw myself over Snorri. "Stop!"

Bjorn wavered, his axe disappearing. "He's dead, Freya," he said. "He can't survive that."

I knew Snorri wouldn't survive, and yet I could still feel the threat to the blood I'd sworn to protect so viscerally I could barely breathe.

I pressed my hands to the wound, gagging at how the burned flesh crackled beneath my palm. Snorri groaned in agony. "Don't. Please don't."

"Don't! Please don't!" Saga mimicked his voice, and then she began to laugh.

She moved, skipping around the perimeter of the square, her midnight braids bouncing against her back.

"Mother, enough." Bjorn was watching her with the same unease I felt.

Saga ignored him and kept skipping, but the tone of her laughter began to change. Shifting and warping into deeper, yet familiar, tones. Wild and cruel.

Not Saga's laugh.

But *Harald's*.

Horror pooling in my guts, because it was Harald's laughter pouring from Saga's lips.

"What madness is this?" Bjorn whispered, even as Saga's features shuddered and blurred, her shape distorting and then suddenly reforming as the king of Nordeland.

"Child of Loki!" Snorri choked out, blood running down his chin. "A shape-shifter. A trickster."

Harald laughed, the sound turning wild and maniacal even as he clapped his hands like a small child and continued to skip around the square. "Long have I waited for this moment," he said when his mirth finally calmed. "And it was more perfect than I'd ever dreamed!"

"Where is my mother?" Bjorn demanded. "What have you done to her?"

Harald snickered, his demeanor entirely different from what I'd ever seen, yet every part of me screamed that this was the real him. That I'd been fooled.

"Most of Saga is nothing more than ash on the wind." Harald's mouth spread into a wild grin. "You can ask Snorri where he buried her bones before he expires. Though I think that will be very soon."

Oh gods oh gods oh gods.

All this time, Harald had been impersonating Saga. Been pretending to be Bjorn's mother. Manipulating him with lies and false sentiment.

Just as he'd done to me. Bile burned up my throat as I realized I'd sat naked in a sauna with this monster, spilling my heart out, and for Bjorn, it was so much worse.

"I'm going to kill you," Bjorn hissed, his axe appearing in his hand. He lunged at Herald, only to stagger backward as he struck the ward.

Fear filled my chest and, drawing my sword, I lifted my hand and walked forward, my worries confirmed as my palm encountered an invisible barrier.

"Silly, foolish girl." Harald laughed. "Racing into your own trap, never stopping to look at the runes before you crossed. Not that you'd understand them anyway, ignorant fishwife that you are." He rolled his eyes skyward. "Pretending to hold you in any level of esteem was more challenging than mimicking Saga all these years."

A thousand curses rose in my throat, but I bit down on all of them, looking instead to Tora. The child of Thor stood beyond, shoulders slumped, eyes dull with resignation. "Tora, help us."

"I cannot," the other woman whispered. "I am sorry, Freya."

"She was another foolish girl." Harald glanced back at Tora. "So quick to make promises she shouldn't have."

"I hate you," Tora whispered, but Harald only huffed out an amused breath. "To be hated holds more power than to be loved. You serve either way, Tora. Now be silent."

Tora's jaw shut with an audible click, bound to obey Harald in all things.

We were trapped.

Behind me, Snorri gurgled out a curse, and Harald said, "It has been a pleasure to steal your fate, old friend. Give my well-wishes to my half sister when you arrive in Helheim, and my thanks for her restraint."

Half sister? I remembered, then: Hel was Loki's daughter.

That was why the roots hadn't attacked him.

And I had no doubt that if I tried to curse him now, Hel would not answer my call.

Whirling away from the barrier, I raced to Snorri's side and pressed his sword into his hand. "You're an arse and I hate you for all that you have done," I said. "But you are no coward. May Odin take you into Valhalla if for no other reason than to put you in your place."

Snorri's hand tightened on the hilt, his eyes fixed on me. "Protect . . . the . . . blood."

"I will or will die trying," I promised, then watched as the light faded from his eyes. Beneath me, the ground trembled, and anger burned in my heart. Pressing my hands to the ground, I whispered, "Hel, grant me your powers."

Simmering strength filled me, and clenching my teeth, I said, "You will not take him."

All too familiar anger smashed against me, my divine mother enraged at being denied something she wanted, but I warred against her. "No."

The ground shuddered, Snorri's body bouncing with the force of it, but I only dug my fingers into the wet earth. "No."

The ground went still.

"Impressive," Harald said. "But in the end, of little consequence. I control your fate, Freya. And soon I will control all of Skaland."

Think, I ordered myself. *Think of a way out of this.*

Yet all thought vanished from my head as Bjorn let out a roar and attacked the barrier. Over and over, he smashed his axe against the barrier, the noise deafening, but each time, the wards threw him back.

Harald threw back his head and laughed, which only enraged Bjorn further. He flung himself at the wards, clawing at the magic, screaming in wordless rage. Harald only came closer, stopping when he was inches away from Bjorn. His eyes burned with delight as he watched Bjorn rage, the pleasure he took in the hurt he'd caused making my stomach turn. "Stop."

In his frenzy, Bjorn didn't hear me. I leaped to my feet. "Bjorn, enough! This is what he wants!"

But all he seemed to hear was Harald's laughter. Desperate to stop him from hurting himself, I waited for the magic to throw him back, then wrapped my arms around his neck and heaved.

Bjorn fell backward on me, weight driving the air from my lungs, but I held on even as I managed to gasp out, "He . . . wants . . . this."

He was shaking in my arms. "He killed her. He killed her."

"I didn't kill Saga, Bjorn," Harald said. "You did. You set the fire that burned her alive."

"Be silent," I shouted at him. "Haven't you done enough harm?"

"It's never enough." Harald's grin was all teeth. "I never grow weary of watching others bring themselves low."

"You were hurting her." Tears ran down Bjorn's face, his knuckles split and bloody from attacking the barrier. "Disguised as Snorri, but it was you hurting her. Threatening her. Why? Was it because she knew that you were a trickster?"

"She did not know." Harald tilted his head, that awful smile still plastered over his face.

"Why, then? What did she ever do but be a friend to you?"

"Yes. A friend." Finally, Harald's smile fell away. "That is what she did—chose poorly by favoring Snorri over me. My goal was to break her bond with him, turn her against him so that she'd come to me of her own free will. Then you spoiled my plans to make her the cornerstone of my cabal by killing her." Hate replaced the amusement. "I considered leaving you to die but it felt too easy an end for what you'd done. You needed to lose everything. Snorri needed to lose everything. And Tyr's fire was no small addition to my cabal. So I brought you to Nordeland and oh, what a game grew from that decision. It has been a pleasure from beginning to end, and I think that the best is yet to come."

There were no words. No words for the depths of Harald's cruelty, so I only tightened my arms around Bjorn and tried to will my strength into him so that he could endure this horror.

"What do you want?" I demanded. "What is the point of all of this? Power?"

He smirked. "As though I can be reduced to one goal, you little fool. My goals are without limit, but the pleasure is in making all those around me dance to my drum and love me while they do it."

"It was your Nameless who kidnapped me, wasn't it?" All the countless ways he'd manipulated me were falling into place. "Not Snorri. You sacrificed your own thralls to convince me that the threat was real and imminent. But it wasn't. Snorri wasn't sailing to Nordeland bent on conquest—he truly believed he was coming to rescue us."

Harald giggled, clearly enjoying watching horror build in me as I came to understand his schemes. Came to understand how cleverly he played his games.

"You're a monster," I breathed.

Harald's expression hardened at my words, but he only snapped his fingers at Tora like a dog. "Come."

Tora walked toward him, visibly fighting the compulsion every step of the way. But whatever magic Harald had used to bind her was too powerful for her to resist. "Yes, my king."

He bent his head, whispering something in her ear. Tora nodded, then lightning exploded from her hands. It shot through the air, striking the ground beneath Snorri's body and launching it through the air.

I gasped as dirt and rock rained down on me, but Bjorn's eyes were on Snorri's smoking corpse, which now rested outside the barrier.

"Kill them," Harald said. "They have served their purpose and are now only a liability to us."

"I'm sorry," Tora whispered. But lightning was already crackling between her palms.

"Hlin." I snatched up my shield. "Lend me your strength."

Magic surged and covered my shield with silver light not a heartbeat before Tora's lightning bolt struck. It rebounded off my magic, nearly striking Harald, who cursed and leaped sideways.

More lightning crackled between Tora's hands, and I could see in her eyes the plan burning in her heart. But so did Harald. "Tora, stop!"

She grimaced, but the flickering light between her palms disappeared. Harald slapped her hard. "You test your limits again, and it will be the death of you," he snarled. "Obey."

"Yes, my king," Tora answered between her teeth. "Do you wish me to try again?"

"No. We've played this game before." Harald eyed us, gaze full of cunning as he weighed his options. I knew what he'd choose. Knew that it would be a slow, painful death for us.

"You want to kill us?" I shouted. "Then come in here and do it yourself, Harald. Or are you too much of a coward?"

He only chuckled. "Such tactics have little use against me, Freya. Especially with no witnesses."

"The gods are watching," I hissed. "They see your cowardice."

"Or my cleverness." He lifted one shoulder. "No one knows you are here. You are trapped within wards with no food or shelter. If the cold doesn't take you, starvation surely will, and my half sister will welcome you both into Helheim, for this is not a death for one destined to enter Valhalla." Crooking a finger, he said, "Tora, fetch the corpse and have my Nameless make ready to sail to rejoin our fleet. Skaland awaits its king."

Tears ran down Tora's face, but she obeyed and slung Snorri's body over her shoulder. Then she and Harald walked away.

"Coward," I screamed. "You're a fucking coward, Harald!"

But the only answer I received was laughter carried over us on the frigid wind. And then . . . silence.

CHAPTER 33

FREYA

I kept my magic on my shield and my eyes on our surroundings, no part of me putting it past Harald to sneak around through the trees and have Tora hit me in the back with a bolt of lightning. Or worse, waiting until I had to sleep and then coming at us again.

"Bjorn," I whispered, taking hold of his hand. "We need to find a way past these wards. We need to escape."

He didn't answer, and I tore my gaze from the trees to look at him, my heart breaking as I realized he was staring at the bloodstains left by Snorri's body. My lips parted to offer some comfort. To tell him it wasn't his fault. That Harald had tricked not just him but everyone. But nothing came out. What comfort would my words be, given that Bjorn had spent the better part of his life serving a man who used him only to damn him in the end? Not just serving, but loving Harald as a father. Through accident, Bjorn had caused the death of his mother, and through manipulation, his father. Had been tricked into fighting against his own people, his own family, every choice he'd made on the basis of endless layers of lies. "I know," I whispered. "I know this—"

"You don't know."

Bjorn pulled away from me, and I grimaced. "Stay close. They might come back."

"They aren't coming back. They don't need to." He crouched down. "Leaving us here to starve means long days of me coming to terms with being the cause of your death, Born-in-Fire. Which is the worst part of all of this."

My chest tightened, because I could only begin to imagine this sort of hurt. To have one's whole life unravel in a moment. I reached for him, but Bjorn held up his hand.

"Don't," he said. "I can't stand the thought of you touching me right now. You are going to die because of me, and I deserve nothing from you but hate."

"I don't hate you." His grief hollowed my own core. "I love—"

"Don't!" he shouted, then pressed the heels of his hands to his face. "Do not say it, Freya. Do not let this nightmare be what gives me absolution from your anger. Pity is not the same thing as forgiveness, and right now, I do not want either."

I slowly lowered my hand to my side, my heart understanding what a terrible taste receiving forgiveness in this moment would be. Every part of me wanted to press my forehead to the ground and weep, for I had never felt more defeated, outwitted, and hopeless in all my life. But I refused to do that. Refused to let Harald win while I still drew breath. "If you wish my forgiveness, Bjorn, then find us a way out of this predicament rather than sitting on your arse feeling sorry for yourself."

His gaze shot to mine, the outrage in his eyes infinitely better than the glassy stare from a heartbeat before. "I have destroyed everything that matters to me and everything that should have mattered to me. How else should I feel?"

Climbing to my feet, I straightened my clothing while assessing our surroundings. "As though you should do something about it."

"What should I do?" His axe appeared in his hand, and he flung it.

Flames flew end over end, but rather than rebounding off the barrier, it flew through to strike a distant tree. "There is nothing I can do!"

"I think that is not the case." I stared at the smoldering bark of the tree. "Your tantrum has yielded results."

Bjorn glared at me. "It was not a tantrum. Children throw tantrums."

"So do men." I crossed my arms. "But I will forgive your outburst, for you have unwittingly found us a solution."

"You drive me to madness, woman."

Shrugging, I said, "With any luck, that will be the case for many years to come. Now hit that tree again and let it burn. It won't be long until a fisherman sees the signal, investigates, then wipes away the runes binding us. Then we will be free to chase Harald down for vengeance." Glancing sideways at him, I added, "Unless you can't hit the tree again. It is quite a distance away."

"I hit it once, didn't I?"

"The tree merely had the misfortune of being in the way of your tantrum. I don't think you can do it on purpose."

He huffed out an irritated breath, axe appearing in his hand. Staring at the tree, he took two quick steps and then threw. The axe flipped end over end, a blur of crimson fire.

And streaked right past the tree to smash against a boulder with a bang.

I laughed and slapped my knee. "Missed."

"Born-in-Fire, for someone whose longevity depends very much on my ability to hit that tree, you seem oddly delighted by my failure."

"You are possessed of too much arrogance and it is unattractive," I replied. "Failure gives you some small measure of humility, which is more appealing. If I am to spend my final hours stuck on a barren island, I would rather it be with a handsome man."

"I see." Shaking his head, Bjorn lifted his axe, which had reappeared in his hand. Exhaling slowly, he took quick steps and threw it again.

And missed again.

Casting a sideways glance at him, I whistled between my teeth and then winked.

"You are the most irritating woman to ever breathe," he growled, then hurled the axe yet again, flames crackling as it soared through the air.

To embed with a *thunk* in the tree's trunk.

Neither of us spoke, and for my part it was because I was holding my breath, but then Tyr's fire ignited the tree. Crimson flame turned to the oranges and yellows and blues of natural fire, and it spread upward until the entire tree was engulfed.

"Well done," I breathed. "But don't let it go to your head or it will be like a bucket of ice water on the flames of my desire for you."

Bjorn laughed softly. "I wouldn't dream of it."

We stood in silence, watching the tree burn down to ash.

But no one came.

"I'll hit another," Bjorn muttered, pacing the perimeter of the square until he decided on a tree a similar distance away.

I said nothing as he took aim. The wind had risen and I was painfully cold, my clothes intended for fighting, not spending hours on an island so small it didn't deserve a name. Bjorn mercifully hit the tree on the first try, the wood igniting, but when he looked at me, he frowned.

"Take off your mail," he said. "It's only making you colder."

Unbuckling my belt, I lifted the heavy vest of metal links over my head, discarding it in a pile. While it was a relief to be free of the weight, it did little to ease the chill and I stuck my hands under my armpits.

"Here." Bjorn set his axe on the ground in front of me. "Try to avoid picking it up." He pulled off his own mail and tossed it next to mine.

I gave a soft smile and sat on my heels to keep my arse dry while I warmed my hands over the axe, slowly regaining feeling in them. Bjorn prowled the perimeter, seeming to be taking account of our stock of trees, their sizes, and the distance he'd have to throw. I noticed how he avoided the crimson stains where Snorri had fallen. But it was better than silence. Better than hopelessness. I had no notion of whether this would work, but it was something, and something was worth clinging to right now.

We would weave our own fates, and I refused to let that fate be death on this rock in the middle of nowhere.

Yet as the second tree burned low, still no one had come.

I ignored the growl of my empty stomach and sipped some water from snow I'd melted in my shield using the heat from his axe. "Which one is next?"

"That one." Bjorn jerked his chin toward a distant tree as he walked past me, axe disappearing only to reappear in his hand. Coldness pressed around me, and I eyed the sun setting in the distance, knowing it was going to get worse. Rising to my feet, I walked the perimeter to get my blood flowing, my stomach clenching each time I heard Bjorn curse, unwilling to watch the process.

Thunk.

I exhaled a breath of relief, allowing myself to look toward the thick tree he'd hit, much farther than the others had been but large enough to burn longer.

Bjorn turned and eyed me. "You're freezing."

"I'm fine." Not entirely true given that my clothes were sodden from melting snow and the wind felt like it was bringing all of winter down upon us, but I didn't want him to worry. "But thank you for volunteering."

"For what?" His eyes narrowed.

Not giving him a chance to step away, I unbuckled his belt and then lifted his tunic, shoving my frozen hands beneath it. He winced as I pressed them against the hard muscles of his stomach. "I would not have volunteered for this."

Yet he belied his own words, wrapping his arms around me and pulling me close, my hands sliding around to his back, the feel of him doing more than the warmth to drive away the chill. I rested my head against his chest, feeling the heat of his axe against the back of my legs as it manifested on the ground near my feet. "I need to tell you something."

"I've been told a few too many things today, Freya."

I nodded my head in acknowledgment but still said, "When I was taken by the Nameless posing as Snorri's men, they drugged me, but I was roused from my stupor by the specter. She said, 'Your name was born in fire. Skaland will be united beneath the rule of the one who controls your fate.'"

"*She*."

I bit the insides of my cheeks. "Her eyes are the same shade of green as yours, Bjorn. Snorri believed Saga was the specter, and I . . . I think he was right."

"So not only did she die in my fire, she still burns in it."

His whole body sang with tension, and while I wished my words had not hurt him, I had a point that needed to be made. "Your mother is trying to help me. The first foretelling about me was the only one she ever gave. All the stories of darkness and death were spun by Harald to manipulate you. And to manipulate me. False foretellings through and through. He doesn't want Skaland united because that will make it strong where it is now weak, and weakness is easier to manipulate. He's been trying to change my fate all my life to prevent anyone who might rival him from coming to power, and I think your mother remained between realms to fight against him. She's suffering in order to keep Harald from winning, and for that reason alone, we can't give up."

"What if he has won?"

His gaze was fixed on the burning tree, though I didn't think he saw it. "We're still alive. He wanted us dead but couldn't see it through, and we need to take advantage of that. Escape and stop him. Make all of Nordeland and Skaland know who and what he really is."

"He's beloved, Freya. It's not so simple."

"I know, but how much of that love is built on lies?" When Bjorn didn't answer, I added, "Tora is not serving him of her own free will, that much is clear. My guess is that she discovered what he was and he bound her to keep the secret. What if he has bound others in a similar fashion?"

"Even if we escape, how do we prove it? It is our word against his, and he has an entire army and dozens of Unfated in his service."

I huffed out a breath. "Obviously I have not thought that far ahead, so quit asking questions about what we will do when we are free when the priority is escape."

"Your plans always have great beginnings, Born-in-Fire, but having barely survived the middles and endings of said plans, it is difficult not to ask questions."

"The question you should ask yourself is why you aren't being more helpful by offering suggestions rather than criticisms. I have a plan. You have no plan. That makes my plan better than yours."

His chest shook beneath my cheek with silent laughter. "Is that a challenge?"

"Yes." I smiled. "Let me know when you come up with an idea, as I will deeply enjoy picking it apart as you do mine."

"Then I should give it some thought." His hand slid down my back, scooping me up into his arms. Then he sat, settling me on the ground between his knees. I leaned against his chest, soaking in the heat of his body.

Wishing it didn't feel as though an obstacle still stood between us, but there was no denying that it did. Because there was still one thing I needed from him.

Silence stretched between us for a long time, broken only when Bjorn said, "I'm sorry, Freya. I should have trusted you with the truth, but I was afraid. Not just of what you'd do with the truth, but of losing you."

With his admission, the last vestiges of my anger crumbled and took the wall between us with it because he'd finally given me the reason for his lies. *The real reason.* "You are forgiven."

Bjorn was quiet. "Why?"

"Because you are very good-looking." Lifting my head from his shoulder, I met his gaze in the darkness, then traced my fingertips down the side of his stubbled cheek. "Are you quite certain that Baldur did not give you some of his blood?"

"It would explain a great deal." He smiled, then turned his face to kiss my scarred palm. Though my skin had little sensation, I felt it all the way down to my core.

"Most especially your arrogance," I murmured, turning my body so that I sat between his legs, wrapping my own around his waist. "I lied before. The arrogance only ever makes me want you more."

"I'll keep that in mind."

I rolled my eyes. "Already I regret my words."

His hands closed around my waist, running up and down my back, sending shivers of sensation through me that had nothing to do with the cold. He leaned forward, and my lips parted, certain he'd kiss me, but Bjorn only said, "You still haven't answered my question."

It was hard to think with his hands on me. Hard to put my mind to anything other than how badly I wanted to be close to him. To be one with him again, because in his absence, I'd felt so empty. "You promised that I was yours. That you were mine. That you'd be at my back until the gates of Valhalla, and though you broke me in other ways, you never broke those promises." I curved my hand behind his head, feeling the silken length of his hair brush my skin. "You hurt me but earned my forgiveness, and to deny it only makes the pain worse. Forgiving you frees me to feel things other than pain. I'm forgiving you for myself."

"I love you, Born-in-Fire," he whispered, pulling me onto his lap, the apex of my thighs pressed against the hard plains of his stomach. "From the moment I met you, I have fought for you. And I'll fight for you every day until I enter Valhalla."

"You have me." I lifted my head to kiss him. "No matter where fate takes me, I will be yours."

His mouth claimed mine, and there were no more words. Only the taste of him on my tongue, the feel of his skin against mine, and the raging heat of his fire that seemed to burn hotter with the fuel of the desire between us.

His tongue stroked over mine, our teeth clicking together, and I didn't care that my head went light from lack of breath because all I wanted was him. All I wanted was to destroy any distance between us, to have him touch me, kiss me, claim me, and oh gods, for him to be in me again.

I tore at my belt, casting it aside, then caught the hem of my tunic and lifted it over my head.

"You'll freeze," he growled into my throat, kissing lines of fire down to my collarbone.

"Keep me warm," I breathed, lifting onto my knees and moaning as he kissed my left breast, drawing my nipple into his mouth and sending a jolt through to my core. My head fell back, my eyes fixed on the stars in the midnight sky, specks of silver light beyond counting, and let all the world fall away but for the feel of his mouth on my breasts. Licking and sucking and biting until I felt swollen and aching and desperate to be sated.

Needing to be filled.

I lowered myself onto his lap, feeling the hard ridge of his cock press against me, and my need for him felt like it was burning me up from the inside. With feral fingers, I tore off his tunic, kissing and biting at his throat, my hands roving over his back and shoulders. Every muscle was hard, his skin like fire beneath my touch, and though I could feel his hands on my naked body, my focus was on touching all of him. Reclaiming that which had always been mine and always would be, because I'd kill anyone who tried to come between us.

Then Bjorn caught hold of both sides of my face. He kissed me, tongue chasing over mine before he pulled back to look me in the eyes. His axe cast dancing shadows over his features, feral and fierce, and he said, "You are so beautiful, Born-in-Fire. You put the goddesses whose blood runs in your veins to shame."

The ground beneath us trembled, and Bjorn gave a dark laugh, one hand sliding from my cheek to my throat, holding me in place while the other unfastened the ties on my war braids. I moaned softly as his fingers unraveled the braids, grinding myself against him. The wind howled over me, but I barely felt it, my body all liquid heat as I traced the tattoos on his muscled arms, wanting to reach down to free him from the rest of the clothes but bound in place by his grip on my throat.

"I want you to fuck me," I breathed, shivering as the loosened lengths of my hair fell across my breasts. "I want you to have all of me."

"I intend to," he murmured, finishing with the last of my braids. "In every possible way."

He released my throat, but before I could reach for him, he caught me by the hips and lifted me to my feet. I looked down at him, all taut skin and tattoos as he unlaced the front of my trousers, catching my bottom lip in between my teeth as he eased the fabric over my hips and slid it slowly down my legs.

I kicked off my shoes, and he discarded my clothes, leaving me naked before him. He kissed my navel once, then leaned back on one elbow, looking up at me while he freed his cock, stroking it as he looked me up and down. I could only imagine how I looked, naked with my hair loose and blowing in the wind, my face still painted for war and my body illuminated by a god's fire.

"I am glad no one has come," he said, his eyes darkening in a way that made my toes curl against the cold ground. "Seeing you like this is worth dying for."

Then he let go of his cock and crooked a finger at me. "Let me have you, Freya."

I dropped to my hands and knees, running my tongue up his length and relishing the groan of pleasure that tore from his lips. But then he caught hold of me and lifted, falling backward until his head rested against the ground with my knees to either side of his face. I gasped as he elbowed my thighs wider, his breath hot against my slick sex.

I trembled, my body all contrasts of hot and cold, but every part of me heavy with anticipation as he pushed my thighs wider still, lowering me farther still. Each breath I took was ragged, because each breath he took seared against the most intimate part of me. His fingers traced up and down my bare legs, driving me so wild that I fought the urge to scream because if I did not have release, I would surely burn to ash from the inside out.

Then his tongue stroked up my sex, lingering on the most sensitive part before he whispered, "Come for me, Born-in-Fire. I want to taste you while you scream my name at the stars."

He pushed my knees apart until my thighs ached, and then he consumed me.

The wind caught my sob of pleasure and tore it away to the wilds of the sea as he laid claim to my body, his tongue inside me before laying siege to my clit, each suck, each stroke, driving me closer to climax.

I dug my nails into my own thighs, my breasts, desperate to hold on to something while I rode him, the ache between my thighs so fierce my body shook.

The wave of my desire crested with such violence that I screamed, howled his name, overcome with sensation as though I knelt at the brink between life and death. Which perhaps I did. Over and over the waves surged through me until I could scarcely breathe.

I slid my hips back and collapsed against him, my skin icy where the wind had kissed it, the heat of him almost painful. His heart hammered beneath my ear, arms warm as they wrapped around me, but the feel of his cock pressing against my liquid heat was fuel for the desire that still raged inside of me.

Lifting my body, I gave him a feral smile, then began to kiss my way down his chest. Down the hard ridges of his abdomen, each intake of breath filling me with wicked delight as my mouth found his cock. I circled it with my tongue, smiling when he groaned, then took him into my mouth. He was long and thick, but I took him as deep as I could, tasting the salt of him as my hands explored his body.

"Freya," he groaned. "You have a wicked little mouth."

I only rolled my eyes up to look at him, then scraped my teeth gently over his tip, his back bowing as I whispered, "What are you going to do about that?"

"Nothing." His fingers tangled in my hair. "There is nothing about you I would change."

A warmth different from desire filled me, because I knew that I was a flawed woman. That there were parts of me that were not good. Yet Bjorn loved me as I was, wanted me to be who I was rather than to shape me into something else, the way so many other people had tried.

I wanted him to know that I felt the same way about him. That despite everything, good and bad, I loved him as he was. Wanted him as he was.

So I showed him.

Took him deep in my mouth again, tasting and relishing him, my fingers exploring the hard lines of his body. Traced the scars and tattoos, reaffirming that he was mine and that I'd never be parted from him again. We'd be together now until we walked into Valhalla, then together for whatever came next.

"Freya," he groaned, and I knew he was close. Could feel the tension in him. But rather than allowing himself release, Bjorn pulled me into his arms and kissed me deeply, his tongue stroking over mine. "You are mine, Born-in-Fire," he growled, "and I will have all of you."

He rolled, and I found myself on my hands and knees, Bjorn behind me. My whole body quivered as he drew my hair over my back, the wind gusting over my hardened nipples and my fingers digging into the ground.

"So fucking perfect," he whispered, his large hands gripping my hips and his thumbs pressing into the muscle of my arse. He pulled me against him, his knees on either side of mine, his cock pressing against me. "Use your magic, Freya. I want to see you while I make you mine."

"Hlin," I whispered, "lend me your power."

Magic surged into me and out through my hands, spilling across the ground in a silver glow. My body was liquid fire, knowing he could see the most intimate parts of me making my breath come in rapid gasps because I needed him in me. Needed to be joined with him in every possible way.

Bjorn's fingers tightened on my hips, drawing me back, and a sob tore from my lips as he pressed into me. Inch by delicious inch, until my body could take no more of him.

"Mine," he breathed, one hand moving around my hip, and I whimpered as his finger circled my clit.

My release was already rising, the snow melting and running down my body in rivulets, juxtaposed with the burning heat of him inside me. My magic seemed to pulse with my heart, silver light climbing the walls of our prison, reaching up to the sky.

He pulled out, then thrust into me again, and I whimpered as he found his rhythm. My arms shuddered with the strain of holding myself up against his strength, but gods, I wanted more. Wanted everything, and I pushed back against him, taking him deeper.

His fingers matched the intensity of his thrust, stroking against my clit, and the aching rise of my climax was a river against a dam on the verge of collapse. My heart was hammering, my eyes filled with nothing but silver light, and I felt like I was drowning and it wouldn't matter if I never took another breath.

His thrusting intensified, and the desperate need in it shattered my control. A cry tore from me as I surrendered to the release. Bjorn screamed my name as he climaxed, arm wrapping around my hips and his cock driving so deeply into me that my back bowed.

I gasped for breath as pleasure claimed me, stealing away my strength, my body limp.

"Freya." Bjorn's arm moved up my torso, lifting me so that my back was pressed against his chest, the light of my magic winking out. He was still in me, still pulsing, and I shuddered against the overwhelming sensations as the darkness wrapped around us like velvet.

"I love you," he said, and I turned my head, feeling my temple brush against the stubble of his chin as I whispered, "You have my heart."

It felt as though time stood still. There was nothing but the gentle fall of snow around us, the wind in the distant trees, and the roar of the sea beyond. A moment that I might wish would last, for we were finally together.

Except as the chill grew, the wind no longer stroked my skin but cut like a knife, and reality came thundering back.

We were alone.

Trapped.

And the place that had brought our hearts back together might well be the place where they beat their last.

CHAPTER 34

FREYA

By dawn, not even Bjorn's heat was enough to keep me warm, both of us soaked from melting snow and no salvation in sight.

It will be better in daylight, I kept repeating to myself as I shivered against him, sensation gone from my toes, my fingers spared only because I kept them wedged under my arms. Yet as the sun rose, it revealed that little about our circumstances had changed.

The runes that held our prison in place seemed impervious to the elements, and though I tried to wash them away with snow melted by Bjorn's axe, the water only ran around them. My magic, bound to my touch as it was, could not help, and though Bjorn's axe could pass through the barrier if he threw it, he could not so much as mar the runes scratched into the earth.

"I've never met anyone who knows as much about runic magic as Harald," Bjorn said, leaning a forearm against the invisible barrier, eyes fixed on the charred remains of the trees around us. "Nor one who plans half as well."

"He did not plan to leave us alive and yet here we are." I held my hands over his axe. "So he's fallible. He can't predict everything."

And yet no matter how I bent my mind to possible solutions, nothing worked. Frustration built in my chest, and needing to do something—anything—I leaped to my feet and shouted, "Help! Help us!"

"Save your breath, Born-in-Fire," Bjorn said. "There is no one who will hear."

Ignoring him, I balled my fists and screamed, "Help! We're here! Help!"

"Well," a female voice said from behind me. "Isn't this an interesting development."

I whirled, about to put Bjorn in his place for mocking my yelling, only for all words to stall on my lips.

Because the woman staring at me with eyes like frozen waterfalls was Ylva.

Dressed in a warrior's attire with her reddish-brown hair in war braids, she stood with Ragnar at her elbow and several warriors to either side, all with arrows trained on Bjorn and me.

"When they say out of the frying pan and into the fire, this is what they mean, Freya." Bjorn bent to retrieve his axe, then bounced the blade of flames against his palm. "Ylva."

"Honorless traitor." She spat on the ground.

"Ylva, if you just listen—"

"You are no better, you faithless whore." She lifted her hand. "Kill them. He's not here."

Slapping my hand against the barrier, I covered our prison with magic, wincing as several arrows bounced off.

Ylva only snorted. "They are trapped, so let them die slowly rather than quickly. Those wards will hold them until they breathe their last. Come, we must continue our search."

"Ylva, wait," I called, unable to keep the desperation from my voice. "Harald is moving to attack Skaland and make himself king."

"That is no revelation, Freya," she answered. "Why do you think we fought so hard against him? If you'd held your faith, we might have held him back, but you were too busy spreading your legs for this one."

"I ran because I thought it was the only solution," I said. "Then Harald took me prisoner."

"Do either of you two know what the word *prisoner* means?" Ylva demanded, looking between Bjorn and me. "Because I do not think you do. The word you are looking for is sycophant. Flunky. Minion." Her lip curled. "You are Harald's pets, not his prisoners."

"Harald trapped us in here!" I couldn't keep the panic from my voice because of all the people who might have come, Ylva was the most ill-fated choice. "Ylva, Harald deceived us! He's—"

But she was already walking away, nearly out of earshot.

Desperate and knowing who she was looking for, I screamed, "Snorri is dead!"

Ylva froze.

"Freya, have you lost your head?" Bjorn hissed, but I ignored him as Ylva slowly approached.

"You know this for certain?" Her voice was unsteady, her jaw trembling, and though she'd never been any friend of mine, I felt a wave of guilt for the grief she was enduring. Especially given that it would only grow worse.

"Yes." I swallowed hard, my eyes flicking to where the bloodstains were obscured by snow. "Harald took his body. Ylva, he's a child of Loki. A shape-shifter. All these years he's been keeping up the pretense that Saga is alive, using her face and voice to tell everyone that it was Snorri who tried to murder her and naming Harald as her savior."

Ylva swayed on her feet. "You were supposed to protect my husband, at all costs," she whispered, not seeming to care about the revelation of Harald's identity. "You swore an oath."

"I tried, Ylva. Truly, I did." I leaned against the barrier, my magic still gleaming bright. "Harald deceived us, but that is not the limit of his trickery, I'm sure of it. We must reveal the truth of his nature to turn his warriors against him."

Tears welled in her icy blue eyes. "Did he die well?"

It was as though she didn't even hear me. Or was just beyond caring for anything beyond her own grief. "Ylva, it is your people Harald aims to make swear to him as king. You are the lady of Halsar and you are sworn to protect them. Let us out and we can help you."

"Their lady no longer, for my husband is dead. Skaland's king is dead." She dropped to her knees, an awful wail tearing from her lips. Ragnar stepped forward to rest a hand on her shoulder, but she shoved his hand away and howled Snorri's name.

"Ylva, where is Leif?" Bjorn had come next to me. "Where is my brother?"

"Do not name him so!" Ylva lifted her face, swollen eyes filled with sudden fury. "You betrayed your family and are no brother to him!"

"That's his decision to make, not yours," Bjorn said. "But as Snorri's heir, it is his legacy at stake if Harald isn't stopped."

"The legacy is already lost," she answered. "For Harald's forces sailed directly to Skaland after the battle. His ships passed me while I was headed in pursuit of our own fleet, and I thought that he must have evaded Snorri's ships on the strait. I believed I'd have a better chance of stopping Nordeland if I could find Snorri and bring him and our warriors back to fight, but a fishing vessel that witnessed the battle told us that Skaland's warriors were lost to the sea. Dragged beneath the waves by black roots." Her eyes fixed on mine. "Lost to you, Hel-child. Don't think to deny it, because word of your power spreads like wildfire on the tongues of every merchant vessel that has recently been in Nordeland. I'd have to be mad to consider setting a creature like you free."

I pursed my lips, understanding now why Harald had done nothing to hide my presence in Nordeland. Done nothing to hide my magic—quite the opposite, in fact. He was ensuring that word of what I was would reach Skaland so that they'd know that I was the one to blame when Harald used me to destroy Snorri's army.

"Leif is in Grindill, which is inevitably Harald's target," Ylva said. "If Harald has not already killed or imprisoned him, it is only a matter of time."

Bjorn cursed, then slammed his fist on the barrier, but my mind was racing. "Negotiate for Leif's return using us."

Ylva went very still.

"Harald wants us dead," I told her. "We served our role in his scheme, and we are now his greatest liability, for we know the truth about him. The only reason we still live is that he was unable to kill us, so he left us imprisoned to starve. Let us out, and then trade us for Leif. We'll kill Harald and avenge Snorri."

"Why would I trust you?" Ylva asked. "Why should I believe any of what you say? How do I know this isn't just a trick to catch me and destroy the last resistance to Harald's rule? Because your word means nothing, Freya."

"What about my memories?"

Ylva didn't answer.

"I remember the runes used for the spell to capture memories and share them with others. I can use them to capture the memory of what happened here," I said. "You can watch and judge for yourself."

"Don't trust her." Ragnar's dark eyes were grim. "They fight for Harald. This is a trick, my—"

Ylva held up a hand, silencing him and, for a long time, the only sound was the sea and the wind. Then she said, "You saw Snorri die?"

The muscles in my jaw tensed because I knew this was a risk. "Yes."

"I want to see everything. Then I will decide."

Keeping my shield up, I turned to meet Bjorn's gaze.

"Do it," he said. "She'll see that you tried."

But also that Bjorn had been the one to slay Snorri, and I didn't think she'd be sympathetic that he'd been tricked into doing so. Yet what other choice did we have?

Sighing, I released my magic, the film of silver light coating the barrier falling away as I dropped to my knees.

"Put the first moment of the memory in your mind as you draw the first rune, and run through events that occurred, ending it with the final rune," Ylva instructed. "And show care, for you may only capture a memory with this magic once."

Nodding, I placed the moment I'd first stepped on this island in my mind's eye, then began to draw the runes. My eyes burned as I forced myself to remember everything, drawing the last rune as I watched Harald and Tora disappear from sight.

"Step to the far side of your prison," Ylva said, then jerked her chin at Bjorn. "You as well."

We obeyed while Ylva scratched markings of her own in the dirt outside our prison, pressing one hand to them. "It will keep me from being caught by the wards," I heard her tell Ragnar, though I noted that he also took a firm grip on her arm, ready to pull her out of reach.

"She'll never forgive what I did nor should she," Bjorn said softly, donning his mail vest. "But she will see that you are not to blame. If she allows only you freedom, take it."

"I'm not leaving you here."

"Yes, you will," he said. "Make a plan with Ylva to get my brother free, and then you can come back for me."

There wasn't a chance I was leaving Bjorn to die in this prison, but the moment to argue was over, because Ylva reached through and placed a hand on the circle of runes. Her whole body stiffened as her mind was filled with my memory, and I had to force myself to breathe.

"Saga?" Ylva whispered, then she shook her head, muttering, "No, please no."

Guilt soured my empty stomach as I watched emotion play across her face, her eyes shifting back and forth, time seeming to stand still. Then, beneath her palm, the runes turned to ash and Ylva withdrew her hand, sitting down hard in the melting snow.

"My lady?" Ragnar gripped her shoulders. "What do you wish for us to do?"

Ylva didn't answer, only stared and stared, and my heart raced, because what if watching Snorri die had broken her? What if my gambit had failed?

Then Ylva straightened, and it was like watching a wall being rebuilt, stone by stone, higher and higher until it was strong once more. She stood. "It is as they say. Harald is a child of Loki and able to take on the shape and voice of anyone he chooses to mimic. A trickster who takes great pleasure in making everyone dance to the beat of his drum, and his heritage must be revealed."

She drew in a steadying breath, then fixed her eyes on Bjorn. "I know your actions were motivated by false beliefs put into your head by Harald, but I still find that I cannot forgive you for killing your father. He was the great love of my life, and part of my heart has died with him."

I tensed, trying to come up with a plan for a situation where she agreed to release me but not Bjorn, then Ylva said, "Yet Snorri died trying to protect you. He forgave you. I will not dishonor him by allowing Harald the victory of your death, Bjorn, but in exchange for your life, I want your word that you'll dedicate it to avenging your father."

"You have it."

Ylva gave a tight nod, then began to move slowly around the perimeter of our prison, etching markings over Harald's, which disappeared with puffs of black smoke. Then she gestured at us. "Come."

I exhaled a breath of relief, for though what would come next would not be easy, at least it wouldn't be dying of starvation and exposure on a deserted island in the middle of the Northern Strait.

"I need to pull you across the wards." Ylva held out her hand. "Harald's magic is complex, and I could not vanquish it entirely."

I started to reach for her, then hesitated, for I did not put it past her to let me out but leave Bjorn trapped as revenge for Snorri's death. "Bjorn, you first. I don't trust her."

His axe flared to life in his hand, and with the other he took hold of Ylva, who pulled him across. He let go of her immediately. "Now Freya."

Ylva reached toward me. But behind Bjorn, Ragnar lifted a heavy cudgel. "Bjorn!" I shouted. "Behind you!"

My warning was too late. The heavy wood struck his skull with a crack. Bjorn dropped like a stone, and I screamed, lunging, only to rebound off a barrier that seemed very much in place.

Ragnar and two of the other warriors flung themselves on Bjorn, binding his wrists behind his back.

"You didn't really believe I'd let you out, did you, Hel-child?" Ylva asked, stepping back. "One with your power cannot be suffered to live, cursing the souls of those who deserve to join the Allfather to languish with your godly mother in Helheim."

Bjorn was stirring, regaining consciousness, and Ylva glanced at him. "I'll trade him for Leif. Perhaps Bjorn will manage to fulfill his promise and will put an end to Harald. Perhaps he'll do it in time to come rescue you before you starve. Or perhaps your fate is to die an honorless death and join your mother in her realm."

I screamed and pounded my fists against the barrier. Bjorn's eyes opened, and he flung himself from side to side as the men dragged him up, his voice garbled through the gag they'd forced into his mouth. But I still understood what he said: *Don't do it. Don't call her name. I'll get you free.*

"Bjorn!" I howled his name, but the name I wanted to scream was Hel's. To curse Ylva and her warriors to Helheim so that we could walk free. But his green eyes pleaded for me to hold my tongue. Pleaded with me to trust him to win me free another way. And even now, that cursed oath bound me to obey.

My knuckles split from hammering my fists against the magic, and Ylva sighed. "I believed Saga's foretelling meant you would accomplish great things. But all you've done is destroy. Goodbye, Freya."

I howled as they dragged Bjorn away, then fell to my knees and sobbed. For him. For myself. For everyone who had fallen victim to Harald's trickery.

Exhaustion finally took me, and I curled up in the driest spot I could find, knowing that there was little chance I would survive the night. That I would freeze to death, my corpse confined until the end of days in the circle of wards that bound me.

Clouds thickened, the sun nothing more than a faintly glowing orb behind them as it was chased across the sky, the wind growing bitter.

I didn't want to die. I didn't want to give up, but there was no way out.

Tears leaked from my closed eyes, my shivers violently painful, and I knew it wouldn't be long now.

"I love you," I whispered into the wind, willing it to carry my voice to Bjorn. "Keep fighting. Don't let him win."

I wanted to tell him that I'd meet him in Valhalla, but Ylva was right: This was not a warrior's death. And the knowledge that I'd never see Bjorn's face again, feel his touch, hear his voice, shattered my heart.

Then a faint crackling filled the twilight, louder than the wind and the sea, and I inhaled the scent of smoke. Peeling open my eyelids, I watched a shadowy figure walking toward me, embers and ash trailing in its wake.

The specter.

No . . . I knew who she was—Snorri had been right all along. "Saga?"

Bjorn's mother passed through the barrier, then knelt before me, green eyes seeming to glow from within. She remained a horror to behold, flesh blackened and burned away to reveal tendon and bone. Harald had done this to her, left her to burn alive in her cabin, and she still suffered that agony even in death.

"I'm sorry," I whispered. "He fooled me."

Reaching out, Saga curved her skeletal fingers around my cheek, but rather than feeling repulsed by her touch, I leaned into it. Took comfort from it.

"I'm trapped," I said. "Ylva is going to trade Bjorn for Leif, and Harald will either kill him or bind him as he has done to Tora, and there isn't anything I can do. I can't help him." I lifted my face, a sudden idea occurring to me. "Can you remove the wards that are binding me?"

"No." As always, her voice was harsh and pained, forced over burned vocal cords, every word agony. "I cannot."

Saga's skeletal hand moved from my face to take my scarred right hand, unfolding my fingers to reveal the tattoo across my palm. Hel's mark, though twisted beyond recognition. "You are not wholly mortal. Her curse will set you free."

Then she was gone.

I forced my numb body upright, staring at the twisted tattoo on my hand. It seemed like madness to consider, but what other options did I have? Better to die trying to live than to die doing nothing at all.

So I said, "Hel, grant me your power." As magic filled me, I donned my chain mail, adjusted my sword belt, and then fastened my shield to my back. Marshalling my courage, I whispered, "I curse myself to walk the path to Helheim."

The ground began to shake.

CHAPTER 35

FREYA

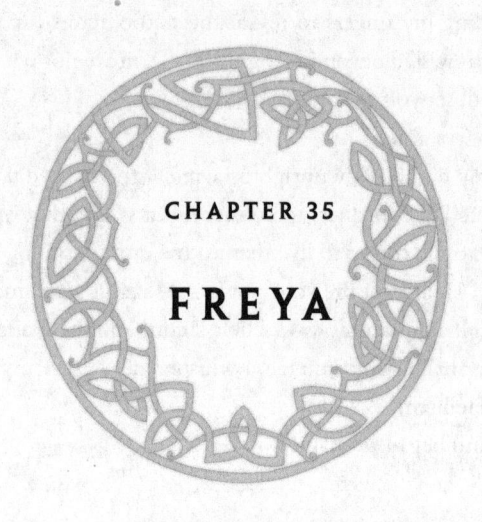

Fear flooded my veins as the roots burst from the ground, black and terrifying. They wrapped around my arms and legs, but I didn't fight them. Didn't struggle. Gave in to them as they dragged me down.

Dirt closed around me, pressing against my face as though I were being buried alive, and that was when panic set in.

I clawed at the roots, desperate to breathe, trying to climb my way back up, but they dragged me down with relentless strength.

This was no escape.

This was death.

My chest was agony with the need for air, and I tried to pull a hand up to carve the dirt away from my mouth, but my arms were pinned.

I'd made a mistake, oh gods, the worst of mistakes.

But then I was falling.

I managed to suck in a breath of air right before my back struck a root, knocking it back out of my lungs. My mouth opened in a scream of pain, but no sound came out as my body bounced and ricocheted off the tangled web of blackened roots, tumbling down and down.

To hit stone with an impact that sent stars spinning across my vision, my shield clattering down next me.

Whimpering, I twisted on my side, the only cares in my head for getting air into my lungs and easing the pain in nearly every part of my body.

Then the scuff of a foot against stone filled my ears, and my eyes snapped open to take in a pair of feet next to me. My still-spinning vision climbed up ankles, then a skirt, higher and higher until it landed on a face I recognized, for I had seen Harald wear it before. "Saga?"

Bjorn's mother smiled, then sat next to me. "You're supposed to climb down, not fall."

"Next time," I croaked, pushing up on one elbow, it taking far too much effort to get my frozen and battered legs beneath me. Only then did I look around, finding that we sat upon a road of stone, all around us blackness and mist, and above . . .

"Yggdrasil," I breathed, staring up into the web of roots that I'd fallen through. "I'm in Helheim."

"No," Saga said. "You are between realms, Freya. On the road to Helheim, specifically. A place for mortal souls, but your body was able to come to this place because of the divine blood in your veins. Only the dead may reside in Helheim, and as I'm sure you are aware, you are very much among the living. So do not enter the golden gates."

Dabbing at a cut on one of my hands that was seeping blood, I had to grudgingly admit that I was indeed alive. "How are you here, Saga?"

"Because my thread is tangled with yours," she said. "I walk the paths between realms, and while I might step into the mortal world, it is not without cost, for I must be as I was when I drew my last breath."

Burned, *burning,* and my stomach twisted at the agony she must endure. "Will you ever be free?"

"I cannot see my own fate," she answered. "Only pieces of yours, which are ever shifting. Ever changing. And right now, you are caught by the trickster's choices, and it is he who determines the future of all. To free us, you must cut his thread short."

Such a simple thing, and yet I knew that to kill Harald would be no easy task because he was as clever as a mortal could be. "I'm sorry," I said. "For not seeing through the mask he wore to mimic you."

In hindsight, it felt so obvious that Harald-as-Saga had been a construct, for she'd been too perfect. Inhuman in her beauty, whereas the woman before me bore the signs of a life lived. Young as she'd been when she was killed, but hands marked with tiny scars, another scar on her chin, and the beginning of smile lines creasing her cheeks and the corners of her eyes. A woman who had lived and laughed and loved, not the marble statue that Harald remembered her as. It made me think he'd never truly known her, nor loved her heart, only desired to possess Saga's body and the gift of magic in her blood.

"He has fooled many."

"Did he fool you?"

"For a time," Saga answered, then sighed. "Harald is not inherently cruel—the suffering of others is not his goal, which is why Nordeland has thrived for so long. Why the people love him as their king. What drives him is the desire to manipulate others, to control them, to outwit them, and suffering is merely the consequence. But above all else, he desires to be loved and adored, and nearly all he does is to achieve those ends. I saw many visions of his future, but they were ever changing and always contradictory, and he did not reveal his bloodline to me. Many times he tried to entice me to join him in Nordeland, but I always declined, for even not knowing what he was, I saw in him the desire to manipulate others. A dangerous trait in all men, but so much worse in a child of the gods, for they have the power to change fate."

"Is that why he killed you?" I only knew what Harald had told me, and I had no certainty it hadn't all been lies.

Saga's green eyes grew distant. "My death was unintended, Freya. He believed that my unwillingness to join his growing cabal was because of Snorri, so he thought to turn my loyalties by making a pretense of Snorri threatening me. The fire was an accident, and though he claims otherwise, I think Harald was motivated by guilt when he took Bjorn with him so as to bring him to a child of Eir for healing. An emotion that faded once he realized my son was a tool he could use, and his nature took control once more."

"How do I stop him?" I asked. "How do I get close enough to kill him? Hel's magic doesn't harm the Unfated, and it won't even touch him."

"Loki is Hel's father," Saga said with a shrug. "Though whether she is motivated by fear or loyalty, you would have to ask her."

My blood chilled, and I looked into the mists around us, half convinced that the goddess of death would appear. But there was only darkness and mist.

And Saga had not answered my question.

"Have you seen what I will do?" I asked. "Do you see how I can stop him?"

"No," Saga answered. "I have only seen you fail. Seen you die. Seen Harald in a crown, king of Skaland and Nordeland both."

My stomach dropped, my tongue incapable of words.

"But you can change your fate." Saga took my hands. "You have the power to save Bjorn. To save Skaland. To save yourself." She gestured to the roots. "Climb a different path than you fell, and you will emerge away from the prison on that island. As to what you do next, it must be a weave of your own making."

Rising to my feet, I stared up at the tangle of roots, not relishing the climb, but as I contemplated how to manage it, a rush of air washed over me like the sigh of a giant. Turning, I looked down the road into the mist. "This leads to Helheim, then?"

"Yes. But only the dead cross the threshold into her domain, and they never return. She does not care to part with what belongs to her."

"I know." I'd heard Hel's voice in my head enough times to have a sense of her . . . *covetousness*. A trait that, for better or worse, I'd inherited.

"Climb, Freya," Saga urged. "Ylva means to trade my son for hers. I fear the fate the trickster will have in store for him. You are his only salvation."

I will be at your back until I cross the threshold to Valhalla, Born-in-Fire, Bjorn's voice echoed in my thoughts because though I'd never said it, my heart had made the same promise to him.

My aching body trembled, because every instinct in my soul demanded that I go to him. That I protect him from whatever horrible fate Harald would invent for him, because I didn't think it would be as easy as death. Reaching up, I took hold of one of the roots. *Save him,* my heart whispered. *You know he would come for you.*

Visions of a future with him filled my mind, of a life beyond this where we could be happy. Gods, but I wanted that life. Wanted it so badly that it hurt to breathe.

"I will weave my own fate," I whispered, then let go of the root and picked up my shield.

"Freya?"

I was already running. Sprinting down the road, knowing that Saga was too afraid of being pulled into the afterlife to follow. Faster and faster, I ran, my boots slapping against the midnight stones forming the road and my shield bouncing on my back, mists pressing in on all sides. Sounds emanated from them, the growls of beastly throats and the scratch of talons, and fear coursed through my veins.

The air smelled of earth and moisture, and above me, the roots of Yggdrasil shifted and moved, though I wasn't certain whether it was because the tree was sentient or if the motion was caused by something else.

Or someone.

I slid to a stop at the sight of a great river stretching before me, waters black and bottomless. Instead of sounding like rushing water, it was as though a battle raged in its depths in an endless clash of steel against steel. A bridge of dark stone that glittered with gold stretched over it, and on the far side, a golden wall reached up to impossible heights. In the wall was a pair of twin gates that would need the hands of giants to open. Before them stood a black hound the size of a bear, its gleaming eyes fixed on me.

Garmr.

The creature let out a low growl, sensing that I did not belong. For I was among the living, and this was a place for the dead.

He prowled onto the bridge, and I swallowed hard as I saw the crimson droplets dripping from his dark fur.

"I am Freya, Erik's daughter," I said to the beast, though I had no notion of whether he could comprehend my words. "Child of Hlin and of Hel. I would speak to my divine mother."

Lips pulled back to reveal teeth as long as my hand, and the hound let out another low growl.

I reached for my shield but then thought better of it and whispered, "Hel, grant me your power."

Magic boiled up inside me, burning hot, and the hound paused, eyeing me with a crimson gaze that I suspected mirrored my own. He leaned forward, sniffing, and it was all I could do to hold my ground. His breath reeked like a week-dead corpse but was somehow cold as a winter wind.

Then he lowered his head and stepped to one side of the bridge.

Taking a deep breath, I crossed and then stopped, my eyes fixed on the closed gates to Hel's hall. Only the dead could enter and, once inside, no one left again. Which suggested that I was best served by remaining here.

"I would speak to my divine mother," I shouted, expecting to be ignored. But no sooner did the words exit my lips than did the gates crack open. Beyond, all I could see was a wall of mist that obscured whatever lay behind the gates, and through it stepped a giant.

I took a staggering step back, my eyes climbing up the giant's form, but even as I watched, she began to shrink. Diminishing in size with each step until Hel and I were of the same height when she stopped before me. Her changed stature made her no more human in appearance. Wiry and stooped, half her face was a beauty to behold, golden hair falling in lush curls to her waist. But the other . . . it was the bluish hue of a bruise or of flesh lost to frostbite, so sunken that I could see the shape of her skull beneath, and her hair hung in wispy lengths of the darkest gray.

Half alive. Half dead. The goddess of death.

"Daughter."

Her voice was the sound of snakes crawling through dead leaves, terrible and horrifying, and I dropped to my knees. "Mother."

"This is not a place for the living."

"I am of your blood," I countered. "It is my place."

Icy cold fingers touched my chin and lifted my face to meet her gaze. One eye was blue, the other was milky white. Not red, as I'd thought they might be, and I didn't know what to make of that. "I need your aid."

Her head tilted.

"I must defeat Harald of Nordeland," I said. "But when I try to send his soul to your realm, you will not take it. Why? Is it because he's Loki's child?"

"Souls of the Unfated are not so easily claimed. To do so risks the ire of my brethren, which I'll not do without worthy cause."

"Fair enough, but at least with the others, the roots appear. For him, you don't even try. Do you fear retaliation from Loki?"

"Fear?" Hel smiled in amusement, and I recoiled at her teeth. Half pristine white and half rotten, but all fangs.

Every instinct in my body screamed that I should run, but I held my ground. "Why, then? Do you favor Harald over your own daughter? Do you desire him to triumph over your own blood? Already he's made a fool of me. Tried to kill me. Imprisoned me. You could have prevented all of it by telling me his nature."

"You are not imprisoned."

I clenched my teeth, annoyance beginning to rise above my fear because it seemed she would give me no straight answers. "Don't you want his soul?"

Hel bent closer and exhaled, the stench of a corpse wafting over me. "Yes, Freya. I do."

"Then why won't you help me kill him!" The words came out as a shout, which I immediately regretted as she bent even closer. The hair on her dead side brushed my hand, and it felt like barrow worms crawling over my skin.

"I have given you power over death," she hissed. "Power to make those destined for Valhalla tremble in terror. Weave your own fate, daughter."

And then she was gone.

I curled up tightly and wrapped my arms around myself, my breath coming in great heaving gasps. Shakes wracked my body and my throat burned with nausea. I'd come here for nothing, and who knew what horrors had befallen Bjorn in the time I'd wasted here.

Then a warm tongue slid up my arm.

I cried out and toppled sideways, my shield striking the ground with a clatter. It was Garmr who'd licked me, and he now stood watching me.

"What do you want?" I asked him. "Do you have a solution?"

He only snuffled my arm with his huge snout, then turned his great head to watch as shadowed shapes climbed out of the river and walked toward the open gates of Helheim, what lay beyond obscured by mist.

"I have to go back," I said to the hound. "I need to help Bjorn."

My voice cracked on his name, because I had no idea how I'd save him. But I had to try. Shoving to my feet, I tried to walk back over the bridge. But Garmr blocked my path.

"Let me go," I snapped at him, trying to go around, but the hound only stepped again into my path. "Bjorn needs me!"

Bjorn.

I froze, his name having drawn up from the recesses of my mind the story of Baldur. Of how he'd been sent to Helheim through Loki's trickery. Hel had agreed to release him if all the world wept, and though that had not come to pass, it struck me that the offer had still been made.

Hel had the power to release souls from Helheim.

I have given you power over death. Power to make those destined for Valhalla tremble in terror. Weave your own fate, daughter.

Slowly, I turned to watch as the gates opened for yet another soul, watching as it disappeared into the swirling mist. Not long ago, I'd sent hundreds upon hundreds of Skalanders through those gates, though they hadn't deserved it. Warriors who deserved a chance at Valhalla.

The gates began to slowly close.

Hel had given me her power. All of her power. But I had one that she did not.

Sucking in a deep breath, I bolted toward the gates and dived through their opening.

Right before they closed with an echoing thud.

CHAPTER 36

FREYA

It was cold.

Colder than the depths of winter, my breath blooming in great gusting clouds and my hands already aching as I climbed to my feet. I pulled my hood over my head and shoved my hands in my armpits, but it made no difference.

Because this was the coldness of death.

All around me were mist and darkness, the former swirling as I lifted my left hand and covered it with Hlin's magic, the silver light revealing a tunnel. Seeing the soul I'd followed, I hurried after her, my shield bouncing on my back. She was old and gray, but when I touched her shoulder, she didn't seem to feel it. "Hello," I said. "Do you hear me?"

She gave no reaction, only carried on walking with a blank expression on her face.

"This might have been a mistake," I muttered, then broke into a run, winding my way through the endless tunnels. I passed dozens of souls, young and old, and none paid me any mind.

I raced onward, the cold piercing deeper with each passing moment, and it occurred to me that I might be dying. That by coming within the hall of the dead, I'd not only secured a new fate but an inglorious one that achieved none of what I'd hoped for. That Harald would rule over all the north while I walked the dark and misty halls of Helheim until the end of days.

Faster, I ordered myself. *Run faster.*

My boots made no noise as I careened through the tunnel, dodging souls, but then my eyes latched onto the broad shoulders of a man ahead. He wore furs and mail, a sword belted at his waist and a shield gripped in his hand, nothing about him like the others that I'd passed.

A warrior.

And judging from the green and black paint on his shield, a Skalander at that.

Putting on a burst of speed, I caught hold of his arm. "Can you hear me?" I demanded, trying to drag him to a stop. "Listen!"

But he kept walking, dragging me onward as though I weighed no more than a feather.

Cursing, I hurried on to the next warrior and then the next, trying to get one of them to see me, but they all kept onward. Lost in a dream. Or in nothingness. I did not know which.

Tears froze on my cheeks, the agony of the cold turning my body sluggish. Though my shield was as light as a feather thanks to Gyda's magic, it suddenly felt as heavy as an anvil on my back.

I'd gambled, and I'd lost.

Everyone had lost.

Desperate, I flung myself at one last warrior only for Hlin's light to illuminate a familiar bearded face.

My brother's face.

He'd been in the battle on the strait.

My own flesh and blood.

And I'd killed him.

Every part of me wanted to fall to my knees and beg his forgiveness, but instead I said, "Geir? Brother, can you hear me?"

He kept walking, stepping on me without care as he carried on down the tunnel.

Fury bubbled up in my veins, Hel's magic seeming to rise with it, and I screamed, "Geir, look at me!"

My brother stopped in his tracks. Slowly, he blinked, and then his eyes focused on me. "Freya?"

"Yes, it's me!" Gripping his shoulders, I looked into his familiar amber eyes. "I'm so sorry."

"Where are we?" He took in our surroundings, alarm rising on his face. "What is this place?"

"Helheim."

Alarm turned to horror. "Helheim? Then I'm . . . we're . . ."

"Dead. At least you are. I will be soon as well, if I don't get out."

"We were fighting," he whispered. "I had my sword in my hand. What did I do to earn this fate?"

"Nothing." My chin trembled. "It's my fault. I . . . I sent you here, along with everyone else in Snorri's fleet. I have Hel's magic in my veins."

His gaze hardened. "Why? Why would you condemn your own people to this fate?"

My grip on consciousness was starting to fade, my hands and feet entirely numb. "It is a long story, brother. This is my fault, but I believe I can make things right."

"By bringing us all back to life?"

"By giving you another chance at Valhalla." I swayed, my strength starting to fail. "I think I can bring you out of Helheim. All of you. Give you a chance to fight to save Skaland and earn a place with the Allfather. But I need you to help me wake all your warriors from the dreams that hold them."

Geir's eyes narrowed as he took in the long column of warriors. Then his hands gripped mine. Hard and cold, yet I felt the connection between us. I'd sent his soul here. Which meant his soul was mine, not hers. As were the souls of every Skalander warrior I'd cursed to this place. "Halt."

They kept walking. Holding his hand tightly, I focused inward, drawing on the power in my blood as I murmured Hel's name, then I shouted, "Halt!"

All around us, the warriors drew to a halt. They blinked as though they had been woken from a dream, confusion swiftly turning to horror.

My elation that I'd woken them was short-lived. Hel had felt the stir of power in her realm, and in the distance, I heard the thud of giant feet.

"We need to go," I whispered. "Need to get back to the gates."

"You are all in Helheim," Geir roared. "If you wish another chance at Valhalla, you will follow me now!"

My knees buckled, but my brother caught me up and started running, my shield slung over his shoulder. He wove through the blank-eyed souls still walking through the tunnel, mist swirling.

My heart was faltering. Each breath was a struggle. This was a place of death, and even with Hel's blood in my veins, my mortal body could not survive here. "Hurry," I gasped. "You must hurry, Geir!"

Ahead, the golden gates gleamed through the mist.

But they were closed.

Open, I willed them, my heart leaping as a gap appeared, growing wider.

We were going to make it.

No sooner did the thought cross my mind did my heart stutter. Then cease beating entirely.

"Geir," I gasped with my last breath of air, and then my vision began to spiral into gloom as my life slipped through my grasp.

Geir leaped at the opening—

And the next thing I knew, I was sucking in desperate breaths of air next to Garmr's paws, my heart stuttering back to life in my chest.

I groaned, trying to find the strength to get to my feet. I was alive, but everything ached.

"Freya!"

I lifted my head to find Geir staring at me from beyond the gates, the rest of the Skalanders amassed behind him. "We can't get through." He flung my shield toward me, the clatter of metal against stone loud. "The gates are closing!"

And my divine mother was coming.

Staggering upright, I shouted, "I call upon the power of Hel!"

Heat roared through my veins, magic flooding my core. Hel's steps quickened as she sensed me calling on her power, but I ignored the rising sense of dread and screamed, "I am Freya Born-in-Fire, daughter of Hel and lady of death! Your souls were sent to Helheim with my magic and it is my magic that will set you free! Agree to fight with me against King Harald, child of Loki, who won the battle with trickery not honor. Fight with me for the sake of Skaland, which was brought low by Snorri's pride. Fight with me for your families, who now stand alone. Fight for me, and I will offer your souls to the Allfather to claim once we are victorious. Fight for a chance at Valhalla!"

There was no hesitation, only a deafening roar of "Born-in-Fire!" and they were flowing through the gates of Helheim in a tide of muscle and steel.

Hel's scream of wrath at my trickery was vicious and terrible. But she'd given me a drop of her blood and the magic that came with it, and short of killing me, she could not take it back.

"Run!" I screamed at the warriors. Scooping up my shield, I joined their ranks as we flowed across the bridge and down the winding path through darkness. "Climb the roots!"

The Skalanders flung themselves at Yggdrasil's black roots, many of their faces familiar, all of them dead because of me. But I'd given them another chance at glory, and all of them had taken it.

I leaped as high as I could, catching hold of one of the roots and heaving myself into the tangled web. Textured like wood and yet hard as steel, the roots were unyielding, catching and pulling at my hair and clothes as I climbed, but to pause meant death. Because beneath me, Hel was reaching into the roots.

Screams tore the air as she snatched warriors from their perches, flinging them violently into the river where they disappeared beneath the surface. I had no idea of what would become of them, and no time to question, because my mother's now-red eyes were fixed on me. "Wicked child," she screamed. "Hlin has stolen your heart from me!"

"My heart is my own," I shouted. "As is my fate."

Her massive hand reached for me, nails like talons. Taking a firm hold of a root, I unhooked my shield and, without a word, drew the power Hlin had given to me. Light burst bright across the silver metal of my shield, and Hel's corpse-blue flesh struck it.

The impact was like thunder, making Yggdrasil shudder, but Hel fell back. Fell through the roots to land with a deafening crash before the gates to her hall. I lost my grip and would have joined her, but Geir caught my arm. I dangled from his grasp, staring down at Hel, and through the roots, our eyes met, hers full of cold fury. "Nidhogg," she screamed. "Claim them!"

A hiss wove its way through the roots, the sound tickling my ears like the tongue of a viper. "Traitorous girl," it seemed to whisper. "I would taste your flesh."

I looked at my brother. "Climb, Freya," he whispered, heaving me up. "Climb!"

Terror gave me strength. Hooking the strap of my shield over my shoulder, I scrambled through the maze of roots, squeezing between gaps and shoving my way higher.

But I could hear something coming.

Something large.

Something that slithered through the dark.

Someone screamed, the sound cutting off with a tremendous crunch of teeth closing on bone. Then another scream cut off. Then another.

If I didn't do something, all the warriors I'd saved from an inglorious afterlife would be lost to something worse, and I couldn't fight what I couldn't see.

Pressing my hand to a thick root, I willed my magic onto it, sending it threading out in a web to shatter the darkness with its silver light.

Part of me wished I had not, for coiled around us was a giant serpent. Its scales were a blue so dark it seemed to swallow the light of my magic, and as it shifted its bulk, the claws on its two limbs tore away chunks of Yggdrasil's roots and sent them falling into the darkness below.

"Traitorous woman," it hissed, turning a head as large as a wagon to look at me with virulent yellow eyes, a mouth capable of swallowing me whole opening to reveal rows and rows of needle-sharp teeth. "Thieving woman."

"I am no thief," I shouted at it. "I claimed their souls. They are mine to do with what I will."

Nidhogg tilted his head, seeming to consider, then hissed, "Lies, for there is but one lady of death. Hel names you thief."

"She's the liar." I motioned at the warriors to keep climbing while I kept Nidhogg's attention. "She gifted me her blood, which means her power is mine to claim."

"Child of two bloods," he answered. "I would chew your flesh. Honorless, traitorous woman."

"You are welcome to try," I said. "Though the list of those who have tried to kill me is long and all have failed."

"I said nothing about killing," he replied, and I swore his serpentine mouth curved into a smile.

Only instinct warned me, and I managed to get my shield in my grip right before Nidhogg spat black venom. Most of it rebounded off my magic, but it sizzled and burned through the roots of Yggdrasil where it struck.

The tree groaned, and I screamed, for a few droplets had struck my leg and eaten through my trousers, my flesh burning beneath.

The serpent spat venom again, and I nearly fell trying to get my whole body behind my shield, my leg in agony. The warriors above me shouted that they'd reached the top, urging me to climb, but Nidhogg gave me no respite, circling and spraying the noxious black substance, the roots crumbling around me.

"Go!" I screamed. "Get free of this place!"

The serpent laughed, coiling tighter, breaking off pieces of root that struck me as they fell.

Think, Freya, I screamed at myself. *You have to fight!*

But what could I do against such a creature? He was a thousand times my size, a thing not of the mortal realm, and I wasn't even certain if he *could* be killed. Not even his own venom seemed to harm him, the black fluid dripping off his scales.

"I shall keep you until the end of days," the serpent hissed, coiling around me. "I shall make you scream and scream and scream!"

He spat again, and as I ducked behind my shield, I noticed his eyes were closed.

A weakness.

Hooking my shield over my shoulder, I scrambled into a thick tangle of roots, then pretended as though I could not get through and started to edge downward.

Nidhogg cackled. "Caught in a web, little traitor."

Gasps of terror escaped my lips that were not feigned as I watched him slither beneath me.

"Perhaps I will eat you after all," he hissed. "Consume the flesh and keep the soul."

Maneuvering my shield beneath me, I called Hlin's magic and then drew my sword, Gyda's runes glowing on the blade. Nidhogg spat, his venom burning through the roots of the tree and raining back down upon him. Peering around my shield, I found his eyes closed to protect them from the black rain.

Which meant he didn't see me as I dropped.

I fell through the ruin of roots toward his massive head, holding my breath to keep from screaming.

And with a meaty *thunk,* my sword, strengthened by Gyda's magic, plunged through his eyelid and into his skull.

Nidhogg shrieked in agony, flinging his head from side to side and sending me flying. I screamed, starting to fall, but hands caught me under my arms.

"I've got you," Geir shouted. "Climb!"

I desperately obeyed, my magic illuminating where the tree roots reached the earth of the mortal realm. Geir clawed his way into the earth and disappeared. But for me, it was not so easy. My fingers dug into the moist earth, rocks and debris falling around me as I climbed, digging higher.

There was no air.

I was buried alive, digging my way out of a grave, but my strength was failing. I clawed at dirt and rock and sand, trying to reach higher. Trying to find the surface and the mortal world.

My chest was in agony, eclipsing the pain of my venom-burned legs, and if I'd had the air in my lungs I would have screamed. Screamed and screamed in frustration at having gotten so close only to die in a grave of my own making.

Then skeletal fingers closed over my wrist and heaved.

My head exploded through wet sand, seaweed clinging to my hair and face, and I had a heartbeat to look upon Saga's burned face before she disappeared, leaving only embers and ash on the wind.

Rolling on my back, I spat out sand and gasped in breath after breath, staring at the sun overhead. Vaguely I was aware of cold seawater lapping at my fingers, which meant I was free of Ylva's prison, but my legs still burned from the venom.

As I pushed up onto one elbow, dismay stole away my elation at being alive, because I was still on the same *fucking* island.

Still trapped.

Still alone.

I rolled into the water so that the venom would be washed away, wincing as the salt water stung my wounds. I snatched up handfuls of sand and hurled them at the waves, screaming in rage that nearly eclipsed my pain.

I'd accomplished nothing.

Changed nothing.

Then a drumbeat reached my ears.

My head snapped up so hard my neck clicked, and I stared out over the strait, searching. Ships were sailing toward me, three large drakkar with oars plunging in and out of the waves to the beat of the drum, and their sails were green and black.

I took a step back, certain that Ylva was on one of those ships. That she'd sensed I'd escaped her wards and had returned to finish me off.

Retrieving my shield, I called my magic to it and drew my sand-crusted sword. I wouldn't go down without a fight.

Yet as the ships drew closer, I spotted motion in the waves ahead of them. Something in the water, though I could not see what through the foam and churning sand.

Then heads emerged from the water. Some helmeted, some not, seaweed clinging to armor and shields and weapons as they marched out of the sea toward me. They bore the marks of death, all a ghastly greenish-gray, many missing pieces either from the violence of war or the scavengers of the deep, but I still knew them. Recognized their faces as the souls I'd liberated from Hel, risen to reclaim their bodies to fight for one last chance at Valhalla.

They strode toward me, the drakkar closing fast manned by more of the dead, their faces grim. And their eyes glowing the virulent green of . . .

Draug.

"Shit," I whispered, knowing exactly what the undead consumed, and I was the only living human for miles around.

The Skalander draug encircled me, the men in the ships leaping out and securing their vessels before joining the masses of the dead surrounding me. Hundreds of men, most dead because of my magic, because of my curse, and fear turned my heartbeat staccato.

They began to pound weapons against shields, fists against chests, their inhuman shouts wordlessly filling the air. Then their ranks parted, a face as familiar as my own walking through them to stop before me. My brother, skin ashen, cheeks bloodless and torn, and eyes no longer amber but the virulent green of the undead.

"Freya." Geir's voice was like nails scratching over stone. "Sister."

"Geir." A sob rose in my throat, because seeing him like this made his death so very real. My niece or nephew would never know their father, Ingrid would have to struggle alone, and no amount of magic could undo that. "I'm so—"

He lifted a hand, cutting me off. "We all went into battle knowing death might be our fate, Freya, and so it has come to pass. You have offered us another chance to fight the trickster's army so that we might protect the families we left behind and earn our place in the Allfather's hall. Will you hold to the promise you made in Helheim?"

"I will hold to it." My chest was tight. "Will you fight alongside me in battle, brother?"

"No," he answered, and my heart skipped. "But I will follow you."

"I don't deserve your allegiance." I looked over all the men and women who'd died because I'd been fooled by Harald. "I'm not worthy of the honor of leading you."

"You escaped the trickster. You outwitted Hel. You defeated the serpent Nidhogg!" Geir shouted. "You have earned our respect, shield maiden, so we choose to follow you for you will weave our fates with glory and Valhalla!"

The Skalander draug pounded weapons against shields, fists against armored chests, their unnatural voices all chanting the same name.

Freya.

Skalander warriors from a dozen different clans stood dead before me, yet united as they had never been before. This was not the future I'd imagined when I'd heard Saga's prophecy, not the glory I'd envisioned, but it was a moment that had been achieved by taking my fate into my own hands. A moment that I'd woven.

Lifting my shield, which glowed fiercely with my magic, I shouted, "For all of Skaland, let us to war!"

CHAPTER 37

BJORN

"It isn't going to work," I said, watching Ylva where she sat next to Ragnar near the helm. She had wept for a time when we'd first boarded her drakkar but now sat in grim silence, eyes blank as she stared at the rolling waves of the strait. "Harald will suspect that you know his secret and kill us all. You're smarter than this, Ylva."

"Harald very likely has my son." Ylva didn't look at me as she spoke. "I will not risk his life with trickery and games. Harald will trade him for you, because you have more value. Whether he kills you or binds you, I care not. I will take Leif, and, with these men, we will sail away to make a home somewhere far enough away that we are beyond concern."

"You'd abandon Skaland to be ruled by Harald? By a child of Loki?" I asked. "You'd abandon all those in Grindill who swore allegiance to you in exchange for your protection?"

"Yes. For my son's life, I'll do what it takes." Her throat moved as she swallowed. "It was Snorri who they swore allegiance to. Snorri who they believed would protect them. Snorri is dead." She blinked once. "By *your hand*."

I needed no reminders of my actions, but I understood her need to give them. Ylva had seen what I'd done through Freya's memory. Had watched my father refuse to fight me, and how I'd cut him down anyway. I deserved her hate and all that came with it, but I felt the same toward her, because she'd abandoned my Freya to die, to freeze alone on that island. The only reason that I'd not called flame to my bound hands and lit the drakkar on fire was that I could no more swim back to the island than I could sail this vessel alone if I killed the entire crew.

Freya had both water and wits, which meant that she'd survive while I found my way out of this situation and back to her. Yet doubt was climbing in my chest that it had been an error forcing her not to call Hel's power to stop Ylva. That I'd overestimated myself and Freya would pay the price.

Except I'd seen what a burden using her magic was to her. Knew that she'd been desperate not to curse anyone else again, for it would only compound the guilt she felt. It hadn't felt necessary in the moment, because I'd been so certain that it would be nothing for me to get free.

It's only been a few hours, I reminded myself. Yet I could not help but think of Freya alone and exposed. She always got so cursedly cold, and a vision of her shivering and suffering while she fought to survive caused Tyr's fire to flare across my palm.

Enough, I silently snarled. *Impulsivity will not save her.*

"He won't let you go free," I said, shifting to alleviate the ache in my arms, my fingers losing sensation as Ragnar had bound them tight. "If Harald has claimed Grindill and taken Leif prisoner, he will be keeping him alive for a reason. He knows that you'll come for your son and, in doing so, walk right into his trap. In one swoop, he'll destroy the last link holding the Skalander jarls together and name himself king. Be smarter."

A tear trickled down Ylva's face.

"You're going to get my brother killed," I shouted at her, the fragile hold I had over my temper evaporating. "You are allowing grief to make decisions for you, and they are the wrong ones. Snorri is dead. I killed him. Neither of us can escape that truth, but wallowing in it helps no one."

"Be silent!" Ragnar roared, and I gritted my teeth as he kicked me hard in the ribs, adding to the multitude of bruises he'd already delivered upon me. He'd been loyal to my father, and though he'd not seen what Ylva had seen, his grief still weighed heavy.

"You know I'm right," I shouted back at him. "You are supposed to advise and support Ylva in all things, yet you let her sail to certain death!"

"What would you have me do, Bjorn?" Ylva leaped to her feet, nearly falling as the ship hit a swell. "What solution do you offer?"

"Fight him! Turn around and release Freya from that prison and we can defeat him!"

"You would have me release death upon the world?" Ylva scoffed in disgust. "Of course that is the solution you offer. Freya has controlled your mind through your cock since the moment you set eyes on her. She killed hundreds of warriors. Worse than killed, for she condemned their souls to Helheim when they might have joined the Allfather's ranks to fight in the glorious last battle. Freya is a *monster*. A curse upon the world who should not be suffered to live."

It had been Freya's magic that had killed them, but it was me who'd forced her to do it. Yet I did not think Ylva would be swayed by that fact. "She is not a monster! Harald tricked her, so the deaths of all are on his hands, yet you care not for punishing him."

"Freya is the daughter of the goddess of death! She is a Hel-child!"

"But also Hlin's!" Fire again filled my palm, but I forced thought of Tyr's name out of my head and it faded. "Harald fears her, that is why he wanted her dead. If he thought there was a way to control her, he would have kept up his deception, tried to bind her in other ways. You have condemned the one person who can defeat him, the one person you know has more cause than any to destroy him, because you are afraid."

Ylva waved a hand, dismissing my words. "Your arguments hold no weight, Bjorn, for I know that you argue only out of a desire to save your lover's life."

"That I argue for her life does not mean that I'm wrong!"

"Gag him, Ragnar," Ylva said. "I no longer wish to listen to this honorless creature bargain for death's life."

"You're a coward!" I snarled. "You condemn Skaland out of fear, not wisdom."

Ragnar shoved a filthy piece of fabric in my mouth, binding it with another strip around my head so that I couldn't spit it out. Not that it mattered. I could scream all the warnings, all the logic in the world, and they would not hear me. Because they believed that the only thing I cared about was Freya.

And they were right.

There was nothing that mattered to me more than her. Nothing I wouldn't do to see her freed. But I also knew that Ylva was wrong, because I knew Freya's heart. In all my life I'd never met anyone who cared so much for the well-being of others, usually to her own detriment, and hearing her named *monster* for it made me seethe. Made me want to show Ylva what real monstrosity looked like.

Burn the ropes, my rage screamed. *Kill them all!*

I could do it. When the ropes caught fire, they'd burn my flesh but I'd fought through worse pain. There were thirty warriors on this drakkar, but if I was quick, I could kill enough of them that the others would capitulate and turn the ship around. I silently calculated the number I'd need to leave alive to sail the vessel.

"My lady!" a voice called. "Torne is in sight! Two of Harald's ships are at the docks."

Only two?

I shoved away the thought, because if the village was in sight, the ship was close enough to shore that I could swim. All I'd have to do was escape into the forest, then steal a fishing vessel once darkness fell. Then I could make my way back to her.

Hold on, I silently willed Freya. *I'll come for you.*

"Run up a white cloth so that they know we come to treat," Ylva ordered.

Ragnar moved to obey her command and with him distracted, I whispered Tyr's name. My axe flared to life in my right hand. The axe itself didn't burn, but as I rotated to press it against the ropes, natural fire took hold. Agony lanced across my wrists and forearms as the ropes burned, the metal of my chain mail heating against my back.

I kept my eyes on Ylva, who was staring at the village.

Come on, I willed the fire even as I strained against the burning ropes. *Burn.*

Ylva's nostrils abruptly flared, and her focus snapped to me. "Ragnar!"

I jerked my arms, blackened ropes falling against the hull. I rolled to my feet and ripped my mail vest over my head. Ragnar leaped at me, axe in hand, but I threw the mail. The heavy vest slammed into his face and knocked him back, giving me the space I needed.

Stepping onto a bench, I put a foot on the edge of the drakkar between two shields. The village was close, warriors running about on the docks, but my eyes were all for the stretch of empty beach.

I sucked in a breath, ready to dive, but then agony stabbed through my shoulder. A green brand, familiar and horrible, was spiked through my right shoulder. Slowly, I lifted my head to see Skade standing at the end of a dock. A smile formed on her face as she nocked the brand that had disappeared from my shoulder and was once again in her hands.

She loosed her arrow, eyes promising pain.

"Tyr," I gasped, blood sluicing down my arm as my axe appeared in my palm. But I couldn't lift it, my ruined shoulder muscles refusing to obey.

Pain lanced through my wrist, then thigh, Skade's shot pinning my arm to my leg. My hand opened, axe falling to hiss against the water, glowing as it sank.

I swayed, then fell backward.

My back struck a bench, bouncing me sideways. Rolling, I got to my feet in time for Ragnar's weight to slam against me. Not just him, but all the warriors in the ship who'd abandoned their oars to pin me down.

"Don't kill him," Ylva shouted. "He's no good to us if he's dead!"

And if Skade had wanted me dead, I would be.

I thrashed and fought, cries of pain filling my ears as I took up my axe in my left hand, the blade cutting. The fire burning.

But there were too many, and with each gush of blood that poured from my shoulder, my strength lessened.

As they restrained me, regret pooled in my chest. I should have tried to escape earlier. Should have killed them all and found a way to sail by myself. Should have tried to *fucking* swim back to her, because then at least there would have been a chance.

For now all chance was lost.

The Skalanders bound me with more rope, the rough fibers rubbing raw my burned arms, and then held me face down in the water pooled in the hull. Ylva bound the wound in my shoulder with strips of cloth while shouting at her warriors to hurry. "We can't trade him if he's dead!"

The world swam in and out of focus as the drakkar bumped against the dock.

"We've come to treat!" Ylva shouted. "To negotiate a trade with Harald. Bjorn for my son, Leif!"

"What makes you think that Leif is alive?" Skade answered, and Ylva gave a soft sob.

Skade laughed. "I jest. Your son is alive and well, Ylva."

A heartbeat later, I heard the heavy thud of someone jumping into the ship near my head. "A trade, you say. That's destined to be an interesting conversation, all things considered."

Then hot breath brushed my ear as Skade whispered, "Your capacity to survive never ceases to amaze, Bjorn. But I think you will regret not dying on that island with the Hel-child."

The gag kept me from any retort, but I turned my head to meet

Skade's gaze, and with it, I promised her death. She only smiled and straightened. "Leif is safe in the fortress. I will escort you to him, Ylva. The king is most eager to see you, of that I am certain."

It's a trick, I screamed around the gag, but everyone ignored me except Ragnar, who hauled me to my feet.

"Bring your full guard," Skade said. "We are all friends here."

What is going on?

I stopped fighting Ragnar in favor of looking around Torne. The salty sea breeze carried the stink of fish and seaweed between the wooden huts with thatched roofs. Fishermen unloaded their catches while seagulls shrieked overhead, the gulls nearly drowned out by a strapping woman shouting at every person who walked by to look at the wares in her cart.

It felt profoundly unchanged, and though it was possible that the people cared not who they swore fealty to or paid tithes to, my hackles rose with the sense that something was very wrong.

On Skade's orders, they wrapped chains around my hands to keep me from calling my axe, and then a wagon was brought over. Ragnar shoved me inside and then climbed in next to me, sword tip digging into my balls. "Try anything, traitor, and I'll unman you."

A dozen possible ways to indicate my indifference to his threat reared in my head, but the distance to Grindill was the last chance I had to convince him that this was folly before we reached the confines of the fortress.

The cart rocked from side to side as the horse started walking, accompanied by the heavy footfalls of the Skalanders flanking either side of the cart. Through the slats, Ylva was visible, her mouth drawn in a tight line, whereas Skade was smiling and gesturing as though she hadn't a care in the world.

Ragnar shifted, the tip of his sword digging painfully into my balls, but when I turned my head it was to find him staring back at Torne, his brown skin creased from his heavy frown. He felt it too.

The wrongness.

The cart hit a bump and I groaned around the gag. Blood was pooling from the wounds Skade had given me, my wrists and forearms already blistering from the burns I'd inflicted upon myself. Survivable, yes, but surviving wasn't enough. I had to get back to Freya.

Or someone else had to for me.

I rubbed my cheek against the wood of the cart and pulled down the strip of fabric holding my gag in place.

The sword dug deeper, but I spat the fabric out even as I met Ragnar's gaze. "Something's not right," I said softly. "I know Snorri didn't leave Grindill entirely unmanned, yet somehow Harald has managed to take both Torne and Grindill with no fight?"

Ragnar's jaw worked back and forth beneath his silvered beard, warring with his dislike for me and his knowledge that I was right. "Might be they surrendered. Leif would have known they could not win in a fight."

"Those who have surrendered have a way about them, Ragnar. You know that. Men and women who are waiting to see what the consequences of capitulation will be. Did the people in Torne look like that to you?"

Skade's head turned to look at the wagon, frowning, and I fell silent.

We pressed closer to Grindill, the breathing of the men and women walking alongside the wagon growing heavier as they climbed the steepening slope.

"This will not go as Ylva plans," I whispered. "Harald will not let you all walk away with what you know, because it puts every scheme of his at risk. Someone who knows the truth needs to stay free of this. Needs to stay alive."

"I suppose you volunteer yourself?"

I shook my head. "Not with these injuries. It needs to be you."

"I'm not leaving Lady Ylva."

"You cannot help her if you are dead," I hissed. "Sneak away. Spread the truth and get aid. That is how you can help her."

"You mean Freya?" He shook his head. "She's probably already frozen to death. Let it go, Bjorn."

My chest clenched painfully, every part of my soul rejecting the notion that Freya was lost to me. I'd know. I'd feel it. And my heart screamed that my Born-in-Fire warred on. "She's not dead."

Exhaling an irritated breath, Ragnar moved his sword from my balls, then stood, his eyes on the fortress that would be visible ahead. Taking in the scene. The man was twenty years my senior, born and bred to fight. He knew Ylva was making a mistake—it was a matter of whether he'd go against her to save her.

"Skade!" he abruptly called out. "He's half dead but needs someone to watch him while I piss. Get up here, would you?"

Skade shrugged, then moved to the back of the wagon and jumped in, Ragnar leaping out and heading into the trees.

Her arrow appeared in one hand, glowing green and malevolent, and Skade began to prune her nails with the tip. "I told him to let me go back and make sure you were dead," she said. "Not like him to leave loose ends. Ylva said Freya was alive when she left, but trapped. After he kills you, I hope he lets me go put an end to the bitch."

Instead of rising to her bait, I tilted my head. "You know what he is, don't you? A child of Loki."

She grinned, eyes feral. "I've always known. Harald trusts me. Knows that I'll do what needs doing and keep my mouth shut. Ground my nerves all those years that he pretended you were his favorite, but I've always known the truth. I'm his daughter. I'm his heir. I'm his blood. You were only ever something for us to use."

"What has he promised you?"

"Power." Skade tapped her arrow against her palm. "Wealth. Status. And when he sees you, I hope he will give me the pleasure of your death."

"And Ylva's?"

Skade shook her head. "Oh, Ylva he wants alive. Needs her alive, if I'm being truthful."

I narrowed my eyes.

She grinned. "If you're lucky, you'll have a heartbeat to appreciate the beauty of his plan before you die." Standing, she leaned over me, forcing the gag back in my mouth. "Not many heartbeats left for you, I'm afraid. We're here."

The cart trundled through the gates. A cheer rose at the sight of Ylva, for many who lived in Grindill were originally from Halsar. The horse stopped, and Skade leaned forward to grab my bound wrists. "Get up. The king awaits."

My knees threatened to buckle, but I managed to keep my feet as she dragged me out. The Skalanders scowled at the sight of me, several shouting, "Traitor!" as I was dragged into the great hall. All of Ylva's warriors flanked her as she walked inside, but I noted that Ragnar was nowhere in sight. Shoving me forward so that I landed on my knees, Skade then turned to put a beam in place to lock the door. "The king will be here shortly." She took Ylva's arm, leading her onto the dais and seating her on one of the fur-covered chairs.

What is going on?

Ylva shifted uneasily, her eyes flicking briefly to mine. "Skade, where is my son?"

"With the king." Skade grinned, eyes bright with delight and a hint of madness. She cupped a hand to her ear. "I believe I hear them coming."

Leif's familiar laugh rang out from the rear of the building, then my brother appeared. He wasn't alone. For walking with a muscled arm slung around Leif's skinny shoulder, hale and healthy as I'd ever seen him, was Snorri.

CHAPTER 38

FREYA

The drakkar skipped over the white-capped waves, the wind filling the sails so strong I swore the gods themselves were urging us on. The vessels were full of undead warriors, their numbers fierce and terrifying.

As, unfortunately, was the smell.

Geir stood next to me at the helm, and though his mind and spirit were as they always had been, the same could not be said of his body, which appeared more rotted by the hour. From battling the draug in the tunnels below Fjalltindr, I knew that it would have no impact on his strength, but it was unpleasant.

"So, you know nothing of Harald's plan?" my brother asked, brushing a piece of blond hair back from his face. It broke loose from his scalp, flying away on the breeze, and I struggled not to gag.

"I believed we were defending Nordeland against Snorri's invasion," I replied. "That we aimed to defeat him, and that would be the extent of things. Harald's plans to defeat him and then force all of Skaland to bend the knee to him as king were hidden from me." The last came out with more sarcasm than I'd intended.

Geir snorted, not the first time I'd seen him clinging to the behaviors of the living. Like breathing. "And on the assumption Grindill has already fallen to Harald, Ylva aims to trade Bjorn for Leif?"

I nodded; it was not lost on me that Ylva had a head start. Bjorn was far from helpless, but Ylva and her warriors were familiar with his magic and would not underestimate him. What if she'd arranged the exchange already? What if Harald had Bjorn? My hands started to shake, because if he was . . .

I refused to allow myself to finish that thought. Refused to imagine life without Bjorn. Besides, it made more sense that Harald would attempt to bind Bjorn the same way he had Tora. Death was final, whereas a life like Tora's gave Harald infinite possibilities for amusement. And as long as Bjorn was alive, there was hope.

"Freya?"

I twitched, realizing that I'd been silent too long. "I think Harald will agree to the trade, but it won't save Leif in the long run. Harald will assume that Bjorn has told Ylva about him being a child of Loki, and he'll not suffer anyone he believes knows the truth to roam free. He'll either bind them or kill them."

"Honorless trickster," Geir hissed, the sound making me wince.

"Yes, but knowing that he is so gives us an idea of what he'll do," I said. "I don't think he will default to force and violence to make people bend the knee. He will use guile." Frowning at the waves, I added, "It's a game to him, Geir. Just like in the stories of Loki himself, Harald wants to manipulate others, trick them, pull strings to make them do things they otherwise would not. It isn't having power that gives him pleasure but the process of gaining it. Violence will only come if his back is against the wall or someone angers him. Or when he grows bored."

"We will not give him a choice," Geir answered. "We will find him and fall upon him like a plague, for we cannot be harmed by the weapons of mortal men."

"But he's surrounded by Unfated who serve him faithfully," I reminded him, regretting having told him about his newfound invincibility. My brother's vaingloriousness had not been reduced by death. Quite the opposite. "If you are struck by Skade's arrows or Tora's lightning, it will be your end."

My brother didn't answer, but I saw more than a few of the Skalander undead turn their heads, my words having reached their ears.

"We have to be clever," I said. "The Nordelanders, they do not know the nature of the man they serve, and I do not wish to see a field of their dead left in our wake in order to reach Harald. We must find a way to reveal the truth to the Unfated who serve him, for without their support, I think he will run rather than stand his ground."

"You've an idea of how to achieve this? They've no reason to believe you, especially if he denies your accusations."

Ylva had told me that the runic magic to capture memory would only work once, and I'd used it for her, so that method was lost to me. "Steinunn." The idea had been forming in my head for some time. "I'll recount what happened on the island, and she will sing it. All who hear will see Harald's change from Saga's form to his own. Hear his trickery from his own mouth."

"You assume they will care," Geir said. "Harald has made their lives good off the bounty taken in raids. His trickery has been to their benefit."

I chewed the insides of my cheeks, then shook my head. "I met many of his cabal of Unfated in my time in Nordeland, and they are for the most part good people. I cannot believe they'd choose to serve a child of Loki."

"Perhaps." Geir shrugged. "The question is, how will you prove this speculation? The moment Harald realizes you are alive and have escaped, all his efforts will be to silence you, and we"—he gestured at all of the warriors—"are bound to you. We exist in this realm because we swore to serve you. I believe our souls will leave our bodies if you die, and Harald will be once again victorious. No doubt he will reward his Unfated handsomely for their loyalty. In their minds, the only people he has tricked are you and Bjorn. Why should they care?"

The coast of Skaland was growing on the horizon, but rather than filling me with elation, I only felt rising unease because I'd thought showing Harald's Unfated what had happened would be enough. That I'd be able to win this without a catastrophic loss of life, because my hands were already red with blood.

"It is better to fight," Geir said. "Kill Harald and all those who are loyal to him. A clean victory, and Skaland will be safe. You have an army of the undead, and we have you to shield us from the Unfated. You will be victorious."

There was logic to what my brother said. It was the way these wars had always been won in the past, but it didn't feel right given that I knew that all of Harald's army was deceived. It wouldn't be glorious victory but murderous slaughter. Though I knew the prophecy of my leaving a field of dead in my wake was Harald's fabrication, not Saga's vision, to walk the path my brother suggested would make it reality.

Changing the subject for no other reason than because I needed to tamp down the rising sourness in my stomach, I asked, "Where is Ingrid? Is she well?"

"Selvegr. She's well, or was when I set sail. She is certain our child is a son."

I gave a tight nod, and I wondered if it had sunk into my brother's soul that he would never go home. That he'd never see his family again.

Silence stretched, then Geir said, "It was a deception, that moment in Grindill when Ragnar held a blade to my neck. Ingrid was never threatened. It was a ruse to try to make you keep fighting for Snorri. Part of the deal I made with him to regain my place. I'm sorry for it, Freya. And not just for that, but for all the other moments that I stood on your back to achieve something for myself."

My eyes prickled with tears. "I'm sorry for killing you."

Geir laughed, and though the sound of it was strange and horrible, my heart felt stronger at hearing it. "Then let us both be grateful for a last opportunity to do right by each other."

We stood in comfortable silence as the coast grew ahead of us, familiar mountains and fjords, though there was no sign of Harald's fleet or Ylva's ship. In my periphery, I saw a flash of movement in the sky, and then a merlin landed on the bow of the drakkar.

"Kaja," I breathed, grief pooling in my stomach because I could only imagine what a blow Guthrum's loss was to her.

Geir was staring at me, and I explained. "She is . . . *was* the familiar of one of Harald's Unfated. He went overboard in the battle. Guthrum was a good man." *Mostly* good, at any rate.

Kaja abruptly flew right at me.

Cursing, I ducked sideways. She flew away from the ship and then circled back around, flying at me again. Geir swatted at her, but I caught hold of his arm. "No! Look!"

He followed my pointing finger to a tangle of driftwood in the distance.

"She's trying to lead us to that driftwood. Change course."

Geir gave the order, and the helmsman changed direction even as others worked to lower the sail to slow our speed. As we drew closer, I picked out the shape of a man sprawled over the branches of the dead tree.

"Guthrum!" I shouted. "Guthrum, can you hear me?"

The man didn't move. Whether that was because he was dead or unconscious, it was impossible to tell. Kaja flew circles above him, though, and she was unlikely to do that for anyone but her familiar.

"Guthrum!"

The swells from the drakkar rolled into the driftwood, and I sucked in a panicked breath as Guthrum slipped off the branches and under the swells. Unbelting my sword, I lifted my chain mail over my head and shoved it into Geir's hands before diving into the sea.

Icy water closed over my head, but I ignored the sting against the venom burns on my legs and swam down to Guthrum, who floated limply below the surface. I hooked my arms under his and then kicked hard. My chest ached with the need for air, but I managed to get him to the surface, where Geir caught hold of Guthrum and hauled him in. Other of the draug did the same to me, and I toppled unceremoniously at their feet. "Is he alive?"

"Barely." Geir pulled a spare length of canvas around Guthrum's body, which was drained of color. "Looks like he's been in the water this entire time. It's amazing he's alive."

"He's strong." Retrieving a skin of water, I sat next to Guthrum and supported his head, trickling a small amount into his mouth. He swallowed, then coughed, and his eyes opened. "Freya?"

"Yes, it's me."

But before I'd finished saying those few short words, his eyes rolled back in his head and Guthrum was unconscious once more. I sighed and tucked the sail cloth more tightly around his body, my own wracked with shivers as I got to my feet.

"He is part of Harald's cabal?" Geir slung an arm around my shoulders, but he was no warmer than the sea and I wriggled free.

"Yes. Harald rescued him from bad circumstances as a boy. He's loyal."

"Then if he lives, he'll be the first test to see if the truth will shift those loyalties." He gave my hand a squeeze. "If not, you will have to make a difficult choice, sister."

"I'm not killing Guthrum." I pulled out of his grip. "I'll tie him up until this is over, if I have to, but I'm not killing him."

My brother shrugged, clearly of the opinion that my thoughts on the matter would change. But I'd had enough of killing, and the only death I sought now was Harald's. We stood in silence as the coast drew closer, though there was still no sign of Harald's fleet.

"You said Harald took Snorri's body," Geir abruptly said. "Do you know why?"

"Proof he's dead, I suppose. Proof that Bjorn was the one who killed him, because his axe leaves a distinct wound." Memory filled my head of the meaty *thunk* that the axe had made, the sizzle of blood and flesh, and the smell . . . "Whatever his reason, it won't be good."

The ships drew closer to the sandy beach and I took in the coast of Skaland, noting that the tree leaves were beginning to change into fall. Reds, oranges, and yellows mixed with the greens of the pines, and a sudden sense of yearning filled my core. Sails lowered in favor of oars as we entered the shallower water. The draug drummer pounded a steady beat and my heart seemed to take up its rhythm until the ship in which I stood ran up onto the beach.

Leaping out, I took up a handful of wet sand, water running through my fingers as I took my first steps back in Skaland.

Control your fate.

Taking a breath, I turned to my army. Undead, yes, but every one of them a Skalander. "This is our home," I said. "Our land. Our families. And though they may not know it, they are in danger. We must discover what we can about the trickster's plans so that we might make one of our own to defeat him."

My brother and one of the other draug had lifted the still-unconscious Guthrum out of the ship and were carrying him up the beach to where another was lighting a small fire. I followed after them, watching Kaja circle overhead and hoping that warmth and sustenance would bring him back to consciousness. But more than that, I prayed to the gods that Guthrum would hear me out. Would believe me. Because I very much needed someone among the living on my side.

And so much the better if that person was unfated.

Geir set to organizing the draug to scout and see what information they might learn, though it was not lost on anyone that the living would likely take one look at them and go running the other direction. We needed a better source of information.

I added more wood to the fire and then lifted Guthrum so that he was resting on my lap. Carefully, I gave him more water. Tiny sips so that he wouldn't choke while I waited for the heat to warm his body. He was ghastly pale, and with his wild hair and beard, he appeared as dead as any of the draug. Yet his chest rose and fell with steady breaths, and his pulse felt strong beneath my fingertips.

Kaja landed on a piece of driftwood near us, yellow eyes fixed on her familiar. "Can you rouse him?" I asked her. "He needs to be awake to drink and to eat, else he'll only weaken further."

The bird's head tilted, yellow eyes regarding me, and then she flew to land on Guthrum's chest and began pulling out hairs from his beard.

"Stop that!" I shoved her away, but as I did, Guthrum stirred and opened his eyes. It took a moment for him to focus, but then he said, "Freya?"

"Yes. Can you drink?"

He nodded and I propped him up more while he guzzled down several more mouthfuls of water. Then with a sigh, he passed out in my arms again.

"Fuck!" I shouted, knowing that it wasn't fair for me to put demands on a man who stood on the brink of death, but Guthrum and Kaja were an asset I desperately needed. They could discover what Harald was up to and where Bjorn was, and it felt like every moment that he slept reduced the chances of me rescuing Bjorn alive.

I lowered Guthrum to the ground and tucked the sail cloth around him. Kaja hopped down on his chest, watching me with her uncanny eyes that saw more than any animal should.

Exhaustion weighed upon my heart as I made my way over to Geir. "Any luck?"

"He roused for a bit." I scuffed my shoe in the sand of the beach, my eyes on the drakkar that formed my tiny fleet. "I'm afraid, Geir. What if Ylva has already traded Bjorn for Leif? What if Harald has—"

"Don't think it." My brother rested a comforting hand on my shoulder. "Harald is clever. He won't kill Bjorn out of hand if he thinks that you still live. He knows Bjorn can be used against you, so trust in that, if nothing else. I have warriors ranging up the coast who will listen for information, but hopefully with warmth and rest, this Guthrum will rouse enough to aid your cause."

"I don't think it will be so easy. He's loyal to Harald, and even when presented with the truth, I am not certain he can be convinced to go against him. Guthrum has a . . . certain respect for monsters." Rubbing my hands up and down my chilled arms, I turned to go back to the fire.

Only to freeze.

Because Guthrum was gone.

CHAPTER 39

BJORN

Snorri stood before me. But not my sire, because I'd watched Snorri die from injuries that I'd given him.

Harald.

"Mother!" Leif bolted forward to fling his arms around Ylva, whose face had blanched an awful shade of gray as she stared at the man masquerading as her husband.

"What possessed you to venture onto the strait? Father and I have been in a panic that you were lost at sea. That perhaps you'd been caught in the Hel-child's curse," Leif said. "The relief I felt when news came that your drakkar had been spotted..." He exhaled a shaky breath. "I'm so happy you are safe."

"I'm fine," she whispered. "Quite fine."

"I told you she'd be fine," Harald said in perfect mimicry of my father's voice. "Njord himself wouldn't dare get in your mother's way. Though I see she has brought us a prize."

Skade shoved me forward.

Leif's head turned, seeing me for the first time. "Traitor!" He reached for the sword belted at his waist, but Harald-as-Snorri caught hold of his arm.

"Your brother is my problem, Leif. His betrayal will be punished in due course." He gave Leif a push toward the rear door. "Go now. Spread the word that the traitor has been caught."

"Ragnar, go with—" Ylva's shaky voice broke off as she scanned the stunned warriors in the room and found the man missing.

I cursed silently as Skade scowled, finally realizing that Ragnar had slipped away. I'd hoped he'd have a longer head start.

Leif hesitated, then obeyed, but as he walked past me, he spat in my face. "You are no brother of mine. You're a traitor. A slave to the Hel-child's will. The blood eagle is what you deserve."

I flinched. There was no question that I deserved his ire, but it still cut like a knife.

"Leif, go," Harald-as-Snorri said wearily. "You must stand in for me while I deal with this ugly matter."

My brother stormed to the rear door, passing Tora as he left.

Her eyes widened in shock at the sight of me, but Harald-as-Snorri said, "Tora, if you'd make sure the rear door is secure. This is not a conversation I wish overheard."

Tora obeyed without hesitation, but I didn't miss the flicker of hatred in her eyes. It made me question whether I'd been oblivious for years that this tension sat between them or if the conflict was new. A question I might never get an answer to, but what I did know was that if there was a way to break the control Harald had on Tora, she'd be an ally. And a dangerous one at that.

Ylva was shaking. Lifting a finger to point at Harald, she cried, "You are not my husband, child of Loki! You are a trickster!"

Harald-as-Snorri sighed. "This is what I get for leaving loose ends."

"Kill him!" Ylva shrieked, and the Skalander warriors unsheathed their weapons. But Harald-as-Snorri only waved a hand and said, "Skade, deal with this, please."

Bound, bleeding, and gagged, there was nothing I could do as

Skade's bow appeared in her hands, the green brand spiraling in loops and arcs around the room, punching through throats in rapid succession until every one of the warriors was on the ground gasping. Dying.

Harald-as-Snorri had clapped his hand over Ylva's mouth to silence her screams. When Skade's arrow had finished its bloody business, he moved his mouth close to her ear. "Behave or I will gut Leif in front of you. Am I understood?"

She gave a tight nod, and he kissed her cheek before letting go of her. Ylva staggered, gagging once before regaining her composure. Harald-as-Snorri walked away from her. Just as before, his skin seemed to move like softening wax, shifting in shape and color, until he was Harald once more.

Motion caught my eye. Skoll and Hati rose from where they'd sat in the shadows, moving to Harald's side. He stroked their fur, tracing a finger over the markings painted onto their heads that ensured their loyalty.

"This is why killing people is rarely the best solution." He gestured to the bodies. "It's always such a mess to clean up. Tora, think of a solution that makes this disappear."

"There are drains for waste that lead into the river," Tora said. "The bodies will be unrecognizable after they go over the falls, and what is left will go to the sea."

"See it done," Harald ordered. "Then clean up the blood. I wish it to be as though they were never here."

"Most have families in Grindill." Ylva stared at the faces of the warriors that she'd brought to their deaths. "There will be questions."

"For which you will provide answers that steer them away from suspicion." Harald stroked Hati's head, again tracing the markings painted on the wolf's fur. It was a nervous tic of his that belied his feigned composure. "Deceit, darling Ylva, is how you will earn your keep and ensure Leif's continued longevity. By being the lady of Grindill, the wife of the king, the queen that all of Skaland trusts without question. You will keep Snorri's rule alive."

"Your rule, you mean," Ylva whispered, her gaze tracking Tora as she carried the bodies of the fallen to the drains.

Harald let out the strange giggle he'd used on the island, then clapped a hand over his mouth. "Well, yes. Though all of Skaland will believe that Snorri and Harald have formed an alliance. Enemies who are friends again after slaying the Hel-child, who cursed Skaland's warriors, murdered Saga, and then turned her sights on the warriors of Nordeland. If only we'd united sooner, your warriors might all still live." He smirked.

My jaw clenched because there was no easy way to prove his lies, given that everyone who had witnessed what had really happened was dead. Harald's gaze drifted to me. "Though I see we may have a problem with the latter part of my narrative. Tell me, is Freya alive?"

"I was told she remained imprisoned where you left her," Skade said when Ylva didn't answer. "I would happily travel there and put an end to her, Father. My arrow doesn't miss."

"No, it doesn't," Harald agreed. "Though the same cannot be said for your eyes. Where is this Ragnar?"

Skade's cheeks colored. "Said he needed to piss. He's likely in Grindill, somewhere."

"Is *likely* good enough given that Ragnar knows where the Hel-child is imprisoned, among other things?" The last came out in a vicious snarl, and I bit down on the gag as Harald backhanded Skade with enough force that she sprawled across the floor.

"Where is your man Ragnar?" he then demanded of Ylva. "What orders did you give him?"

"I know not," she answered. "It wasn't under my order that he departed."

Seeing violence rising in Harald, I coughed around my gag and Harald turned his glare on me. Closing the distance between us, he wrenched the gag out of my mouth. Then he backhanded me. "Where is he?"

"Go fuck yourself." I spat on the floor before him.

Reaching down, Harald unraveled the bandage around my shoulder, then shoved his fingers into the hole left by Skade's arrow. I bit down on a scream even as the world around me spun with pain and stars, and when they cleared, I was sideways on the floor.

"You are predictable, Bjorn." Harald loomed over me. "Your loyalty to those who earn your affection makes you so, just as it makes you easy to manipulate. There is only one place you would have sent Ragnar, and that is to liberate your lover."

He turned away, and I started to laugh, spitting out blood as I did. "I told him to spread the word, child of Loki. To whisper into the ear of every person he sees that Snorri is dead and that it is Harald of Nordeland who wears his face. I told him to seek out the village gossips, the fishwives, and orphans who trade in information. To buy a cup of mead for every foreign merchant or sailor he meets and tell the tale of the king who wears faces and trades in lies and deception. Harald, king of tricksters, king of lies, and soon, I wager, king of nothing."

A desperate lie, but I wanted them to search everywhere but the island where I'd left Freya. Ragnar was her only chance.

"He's spinning tales," Skade spat. "He'd not sacrifice his only chance to save Freya. Send me after her, Father, and I will lay a trap for Ragnar."

"Ragnar would not free Freya," Ylva said, and I wasn't sure if she believed that or if she was trying to buy her warrior time to escape. "He knows what a danger she poses to us all."

"Born-in-Fire *is* very dangerous." I dragged my legs under me, managing to get upright even though blood was running fresh down my chest and back. "And she has grown to be very cunning. Do you really think the daughter of death is so easily defeated, trickster? You should have killed her when you had the chance."

"I tied the wards to Freya's life," Ylva said. "They will hold until she breathes her last. My wards are good—that monster will never walk free."

I scoffed at her. "You think death will stop Hel's daughter from having vengeance?"

My words were bluster, yet the entire hall fell entirely silent.

"Oh, gods." Ylva lifted a hand to her mouth in horror that I was fairly confident was feigned, for she was not a woman easily shaken.

"What?" Harald demanded. "Spit out your concerns, woman."

"Runic magic only holds power over the living. If Freya dies, the wards will not hold her."

"Are you suggesting Freya might be loose?" Harald demanded. "That she's dead . . . yet living? An unfated draug? Or something else?"

"I don't know!" Tears rolled down Ylva's face. "I do not know the extent of the powers Hel has granted her. You know more of her magic than I do. Do you believe she might have escaped?"

Harald's fingers twitched, and though his face was a blank mask, I could feel the tension seething out of him as he weighed which threat was greater: stopping Ragnar from spreading his secret or ensuring that Freya was no longer a threat.

"You will hunt Ragnar down," he finally snapped at Skade. "Silence him, and then sail to the island and kill the Hel-child, then burn the corpse. Take Skoll and Hati, and go!"

"Yes, Father," Skade whispered, wiping blood from her split lip and hurrying past Tora, who didn't hide her smile at seeing the other woman brought low. Harald noted it as well, his glower deepening, and he snapped, "Ensure the door is secured behind her else you'll have more bodies to dispose of."

"Yes, my king." Tora heaved a corpse over her shoulder and followed after Skade and the wolves, leaving bloody footprints in her wake. Harald glared at the mess in frustration.

Ragnar, for all his skills, was a dead man, because Skade always caught her quarry. But he'd bought Freya more time. More than that, he'd revealed that Harald was not in control, his plans coming apart at the seams. The secret he'd kept his whole life, on which hung every one of his schemes, was loose in the world. If I knew anything, it was that nothing infuriated him more than losing control.

"I think your ambition has stretched beyond your skill, *Father*," I said. "It's one thing to keep up the pretense of the life of a reclusive woman no one ever sees, quite another to keep up the pretense of the life of a king. I see your plans fraying like a poorly made tapestry, and with it your control over your own fate."

He backhanded me, but I just spat blood and laughed. "You spent too much time in my mother's form, Harald. You hit like an old woman."

Harald drew the knife belted at his waist. "You have outlived your usefulness. Just as your mother did." His smile was vicious. "I still remember how she screamed as she burned in the fire of your making. It was not quick. But I've learned my lesson about indulging in the pleasure of slow deaths."

I had not known it possible to hate someone as much as I hated him, and it drowned out any fear I might have for my own life.

Harald lifted his knife. "Give my regards to your mother when you reach Helheim."

Ylva caught his wrist. "Wait. He is still useful."

Harald turned his head, listening.

"If the Hel-child has escaped," Ylva said, "we must catch her and kill her. Use Bjorn as bait, Harald, for Freya will surely come for him."

"I distrust your wisdom, Ylva." Harald crossed his arms. "And feel inclined to do the opposite."

Tora came back into the hall, bending to collect another body. Though no one paid her any attention, I knew that she was listening to everything that was being said.

"Bjorn killed my husband." A tear trickled down Ylva's cheek. "Killed him in cold blood. There is no one who wishes him dead more than I do, but not at the cost of my son. All things that I do are for Leif's well-being, which means I must set aside matters of the heart in favor of cold logic. To rule Skaland, you need me. To keep me, Leif must be well. Knowing this, I believe that your success will be my son's success. And," she swallowed hard, "if Freya has escaped through means other than death, Leif has the capacity to control her. She is bound to serve his blood."

My jaw clenched, because even with Snorri dead the burden of those oaths remained on Freya's shoulders.

Rather than appeasing him, Harald turned on Ylva, pressing the knife to her throat. "Understand this, woman. If you try to cross me in any way, your son will die. Die badly, die slowly, and I assure you, there will be no honor in it. Do you understand?"

"Yes, my lord." Ylva inclined her head. "I suggest you make a spectacle of Bjorn's death. A traitor's death, for all those his actions harmed to witness. If Freya is free, she will aim to rescue him and we will catch her. We need a few days to set our trap, but also to ensure Bjorn is strong enough to endure the worst of tortures."

Ylva was buying me time. Freya time. Not because she'd forgiven what I'd done to Snorri, but because she had realized that Freya was our best chance at salvation. Ylva was nothing if not pragmatic, and she knew she had erred in her decisions. But her regret was not enough to risk Leif, so time was the only thing she'd give me.

Harald was silent, eyes distant as he considered, then his face began to melt like wax, re-forming as Snorri. Lowering the knife, he leaned down and kissed Ylva on the lips. "I see why my old rival valued you so, Ylva. You will be a good queen."

It was a struggle not to look away.

"Yes, my king." The slight tightening of Ylva's jaw was the only emotion on her face. "I will not disappoint you."

"Tora, have Volund patch Bjorn together so he doesn't bleed to death. He is to be confined under your watch and you will do whatever it takes to keep him from escaping," Harald-as-Snorri said. "Come, wife. Let us announce our plans to Skaland. What better way to celebrate the union between Skaland and Nordeland than to execute the man who betrayed both?"

Keep fighting, Born-in-fire, I silently whispered, then my strength finally failed me and the world fell into darkness.

CHAPTER 40

FREYA

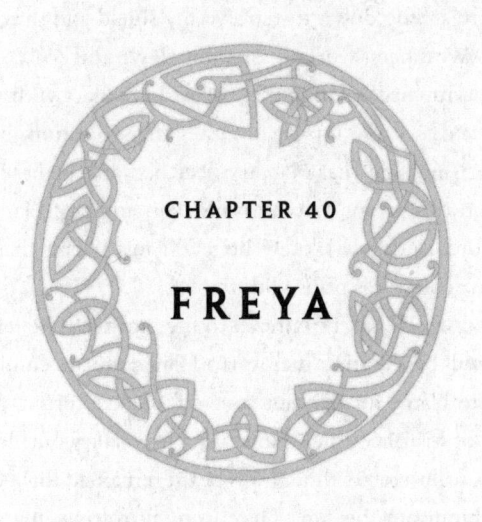

"No signs of Harald's fleet, nor his warriors, shield maiden," the Skalander draug rasped in the strange voice of the undead that I still hadn't gotten used to. "Nor sign of the child of Jord or his familiar."

It was no shock to me that they hadn't managed to catch Guthrum. He was a man who belonged far more to the wilds than to civilization, and the only way we'd manage to find him would be if he was dead. I was still struck with anger at myself whenever I thought of how easily he escaped, but in truth, not only had I believed him too unwell to run, I'd also not thought he'd have the desire to. A mistake on my part, because Kaja had obviously told him enough that he'd decided fleeing the best course. There was no doubt in my mind that he'd go to Harald, which meant that my enemy would soon know I had escaped and that I had an army of my own.

"We'll continue pressing down the coast toward Torne," Geir said. "If Ylva was correct that Grindill was his target, Torne is where his ships will be beached."

I nodded, reaching down to retrieve my shield and slinging it over my shoulder. We'd been working our way down the coast, the undead nature of my army necessitating that we avoid contact with villages lest we be perceived as cause for alarm rather than salvation, but thus far there had been no sign that Harald's fleet had attacked. Many of the draug believed this meant Ylva was mistaken and that Harald had returned to Nordeland, but I knew better. It just meant that he wasn't attempting to achieve his plans with force.

"Gods, you smell bad," I muttered to my brother as he fell in alongside me. "It will be the stink that warns Harald we are coming."

"No one to blame for that but yourself," Geir retorted, rubbing his head. Much of his once thick blond hair had fallen out, leaving bald patches of his scalp visible, though his beard remained thick as ever, the rings on it shining in the sun. They were all rotting, my army, their bodies decaying with every passing hour, and though it didn't seem to hinder their mobility, I knew it must impact their sanity. What I was doing to them couldn't go on forever, which meant the time I had to defeat Harald was limited.

Climbing into a drakkar, I scanned the horizon while the oars dug into the waves, pulling us toward Torne. We passed the entrance of the fjord on which Selvegr, the village I'd once called home, was located.

"Did you see her?" I asked quietly, knowing that Geir had gone to ensure that Ingrid was unharmed and safe, living with her father.

"Yes." His fingers tightened where they gripped the edge of the ship, skin a terrible hue of gray. "She is well."

I bit the insides of my cheeks. "Did you . . . Did you speak to her?"

My brother shook his head. "I didn't wish to frighten her." Lifting his hands, Geir examined them with his glowing green eyes. "Better for her to remember me how I was than like this."

Part of me agreed. To see the one you loved as the undead, rotting and horrifying, was not the last memory you should have of them. But another part of me wondered if it would be worth it to have a chance to say goodbye. To have one final moment and the closure that came with it.

Something that I'd been robbed of with Bjorn.

My eyes burned, and I scrubbed at them, angry at myself for even considering that he might be dead. Yet grief and fear still clawed my insides, because it felt like such a cruel twist to have united our hearts once again only to be torn apart for good.

"Not for good," I hissed at myself, then shook my head when Geir looked askance. "You know her heart, Geir. Whatever choice you made is the right one."

"Will you tell her that I love her?" His eyes met mine, and though they were entirely inhuman, I saw the grief in them. "Take care of her once the day is won?"

I nodded, then forced a grin onto my face. "When your child grows older, I shall tell them how you fought back from Hel's grasp to win a great battle and a place in Odin's hall. It will be a story for skalds to tell through the ages, and your child will have the honor of bearing your name."

Geir frowned, and I winced, afraid I'd said the wrong thing, but then my attention was caught by the true source of his concern. Two riders galloped down the beach, one in pursuit of the other. It was too far to make out their faces clearly, but as I lifted my hand to shade my eyes, the pursuer straightened on her horse, a glowing bow and arrow appearing in her hand. And to either side of her ran Skoll and Hati.

"Skade!" I snarled. "Head for shore!"

Geir called the order, the rowers picking up speed. Yet as they did, Skade let loose her bowstring. The green arrow flew through the air, striking the pursued horse in the haunches. The animal went down, the rider flipping through the air. He hit the sand and rolled, on his feet in a flash and running.

"It's Ragnar!" one of my warriors shouted.

My heart lurched, because if Skade was pursuing Ragnar, it meant that Ylva's plan to exchange Bjorn for Leif had not gone as planned. "Faster!" I shouted. "Archers, shoot her!"

The drakkar's drums caught Skade's attention, her eyes widening as she recognized me.

"Try it, you murderous bitch," I hissed, calling magic to my shield. But instead of shooting her brand toward me, Skade aimed at Ragnar's back. Ragnar, who might well be the only person alive who knew Bjorn's fate. "Kill her!"

My archers shot arrows, but they fell short. I screamed in fury as she released her bowstring, the deadly slice of green flying through the air to punch through Ragnar's back. He fell, and rolled, then lay still in the sand.

The drakkar ran up on the beach, my warriors spilling out in pursuit of Skade. I joined them, sword in hand, chasing her up the beach. Hel's name started to rise to my lips, but I knew it would be wasted words. The goddess of death would not claim an Unfated without a reason worth angering the other gods, and I highly doubted this situation warranted it. But on horseback, the huntress swiftly outpaced us, cutting onto the road at a gallop. She looked over her shoulder and screamed Skoll and Hati's names, but the wolves had paused on the beach, their eyes on me.

"Geir," I shouted. "Have some of your men follow her. She'll lead us to Harald!"

He nodded, calling out orders that I barely heard as I raced to Ragnar's prone form. Two of my warriors had stopped next to him, rolling the man over. Sand clung to his skin, and blood oozed from a hole just below his collarbone.

But he was alive.

Brown eyes jumped from me to the undead surrounding me, many of them individuals he knew well. "Hel-child," Ragnar whispered. "What have you done?"

"United Skaland. These warriors fight for their families and another chance at Valhalla. Tell me what has happened?" Kneeling next to him, I asked, "Did Harald attack you?" And because I could not help myself, "Where is Bjorn? Is he alive?"

"Grindill," Ragnar said between his teeth. "He's alive but injured. I escaped because of him."

My stomach clenched, fear making me want to vomit. "Harald has him?"

Ragnar shook his head, breathing shallow and rapid, not long for this world. "Snorri."

"Snorri's dead," I snapped. "I watched him breathe his last."

"All say he is alive. Snorri made an alliance with Harald, united by a common enemy." Blood oozed out of his lips. "You."

I cursed, seeing to the heart of Harald's plan because there was no doubt in my mind that he played both roles. "It is not Snorri, but the trickster wearing his face."

"Perhaps so, but all believe that after you cursed Skaland's warriors that you attempted to do the same to Nordeland's fleet, only quick thinking allowing Harald and Snorri to work together to slay you," Ragnar whispered. "Word has spread that a celebration of the alliance is planned. Steinunn will sing the song of what you did. Bjorn will be executed. The blood eagle for your traitorous lover."

The world spun around me, terror strangling me, but I managed to say, "When?"

"Soon." More bloody foam to Ragnar's lips, but he managed to say, "Ylva lives. Leif as well. Save them. Redeem yourself. Save . . ."

The final word never came, Ragnar's chest falling still.

"I look forward to seeing you in Odin's hall when the time comes, brother," Geir murmured, and I saw that he'd pressed his own sword hilt into Ragnar's hand. "Have a cup waiting for me."

I sat back on my heels in the bloody sand. "Soon . . ." I couldn't finish my sentence. Couldn't repeat what Ragnar had said, for Bjorn would be executed in the worst way imaginable.

"Are you certain that Snorri was dead, sister?" Geir asked. "Because child of Loki or not, Harald cannot be two men in one room at the same time."

"He doesn't have to be." I got to my feet. "He has Ylva, who ruled with as much power and influence as Snorri ever did. What's more, the people love and trust her, so there will be no doubt in anyone's mind that Snorri is alive and well. And with threats to Leif's life, Ylva will do as Harald says. Fuck!" I kicked the sand.

"Little has changed," Geir said. "We can reach Grindill swiftly, and we know the fortress. It will be easy to take it from Harald."

"Who do you think will be defending the walls of Grindill?" I demanded. "It won't just be Nordelanders. It will be our people we must fight. Friends. Families. And given that Harald has made me the common enemy of all, they'll fight with everything they have to defend against me. Gods." I buried my face in my hands. "He is so clever. So painfully, cruelly clever, and what advantage we might have had is lost. It is uncertain if Guthrum has rejoined him, but Skade will certainly ensure he knows that I'm free. That I have an army. That I'm coming."

"What of the other Unfated in his service?" Geir asked. "You say that Tora knows the truth of his shape-shifting but her loyalty to him is forced by magic or oaths. Perhaps both. Guthrum may or may not know, depending on how much his bird witnessed. What of the others?"

"If I had to guess, it would be that Skade knows everything," I said. "But I do not think anyone else does because the secret would inevitably get out. Necessity would demand that he keep the information as close as possible."

"Who among his cabal do you believe most likely to turn on him if they learn he is a child of Loki?"

"I don't know." I considered what I had learned during my time with them. "Harald has not used his magic to hurt them. It's possible some might see his magic as an asset, given it has allowed them to thrive under his rule."

"Then our only choice is to turn our own people against him, because everyone has suffered from Harald's raids over the years of his rule. Snorri forming an alliance with him won't have erased that," Geir said. "We need to find a way to reveal to them the truth."

Except that it would be the word of the Hel-child and her army of draug against Harald, Snorri, and Ylva. No one would believe us.

I squeezed my eyes shut, trying to think through my desperation.

"Freya," Geir murmured. "Show caution."

My eyes snapped open, and I tensed at the sight of Skoll and Hati approaching.

The wolves hadn't gone back with Skade.

Skoll moved next to me and licked my hand, while Hati sat on his haunches with his tongue hanging out, panting from their exertions.

Stroking my hand over Skoll's fur, I noted that the painted runes that typically stained their fur were faded. "He controls you too, doesn't he," I said softly. "You were never meant to be pets."

Not only could I not risk them spying, these animals deserved to be free.

I removed their collars, then, extracting Gyda's seax from my belt, I carefully trimmed away the stained fur on Skoll's head. No sooner was I finished did he jerk out of my grip, racing away to stop on the sand. I did the same for Hati, who then raced after his brother. "Be free," I said. "I know what it's like to be bound." For I was still bound by my own oaths, given that Ylva still lived. What pain that might yet cause me was unknown.

The wolves raced away into the trees, and as they did, an idea occurred to me.

"Ragnar said that Steinunn is in Grindill, or at least will be soon if a performance is planned in conjunction with Bjorn's execution. If she sings the tale of what happened on that island in front of the whole crowd, all who hear will see the truth."

"So we head to Grindill and capture the skald?"

"But how do we get to her without him knowing?" I paced up and down the beach. "Harald will know we are coming, so he'll be watching. There will be no way to sneak through Grindill's gates, and there is no other way into the fortress."

"There is one way." Geir pursed his lips thoughtfully. "There are drains in the city that pour into the river Torne. We just have to find the opening and crawl inside."

I huffed out a breath. "And just how are we to find them without anyone noticing? The river is fast and deep, and one misstep, and you'll be over the falls. Trust me, that is not a thing you wish to experience."

"Ropes moored upstream. We do it at night. As to how . . ." Geir shrugged. "It is of good fortune that you have an army that does not need to breathe."

CHAPTER 41

BJORN

I woke face down in a pile of moldy straw, my nose filled with the stench of piss and shit. Opening an eye, I took in the bars within arm's reach of my face and realized I was in one of the cells beneath Grindill.

"You want something to drink?"

I turned my head, finding Tora seated on a stool facing the bars, her elbows on her knees. Her face drooped with misery and her eyes were dull.

"Yes." My mouth tasted like something had died in it. And my body felt worse. "How long have I been out?"

"Long enough that I wondered if you'd ever wake."

She dipped a ladle into a bucket and held it through the bars as I pushed myself to a seated position. I drank greedily, and it tasted like the nectar of the gods, I was so parched.

"Volund put you back together." Tora refilled the ladle for me. "More or less, at any rate. He wanted to let you die, but Ylva was insistent."

I finished off the ladle of water and said, "What has Harald told everyone? Or are you able to say?"

"Changes by the hour." She gave a frustrated shake of her head, blond braids swaying. "Too many moving parts. Too many players he can't control. But everyone believes that you and Freya conspired to gather the armies of both Nordeland and Skaland together so that she could send them all to Helheim, and that it is only because the gods intervened that she was limited to slaying the Skalanders. He told them that it was a desperate union between him and Snorri that saw Freya killed and you captured, though I am not sure how he'll handle her return to the realm of the living if she escapes before Skade can reach her."

I ignored the latter in favor of the former, because thinking about Skade finding Freya trapped in that prison made me sick. "Why would we want to kill the armies of two nations?"

"Freya is Hel's child and desires to steal souls deserving of Valhalla for her divine mother. And you are just a lovesick fool who does her bidding." Tora shrugged. "Steinunn has been singing herself hoarse showing Freya at her worst. Red-eyed and rage incarnate, the midnight roots of Yggdrasil bound to do her bidding. It is easy for them to see her as a monster, and no one questions *why* a monster does evil deeds. As for you, it is agreed that you have been thinking with your cock."

I made a face, weary of everyone assuming that my only motivation in life was to get between Freya's legs.

"He's not as in control as he likes to be, but once you're dead and Freya's dead, it will be easier. He'll tighten his hold on two nations and then find a new game to play. It's his nature." She spat on the floor. "Loki."

"How long have you known?" I asked.

"A little more than a year." Tora picked at her nails, the cuticles bleeding. "I wanted to ask Saga some questions, so I traveled to her without asking for his leave. Despite him having claimed to have visited her not a week prior, it was clear to me upon arrival that no one was living in that cabin. Weeks of dust and mouse shit everywhere. No stores. The path overgrown. In truth, I thought she'd died and that he was feigning that she still lived for reasons of his own."

"Not far from the truth," I said, my eyes filling with the horror of my mother's face melting and re-forming as Harald.

"I made the mistake of telling Skade what I'd discovered," Tora continued. "She feigned concern but then told Harald my suspicions. And that was when he began the process of binding me to his will." Her lip quivered. "I had a lover in one of the villages. She came to Hrafnheim to see me and we spent the night drinking. Making love. When we were deep in our cups, she said that we should bind ourselves together for life. Pledge something deeper than troth. I loved her so much that I didn't hesitate to agree. She wrote runes in blood and I swore vows to her, bound myself to her in every possible way. But when it came time for her to swear the same to me, she started to laugh."

The water I'd consumed started to rise in my throat, the story making me sick to my stomach.

"She laughed and laughed, and then her face began to melt." Tora clenched her teeth, fighting back tears. "I started to scream, but my lover snarled, 'Silence!' and the scream was stolen from my lungs because I'd sworn to obey. And then she re-formed as Harald and I knew. Knew what he was, and that I'd not been making love to my sweet Tove but to *him*. That I'd not sworn oaths to Tove but to Harald. And he laughed and laughed, because nothing delights him more than one of his schemes coming to fruition."

"I'm sorry, Tora." My words felt deeply insufficient for the nightmare she'd suffered. Horror that I understood all too well.

"Every time I'd find a way to worm my way free, he'd only make me swear another oath," she said. "I am so bound to his will that there are times I feel that I can barely breathe without his permission. And the things he's made me do . . ." Tears trickled down her cheeks. "I am like one of his Nameless. Bound to his will and destined to do all his dark deeds. I hate him but I also love him more than life, and I will continue to love him until the end of my days, because I swore it to him when he wore my sweet Tove's face."

Tora had been a sister to me most of my life, and to know that the man I called Father had done this to her made me see red. "How is it you can speak of this to me now?"

"Because I swore to keep his secrets, but the truth about his bloodline and magic he revealed to you himself." Her hands fisted. "It is his weakness, always wanting those he manipulates and tricks to know it was him. It is the sweetest moment for him, and watching him . . . *relish* what happened to Snorri, you, and Freya on that island was—" She broke off and took a deep breath. "Suffice it to say that he took the greatest of pleasures from that moment."

So much made sense now that I knew it. I'd always questioned why we just didn't kill Snorri and be done with it: My *mother's* convenient prophecies and foresights and opinions of why that was not possible were now revealed as Harald's lies. Death was no satisfaction to him, no vengeance, and watching how easily he'd played me when dressed as my mother made me cringe.

"The only foretelling Saga ever gave about Freya was the first," Tora continued quietly. "That she'd unite Skaland beneath the one who controlled her fate. All the rest was lies created by Harald to manipulate you and, ultimately, Freya herself."

Harald had made Freya believe that she was destined to be a monster.

No. I had made her believe that.

I rested my head on my knees, knowing that I'd made Freya believe that her fate was to be a plague. That she'd leave thousands dead in her wake. I'd made Freya believe she was to be hated and reviled, and that her fate was dark and full of horror. That I'd been manipulated didn't absolve me of that fact. Everything that had happened on the strait, every Skalander who'd died, was because of my choices. Because it hadn't just been Freya who believed she was destined to become a monster—I'd believed it too.

"Can you help her?" I asked. "Can you stop Skade?"

"No." Tora sighed. "Even if it were possible to catch Skade, he was very clear in his orders. I am to keep you imprisoned in this cell, even if it means my own life. But to be clear, if you are able to kill me and escape, I will thank you with my dying breath, because this is no life, brother."

The sound of wings flapping caught my attention, and shock filled me as Kaja landed on the bars of the opposite cell. Tora held out an arm and the merlin swooped onto her wrist. "What are you doing here, Kaja?"

"Guthrum is alive?" My chest tightened because I'd seen my friend fall from the drakkar and go beneath another vessel. The chances of him surviving hadn't been good.

"I did not think so." Tora gently stroked the bird's feathers. "But if he is, he's not made himself known to Harald. At least, that I'm aware of."

It was possible Guthrum had managed to escape the sea and Harald had told him to remain hidden while Kaja spied, but if that was the case, why had the bird shown herself to us? Guthrum was not one to risk his familiars, and entering such a confined space with us put Kaja very much at risk. Alternatively, Guthrum was dead, and the bird had merely sought the comfort of those she knew well. But the uncanny intelligence in the bird's eyes told me otherwise.

Which left one other option: that Guthrum had sent Kaja to me of his own accord. Which meant that my friend might yet be turned into an ally.

"I won't kill you, Tora," I said. "But that doesn't mean I'm going to go down without a fight."

Her eyes met mine. "Don't tell me any of your plans. I'm bound to protect him, and I swore never to keep any secrets from him."

She'd sworn those words believing them vows to the woman she loved. Harald's perversion of those vows was fuel to my anger, and I climbed to my feet, ignoring the pain from the injuries Volund had only half healed. "Give me the bird."

Tora eased Kaja through the bars and she flapped to land on my knee. It was impossible to get comfortable with my wrists and hands bound with chains behind my back, but I leaned one shoulder against the cold walls as I stared into the bird's golden eyes, praying to the gods that Guthrum saw through them. "Hello, old friend," I murmured. "There is a story I need to tell you, and then I need your help."

CHAPTER 42

FREYA

We waited until night was fully upon us, then crept down the river Torne until we were in sight of Grindill's walls. A thick rope was tied to a tree and the other end secured to one of the sturdier warriors who then trudged out into the water carrying a heavy rock to keep him on the riverbed. The others eased him downstream, running out the rope until he reached the base of the fortress.

I paced back and forth through the trees, each passing minute feeling like a lifetime while we waited for him to find the entrance to the tunnel that led under the fortress.

"There's the signal," Geir said, letting go of the rope. "Two long pulls followed by three short. He's in." My brother gestured to the group of warriors he'd selected. "Go!"

The warriors waded out into the depths and disappeared beneath the surface, using the rope to guide themselves downstream.

"Our turn." Geir began fastening another length of rope to his waist before handing the other end to me. "You sure you wish to do this, Freya? I can speak to Steinunn as surely as you."

"She has to hear the story from me for her magic to work." I fastened the rope around my own waist, checking my knots twice. "I'll be fine. Just don't let go of me."

My brother checked his own knots again, then took hold of the main rope. "Let's go."

The chill of the water bit into my skin as I followed him into the river and took hold of a large piece of deadfall that one of the other warriors handed me. "Keep low and behind the branches," the female draug said. "They have patrols on the wall and they watch the water."

I gave a tight nod, shivers wracking my body. "I won't let them see me."

Geir disappeared beneath the surface, and I held my position until he gave a firm tug. Then I lowered myself into the water and let the current take me. It took only a moment for me to overtake Geir, the rope between us going taut. Keeping behind the branches I clung to, I kicked against the current and prayed to all the gods that those on the walls wouldn't notice a branch moving slower than everything else on the river as we pressed nearer to Grindill.

I sank lower in the water so that only my nose was above the surface as we drew closer. The walls were well lit with torches, and I counted at least seven warriors on the side facing the river, all attentive at their posts. One man's eyes latched onto my piece of wood and my heart lurched, but then his gaze jumped away from me. Hopefully drawn by the light of the fires in the distance that other draug had lit as a distraction.

I slipped alongside the wall, the branches no longer enough to hide me from anyone who looked down.

My pulse roared in my ears because this was the moment. Drawing in a deep breath, I let go of the branch and dropped beneath the surface.

All around me was blackness and cold, and if not for the rope around my waist that kept me from being swept away, it would have felt like a void of nothingness.

I pulled myself toward Geir. Hand over hand, the effort it took far greater than I'd anticipated.

The need to breathe grew with every passing second, as did my panic that I'd mistimed my dive.

Then I collided with something solid.

Geir.

Feeling along his arms, I found the rope that would lead me to the tunnel opening and swiftly drew myself along it.

My chest was burning, instinct screaming that I swim back to the surface.

Except that if I did, I'd be seen. All it would take is one arrow shot from the wall and my destiny would be cut short.

The fibers of the rope cut into my palms as I desperately pulled myself along. The darkness grew more absolute, the current diminishing.

I was in the tunnel.

Except it was completely submerged and thick with debris.

I had to move faster. Had to find air.

But as I tried to hurry through the debris, I was jerked back by the rope fastened between me and my brother.

I clawed with desperation at the knots binding it around my waist.

Air. *Air.* I needed air!

The knots came loose and I half swam, half dragged myself down the tunnel. My chest was spasming, the need to breathe terrifying. Agonizing.

Then hands closed around my wrists and I was jerked upward.

My head broke the surface of the water, and I gasped in a mouthful of air. For the first few breaths, all I felt was relief. Then the stench of shit, piss, and worse accosted me. Gagging, I called my magic and covered my fist with it, illuminating the tunnel.

And the dead around me.

Not undead, though my draug were present, but the warriors who'd accompanied Ylva. I bit down on my other hand to curb the scream that threatened to rise, because they were bobbing around me, cold limbs bumping my body, eyes sightless yet staring.

Geir emerged from the depths. He looked around, then took my arm and led me farther along the tunnel where I had only filthy water to contend with.

"They must have thought the corpses would go into the river, over the falls, and out to sea. But no one has cleared the tunnel in so long that they got caught up in the debris," he whispered. "But their mistake is to our advantage, as it is yet more proof that Snorri is not Snorri, for why would he murder his own men?"

I gave a tight nod and kept moving, sloshing through the murk to where the tunnel curved and turned vertical. Light filtered in from above, along with laughter and voices.

"The great hall," Geir whispered. "We wait until they go to sleep, then climb and find Steinunn."

The person I was desperate to find was Bjorn, but he'd be the one under guard. If I took him, Harald would know that we'd infiltrated Grindill and my plans to reveal his secret to all those who gathered for the execution would be ruined. I was risking Bjorn's life to defeat Harald, and that fact was like a knife twisting in my gut, but I knew he'd tell me to do it with no hesitation.

We stood in silence listening to shouts and laughter, the only break in the monotony when the servants tossed waste down the opening into the drain. I was glad for the darkness so as not to have to see what floated past. But then a familiar voice filtered down from above.

"You promised I would have vengeance, Harald." Steinunn sounded close to tears. "You promised that at the end of this, Snorri would suffer for murdering my family. Instead, you've formed an alliance with him, and rather than suffering, he is currently drunk on mead and servicing Ylva in the comforts of his room! Worse still, you promised that the shield maiden who gave him power was dead, yet Skade has revealed that not only is Freya alive, but she has also returned to Skaland with an army of the dead."

I caught hold of Geir's arm, a sudden thrill running through me because if they were at odds, this would make my task far easier.

"It is a mystery to both Snorri and me how she survived," Harald answered, and I could tell he was struggling to reconcile the lies he'd told with all that had happened since. "She was imprisoned by magic on an island in the middle of the strait with no shelter and no sustenance. Anyone who attempted to approach her risked being dragged to Helheim, and we were certain that the elements would see her swiftly to her death. No one is more shocked than I am to discover she yet lives."

"And your alliance with Snorri? Are you equally shocked by *that*?" Steinunn's voice was full of venom, and Harald was silent.

"Sweet Steinunn, I know this pains you," he finally said. "I know that seeing Snorri thrive is a knife to your heart but have faith that the fate he deserves will soon be delivered upon him."

"You're saying this is a ruse?"

"Of course it's a ruse." Harald's voice was soothing. "For me, but for Snorri as well. Freya sent most of his warriors to Helheim, so he has no choice but to accept the pretense that we are now friends, united by our common enemy, the Hel-child. Nothing would please me more than to slaughter him in his bed for the harm he has done to those I love, but that would be oil on the flames of the conflict between Nordeland and Skaland. More war, more violence, and more families torn asunder. I don't want that any more than you do, so I have set aside my own hurts and work to establish a lasting peace between our nations before I give Snorri his due."

"I do not know how much longer I can endure this." Steinunn was crying now. "Every moment spent in his presence makes me sick. I want it to be over."

Harald sighed. "I know you do. But I also know that you have the strength to press through this trial for the sake of protecting others who might be forced to endure the same pain you did if we immediately turn to violence. Skaland and Nordeland both need to heal after the horror that Freya has inflicted, so we must turn to guile."

More voices approached, and Harald and Steinunn fell silent until they passed. Then Harald said, "Allow me to escort you to your bed, Steinunn. You must rest, because I need you, as I always have. Please do not allow your faith in me to falter."

"I will stand strong," Steinunn whispered. "You have never failed me, my king. Not ever."

They departed, and I released my grip on my brother's arm. "She doesn't know," I whispered. "She has no idea that he's a child of Loki and playing both parts."

It felt like it took an eternity for the revelers above to drink themselves into sleep, but finally, in what must have been the hours just before dawn, the great hall fell silent.

Geir took hold of my waist and lifted me, my feet finding his shoulders as I reached for the lip of the opening and then heaved myself out. Nervous sweat added to the dampness of my palms, and the second I stood straight, both my knees cracked, the noise deafening.

I grabbed Geir's wrist as he jumped up, gagging as skin gave way beneath my palm so that I was gripping tendon and bone. But it seemed to cause him no grief, and my brother climbed out, whispering to his warriors to hold their ground unless they heard trouble. Then we both put on the cloaks we'd brought, lifting the hoods. Hiding our identities, but not the stink we'd picked up in our passage through the drains.

Geir linked arms with me, both of us walking with the swaying gait of people deep in their cups and looking for a bed. The hall was quiet but for the distant sounds of people coupling, and Geir whispered, "You know where her room is?"

I nodded, leading him toward the stairs. Unlike most great halls, Grindill was built with a great deal of stone, and the building was massive. Heading up the stairs as though I belonged, I started down the hallway, passing the door that had once led to my own chamber. But before we reached Steinunn's chambers, the door at the far end of the hallway opened.

Reacting without thought, I pulled Geir toward me, my back against the wall. Geir put his hands on my waist, hood falling against mine, and if I hadn't been half dead from fear of being discovered, I would have died of mortification at having to pretend like this with my own brother. That his face was rotting mere inches from mine did not help the situation.

Twin footfalls approached, and I heard Ylva say, "More jarls will arrive by tomorrow, my lord. All blame the Firehand and the Hel-child for the loss of so many warriors, and they desire the pleasure of seeing at least one of them punished in such appropriate fashion."

My teeth clenched, fury rising in my chest at how swiftly Ylva switched sides to save her own skin.

Then Snorri's voice said, "We will make their travels worth their time. You must keep a tighter rein on Leif. He's tried to enter the prison, but I don't want him near Bjorn."

"He's angry and hurt by his brother's betrayal, but he wants answers. He's not satisfied by the explanations he's been given." Ylva hesitated, then added, "I'll keep them apart."

"Do so."

Their footsteps neared us, and paused, and Snorri's voice snarled, "Find another place to fuck, you fools!"

"It's raining, my lord," Geir mumbled, and I cringed, certain the strange tenor of his voice would be noticed.

"Go stand in it for the rest of the night," Snorri's voice said. "Perhaps it will wash away the stink, since you clearly don't wash your own arse."

Then the footsteps carried on, heading down the hall and descending the steps, their conversation too low for me to hear.

"It was Snorri," Geir whispered to me. "That was *Snorri*."

I shook my head. "It was Harald. But perhaps you now understand his mastery of deception."

Catching hold of my brother's arm, I dragged him down the hall to Steinunn's room, praying to every god that she'd retained the same location upon her return. Opening the door, I eased into the dark room, walking on silent feet. Geir followed, closing the door behind us.

All I could see were shadows, but I crept across the room toward the bed. I waited for my eyes to adjust, searching the furs for a form, but they were empty. I reached down to touch the bed to confirm my eyes weren't deceiving me.

Definitely empty. But also very warm.

Realizing my mistake, I whirled in time to see the door open, a slim shape outlined by the lamps in the hall. I lunged, but Steinunn was too quick for me to catch.

But not too quick for Geir.

Whether it was luck or some preternatural speed, he caught the skald around the waist even as he clapped a hand over her mouth. I hurried to shut the door, then lit a lamp. Steinunn thrashed and kicked in Geir's arms, thumping her bare heels against his shins.

"I'm here to talk, and I want you to listen," I told her. "And believe me, you should quit trying to bite my brother because you're going to come away with a bigger mouthful than you hope for."

Steinunn stared at me, then rolled her eyes up to look at Geir. Immediately she began thrashing about in a panic, no stranger to draug given she'd followed me and Bjorn through the tunnels beneath Fjalltindr. I waited for her to give up trying to escape, exhaustion forcing a degree of calmness back into her, then I said, "It's true what you've been told. In the battle on the strait, I used Hel's magic to pull the souls of most of Snorri's army down to Helheim. What you don't know is that it was Harald who manipulated me into doing so."

Steinunn stared at me, eyes filled with angry skepticism.

There was no good way to explain everything, so I carried on. "Harald is a child of Loki. A trickster and a shape-shifter. Snorri is dead. I know this, because I watched Bjorn kill him." As quickly as I could, I told her of what had happened on the island, the truth about Saga, and how Ylva had taken Bjorn. My throat was dry as I explained how I'd gone into Helheim and brought back the souls of the warriors I'd cursed, promising them another chance at Valhalla. When I was finished, I said, "I need your help revealing the reality of what has happened when everyone gathers tomorrow for Bjorn's execution. Your song will reveal the truth. Now, if Geir removes his hand, do you promise not to scream?"

Steinunn gave a tight nod, remaining silent as my brother moved his hand, though she scrubbed at her mouth. I didn't blame her for that.

"Harald is wearing Snorri's face," I continued. "It's a clever way for Harald to rule both nations. He's manipulating you and everyone else."

"That's impossible. They are both here. I've seen them with my own eyes, and Harald—" Steinunn broke off, likely unwilling to reveal to me that Harald still intended to kill Snorri, little knowing that Geir and I had overheard them.

"But have you ever seen them together?" Geir asked. "Has anyone seen them together?"

"Ylva—"

"Ylva knows the truth." Sweat was pouring down my back because I'd been so sure that Steinunn would believe me. "I can only assume that Harald has secured her cooperation with threats against Leif's life. *Think,* Steinunn. Have you once seen them together since the battle? Or if that is not compelling enough proof, ask yourself this: Did you ever see Harald and *Saga* together?"

Silence.

"You're a skald, Steinunn! You know the lore. You know what Loki's children can do!"

For a moment, I thought that I'd have to slap her to get a reaction, but then Steinunn whispered, "So Snorri is dead? Dead by Bjorn's hand?"

"Yes." My fingers balled into fists of frustration because this was not the reaction I'd hoped for. "Harald is a child of Loki and he has worn many faces not his own. Compose a song about what happened to me on that island and you'll see the truth. That is the power of your magic."

"The man who killed my family is dead," she breathed. "Killed by his own son. The son he was trying to steal back when he attacked my village. Justice has been done."

My stomach dropped and I abruptly realized that I had erred. None of Harald's trickery mattered to Steinunn because he'd given her the thing she wanted more than life itself: revenge.

"He's lying to you! We overheard your conversation—Harald lied to your face."

"Freya, keep your voice down," Geir hissed. "You're going to get us caught."

"But did he lie?" Steinunn stepped closer to me, breath hot against my face. "He said I would have my justice, I needed only to be patient. He planned to tell me the truth."

"He doesn't tell anyone the truth!" It took concerted effort not to shout, because why didn't she understand? "But you can help us reveal what he is to everyone. You can help me fix this."

"No," Steinunn whispered, then she opened her mouth and screamed.

Geir clapped his hand over her mouth, but I knew that it was too late. Someone would have heard her scream and would come to investigate. Worse still, Steinunn had proven my brother was right.

No one cared about the truth. No one cared about the lies that had been told. Because it was in their best interests not to. "Let her go."

Geir looked ready to argue but Steinunn wrenched away from him. "Snorri and Skaland took everything from me when they killed my family," the skald snarled. "I swore vengeance, and now I have it."

I shook my head and stepped back, my heart filled not with fear or anger, but sorrow at seeing how grief had eaten her up inside and turned her cruel. Turned her selfish. "Then all the Skalanders have the right to know the reason you hate them so much. Compose your song, Steinunn. Show them why Snorri deserved to die. Show them why you deserved vengeance."

She blanched.

"That's what I thought." I shook my head. "Coward."

"Freya, we must run!" Geir hauled on my arm, dragging me out the door. Shouts were sounding in the great hall, voices demanding that the scream be investigated.

"We need to get Bjorn!" I hissed after I shut Steinunn's door. "She'll tell Harald that I was here. He might kill him before tomorrow."

"He won't," Geir snapped. "Bjorn is bait for you, Freya. He won't kill him until he's caught you."

Logically, I knew that. But there was a lot of pain that could be inflicted before death, and leaving Bjorn to suffer while I escaped wasn't a thought I was willing to entertain. Especially with all my plans to rescue him in shambles.

Geir gripped my shoulders. "We can't help him if you're dead. We didn't bring enough warriors to get him out by force and it's Skalanders we'll have to fight. It was you who said you didn't wish innocents to die because they had the misfortune of being deceived."

I swayed on my feet, warring with myself. Knowing what Bjorn would want me to do, if given the choice. "We run. But I'm not letting him die, Geir. If I have to kill them all to save him, I'll do it."

Geir drew his sword. "We'll come up with another plan."

I drew my own blade, fighting tears, because I had been so certain this would work. So certain that I could outwit the trickster, but my plan had failed spectacularly. More screams of terror echoed up from below, boots pounding this way and that, Grindill waking up in the commotion.

We raced down the stairs only for a crying thrall to run by. "The dead are walking!" Her eyes landed on Geir, and she screamed, then bolted into the main hall.

It was a chaos of people running all different directions, warriors staggering out of beds, most still heavy with drink. Geir latched his hand onto my wrist, dragging me through the hall to the drains. He shoved me in the opening, and I landed with a splash in the water before swiftly staggering out of his way.

The rest of the draug followed, their laughs clawing the insides of my ears and made all the worse because I took no humor from the chaos. Our one opportunity to sneak inside Grindill had been spent and it had been for nothing.

And Bjorn would be the one to pay the price.

CHAPTER 43

BJORN

It was hard to tell the passage of time in the darkness beneath Grindill. Minutes felt like hours. Hours like days. Days, I had no doubt, would feel like years despite them being very much numbered.

I'd told Kaja all that I could about Harald's duplicity, and while I had no doubt she'd relay it back to Guthrum, what he'd chosen to do with the revelation was unknown to me. I'd pleaded that he liberate Freya from her island prison, but it was not lost on me how much time had passed. That Freya would not only have had to endure cold and hunger, but that Skade might well have already reached her. How long could she defend herself in such a state against Skade's arrow?

Sleep was the only release I had from the sickening sense of helplessness I felt, though it was sleep plagued by fitful dreams. It was from one such dream that I was dragged awake by shouts of alarm coming from the fortress above.

Tora rose from where she sat guard near my cell, then went a few paces down the hall. My heart thundered with anticipation that something was happening to our benefit. That Harald's schemes had been discovered, and that even now, everyone was turning against him. Hopes that faded along with the commotion.

"Must have just been drunks." Tora came back to my cell and leaned against it. "They were feasting tonight in the great hall. I'd go up to check, but I have to keep you in my sights."

She sat down again, head resting against the bars, and the thought of escape rose to the forefront of my mind. Except to do so would require killing Tora. Would require killing the woman who was more family to me than my own blood for the sake of saving Freya. It would be one thing if Tora was like Skade and had chosen to support Harald's deception, but she was as much a prisoner in this situation as I was.

"Just do it," Tora whispered, seeming to sense my thoughts. "I'll fight to stop you, but I know you can kill me, Bjorn. You've always been the better warrior."

Rage and hate burned sour in my stomach, because there was a reason Harald had set her to this role rather than his Nameless. He had known that it would come to this and that freedom would demand a piece of my soul. This was all a game to him—an amusement to discover how far I'd go to save Freya.

You're out of time.

There is no other choice.

My hands were encased with chains that kept them compressed into fists, so I wasn't even sure I could call my axe. Wasn't sure whether it would force its way into my palm and crush my fingers against the steel chains. Whether I could endure the pain long enough to melt through the metal. And even if I could stomach the agony, how well would I be able to fight with my hands broken and burned?

Do it, I snarled at myself. *Don't be a fucking coward.*

I drew in a breath to whisper Tyr's name, but the soft pat of shoes filled the air, and the moment was lost.

Steinunn approached, and though Tora eyed the skald she said nothing as Steinunn stopped before the bars of my cell.

"Why are you here, skald? Don't you know that I've no interest in giving fuel for your caterwauling?" Spitting on the floor between us, I added, "Your duty is to create stories of truth to spread through the generations, but you only give truths that benefit you and, in doing so, spin lies. You're a traitor to your birthright."

Steinunn ignored my taunts and rested her hands against the bars. "Freya was here tonight. That was the cause of the commotion. She has raised all the Skalander warriors she cursed to Helheim as undead, including her own brother."

I straightened, shock driving my anger. "Freya is alive? She's free?"

"Yes." Steinunn wrapped her red cloak more tightly around her body, and I noticed that she was shaking. "Which was already known. Skade saw Freya and her army when she hunted down Ragnar."

My teeth clenched, a flash of guilt filling me that Ragnar had fallen to Skade's arrow. "Where is she now?"

"Gone." Steinunn kept well back of the bars. "She came to me thinking that the truth about Harald's identity and his deceptions would turn me to her cause, but in doing so, revealed to me that I finally had my vengeance against Snorri. The man who killed my family is dead by your hand, and though he has kept it from me, it was Harald who ensured I had justice. When Freya asked me to turn on him, I revealed her presence, though she and Geir were able to escape. He's undead—a draug raised by her magic, is my guess."

Anger burned hot in my veins and, ignoring the pain in my body, I got to my feet. The chains binding me rattled as I stepped close to the bars. "You bitch. Is your revenge worth so much? Snorri is dead! What more do you hope to gain by furthering Harald's deceptions?"

"Harald delivered me from the worst moment of my life," Steinunn said softly. "Without him to give me a reason to live, I would have surely died of grief. Trickster or not, he has given me everything he promised."

"So because he's given you everything you wanted, you are willing to turn a blind eye to *everything* he's taken from everyone else?"

"Weren't you willing to do the same?" Steinunn's head tilted. "You knew he was not a good man, not really, and yet you ignored all the signs because he offered you the chance to avenge what had been done to your mother. That it was a fabrication doesn't matter, because you still trod over innocents without mercy in pursuit of your vengeance. We are the same, Bjorn. And perhaps if you had not betrayed your loyalty to Harald for Freya's sake, you and I would yet still be on the same side of the bars."

"He betrayed me. I swore loyalty to a lie." The muscles in my arms flexed as I strained against the chains. "He wore Snorri's face when he attacked Saga, and all because he couldn't bear her rejection. It cost my mother her life, and eventually cost my father his as well."

Both dead at my hands.

"I know your story, Bjorn. I know the stories of everyone in Harald's cabal of Unfated." She sighed. "Do any of you know mine?"

"I don't fucking care about your story, Steinunn," I snarled. "I don't want to hear your justification for all that you have done."

Silence stretched, and Steinunn was the one to break it.

"I have always told myself that no one cared to hear my story when the truth has always been that I am too afraid to tell it," she whispered. "And so I sing the songs of others but never the song of myself. But the words have always been composed in my heart."

Her tragedy did not justify her actions and I didn't want to hear it. "I know enough."

Then Tora reached through the bars and took hold of my shoulder. The tension in her face told me that she could not speak the thought in her mind, her tongue bound by Harald's magic, but not every truth was told with words.

"Fine." I rattled my chains, then sat back down. "Sing. It isn't as though I have anywhere else to be."

Steinunn sat on the floor, a small drum in her lap. The rhythm she beat upon it was soft, and as she began to sing, it was not just my ears that filled with the skald's story but my eyes. And though I wished otherwise, my heart.

A story of a hard youth, liberty won through the love of a good man, and a year later, came a child. A boy with red curls and a large smile, blue eyes beaming at me. A ghost's eyes, because death came and though death carried the colors of Skaland, Steinunn's magic revealed the true villain's face. He destroyed all that he touched, laughing as he did, and as the last lines of song poured from Steinunn's lips, the child's blue eyes were glassy and still.

A tear ran down my face. "Harald killed your family. Not Snorri. Harald and his Nameless. Harald wearing Snorri's face."

Steinunn's face was dry. As though she'd already wept every tear she would ever have. "I'd long refused to join Harald's service because I wished to remain with my husband and child. He killed them so that he could make me part of his cabal. So that he could use me in his machinations. He created my tragedy and then allowed me to weep on his shoulder and name him my savior. And because I was too much of a coward to sing of my own loss as it would mean watching them die, I did not know the truth until now."

Tora reached into her pocket and pulled out balls of wool. "I cannot speak of plans that I have not heard," she said, then shoved the wool into her ears and turned her back on us. Doing all that she could to aid us within the boundaries of the oath she'd sworn.

"I know the stories of everyone in the cabal." Steinunn gripped the bars of my cell. "And I think it long past time I composed a song to honor our king. Our father. Our savior. But there is one more tale I must learn in order to ensure the song is complete. Will you help me, Bjorn Firehand?"

We would never be friends, this woman and me. There was too much ugliness, too much betrayal, between us. But in what might be the final hours of my life, Steinunn and I would be allies.

CHAPTER 44

FREYA

Geir and the other Skalander draug hauled me out of the river and half carried me at a run through the trees, the shouts of pursuit filling our ears.

"Skade led those who came after us," Geir told me after we'd reached our camp, which was nothing more than a few tents and a single fire, for the draug needed neither rest nor warmth. "But she broke off chase. Likely because she does not care to face us in the dark."

"Do not allow your confidence to get the better of you." I crouched next to a small fire, warming my shaking hands. I was frozen to the bone, the sensation made worse by the hollowness in my chest. "I cannot believe Steinunn did not listen. That the truth did not matter."

"You assume that everyone is like you, sister." Geir muttered orders to the other Skalanders to keep a strong watch in case Skade had continued her hunt alone. "You assume that everyone will fight for what is right and make sacrifices for others, but that is not the nature of most people. They are selfish, and they always choose the path that is best for them and call it wisdom. But it is cowardice. Let them call you the fool for trying to do better—the gods see the truth of their nature and they will be judged accordingly. Odin has no place for cowards in Valhalla."

It was cold comfort. I'd spent my one chance to extract Bjorn on a failed conversation with Steinunn, and in the coming day, he'd be executed unless I found a solution. Exhaustion dragged upon me, but there was no chance that I'd waste these last few hours when I might yet win Bjorn free to do anything as useless as sleep.

A sharp whistle split the night, and as I lifted my head, it was to see that the first hint of dawn glowed through the dense trees of the forest. Yet that was not the reason for the whistle. Two of my draug were coming toward us with a man between them.

"Guthrum!"

I clambered to my feet, and one of the draug said, "He approached and asked to speak to you."

I waved a hand at them to let Guthrum go, then motioned for him to join me at the fire.

Guthrum was silent, holding his hands above the flame. He was skinny as a rail, and his ill-fitting clothes looked to have been stolen from a clothesline. Yet he was also alive, and though I was not certain what side he was on, there was comfort in standing next to the living.

"I'm sorry I ran," he finally said. "It felt like I was caught in a trap, and so I thought only of escape."

"In fairness, you did wake up surrounded by corpses." I tried to laugh but it sounded more like a sob. Sitting before my knees could betray me, I motioned for him to sit next to me. "Where have you been?"

"In the wilds." He rested his elbows on his knees and stared at the fire. "Kaja showed me some of what happened during the battle on the strait, though once I fell from the boat all she looked for was me. She told me that it was you who pulled me from the water and chastised me for not listening to you, but I have not lived this long by ignoring my instinct to run." He shrugged. "We've been watching you and yours. Watching those at Grindill. The alliance between Snorri and Harald. Nothing made sense to me, and so I sent Kaja to speak to Bjorn."

I sucked in a sharp breath. "She saw him? Is he well?"

"*Well* is a stretch but he's alive and in the cells beneath the fortress with Tora as his guard. He told Kaja all that had happened and she relayed it to me, along with his request that I aid you. It was . . . quite a story." He stuck a hand in his pocket and withdrew a handful of berries, which he ate in silence. "I struggled to believe it. Still struggle to believe it, for I have been in Harald's company most of my life and never once had cause to question he might be a trickster. Kaja has since watched for proof of such a nature but has seen nothing."

I kept silent, for if Bjorn's story and days of watching had not given him the proof Guthrum needed, then nothing I said would.

"But what she has seen, time and again, is Harald and Snorri referring to you as a monster." He ate the last of his berries. "You and I once talked about what it means to have a monster in you, Freya, and I said that we all do. But I think I was wrong, because no part of you is the villain. I was on that drakkar. I know the lengths to which you went not to use Hel's magic, and I know that it was Bjorn who forced your hand, just as I know that it was Saga who drove him to it. Saga, who has mysteriously vanished from the world with nothing but a vague explanation that Bjorn or you killed her in the battle."

I kept silent, waiting to see where this would go.

"Harald saved my life. I owe him a life debt and I will not turn against him," Guthrum said. "But neither will I fight for him in this, because my respect for him is tarnished. I know your goal is to rescue Bjorn, but the cost of doing so will be high." He hesitated. "Kaja has overheard that Snorri intends to send you a message offering you the chance to surrender. If you do, he will give you a swift and merciful death, and Bjorn will be sent into exile. If you decline, it will be the blood eagle at dusk for him."

My despair swelled at the reminder of the fate that Bjorn would face if I failed to rescue him. The most torturous of deaths where the victim's ribs were separated from their spine, skin and bone pulled outward to form macabre wings before the victim's lungs were removed from their chest. A horrible and slow way to die, and one that surely denied the victim Valhalla.

Guthrum rose to his feet, so I did as well. "I will leave you to debate your course of action. Goodbye, Freya Born-in-Fire," he said, then melted into the darkness.

Geir moved into the firelight. "Do not agree to this offer, sister. Not only would you grant victory to the enemy, there is no certainty that Harald will hold to his agreement. Already crowds gather to see the brutal end to one of the named traitors, so imagine how many would come to see the blood eagle of two."

"I know." I resumed my spot in front of the fire, rubbing at my scarred hand as I tried to swim above the fear that threatened to drown me. "Grindill's walls are manned mostly with Skalanders. If we attempt to take the fortress by force, many of our people will die. Bjorn might be killed in the chaos of the battle, and if it looks as though it is going badly for him, Harald will merely change form and escape with the masses. It will all be for nothing."

"What about your magic?"

"It won't work on the Unfated," I muttered. "And it especially won't work on one of Loki's children. Hel feels some degree of solidarity with her father, I think."

Geir toyed with the hilt of his sword. "I know you love Bjorn, but maybe it's time—"

"No." My scarred hand balled into a fist. "I'll not sacrifice him. I'll die to save him."

"Your death will not save him," my brother muttered. "Even if Harald allows him to go free, he'll only get himself killed trying to avenge your death. You know this."

I did know it, but I said nothing.

"We can try to climb the walls while it is still dark," one of the other draug suggested. "They may not know the capabilities of the undead.

It may be that we can break Bjorn free before they even realize we are inside."

"Steinunn knows the capacity of the undead." My voice caught. "And she is no friend of ours. What's more, if Skade gets any of you in her sights, her arrow can easily end you. Likewise Tora's lightning, and it is she who stands guard over Bjorn." Although there was no doubt in my mind that Tora did so under duress.

"We are dead, Freya Born-in-Fire," he answered. "Life in this realm will never again be possible, but what comes next is unknown. I, for one, would gladly take that step for the sake of avoiding battle with our friends and family who stand against us on Grindill's walls."

It didn't feel right to ask the draug to take such a risk when I'd already taken so much from them, but I knew he was right. This was why they'd come back. Not to hide in the woods, but to do battle against Harald and win a place in Valhalla. To deny them that was worse than killing them in the first place. "All right. But we must be quick. In another hour, there will be full light."

Geir sent his best warriors to attempt to infiltrate the fortress, but it was for naught. After our failed attempt to sway Steinunn, Grindill had been rendered virtually impenetrable. No one was allowed in or out, the gates were kept shut, and the patrols on the walls were doubled. Even so, the draug might have succeeded.

If not for Skade.

She was called *the huntress* for a reason, and the magic in her blood proved its worth, for she shot all four draug who made the attempt. They burst into ash just as had those beneath Fjalltindr when they'd encountered Bjorn's axe, and I sent a prayer to the Allfather that he honor their bravery.

As the sun moved high in the sky, a single rider approached the new camp we'd made on the ridgeline overlooking the fortress, it now seeming pointless to attempt to hide our presence.

"King Snorri offers terms," the messenger shouted. "If the Hel-child known as Freya Born-in-Fire approaches the gates alone and surrenders herself, she will be given a swift and honorable death and her lover will be granted exile. The Hel-child has until dusk to surrender, else her lover will die a traitor's death. A blood eagle in front of all he betrayed." Without waiting for a response, she rode back to the gates of Grindill.

"I had hoped it would be Skade who brought the message," Geir growled. "That one deserves death for what she did to Mother."

"Skade is too clever for that." I paced back and forth, wearing a track in the dirt. "She knows we're here and won't race into a trap. Not when she is equally certain that I will walk into theirs."

"Time runs short." Geir watched me pace, rotting thumbs hooked on his belt. "What do you wish to do, Freya?"

Noise from inside the fortress reached my ears. Shouts of celebration and calls for blood, hundreds of Skalanders lifting their cups to Snorri. To his renewed friendship with Harald. Toasted to peace between Nordeland and Skaland. Toasted to the imminent execution of a traitor.

It turned my stomach sour. "How quickly Harald has become the hero. How quickly our people forget the long years he raided Skaland's coast, plundering and killing."

"He's painted himself as a victim," Geir replied. "A victim of the monstrous Hel-child and her hapless lover. It was not visions of Harald or Nordelander warriors that Steinunn's song showed dragging their loved ones beneath the waves, Freya. It was you, with Bjorn at your side."

"Nothing is more powerful than the truth." I wished desperately to see a path through this. A path to defeating Harald that wouldn't make truth out of his fabricated vision of me as a plague upon both nations with scores of innocent dead left in my wake. "But the truth refuses to be our weapon. There is no choice. We must go over the walls and take control of the fortress to rescue Bjorn and kill Harald."

The draug shook their heads restlessly, and Geir watched them, some form of silent communication passing between my brother and the dead Skalanders. "No, Freya," he finally said. "It would be one thing if doing so yielded victory, but we know that Harald will only shift forms and escape. We might save Bjorn, but it would come at the cost of the lives of those we call friends and family, for they all believe that we are the enemy. That we are ruled by a traitor. They will fight us, and none here wish to harm our people."

Whether it was my oath or just my frustration, I didn't know, only that emotion rose in my chest, wild and furious.

"You promised me!" The words tore from my lips as a wild shriek. "You swore to fight for me!"

"To fight for Skaland!" my brother shouted back. "To fight to defeat the trickster whose plots put us all in Helheim. To fight for a chance at Valhalla. But what you suggest has no honor—to kill those we love for the sake of the one *you* love."

A ragged sob tore from my lips, because he was right. I couldn't ask them for this. All I could do now was choose between fighting this battle myself or surrendering on the hope Harald would hold to his word and allow Bjorn to go free. Hooking my shield over my shoulder, I started walking toward Grindill.

"Freya," Geir called before I'd gone more than a few paces. "Wait! The wolves have returned!"

Turning my head, I found Skoll and Hati sitting in the trees, watching me. Their presence changed nothing, yet I stopped walking and waited as they made their way in my direction. It was not lost on me that both creatures were larger than I was. More than capable of ripping out my throat. Yet I felt no threat as they neared, not even when they sniffed my hands, massive teeth clearly visible.

Sniffed with their large noses. Their *keen* noses.

I went still, watching the wolves lick my hands. "Harald changes shape," I murmured. "But does he change smell?"

Geir and the others exchanged looks but then shrugged.

It was a long shot, but desperation drove me to take it. "Get me a stick of charcoal." When one was brought to me, I dropped to my knees before the wolves, a cold fall wind tugging and pulling at my hair. "Will you trust me to wash away the magic when we are through? I have no desire to bind you to my will, only to offer you the chance for revenge against the one who kept you bound for so long. And for that, I need you to be able to understand me."

They only sat with lolling tongues, showing no resistance as I replicated the runes that Harald had once used to bind them. Immediately, their eyes sharpened with intelligence. "Can you smell Harald no matter his shape?" I asked them.

Hati gave a soft whine.

Geir frowned. "Is that a yes?"

I nodded, understanding them as easily as they understood me. "Will you help us?"

Both animals circled me with wagging tails, and resting my hands on their heads, I looked at Grindill with a different light.

"We flush everyone in the fortress out with smoke," I said. "Force them through two gates as choke points. Harald doesn't know we have Skoll and Hati, so he'll not hesitate to try to slip through. But they will know it is him no matter what face he wears."

"He'll know it's a ploy," Geir argued.

"Every part of Harald's strategy here has been predicated on his belief that he knows how I will act. On his certainty that I will not voluntarily attack my own people. On his certainty that I'll risk myself for Bjorn's sake. That I'll die for him." I swallowed hard, wishing I could tell Geir about my oath, although in truth, even without it, I'd have made the same choices. "Harald was right in his assessment of my character. But I also know *him*. He has consistently fooled everyone by taking on another's form and it will not occur to him that his magic will fail him. When it seems as though he has erred in his judgment of me, that we are attacking the fortress in truth, he will change form and try to run. It is his nature."

"And once he's caught? Then what?"

Every part of me wanted to force Harald to reveal the truth of his nature. For all to know who and what he was. But that might well be a dream out of reach for me, so I said, "I'll kill him."

Geir rubbed at his beard. "We need to think of a way to fill the fortress with smoke without setting it ablaze so quickly that no one has time to flee."

"We need to get the smoke to the center of Grindill," I said. "The gates we wish them to escape through must be kept clear of flame. And we have only a matter of hours to figure out how to do it."

The draug set to work while I stood with Skoll and Hati, listening to my people in Grindill call for my blood. For Bjorn's blood. They patrolled the battlements, Skade in their midst, all forewarned that I was coming. All forewarned that I'd raised an army of the dead that was bound to do my bidding.

They would wait no longer.

"It's time." I called magic to my shield and drew my sword, the runes glowing in the presence of the draug surrounding me. "To Harald, this is all a game and we are but pieces on the board. Today the pieces rise against him, and he will taste what it is like to lose!"

My army of the undead flanked me and, as one, we stepped out of the trees and into the open.

CHAPTER 45

BJORN

I paced the length of my cell, sensing that dusk was coming despite the sun never reaching the bowels of the fortress.

"Freya is here!" Harald's voice carried down the dim hall toward me, singsong and cruel. Then he appeared, the grin on his face making me want to break the bars between us so that I might strangle him with my bare hands.

"She lurks with her rotting army of the dead, desperately trying to think of a way to rescue you that won't necessitate her killing every Skalander I've manned Grindill's walls with."

"And what will you do if she does?" I asked. "Fighting draug is no easy task, I would know."

Harald waved a dismissive hand at me. "She won't. Her morality won't allow it. Just as it won't allow her to drag all those who oppose her down to Helheim because she perceives them as victims of my trickery." He stretched his arms above his head, sighing as his back cracked. "She'll try every ruse she can think of and then take my offer to accept her surrender in exchange for your life in exile. It's just a matter of stymieing her until she reaches that depth of desperation, and then she'll come close enough that Leif can order her to stand down. And I think we are nearly at that moment."

It was a struggle to keep dismay from my face, because Freya's *fucking oath* would drive her to surrender. To sacrifice her life for mine. Though in truth, even without it, I knew she'd do the same. With Leif rightfully angry at me—and Freya—he'd be easy for Harald to manipulate and use as his tool against us, and Ylva had risked as much as I suspected she would to aid us. Her goal now was survival. For Leif. For herself. And for all the Skalanders who trusted the former lady of Halsar to protect them.

"And what will you do after we are defeated?" I asked. "You can't really believe that you can maintain this farce. It is one thing to be two men, quite another to be two kings. More and more people will begin to ask questions, and the seeds of truth that Freya has no doubt been sowing in towns and villages will take root. They'll realize they are all pieces in your game, and they'll come for your blood."

"What fun is there if there is no risk?" Harald cocked his head. "I remember when I first met young Harald of Hrafnheim many long years ago. I listened to him weep and moan about his lot in life, despite being heir to his father's jarldom back in Nordeland.

"Before I consumed him, he told me that I was mad if I believed I could become him. That those who knew him would suspect and that I would be swiftly discovered. Except I learned well and learned early that people do not doubt what they see with their eyes, even when every other instinct tells them something is amiss. Sight is truth, and so no one ever suspected when I returned to Hrafnheim and challenged *my dear father* and killed him. No one believed me to be anyone other than the Harald who had left them."

Shock filled my core. "You aren't even Harald in truth?"

"I have been Harald for so many years that I've become him." He tapped his chin. "Or he became me. Either way, we are one in a way that I've never achieved with another skin. Perhaps it has to do with the amount of him I consumed, for I let not a piece go to waste. Either way, what you see before you now is the true me."

Bile burned in my stomach as I understood his meaning. And also why he had taken Snorri's corpse. I did not want to ask. Did not want to know. But I needed him to reveal the full story so that Steinunn would hear it from where she hid in the next cell. "You . . . eat them? Why?"

Harald shrugged. "Loki's blood allows me to take the shape of anything I wish, anything I can envision, but there are other sorts of magic that allow me to take on more than just a shape. The sagas sung in Islund taught me that to truly take on something's attributes, you must take them into yourself."

"My mother . . . Did you . . ." I couldn't say it. Couldn't allow myself to put voice to that horror.

A slow smile climbed onto Harald's face, and turning away from him I fell to my knees and vomited. Over and over, my body trying to rid itself of the knowledge that was surely stamped across my mind for eternity.

When the heaving ceased, I slowly looked up at him as I wiped my mouth against my shoulder. "Who are you really?"

He held his hands wide. "I am everyone and everything." The grin fell away. "And nothing and no one. As Nameless as my Nameless, cast aside the moment my mother realized what blood flowed in my veins. Unloved and unwanted because of what I was, and so I made myself into someone new. Over and over again, learning from my mistakes and discovering pieces of lore until I had mastered my art. Harald is my masterpiece, your mother a close second, but Snorri . . ." He sighed happily. "All of Skaland will sing my name even as they dance to the beat of my drum."

"You are a monster," I whispered. "Your mother should have strangled you and spared the world."

Harald's eyes hardened for a heartbeat, but then he smiled. "It's time, Bjorn. Time to lure your Freya in."

"She'll kill you."

"Not with my Unfated to protect me." He snapped his fingers, and Tora came down the hall, head lowered. Four of Harald's Nameless followed her. "Gag him and then bring him. If he puts up a struggle, feel free to make him scream."

"Yes, my king," Tora responded tonelessly. "Ylva is looking for her husband."

Harald cast his eyes skyward in irritation. "Fine."

His face melted, then re-formed as Snorri. Pulling his tunic off, he turned it inside out, revealing a second garment sewn within that was not green but gray. Straightening it and loosening his belt to accommodate Snorri's greater girth, he departed without a word.

Tora met my gaze. "It's time."

CHAPTER 46

FREYA

I had no doubt that we painted a picture of Helheim itself as we walked out of the trees and stalked toward Grindill. An army of rotting dead pulling swiftly built war machines, torches held in the hands of many of the warriors.

And the Hel-child, eyes burning crimson and shield ablaze with magic at their head.

I had called the power of both goddesses into my veins, though I had no intent to use Hel's magic against my own people. Never again would it be a weapon of war, but those on the walls didn't know that.

And I could all but smell their fear in the glow of the setting sun.

Skade was among them, bow and arrow glowing bright, though she did not shoot. No doubt she'd been ordered not to so that Harald could have the satisfaction of my surrender. Except Skade was no fool—she knew that I was not yet defeated, and her bow wavered.

Leaving my draug to ready the rough catapults, I approached on foot to stop in the same place where Harald once had. Back then I'd stood in Skade's place, defending Grindill.

"Here to surrender, Freya?" she called down. "Or did you just wish to be close enough to hear Bjorn's screams when they split him open like a hog?"

"I do wish to be close enough to hear the screams, Skade," I called back. "Though it will not be Bjorn's lips from which they come." I gave her a feral smile.

Vaguely I could hear a drum beating, audible because the crowd of hundreds within the fortress had fallen silent.

"He has misjudged you, hasn't he?" Skade's braid fell over her shoulder as she tilted her head, considering me. "You know that surrendering yourself will not keep Bjorn alive, for he'll never accept your death. So you'll kill your own people to save him, won't you? Is it your oath that forces you or do you love him that much?"

"Does it matter?"

"No." She drew her bowstring. "It doesn't."

Her magic arrow sped toward me with a god's deadly accuracy, but I did not move my shield to block it. Instead, I moved my magic from the shield to my hand and caught the arrow midair.

Skade gaped at me in shock as I covered her arrow with my magic and held tight. A war of wills, a war of gods, as she tried to call it back and I refused to let go.

"Now, Geir!" I screamed, and the draug raced into range. Working swiftly, they launched loads of smoldering pine boughs over Grindill's walls. "Again!"

More smoking fuel was hurled through the air, but as it flew over the heads of the warriors on the wall, I stiffened. They were not watching me or the draug. Instead, they were turned inward, focused on whatever was happening within Grindill. Arms slack at their sides.

The war for control over the arrow in my grip lessened, and as my attention shot to Skade, it was to discover that the huntress had turned her back to us as well.

Her bow disappeared and her arms slackened. Like she was lost to everything that was going on around her, not the least of which was the undead army at her back.

"Freya!"

Guthrum's shout caught my attention. He burst between the line of draug, racing my way. "Stop! Steinunn is singing! She has them in thrall!"

Which meant none of the people inside the fortress, not even the skald herself, were aware of the choking smoke rolling over them.

Guthrum staggered into me, catching hold of my arms. "Kaja is caught in Steinunn's magic. She's caught in the smoke." His eyes abruptly turned the same yellow as his familiar's, and his body stiffened. "I can see the visions."

"Hold!" I shouted at Geir. "Everyone inside is in thrall!"

As I turned back to the fortress, I knew my orders were in vain.

Because through the clouds of smoke, I saw the first flickers of flame.

CHAPTER 47

BJORN

"Turn around," Tora ordered me, and I obeyed. The hinges on the cell groaned as she opened the door, but I offered no resistance as she took hold of my chained wrists. One of the Nameless gagged me, and then they led me out of the cell and up into the fortress where Troels waited.

"I'd kill you myself for what you and the Hel-child intended to do to our people," my friend whispered. "But death at my hands would be too quick."

I wanted to shout that Harald's words were lies. That my friend was deceived, but with a gag in my mouth, there was nothing I could do but lower my head and pray that Troels would understand once he knew the truth.

The streets of Grindill were packed with people, mostly Skalanders, and it took a dozen of the Nameless to carve a path toward the square. People screamed and jeered at me, throwing rotten vegetables and shit at me as I passed, but I kept my head down and ignored them as best I could as Tora and Troels dragged me onward.

We reached the square, which was set up with a dais, much as it had been when Steinunn had performed her song about the taking of Grindill. Torches burned around the perimeter, and the crowd was pressed so tight that it was a wonder the people could breathe. Harald-as-Snorri stood with Ylva and Leif on the dais, along with his cabal of Unfated. Nearly three dozen men and women with the blood of gods in their veins, and while only some were warriors, all were loyal to Harald. He was their king.

Their savior.

Their father.

I wondered if any of them questioned why the man himself was absent for this moment.

Troels dragged me onto the dais and unfastened my wrists, the Nameless shoving my fists into heavy steel gauntlets fixed to wooden posts that had been set into the platform we stood upon. As I looked up, my eyes skipped past the screaming crowd to the bird perched on one of the buildings. Whether Guthrum had helped Freya, I did not know, but he was watching now.

The crowd screamed and taunted me, naming me traitor and worse until *Snorri* held up his hand for silence. "We will have justice today," he proclaimed. "This man betrayed all of Skaland for the sake of lust for a monster. Our brothers and sisters perished upon the strait at his command and now endure the worst sort of torture as undead slaves to his mistress. Unless she surrenders, we will take her lover's heart as punishment, and tomorrow we will hunt her down and do worse to her!"

The crowd cried for Freya's blood.

Gyda approached and handed *Snorri* a knife. "A gift from my liege, your ally," she said. "It burns like acid as it cuts, ensuring the traitor will scream for mercy and be turned aside at the gates of Valhalla for cowardice."

The smith cast a dark glare of hatred at me as she stepped aside, leaving *Snorri* to gaze upon the knife. Then he held it out, hilt first, to Tora. "It was not just Skaland he betrayed. He aimed to put Nordelander warriors in Helheim as well. I would have you do the honors in Harald's name."

Gods, but he was cruel to the last.

Tora reluctantly took the knife, but as she stepped behind me, Ylva said, "My love, Steinunn told me that she has prepared a song. A story to remind all who listen of why justice must be done today."

Snorri's eyes narrowed in a way that wholly belonged to Harald, and I wondered how many other flaws in his performance that I'd failed to notice over the years. Or noticed, and disregarded. "She honors us."

Steinunn stepped onto the dais with her drum, striking it with a heavy beat. Drawing every eye down upon her as she huffed breaths of air in a rhythm that cast her spell, drawing all of us into the story she told. Instead of tuning her out, as I always did, I allowed her magic to wash over me as she sang the tale of *Harald the Savior*.

She began at the beginning, the story she'd overheard while hiding near my cell beneath Grindill, and visions of a young Harald appeared before me, weeping on his knees before a man-shape of white wax and glowing eyes. "They'll know," young Harald sobbed. "Gyda will know it isn't me!"

"People believe what their eyes tell them," the wax creature whispered. "And I will be a better version of you, so none will have cause to question whether the face they see is false."

"Stop, Steinunn!" Harald-as-Snorri shrieked, but his voice was drowned out by the screams of young Harald as the wax creature tore off his face, its maw slick with crimson as it gulped it down. The wax creature melted, and slowly, it re-formed wearing young Harald's face, lips still stained with red.

The crowd screamed in horror, many shouting, "Child of Loki!," the powers granted to the trickster's children well-known lore.

I tried to rip myself from the vision so that I might see what was happening around me, but Steinunn's magic held me in thrall like it never had before, and all I could see was the story she sang.

The child of Loki wearing young Harald's face appeared before me, and he embraced a far younger Gyda. "I missed you terribly, my dearest friend," he said to her. "But oh the adventures I have to share with you. My greatest regret is that you were not there to experience them with me." Young Gyda embraced him tightly even as the Gyda who watched on cried in dismay.

I could not wrench myself free of the skald's magic though I heard tumult near me. Heard Harald-as-Snorri screaming at his Nameless to make Steinunn stop, but no one could intervene. No one could break free of the story that the skald told, her magic holding all of us in thrall.

A young Guthrum appeared before me, skipping down a path with a large hound at his heels. Laughing and happy, only to return home to find his mother on her knees, weeping.

"Father, what is happening here?" he demanded, because it was not Harald he saw but his own father terrorizing his mother. Yet Steinunn's vision showed the truth—it was the child of Loki.

"You will give Guthrum over to serve the jarl," the child of Loki shouted. "In the jarl's service, our son will reclaim his honor."

"No," Guthrum's mother answered. "I will not. He belongs here with me, in the wilds. I will not send him to Hrafnheim."

The child of Loki beat her with heavy blows while young Guthrum screamed and cried, "Father, stop! Please stop!"

Around me, I heard gasps of outrage from the Unfated, because Guthrum's story was well known. Everyone believed that it had been his father who had beaten his mother, and Guthrum's hound had killed him out of vengeance.

But we all watched in silence as Guthrum prowled through the trees at the heels of his dog, following the child of Loki's trail until they came upon their prey. The man on the ground was disoriented and bleeding, and I saw that his wrists were marred with scrapes, as though he'd been kept bound for some time.

"Guthrum, help me," the man pleaded. "I've been kept prisoner."

"You hurt her!" Guthrum screamed. "I hate you!"

"I haven't hurt anyone!" his father pleaded. "Help me!"

But young Guthrum only turned to his hound. "Kill him."

The hound hesitated, but young Guthrum only howled, "He hurt my mother! Kill him!" and the hound obeyed, screams filling my ears as it tore an innocent man to shreds while he begged and pleaded for his life.

A scene orchestrated by the child of Loki to gain loyalty from one of the Unfated, as Harald swept in to play the savior, young Guthrum weeping at his knees as he promised a lifetime of allegiance.

A younger version of Troels came next in Steinunn's tale. My friend was laughing and calling out his brother's name, but as he raced around a corner, it was to fall into a pit lined with stakes.

"Help me," he screamed, legs punctured in three places. "Aksel, help me!"

He looked up out of the pit at the child of Loki, who was laughing. "Aksel, brother, please help me!"

But the child of Loki only said, "Why do you need my help, brother? You are unfated. Help yourself." Then walked away, leaving Troels to scream and scream until Harald appeared, pulling him out of the pit and seeing him healed.

And the real Aksel, begging innocence, was hung from a tree until he could plead no more, all while Troels pledged allegiance to the one who had masterminded the worst moment of his life.

The stories unspooled, visions rising for each of the Unfated in Harald's cabal, and it was clear as day that the child of Loki had orchestrated every tragedy by taking on the faces of friends and family and turning them into villains that *Harald* could rescue the victim from. Except the only thing *Harald* saved anyone from was himself.

Tears ran down my face as my own story unfolded, Harald pretending to be Snorri as he savaged my mother. Myself as a child bursting from my hiding place to call Tyr's flame, the cabin turning into an inferno as my mother screamed, then Harald, dressed in my mother's clothes, carrying me away from the smoke and flame.

Vaguely I heard Harald-as-Snorri shrieking and thrashing, trying to escape Steinunn's magic so that he could hunt her down and silence her, but then the skald's village filled my eyes. People ran in terror from warriors dressed like Skalanders bearing Snorri's banners, yet as one opened his mouth to scream, the brand of Harald's Nameless was clearly visible on his tongue. The child of Loki led them, laughing as he cut down Steinunn's husband and then set the blade to her young son.

It was not Snorri who had murdered them.

It was Harald, or whatever his true name might be. The child of Loki wearing Snorri's face.

The trickster.

Even though Steinunn had shown me these visions in my cell, her grief in this moment was thick and choking as smoke. Making me desperate to be free of her thrall.

But Steinunn had not yet finished her song.

CHAPTER 48

FREYA

My plan had depended on everyone inside fleeing the flames, but my intentions were in shambles, because though the flames grew, not a person on the wall stirred.

Next to me, Guthrum dropped to his knees. Tears ran down his cheeks and his body shook with heaving sobs as he moaned, "No, no, no!"

"Guthrum, what is happening? What do you see?"

"The truth," he whispered. "Steinunn reveals the truth. Harald is not our savior—he is our curse."

The desire for truth had driven me during so much of my journey. The desire to know it. The desire to reveal it. Now both had been achieved, yet rather than winning the day, the truth was going to see every Skalander in Grindill burned alive.

"Go!" I shouted at Geir, my voice barely audible over the draugs' shouts of dismay. "Break open the gates! Do what you can to find Harald, but it is more important to get everyone out!"

Geir didn't hesitate, his rotting face set in grim determination as he barked orders to the draug warriors. They surged past me with preternatural swiftness, their speed driven by the same desperation that fueled my own. It was their families and loved ones caught in Steinunn's thrall, and with every heartbeat, the smoke thickened. I ran with them, my legs pumping over the uneven ground, but my mind was fixed on only one thing—finding Bjorn.

The draug, their skeletal hands gripping the stone walls, scaled the fortress with grim efficiency, their movements eerily silent. The enthralled Skalanders stood like statues on the battlements, oblivious to the threat as the draug raced between them.

Open the gates, I pleaded. *Get them out!*

The gates exploded open with a thunderous crash, and the first screams of panic filled the night air. Steinunn must have finished her song, and the people of Grindill had been released from her thrall to discover themselves surrounded by smoke. Fear took hold, spreading through the crowd like wildfire as they raced to escape the flames, only to find their paths blocked by the draug. But the undead warriors did not strike them down. Instead, they herded them toward the gates, pushing them toward safety. Saviors, though few understood it.

"Skoll! Hati!" I dropped to my knees at their approach, coughing as the smoke filled my lungs. Placing my hands on their heads, I said, "Stay at the gates. Harald will try to sneak out, and you must find him. When you do, signal the draug as we planned. We might yet have victory here."

Skoll growled in understanding, and Hati raced toward the far gate, his dark fur blending into the smoke and shadow. I lifted my shield and sprinted with Skoll into the chaos before me. The fortress was a nightmare—a place where celebration had collapsed into confusion and fear. Villagers and warriors alike shoved and stumbled in their frantic attempts to escape, their faces twisted in terror. I fought my way through the crowd, heart pounding, my eyes stinging from the smoke. I had to reach the center of the fortress. I had to find Bjorn.

The smoke thickened, turning the world into a suffocating haze of gray and black. I could barely see, and each breath was a struggle as the acrid air burned my lungs. Though only a few rooftops had caught ablaze, it felt like a deathtrap. Every second counted, and yet the winding paths through Grindill seemed endless.

"Bjorn!" I screamed, my voice breaking. "Bjorn!"

But there was no answer, only the cries of those fleeing. The draug were everywhere, their rotting forms moving with purpose, guiding the villagers toward the gates, away from the flames.

Please be alive.

Panic clawed at my heart, threatening to overwhelm me. I shoved my way through the crowd, shield bouncing against my back, but it was like fighting against the flow of a river. The smell of burning wood and thatch filled the air, mixing with the stench of fear.

"Bjorn!" I screamed again, a raw, desperate plea. *Please let this not have been for nothing. Please let him at least be alive.*

The square was empty when I reached it. Empty except for a single figure strung between two posts, his fists encased in steel.

A shriek of horror tore from my chest, certainty that I was too late filling me. But then the figure moved.

I stumbled up the steps onto the dais, the torches casting shadows on Bjorn's skin. *Please be alive,* I prayed. *Please don't be gone.*

I fell to my knees before him, my hand curving around his face, lifting it. His skin was warm, and my heart leaped as Bjorn slowly opened his eyes. "Freya?"

"Oh, thank the gods," I breathed. Pulling the steel contraptions from his fists, I then cut the cords binding him and nearly fell backward beneath his weight as Bjorn collapsed onto me. Wrapping my arms around his shoulders, I buried my face in his neck. "I'm sorry it took so long to get to you."

"It's fine, my love." He kissed me, his fingers digging into my hair. "We will always find our way back to each other."

It felt as though my heart would burst from my chest, because despite every obstacle, we were together. And I refused to let go of him ever again.

But clouds of black smoke rolled over us, and a cough wracked my body. "We need to get out," I said. "Grindill is burning."

Wedging my shoulder beneath his arm, I helped Bjorn stand. All around, roofs were crumbling, flames reaching into the sky. Each breath was more difficult than the last, both of us coughing violently.

"This way!" I dragged him toward the gate.

A roar sounded, and with a rush of hot air and smoke, a building collapsed in our path, driving us back. My eyes stung, bits of ember singeing my hair and skin, and I could not see which way to go through the smoke.

We were trapped.

"Into the great hall," Bjorn choked out, catching hold of my hand and pulling. We stumbled through the smoke and into the stone building, the air blissfully cool after the inferno outside. But the smoke was still thick, the roof no doubt aflame, and it would not be long until the flames found us even here.

"There is a drain that leads to the river," I said between coughs. "We can hide down there until the fires ebb."

Bjorn nodded, his grip on my hand tight as we climbed into the hole. The stink was as horrible as it had been before, filthy water and murk sloshing around us. Bjorn tripped and stumbled in the darkness, so I covered my hand with magic to light our way. We pressed deeper, the smoke clearing. Someone had been down here since my ill-fated plan to speak to Steinunn, and the bodies and debris had been cleared. The lower water level allowed us to nearly reach the river.

"We can wait here," I said when I started to feel the current tugging on me, my magic reflecting off the water.

Bjorn gave a tight nod between coughs, and I pulled him against me. For the first time since I'd met him, his skin felt cold against my hand. My heart skittered, because his injuries must be worse than I'd thought. "Our friends will find us when the fires ease. It's over. We've won."

Yet for all my words, my heart was thundering in my chest, because it wouldn't be over until I was certain Skoll and Hati had found Harald.

That he was finally dead. My skin was crawling, and I had to keep fighting the urge to reach for a weapon. "Bjorn," I whispered, looking into the shadows of the tunnel. "Something isn't right."

He didn't answer. I turned to see him sway backward, and then he slumped beneath the surface.

Gasping, I reached for him. But I was too late.

The current had him.

I dropped my shield and dove after him, the river like ice as it closed over my head. I swam hard with the current, reaching my glowing fingers through the darkness, desperate to find him.

Breaking the surface, I screamed, "Bjorn!"

But I couldn't see him, and worse than water lay ahead. For the roar of the falls was already audible, and without me, there was no hope of Bjorn surviving the plunge.

"Freya!"

I scanned the darkness, then saw Bjorn bobbing ahead in the water. "Hold on," I screamed, swimming as hard as I could toward him.

With the roar coming ever closer.

Please, I prayed. *I only just got him back.*

Yet I knew what fate would come for us was mine to be woven, good or ill. Actions not prayers would be what saved him, and I swam harder, reaching.

Our fingers locked right as we were swept over the falls.

Having done it once before hadn't prepared me for doing it again. My stomach rose in my throat as we fell and fell, my magic cocooning around us. Even protected as we were, the impact of us striking the water rattled my teeth.

We plunged beneath the surface and were immediately caught in the circular flow at the base of the falls.

Black water roared around us, but I dug my nails into Bjorn's arm and swam down. He fought against me, but I gritted my teeth and held on, pulling him to the bottom of the river and then clawing my way along it until we were free of the churn.

Pressing my feet to the bottom of the river, I kicked off, my head breaking the surface.

Bjorn appeared next to me and gasped in a breath.

"This way," I called to him. "To the bank! Swim!"

I kicked my way to the river's edge. A frosty north wind blew over us, turning me so cold that I could barely feel my hands. "Bjorn!"

To my left, a shadow moved, Bjorn crawling up the bank in the darkness, coughing and cursing. I covered my hand with magic and the silver glow illuminated his face. "Are you all right?"

"Fine," he snapped, spitting river water onto the bank. "It's freezing."

Not once in the entire time I'd known him had Bjorn complained of being cold. Nor had he ever spoken to me in that tone.

My skin crawled, and I sat back on my heels as sickness rose in my stomach. "Light a fire."

Bjorn turned his head to regard me, and though he was cloaked in shadows there was a cruelty to his gaze that made my hackles rise.

I reached for the hilt of my sword, only to find it missing, lost to the river.

His mouth twisted into a smile I'd never before seen on his face, and Harald's voice said, "Clever girl, Freya."

CHAPTER 49

BJORN

Steinunn's finale showed Harald's confession to me in the prison beneath Grindill, cries of disgust and fury escaping the crowd's lips as they came to understand that Snorri had not only been murdered but *consumed* by Harald. That the man on the dais was not their king, but the child of Loki himself.

The vision spooled out before me, and I watched Harald lean against the bars of my cell, seeing my own face sick with disgust. "I am everyone and everything," Harald said with a grin. "And nothing and no one. As Nameless as my Nameless, cast aside the moment my mother realized what blood flowed in my veins. Unloved and unwanted because of what I was, and so I made myself into someone new. Over and over again, learning from my mistakes and discovering pieces of lore until I had mastered my art. Harald is my masterpiece, your mother a close second, but Snorri . . ." He sighed happily. "All of Skaland will sing my name even as they dance to the beat of my drum."

The vision focused on his laughing face, then faded with Steinunn's voice as her magic released us from its thrall.

Into a cloud of choking smoke.

Grindill was aflame.

For a heartbeat, no one reacted. Every face in the crowd was tight with horror, none more so than the Unfated, the truth of their tragedies now revealed, and all united in their expressions of disgust. Grief. Pain. Emotions swiftly replaced by anger, eyes sharpening as they searched the dais for the creature who'd torn apart their lives.

But Harald was gone.

"Fire!" someone screamed. "Fire!"

Everything turned to chaos.

"Where is he?" Gyda roared, the smith showing no care for the choking smoke as she drew her blades.

Everyone who'd gathered to watch my execution was crying out in panic, terrified by the clouds of smoke and uncertain which direction to flee.

I tried to pull my hands from the steel gauntlets fixed to the posts, shouting around my gag for someone to free me.

It was Leif who approached, pulling the gag from my mouth. "Father is dead, then?"

Steinunn had purposefully excluded what had happened on the island from her song lest my actions inspire any watchers to take inopportune vengeance. Yet Leif added, "You killed him, didn't you? Because you believed he attacked your mother and caused her death. But it was Harald, wearing Father's face."

It was neither the time nor place for this conversation, but I refused to lie to him anymore. "Yes."

"I want to hate you for killing him." Tears ran down Leif's cheeks. "I want to hate you for being tricked by Harald all these years and doing the things you did, and yet how can I judge you when he had me just as fooled? I never questioned why he wanted me waiting to command Freya using the oath when she surrendered—he made me feel like it was an honor."

"He's a child of Loki." I spat the foul taste of the gag onto the platform. "He tricked us all and we will have his blood for it."

Leif gave a sharp shake of his head, then unfastened the straps holding my fists in the metal gauntlets. "It is clear to me now where the blame lies."

I pulled my fists free. "I'll hunt him down. But you need to get everyone out of Grindill. Freya is not the enemy here, nor her army. They are your allies." I clasped his shoulder, and beyond, I saw Ylva watching. "Make Snorri proud."

Stepping away from my brother, I shouted at the Unfated on the platform. "Harald has manipulated us all and must be stopped, but it will not be an easy hunt. He can take any face, any form, and he has Tora bound against her will with oaths. She will fight to the death to protect him, but not by choice."

Their eyes blazed with fury, but their wrath was no longer directed at me.

"Those of you who cannot fight, lead the people out of Grindill before it burns," I shouted, only for a Skalander warrior to approach, his eyes the glowing green of the draug.

"This is an attack on Harald, not on the people of Grindill." His voice was like knives to my ears. "We will help you flee even as we hunt him down!"

Ylva was the first to react. Her voice reached above the tumult, filling the ears of all. "The enemy is within Grindill, not without! Leave through the gates! No harm will come to you from Freya Born-in-Fire or her army!"

The crowd mercifully obeyed her, following the draug toward safety.

"Those who can fight, we must hunt down the child of Loki!" I shouted, and the Unfated moved around me.

"How do we find him if he can take the form of anyone?" Gyda demanded. "He could have disguised himself as a crone and be fleeing with the masses as we speak. Once outside the gates, we'll never be able to find him again."

"Look for Tora." I scanned the fleeing crowd for her tall form. "He's a coward. He'll keep her to protect him. Go!"

We dispersed in all directions, everyone with murder in their eyes.

And weapons gifted by their gods in hand.

"Tyr," I growled, and my axe burned bright. The smoke had grown so thick it was difficult to see, but I pressed on through the crowd. It was possible he was hiding in one of the homes, but instinct told me that Harald would escape while he had the chance.

Through the smoke, the crowd was slowing ahead. I wiped away stinging tears and saw that Freya's draug were holding them back and allowing them through only a few at a time. I understood immediately when I saw Skoll standing among them. The wolf was sniffing everyone who passed, and while Harald could lie with his form, I was willing to bet he could not alter his smell.

"Clever, Freya." I searched for her among the draug, but she was nowhere in sight. Part of me wanted to seek her out, ensure she was safe, but Harald had to be my priority. Cutting down an alley, I scanned the crowd gathered around the other gate, which was controlled by Hati and the draug.

But there was no sign of Tora or Harald.

I cursed, then coughed on the thickening smoke as I picked my way through the fortress. Searching.

Only to see a familiar tall figure duck down a narrow path between buildings.

My chest tightened because the last thing I wanted to do was hurt Tora, but there might be no other way.

I broke into a run, great wafts of black smoke drawing coughs every few steps. Rounding a bend, I slid to a stop at the sight of Tora and an unfamiliar man dressed in a gray tunic trapped at a dead end.

I did not hesitate.

My axe flipped through the air, end over end, embedding in the back of the man's head. He dropped like a stone, but as he did, a blow struck me and I staggered back.

Pain lanced down my arm, and my gaze latched onto Skade's arrow, which was embedded in my right shoulder.

A trap.

The arrow disappeared, and blood welled to a stream down my arm.

Tora stared at me with miserable eyes as Skade jumped down from the rooftop to land with catlike grace next to the dead man. "Don't feel too badly, Bjorn," she said, nudging the dead man with her foot. "The Nameless all have done things that earned them inglorious deaths. They serve a purpose, but I've always hated them."

"Where is he?" I recalled my axe to me, holding it in my left hand. Well aware that I was at a heavy disadvantage against her. Especially if Tora had been ordered to help.

"You'll not catch him." Skade's smirk grew. "He's far too clever for that."

"Freya will catch him." I moved toward her but she raised her bow, glowing arrow leveled at my chest. "He can wear whatever face he likes—Skoll and Hati still know the stench of arsehole when it hits their noses."

Skade lifted one shoulder. "Your woman does better thinking when you are not around, I'll grant her that. But Freya is not clever enough to outwit him."

Through the smoke, I caught sight of a shadow crawling down the side of the building. Inhuman and strange, yet familiar to me. Lifting my axe, I took another step closer, keeping Skade's attention on me. Tora caught sight of the shadow but said nothing.

"Why are you loyal to him, Skade?" I asked. "Tora has been forced, and the rest of us duped, but you support him of your own free will."

"Because I am his trueborn child." She bared her teeth. "I am his daughter and the heir to all that he has built. I suffered his favoritism of you because I knew the truth. Knew it was but a ploy to take control of Skaland so that he might be king of all the north."

"You are not his child. You cannot be."

Gyda's voice filled my ears, and I turned my head to see the smith behind me.

"I remember when you were born, Skade," she said. "Perhaps Harald of Hrafnheim was your father, but he fled his father's fists while you were still in your mother's belly. Which means the creature you serve shares no blood with you. He killed your Harald, girl. Took his face and his life, and then tricked you the same as the rest of us."

"Lies!" Skade shrieked. "My mother told me Harald was my father before she abandoned me, and he told me that she spoke true. He claimed me as his trueborn heir!"

"Steinunn's magic can only show the truth, and I know your mother was pregnant when my friend fled Hrafnheim and the creature who came back was not him," Gyda answered. "The man you claim as father is dead, and you serve an imposter. You have been deceived."

"No!" Skade lifted her bow, arrow trained on Gyda's heart.

But Geir was faster.

With a draug's preternatural speed, he hurled himself off the side of the building and slammed into Skade, twisting her head as she fell.

The snap of her neck was as loud as thunder.

"For my mother," Geir hissed, looking into her eyes as the light in them dimmed. "I hope Nidhogg consumes your soul."

Silence fell, broken only by the crackle of flames as Grindill was consumed around us.

"Tora, where is Harald?" I demanded. "Can you tell me?"

She shook her head. "I don't know, Bjorn. Truly."

A string of curses tore from my lips. "Geir, where is Freya?"

"I was looking for her when I came upon you." Geir rose to his feet. "She raced in to rescue you."

"Have the wolves found Harald?"

Geir shook his head.

"Keep hunting. Have the draug track down all the Nameless they can and kill them. You'll know them by the brands on their tongues. They are bound to his will. I'm going to find Freya." I broke into a run, weaving my way to the gates only to collide with Guthrum.

"I'm sorry." My friend's face was wet with tears. "I'm sorry I didn't believe you."

As though any of that mattered now.

Grabbing his shoulders, I forced him to meet my stare. "Freya is missing. I need Kaja's help to find her."

CHAPTER 50

FREYA

"Where is he?" I demanded, only to gag as Bjorn's face melted, only to re-form as Harald's.

"Burned alive in Grindill, I expect." Harald took up a large rock in one hand.

No. No no no.

"Thank you for rescuing me, Freya. I dare say, I'd not have escaped if it weren't for your bravery. Never mind that you ruined a lifetime of work, you little bitch." The last came out as a snarl, and he took a step in my direction, bouncing the rock in his hand.

"You wove your own fate, Harald." Hate and grief burned in my chest, but I drew the seax Gyda had given me. The knife was the only weapon I had. "By manipulating the lives of everyone around you with no care for the hurt you caused, only for the control you gained. You destroyed lives for nothing more than your own amusement, and if your cabal has turned on you, it is your own doing."

"I made them powerful."

"You made them slaves to vengeance." I circled, desperately wishing I had my sword and shield. "Then used them to further your own schemes. You might have succeeded for many years longer, but your ambition outreached your skill."

"The only mistake I made was not killing you when I had the chance," he hissed. "You ruined everything!"

"It's a talent." I readied for the attack. "And I'm not finished yet."

Harald's lip curled in a snarl, then he threw his rock. It struck my magic-coated hand and exploded off, landing with a splash in the river.

"Nice attempt—" I broke off, because Harald hadn't been trying to hit me. He'd been trying to distract me.

While he shape-shifted into a monstrous version of Hati.

Fear filled my chest, and I took one step back. Then another. All while the black wolf prowled closer, lips pulled back in a snarl that revealed cruel fangs.

I held up my hand, Hlin's magic glowing bright. Wolf or not, if he leaped at me, he'd be thrown back with twice the force.

Then my ankle twisted in the river rocks, pain spiking up my leg. As I fell, my arms went back to brace myself and all I saw was a flash of midnight fur and murderous fangs.

A scream tore from my lips as I tried to move my magic back between me and death. But I was too slow.

Then fire flared above me. It slammed into the wolf and sent it toppling sideways with a yelp of pain. I scrambled to my feet and snatched up a rock, ready to throw myself at the wolf-Harald and beat him to a pulp, but he disappeared into the trees and was gone.

"Freya!"

I turned. "Bjorn?"

He was on the far side of the river, axe once again in hand. Our eyes locked, then he was running. Wading through the rushing water and out the other side, and then I was in his arms. Wrapped in the warmth of him, his familiar scent filling my nose as I buried my face in his neck and wept. "You're alive," I sobbed. "You're alive, you're alive."

"I told you that I'd have your back until we step through the gates of Valhalla." He pressed his face to my hair. "Death was never an option."

I clung to him, unwilling to let go even as part of me thought that it must be a dream for him to even be here. "How?" The word was choked. "How are you here?"

"Kaja." Above us, the merlin gave a fierce cry, then soared back to the fortress. Bjorn lowered me so that my feet were again on the ground, though his arms remained wrapped possessively around me.

I illuminated my hand, grimacing at the wound in his shoulder. "You're hurt."

"Skade's arrow, so the wound is clean." He let go of me with obvious reluctance, and I noted that it was in his left hand that his axe appeared.

"I'm going to kill her. I'm going to cut out her heart for doing this to you."

"You'll have to bring her back to life." Bjorn lowered his head to kiss me. "She's dead. Geir killed her."

I'd have liked to kill her myself, but it was fitting that it had been my brother who'd delivered vengeance to the one who'd killed our mother. Yet we had more pressing concerns, and my gaze turned to the forest wolf-Harald had disappeared into. "You hit him."

"It wasn't a good blow." Bjorn lifted his axe and took several steps away, revealing a splatter of blood on the rocks. "Injured but not badly enough to kill him. Just badly enough to make him dangerous."

I glanced at the cliff tops. "Does anyone know you're here?"

"Guthrum. He'll bring the others, but if we wait for reinforcements, we'll lose Harald's trail and never catch him again. He can become anyone but no matter who he becomes, he'll never let this go. We need to put an end to him now."

The only weapon I had was my seax. No shield other than magic on my hand. My Hel power would not harm him, and in this form, Harald was lethal.

But so were we.

"Then we hunt." I adjusted my grip on my short blade. "Do you want to go first or shall I?"

"You, I think. You're braver." Bjorn grinned and started into the woods, following the trail of blood. I rolled my eyes and kept to his heels, my eyes on the shadows for any sign of motion.

The woods were strangely silent, all the animals who normally filled the night with their calls seeming to be holding their breath. I didn't blame them. Too easily could I call to mind Harald's wolf form, bigger than any I'd ever seen. Yet it was the mind behind the teeth that I feared, for Harald was clever.

"Where did you hit him?" I asked, noting the irregularity of the wolf's tracks. "He's running on only three legs but there is little blood."

"Shoulder." Bjorn bent to examine a drop of crimson. "But the fire will have cauterized it to some extent, which might explain the lack of blood."

His eyes flicked to mine, suggesting another alternative, which was that Harald was not injured nearly as badly as the tracks indicated.

My pulse escalated, my hand icy yet slick with sweat around the seax's hilt. Because there was a possibility we were not the hunters.

But the prey.

"Do you think he can see in the dark?" Every shadow seemed to be moving. "And hear with the skill of a true wolf?"

"Likely," Bjorn replied. "But given that you are glowing and keep asking questions, I'm quite confident he knows where we are, Born-in-Fire."

My cheeks warmed, but his teasing eased my fear. "Should we extinguish the magic, then? For the sake of stealth?"

"Let's try silence, first."

I drew in a steadying breath and stepped carefully through the woods, watching to the sides and behind, but with my magic covering my hand, there was nothing but blackness beyond the pool of light.

A snapping branch echoed to my left, and I jerked in that direction, heart in my throat. Certain I heard panting breath, I held my own, but silence once again reigned over the forest, and Bjorn pressed on.

Only to draw to a stop a dozen paces later. "Trail ends."

I moved next to him, noting that the trail of paw prints and blood had vanished, almost as though he'd taken flight. Catching Bjorn's eye, I flapped my arms like a bird only for him to shake his head and gesture to his shoulder. No flying, then.

Yet how did we hunt a man who could become any creature, take on any living shape? In the songs, Loki himself took on the shape of a fly, and how did one hunt something so small in the darkness? I did not know the rules his kind were bound to, and frustration began to take hold.

Then a drop of something warm splattered against my cheek.

I yanked my arm upward, magic illuminating a large shadow falling, all fangs and teeth. No longer a wolf but a giant cat. A scream tore from my throat, death seeming certain, but the shadow struck my magic and flipped through the air. It slammed into Bjorn with a feline shriek of rage.

A gasp of pain filled my ears.

The sizzle of burning fur.

Then it was gone into the night.

"Oh gods," I breathed, seeing claw marks forming crimson rows down Bjorn's chest, blood already dampening the waistband of his trousers. "This is madness. We need to get Geir and the others to help us hunt."

"By the time we find them and return, he'll be long gone." Bjorn lifted his axe, moving in the direction the cat had gone. "We kill him now."

He broke into a run, weaving through the trees. I could not see what trail he followed or how he knew which way Harald had gone, but I had no choice but to chase after him.

I tripped and stumbled over deadfall and roots, nearly sprawling more times than I could count. "Bjorn!"

"I can see him. I can see him running and I'm going to fucking kill him!"

"Bjorn!"

No sooner did his name leave my lips did Bjorn disappear from sight, and I only barely managed to slide to a stop, teetering at the edge of a pit.

An old game trap, hastily covered by Harald. From its depths Bjorn looked up at me. "Are you all right?" I demanded. "Are you hurt?"

"Behind you!"

I whirled, lifting my seax, but claws raked across my back. I shrieked and lashed out at the dark shape, but Harald was already slinking back into the shadows.

Neither cat nor wolf.

Not any creature of this world, but a monster of Harald's creation.

I'd never really seen Harald fight, which meant that I'd badly underestimated how dangerous he truly was.

"Freyaaaaa," the creature whispered, voice distorted through inhuman vocal cords. "Freyaaaa!"

"Just defend yourself," Bjorn shouted. "I'm climbing out!"

"Hurry," I whispered, watching the creature circle. It glittered with spines and midnight scales, red tongue flickering out between rows of fangs. Muscled limbs were tipped with claws as long as my hand, and though a deep wound in its shoulder seeped blood, the injury seemed not to trouble it in the slightest.

And I was armed with a blade only the length of my forearm.

"Finally adopted your true form, I see." I kept circling, one eye on the hole in the ground, the other on the beast. "Much more suited to your character."

The creature made a noise that might have passed as a laugh. "Long have I desired to cut out your foolish tongue," it hissed. "To silence the endless idiocy that pours from your mouth."

"Is this to be death by a thousand insults, then?" I asked, willing Bjorn to climb faster, though I knew he'd be hindered by his injured shoulder. "If so, you should have asked Ylva to stand in for you in this as well. She's much more cutting."

Harald snarled, then spat, and I stepped away from the spraying black substance. It sizzled where it struck the ground, and my pulse ratcheted up a notch. Gods, what I wouldn't have given for my shield. For my sword. To not have run headlong into a fight where it seemed I was woefully overmatched.

It swiped a clawed foreleg at me, and I struck, but it was already skittering back only to do the same again. Wearing me down.

But I wasn't the one who was injured. I could keep deflecting attacks until Bjorn got out of the hole, and—

The thought died on my lips, for Harald had withdrawn, serpent's eyes considering. Then he changed, melting and re-forming. Himself again but with multiple tentacles sprouting from his body, each with a talon on the end.

"Bjorn!" I screamed. "Fucking climb!"

A tentacle lashed toward me and I blocked it, but another one was already flying at my side, talon gleaming. I dived away, rolling to my feet and barely managing to block another strike.

Only for another to swipe at my legs.

I fell onto my back, and the impact nearly knocked my seax from my grip. Cursing, I rolled, a talon glancing off my chain mail vest. Another scaled tentacle swiped at my head, and I lifted my seax to slice off the tip.

A heartbeat later, pain lanced through my thigh and I realized my error. Harald laughed through his fanged mouth as he backed away.

My thigh was pulsing blood in the light of my magic, but it was the horrible burn that sent terror rushing through my veins. The talons were venomous.

"Foolish girl," Harald cackled, sitting back on his haunches, clearly content to watch me slowly die. "Useless magic of a minor god, and what valuable magic you have is ineffective. Hel will not harm me out of . . . *familial loyalty.*"

I pushed up onto my hands and knees.

Harald only laughed. "One must admire your determination. But it is I who will weave your fate, Freya, not you. Mine is the stronger thread."

"Is this the fate you desired, Harald?" I got to my feet. My leg was in agony, so weak it would barely hold my weight. "Your cabal, lost. Your kingdom, lost. Your power, lost."

His tentacles quivered, revealing his anger, and I kept a wary distance, circling. My eyes on the glow of fire in the hole.

I limped sideways. "I achieved my destiny, Harald. I united Skaland by controlling my own fate, which means that all of this is my doing, not yours. Saga's vision has come to pass, and I wonder how it feels to know that despite everything you have done, all your tricks and manipulations, that you could not change the future she saw. *Mine* is the stronger thread."

"Then allow me to cut it short!" He lunged at me, tentacles flashing through the air and knocking my seax from my grip, the weapon lost to the shadows.

But as he did, Bjorn's axe cut into the earth next to the hole and he dragged himself out. Muddy and bloodied, he lifted his axe and hurled it.

Flame flipped end over end through the air, and Harald shrieked as one of his tentacles was severed, another nearly so.

"I hope that part wasn't important to your man-form," Bjorn said, axe reappearing in his left hand, right arm dangling limp at his side. "I'm not entirely certain what goes where."

Harald snarled, and more tentacles exploded from his sides, lashing out wildly. Bjorn sliced and severed, but there were too many. It was only a matter of time until one struck true, Bjorn's fate determined by that awful black venom at the tips of those talons.

Mine already was.

There was only one way to end this.

Guile. Not force.

Feeling my strength fading, I flung myself on the creature's back and wrapped my arms around its neck.

"I curse myself," I whispered, feeling my magic surge. "Hel, take my body from this mortal realm."

Roots erupted from the earth, wrapping around my body and pulling me back. Harald tried to extricate himself from my grip, but I got my good leg around him and held on. The roots dragged me into the earth, and because his blood was as divine as my own, I took Harald with me.

Dirt pressed in all around and denied me breath, but then we were falling.

I let go of Harald and caught hold of Yggdrasil's roots, stopping my plunge while he carried on and on. My leg burned, and I could feel his venom stealing my strength. Slowly killing me.

"Freya!"

Bjorn's voice was distant. So very distant, and yet I still looked up, imagining that I could see him digging. Trying to go after me, though his magic did not give him the power to cross between realms.

I could climb back up to him, and maybe we could get help. Maybe Volund would reach me in time. Maybe I could have the future I dreamed of for myself, a life with the man I loved that wasn't touched by terror and violence.

I could weave that fate.

Reaching up, I heaved, dragging myself higher. Only to hear motion below.

Peering through the roots, I saw that Harald was alive and back in his human form, though he was bleeding heavily from several wounds, one hand almost entirely missing. Still, he rose to his feet, and I heard him whisper, "Sister, I need your aid."

And beyond the gates to Helheim, I heard the soft thud of giant feet approaching.

No.

No, I could not let this happen. Could not let Hel aid her mortal half brother and set Harald loose again upon the world. I refused.

"Freya!"

The desperation in Bjorn's distant scream tore at my heart, and I cast one last look up into the darkness, silently whispering, *Please forgive me.*

Then I began to work my way down the tree's mighty roots, arms and legs trembling as Harald's venom continued to work its way through me.

His heavy breathing betrayed his distress, but Harald was walking toward the gates to Hel's realm beyond which the sound of the goddess approaching was growing.

I had to put an end to him, and time was running short.

Sliding the rest of the way down the roots, I dropped through empty air to land with a thud on the road. My legs buckled, and I fell to my knees. When I lifted my face, Harald was staring at me with a strange mix of fear and rage.

For a heartbeat, I thought he'd move to attack, but instead he stumbled down the road toward the bridge, the gates to Helheim on the far side. My body was weak, each breath a struggle, but Harald was leaving a heavy trail of blood.

The noise of the river grew louder, black waters rippling beneath the bridge, and the hound who guarded the gates rose to its feet and approached, eyes full of interest.

And recognition.

Garmr's lips curled back at the sight of me, but I ignored the creature and flung myself at Harald's back. We went down in a heap, grappling and rolling, fists flying. Though we were both too weak to do much damage to each other.

His skin rippled beneath my grip as he tried to change form, but it was as though he could not grasp other shapes, mutating between half-formed beasts with no reason to them.

My breathing was ragged, the world spinning in and out of focus and my heart stuttering.

We were both dying—it was only a matter of who would pass first.

You can do this, I silently chanted. *You can stop him for good.*

Harald went still.

He's dead. You did it, he's dead.

My strength abandoned me in that moment, my grip loosening on his body. I'd defeated Harald, and not a moment too soon, because my own end felt near.

His corpse shuddered.

I stiffened, praying to the gods it was nothing more than muscle spasms after death.

But then Harald's body began to lengthen.

Elongating into a horrifying mix of man and serpent, it slithered onto the bridge. Re-forming, Harald coughed up blood. "You cannot win this."

And the moment to try to defeat him was over, for the gates to Helheim had opened and Hel emerged. As before, her enormous form began to shrink as she walked away from her realm, and she was human-sized when she reached Harald.

"Aid me, sister," he begged. "Please."

Hel cocked her head, the living side seeming bemused though the dead side of her face was impassive as always. Instead of answering him, she growled, "I have not forgotten that you stole from me, daughter. You owe me a debt. You owe me your soul."

My throat moved as I swallowed, for I had known this was the risk. Not just to be parted from Bjorn in life but in death as well. "If you agree not to aid him, you can have me."

"You are in no position to bargain. Your mortal life fades, and I will take what belongs to me."

"Freya does not belong to you," a female voice said from behind me. "I made sure of that twenty-one years ago when I tempered your blood with my own."

Hel's amusement fell away even as shock struck me silent.

For striding toward us was a warrior goddess. Her blond war braids hung down to her waist, a shield resting on her back and a sword belted at her side.

It was like looking into a face I'd known all of my life. Like looking into the eyes of my mother.

"Hlin," I croaked out. "You're here."

The goddess's mouth curved up in a half smile. "I once told your mortal mother that if you were only given avarice, your words would be curses. But if you were gifted altruism, what divine power you might make your own was a fate yet unwoven. Except my blood was no more a gift than Hel's, was it?"

Hlin knelt on one knee before me, then her hand curved around my cheek. "To care for others is a burden, but you have shouldered it better than I dared to hope. You tore apart the grim weavings the Norns had for this land and its people beneath the rule of Loki's son, and their fingers work swiftly on their looms to rebuild the tapestries of fates around your thread, which shines silver-bright. I am proud to call you daughter, Freya Born-in-Fire, for you have honored my blood."

Her expression cooled as her gaze returned to Hel. "That you fell for Freya's trick does not put her in your debt. If you want her soul, you must fight for it."

"Fight whom?" Hel's mouth twisted in a sneer. "No one else stands ready to claim her and you have no hall for the dead. Freya is mine."

Hlin didn't answer, only smiled.

The ground quivered, enormous figures appearing all around, and the air seemed to compress with the weight of so much divinity. It seemed as though every one of the gods had come to witness this fight, just as they had all come that night on Fjalltindr.

Hel's lips pursed in irritation and, reaching down, she touched Harald.

In a heartbeat, he was made whole.

Snickering, Harald stood with his hands on his hips. "You still lose, Freya."

Turning, he started down the far side of the bridge, laughing as he went.

Pushing to my feet, I covered my hand with Hlin's magic and then met the gaze of one of the gods who stood watching on, fire dancing across his palms. "Tyr," I whispered. "Can you lend me his flame?"

The corner of the god's mouth turned up, then he reached into Yggdrasil's roots and pulled.

Bjorn's axe appeared in my hand, burning with deadly intensity, but the fire did not touch me through my magic. Lifting it over my head, I heaved, watching it flip end over end, my aim as true as it had been the first time I'd thrown the weapon.

Silence stretched, broken only when Harald cackled, "It was a good attempt, *Born-in-Fire*."

He took two quick steps back, appearing ready to run, but then his gaze fell upon the corpse at his feet.

On his own skull, severed in half by Bjorn's axe.

"No," he whispered. "Not possible."

"You are nothing more than a soul now." I let go of Bjorn's axe and it vanished. "You have lost."

Harald's eyes desperately searched the darkness as though he might find salvation. "Father? Father!"

"Loki is not here," Tyr answered. "He mislikes watching his schemes come to unsatisfying ends."

"It isn't over!" Harald shrieked. "This is not the end!"

He turned to scamper off into the mists, only to draw up short, Saga blocking his path.

"You!" He recoiled from her. "It's not possible!"

"I've been waiting for this moment for a long time, Harald." She shoved her hands into his chest, driving him back. "You took my life."

Shove.

"You killed my people."

Shove.

"You hurt my son!"

Saga gave him one final shove, Harald stumbling and nearly falling.

Her eyes then locked with mine, and Saga said, "Tell Bjorn that I love him."

My lips parted, every part of me wanting her to tell Bjorn herself, but Saga flung herself at Harald, knocking him back.

"Thank you, Freya," she whispered as they fell through the gates of Helheim, souls now bound to the realm of the goddess of death. The gates slowly shut behind them.

I dropped to my knees.

"Your end is near, daughter," Hlin murmured. "I have not the power to change that, and I think that Hel will not aid you as she did her brother."

With the way Hel was watching me with greedy eyes, she would do anything to claim the opportunity of taking my soul into her keeping.

"You are mine, Freya." Hel smiled. "You will wander my halls until the end of days."

Then the ground beneath me trembled, and all the gods around me lowered their heads as yet another appeared.

A warrior with but one eye held out his hand to me. "I claim you, Freya Born-in-Fire. You will fight well in the last battle."

I stared at the Allfather's palm.

The offer of Valhalla.

Hel shrieked in fury, but Odin only cast a dark look in her direction, and she scrambled back, cowering.

Meeting Odin's eye, I shook my head. "Not yet. I'm not finished. I have to try to get back to him."

Turning to Hlin, the goddess who had shaped the light part of my soul but also the one who had caused me the most pain, I asked, "Will you help me climb, Mother?"

Hlin nodded. "I will bring you to the base of Yggdrasil, Freya. But you must win yourself free of this place."

Putting her shoulder beneath mine, Hlin lifted, and then it was as though I were flying. She leaped from root to root, climbing with a speed I could scarcely comprehend, everything around her illuminated by silver light. The scent of damp earth filled my nose, and Hlin arrested her momentum before steadying me on a thick root.

"I cannot see your future," she said. "I do not know what will happen next, Freya. Show me."

Then she was gone.

I reached for the earth above me only for my strength to falter. Suddenly, I was certain that Hlin had not seen my future because I had none. That Harald had struck the final blow, his venom the death of me.

"If I cannot have your soul today, then I do not wish for Odin to have it either." Hel's voice filtered up through the tree's roots. "You have power over death, daughter. Power over the dead. And the Unfated never lose their magic just as they never lose the power to choose the weave of destiny. Use that knowledge to save yourself."

"How?" I tried to shout but it came out as a whisper. And Hel did not respond, the only sound the thud of the gates to Helheim closing behind her.

Power over the dead.

My eyes squeezed shut. *Think.*

And the answer came.

"Hel," I whispered. "Grant me your power."

Heat roiled through me, and though I knew not his name, I knew his face. Knew the feel of every soul I'd sent to her, and I called. The roots of the tree shook, and the leader of the Islunders that I'd cursed climbed next to me, still wearing his bear helm.

"We underestimated you, shield maiden," he said. "And paid a heavy price. Though, judging from the corpse below, not as heavy as Harald of Nordeland."

"I need you to do something for me," I whispered.

"Why should I?" he asked. "You cursed me to Helheim. Denied me Valhalla."

It was tempting to remind him that those who turned children into thralls did not deserve glory, but for once, I held my tongue. He met my gaze for a long moment, then gave a resigned sigh.

"My brother was one of those whose name Harald stole, bound, and forced to serve. One of his Nameless," the Islunder said. "In killing Harald, you killed the volva whose magic imprisoned him. In killing

Harald, you freed my brother, and if he yet lives, he is free. For that, I will grant you one favor, shield maiden."

"I need you to find me someone." And with what was near to the last of my strength, I whispered a name.

Seconds passed. Or a lifetime. I didn't know. Only that when I opened my eyes again, Liv perched next to me on a root, the healer's familiar smile tearing a sob of relief from my throat. "This is what you get for allowing yourself to be won over by good looks and a charming smile, Freya," Liv said. "I hope you've learned your lesson."

"One would think," I whispered. "But wisdom has never been my strength."

Liv laughed and then took hold of my hands. "Eir, give me the strength to help my friend."

Her hands glowed, warmth filling me, and Liv smiled. "If you can fight your way free of this place, you will leave behind his poison." She let go of my hands. "Climb!"

I punched my fist into the dirt above me and heaved. A groan of pain tore from my lips because the venom Harald had put into my veins was like a leash holding me back. Yet as I heaved upward, a glance down revealed strands of black ichor stretching between my body and Liv's hands.

Tensing my muscles, I dug my other fist into the dirt and pulled. The pain was like nothing I'd ever felt before and I screamed.

I could not do this.

I could not.

"Freya!"

"Bjorn." His name came out as little more than a whisper and, sucking in a breath, I shouted, "Bjorn!"

Digging my hands into the damp earth, I began to crawl back to him. Clawing through earth and stone, I dragged my dying body back into the mortal realm, fighting toward the sound of his voice even as my strength failed, my heart stuttering in my chest. Breath kept from me by more than just the dirt pressing all around.

If I could just make it to him, I would live.
If we were together, we could have a future.
I controlled my fate.
I controlled my fate.
I controlled my—

CHAPTER 51

BJORN

As the roots exploded from the earth and wrapped around Freya, I lunged. Cutting and slashing at them, but more appeared to take their place. I reached for her, my fingers brushing the side of her face as the roots dragged her, and the beast that was Harald, down into the ground.

Leaving only undisturbed dirt in their wake.

"Freya!" I screamed, flinging myself down and clawing at the ground. "Freya!"

I couldn't lose her. Not like this, knowing that she'd sacrificed herself. Not for any reason, because she was my life. My heart. Where she went, I went with her, yet she'd gone somewhere I could not follow.

"Freya!" I howled, digging down and down, but there was nothing but dirt and rocks and roots from the trees around me. "Freya!"

"Bjorn!" I turned my head to see Tora running toward me, Guthrum and Voland on her heels. "What has happened?"

"She's gone." My nails tore from my fingers as I dug, flinging aside rocks and earth. "Hel took her and Harald."

Then cold hands closed over my wrists, tendon and bone visible where skin had fallen away, and I looked up into what had once been Geir's face, now barely recognizable.

"She has gone to the place between realms." His voice was awful and strange. A draug's voice. "No matter how deep you dig, you can't reach her."

I ripped my hands from his grip and kept digging. "I'll find her. I have to. She can't be . . ."

"She's not dead," Geir said. "Else our souls would be liberated from the shells she bound us to and we would have moved on to Valhalla."

Cold comfort, because I'd seen the wound on her leg from Harald's stinger. How she'd staggered beneath the weight of the venom. How her skin had been deathly pale. She needed a healer. Needed a child of Eir to save her life, but I needed to find her first. "Freya!"

"She can't hear you. She's beneath Yggdrasil."

His words were noise in my ears, because I needed to find her. "She's hurt."

"As are you," Volund said, the healer stepping closer. "You are no good to her if she returns to find you dead."

They didn't understand. If she didn't come back, life meant nothing. My path was at her side. That was my fate. The only future I wanted. "Freya!"

Next to me, my glowing axe disappeared, casting us in darkness; but I didn't care. I kept digging. No one stopped me, and I cared not for their silence. Their pity. Because as long as Geir and the other undead were still standing, she was alive. And I'd never stop fighting my way to her. "Freya!"

"Bjorn!"

I froze, not certain if I'd heard my name or imagined it, only that it had been Freya's voice. "Did you hear that?"

Geir shook his head.

"I heard her," I whispered, then shouted, "I hear you, Freya!"

My fingers were a bloody mess, but I didn't care as I clawed at the earth. Geir dug too. Everyone around me dug to find the woman who had fought to save us all.

I ripped away a rock, then sucked in a breath at the sight of pale scarred fingers smeared with dirt. Still fingers.

No.

All the world fell away. Nothing else mattered but getting her out of the ground. Having her in my arms. But above all else, her still drawing breath.

"Freya!" I roared. "I'm here!"

Her arms were free, limp, and my fingers caught in her tangled hair as I struggled to expose her face.

She was so still.

Her face was cleared now, eyes closed. Someone was screaming. I was screaming. Struggling to pull her free, Geir and the others digging around her body.

Then she was in my arms.

Her skin was cold.

I'd lost her. Lost my heart as surely as I'd cut it out of my chest. "Please, Freya," I pleaded, holding her close. "Do not make me walk alone."

Then she stirred and sucked in a ragged breath, blinking up at me with dirt-crusted eyelashes. "Bjorn?"

CHAPTER 52

FREYA

All around me were people, living and undead, but I saw nothing but Bjorn. Nothing but his muddy cheeks streaked with tears and his hands with so much blood.

"I thought I'd lost you," he breathed, pressing his forehead to mine. "Never do that to me again."

If I had my way, I'd never go back to that place. Not even in death. "Harald is dead. I killed him with your axe."

Bjorn blinked. "How . . ."

"It's a long story better told with a cup of mead in hand."

Geir stood back from us, and though it was hard to tell given how much of his face was now missing, I swore he was smiling.

"You did it, sister," he said. "You united not just Skaland, but Nordeland along with it, and defeated the trickster who sought to twist all our fates. All skalds will sing of your story, for it is one to be passed down through generations to come."

Once, that had been my dream. But now I dreamed of different things.

"You fought with honor at my side." My voice was rough, and my mouth tasted like dirt. "You have earned a place in Valhalla, brother. I would release you to join the Allfather unless there is something else that you would do before you leave the mortal realm?"

Geir shook his head. "Take care of my family for me. Tell them my stories."

"I will," I promised. "They are mine to protect until I follow you to Valhalla. Have a cup waiting for me."

Geir nodded, then pulled his sword and lifted it into the air, all the other Skalander draug doing the same with their weapons as they approached from the shadows. Men and women that I'd killed as enemies, brought back as allies, but now released as friends. My brother shouted, "Honor to Skaland! Honor to the shield maiden! Honor to Freya Born-in-Fire!"

My army screamed his words in their awful voices, and my heart swelled with pride to have fought alongside them. "I release you."

Bodies crumpled to the earth all around me, mist swirling on the wind, a charge sharpening the air. Then they were gone.

My brother was gone.

Sorrow filled my chest, for though Geir had been dead for many days, he had still been with me. Had been a stalwart presence at my side. We'd reconciled our differences, and I grieved for the lost chance to live as a family without conflict between us. To watch him become a father. Twin tears carved their way down my cheeks, brown with mud as they dripped onto Bjorn's shoulder.

"You'll see him again," Bjorn said. "He earned his place and he'll be waiting for you."

I believed that. Believed that the Allfather would want Geir in his army at the last battle and that, one day, I'd have the chance to fight alongside my brother once more.

But the afterlife would not reunite us with everyone we'd lost.

"Your mother has gone to Helheim. She took Harald's soul with her to keep him from pursuing more trickery, but her last words to me were to tell you that she loves you."

Bjorn's jaw tightened, eyes turning liquid for a moment before he blinked. His voice was steady when he spoke again. "She'll be at peace there. She was not meant for violence and war, and I think she's suffered enough pain for two lifetimes." The corner of his mouth curled up. "And she'll keep Harald in check, that we know."

Peace.

Oh, how that word sang to my soul, and as I looked around me at the Unfated who'd been my allies and enemies in equal measure, I longed for it. Longed to cast aside magic and weapons and violence and just live. Longed to be happy.

Footsteps approached, and I lifted my head to see Steinunn. The skald's face was pale and splattered with blood, a bandage wrapped around one arm, but she also had my shield hooked over her shoulder. She must have found it near the river. The others allowed her to pass, and she dropped to her knees next to me and Bjorn. "I am sorry." She handed me my shield, the silver metal dented from going over the falls. "Sorry for aiding him. Sorry for everything."

"You were deceived," Tora reminded her. "As were so many."

"Yes, but I was also selfish. I cared not for Harald's deception of others because I believed he had given me vengeance for the family I'd lost. I took no action until I learned that the person who deserved my vengeance was him." Steinunn's chin quivered. "I do not deserve your forgiveness, Freya, and do not ask for it. But please know that I am sorry, and that I will accept your punishment."

What she said was true, and yet I did not have it in my heart to fault her for it. Not because her final song had unveiled the truth but because her weakness was one I bore as well. Was a weakness all of us here bore, for we all let our hearts make choices for us. It was only those who refused to acknowledge their weakness that I could not forgive. "I have decided on what your punishment will be."

I could feel her fear, smell it in the sweat that dampened her clothes, but Steinunn nodded.

"I would have you compose a ballad of all that has happened. A ballad that you will sing all over Skaland and Nordeland so that everyone will know the truth." I tilted my head. "And you must include your part in it as well."

Steinunn lifted her face.

"You told me once that no one cared to hear your story," I said. "But it was that you were too afraid to tell it. Your punishment is to confront that fear, Steinunn, and, in doing so, forgive yourself. Your destiny is your own, my friend."

Tears rolled down the skald's face, and she nodded. "A ballad for the ages. The Saga of the Unfated."

"More caterwauling," Bjorn grumbled. "But it is a good title."

Laughter spilled through the group, dispelling the tension, and with it gone I felt exhaustion take hold. Seeming to sense it, Bjorn tightened his grip and lifted me into his arms. "You need warmth and rest and healing."

"I can walk and you are too injured to carry me." I was not entirely sure if that was the truth or a lie, because I was weary to the bone. "Put me down."

"I'm fine. And after what you put me through, I have no intention of ever letting you go."

I wrapped an arm around his neck, mindful of his injuries. "You do understand that isn't practical."

"I am not a practical man," Bjorn retorted. "In fact, I would argue that I am one of the most impractical men you will ever meet." He cast a sideways glance at Steinunn. "You may put that in the part of your song about me."

"If there is space." Steinunn adjusted her bandage. "There are only so many lines that I can dedicate to minor players, or the listeners may become bored."

Bjorn burst into laughter. "I may revise my opinion of you, skald. You have more spirit than I once thought."

I smiled, relaxing against him as the group laughed and bickered. Silence was never allowed to rule, and I knew that it was because all the Unfated present were coming to grips with the painful revelations that

Steinunn's song had delivered upon them. Many had spent most of their lives twisted up in Harald's lies and were now faced with uncertain futures. I wondered how many would return to Hrafnheim and how many would move on to other places and find other jarls to serve.

Tora walked with a determination I'd never seen in her before. Finally unleashed from Harald's runic magic, she seemed like another person entirely. Ready to take her fate by the horns with the same strength as her godly father, and I hoped that she'd guide the others to do the same.

Because I didn't want any of them looking to me to weave the rest of their futures. I had my own to manage.

With Grindill having burned to the stones it was built upon, all had gathered in the village of Torne, and our group made its way to the mead hall where some of the jarls who had been sworn to Snorri had congregated.

"Put me down, Bjorn," I said softly when we reached the doors. "This is a moment I must face on my feet."

He set me down carefully, though his arm remained tight around my waist as I walked inside. All fell silent at the sight of us, and my eyes went immediately to Ylva, who stood at Leif's elbow. We would never be friends, she and I, but we were no longer enemies. She gave me a nod of respect, and I reciprocated, because while she'd caused me a great deal of trouble, she was also a woman who fought for the well-being of her people. But most of all, she fought for those she loved.

"Harald is dead," I said. "His soul is in Helheim, under the watch of the seer Saga, who will keep his trickery in check lest he trouble those who live in that realm."

Conversation and exclamations turned the hall into a riot of noise, and I waited for it to quiet before I continued. "The story in its whole will be told to you with a child of Bragi's magic so you may know the truth to it."

Steinunn nodded. "A tale that will immortalize the heroism of all until the end of days."

"What now?" a jarl demanded. "Do you claim both thrones, shield maiden? Are we to bend the knee to the queen of Nordeland and Skaland?"

I shook my head. "Our people were never meant to be ruled by one man or one woman. We are meant to be led by individuals who know the names of every soul in their jarldom. By men and women who know the needs of each village and farm, for we are clans. Families. Those who seek to change that do so not for the good of the people but because they desire power and influence, which makes them the worst sort to follow."

Accepting a cup from Tora, I took a sip, finally washing away the taste of mud. "We united for the sake of defeating a common enemy. Now he is dead, and so we must turn back to our clans. Work together to heal after the losses of so many who have gone on to the halls of Valhalla to join the Allfather so that they might fight for us again at the end of days."

"What of you, Freya?" Ylva asked. "It was foretold that you would unite Skaland."

"But not that I would keep it that way." I drew in a steadying breath. "We united for a purpose. For a moment when the strength of one clan was not enough, and it needed to be the strength of all. That moment has ended, and what will come next is unknown."

Taking another sip, I lifted my cup. "Jarls, take our people home and look to your own clans and hearths, but never forget the moment when we stood side by side as allies. *Skol!*"

"*Skol!*" Everyone in the room shouted, lifting a cup, and I stepped back so that they'd understand that the moment I'd stood above them was over, and that I was now one of them once more.

Or nearly so.

Tugging on Bjorn's arm, I led him to Ylva and Leif. Inclining my head, I said, "Jarl Leif."

The boy blinked. "I . . ."

"You are Snorri's heir," I reminded him. "But more than that, you are Ylva's heir, and I have faith that she will stand at your shoulder until you are ready to stand on your own."

Ylva drew in a deep breath. "Thank you, Freya. I do not deserve your generosity."

"You are one of the most unpleasant women I have ever met," I said. "But though I often wished to drown you in a pool of pig shit, I never doubted your commitment to those who matter to you."

"I would be honored to have you both as members of my war band." Leif looked between me and Bjorn. "No word of what you said was an untruth, but there will be jarls who see an opportunity to be had. Raids will follow. And with Grindill in ashes, we are an easy target."

I went still, remembering when such an offer had consumed my dreams, asleep and awake. But now knowing the taste of war, the smell of it, the hurt of it, I found myself not wanting any part of it. I looked up at Bjorn, and I could see in his gaze that he felt the same.

Clearing his throat, Bjorn answered, "With respect, brother, we must decline."

"But you can't!" Leif's eyes were full of panic. "I need you. You must stay."

Despair filled me because of my sudden certainty that although Snorri was dead, I remained leashed. Forever to be used by those who desire my magic as a weapon. Yet as I forced myself to breathe, I discovered that the compulsion was not there. My gaze shot to Ylva's. "The blood oath . . . How is this possible? It can only be broken by your death."

"Or yours," Ylva answered. "Runic magic is a power of the mortal realm. Death breaks its hold."

"You were cold when we pulled you out of the ground, Freya," Bjorn said. "Maybe . . ."

"It was before then." My mind drifted to when Geir had been carrying me out of Helheim. How my heart and breath had stopped, my life slipping through my hands. For a moment, I'd been dead. "All this time, I've been free and I didn't even know it."

The revelation was a weight off my shoulders and, squaring them, I glared at Leif. "Don't presume to order me about, jarl. If you want something from us, learn to ask nicely."

Leif blinked, then gave me a respectful nod. "I will keep that in mind. But . . . where will you go?"

"Time will tell."

Without another word, we turned and left the mead hall. Volund followed after us and saw to Bjorn's injuries, and then we bid him farewell. There were no beds to be had in Torne, the now-homeless families of Grindill sleeping many to a bed in every spare room in the small town. Instead of taking space in the barn, Bjorn took a horse. "Can you ride, Born-in-Fire?"

Curious, I nodded. "Where are we going?"

"Somewhere we can call our own."

We rode at a walk, Bjorn's axe illuminating the darkness until dawn lit the night sky, and when it did, a smile lit my face, for I knew where we were.

"I've thought a fair bit about where you would want to live, Born-in-Fire."

"Oh, you did?" I examined the burned remains of Saga's cabin, nearly consumed now by vegetation. "And between which instance of fighting for your life did you do this thinking?"

"I can do two things at once."

I snorted, and he shrugged. "When I was locked up at Grindill, I had a great deal of time on my hands while I waited for you to rescue me. Time to think about what might come after you defeated all your enemies."

Warmth suffused my chest at his admission that he thought about our future the way I did. Fantasies about what our life could look like if we only persevered. That I was the future he reached for in his darkest hours, just as I reached for him.

"It doesn't have to be here. If you want to be nearer to Selvegr, we could rebuild your parents' home."

I turned my head to hide my smile at the faint hint of nervousness in his voice, unfamiliar because Bjorn was nothing if not wholly confident. But this was new. For him. And for me.

"Here is perfect," I said. "I like the idea of having a warm bath whenever I desire it."

"Do you desire it now?" His hands closed on my waist, lips brushing my neck. "Please say yes, for you taste like a mouthful of dirt."

"You should look at your own reflection before you cast stones." I turned in his arms, kissing him deeply and burying my fingers in his hair, not remotely caring that both of us were filthy with mud, blood, and worse. "Actually, I take that back. You are vain enough without getting in the habit of admiring your own reflection."

He laughed, allowing me to walk him backward in the direction of the cave with the hot springs, leaving clothes in our wake.

"Marry me, Born-in-Fire," he whispered as he drew me into the warm water, the current washing away the filth of our ordeals if not the memories. "Be my wife. Build a life with me in this place."

"Are you sure?" I curved my hand around his face. "Are you sure you will be content with a quiet life?"

Because I needed peace. Needed to put away weapons and chain mail. Needed to hang up my shield. Needed to heal my body and my soul, and I did not foresee a time that I'd ever want to go back to the life I once dreamed of.

"The life I dream of is with you, Freya," he replied. "It doesn't matter where we are or what we are doing. As long as you are in my arms, I will be whole. Will you marry me?"

I smiled as the warm water wrapped around us, the darkness holding us close, because I'd fought for this fate and won. "Yes."

EPILOGUE

FREYA

A drop of water struck my forehead, and I frowned up at the ceiling of the home Bjorn and I had built together. "The roof is leaking again."

Bjorn muttered something that sounded distinctly like *we should burn it down and try again,* and I elbowed him in the ribs. "We will do no such thing."

"It would be easier than fixing that leak." He rolled on top of me, his loose hair falling down to brush my cheeks as he kissed me. "We could go back to living in a tent."

"The tent was cold," I reminded him.

"I don't recall hearing you complain."

His lips moved to my jaw, then my throat, and heat kindled between my thighs though the gods knew that the reason we'd slept so late was that we'd been up past the midnight hour doing just this. I traced my fingers down the muscles of his back, as hard as they'd been a year ago despite neither of us having wielded a weapon since swearing loyalty to Leif as our jarl.

This life was harder, in its own way, laboring to survive rather than fighting, but I'd relished every moment of it. Falling asleep in my husband's arms, his breath warm against my cheek in the winter night, only to wake to the feel of his touch. A touch that made me burn as much now as it ever had, the love I felt for him giving life to me more thoroughly than the air in my lungs.

A droplet of water splattered against Bjorn's bare back, but he ignored it, moving his way down my body to my breasts. Outside, the goats were raising a racket in their desire to be milked, the rooster reminding us that it was past dawn and he wished to be fed, the horses adding to the cacophony of noise.

"There is work to be done," I murmured, my smile growing as he growled, "It can wait."

"You're a terrible farmer."

"I only pretend to be a terrible farmer so as not to provoke the jealousy of our neighbors." His cock pressed into me, a soft sigh escaping my lips as my body stretched around his girth. "Keeps the peace, else they might seek vengeance against me for having nothing to . . . *hang their shovels upon* when their wives make comparisons. It is a kindness."

"Gods know, I wed you for your altruism." I wrapped my legs around his waist, pulling him deeper, every part of me wanting more.

"Liar. You married me for my good looks."

"Well, it certainly wasn't your modesty."

Bjorn gave a low laugh, then shifted his weight, the angle of his thrusts making me gasp, my climax already rising, the ache of standing on the brink of pleasure stealing wit and words from my tongue as my husband, my love, my life, claimed me. I fell over the edge, taking him with me, my heart aching with as much pleasure as my body when he murmured, "I want for nothing in life because I have you."

Wrapped in furs and in his arms, I closed my eyes, no part of me wanting to move. But then I heard a faint snap of shifting rushes, and Bjorn yelped as a melting crush of snow broke through the roof, landing square on his head.

Covering my mouth to keep from laughing, I watched him brush snow from his hair, glaring at the beam of sunlight streaming through the roof.

"I really ought to burn the whole thing down," he growled, then his green eyes flicked to mine. "Enough laughter, Born-in-Fire. I'll fix it today."

"Animals first." I reached for my dress, no longer trying to curb my laughter. "Else they'll burst in the door looking for you."

Bjorn sighed, then availed himself of the water in the wash basin before pushing aside the curtain that hid our bed from the main room. I watched him as I washed, noting how he avoided looking at the weapons chest that sat against one wall, my shield, wrapped in cloth, hanging on the wall above it.

Both the weapons chest and shield served as ever-present reminders of our life before. The terror, pain, and suffering that came with them. Danced around but never acknowledged. The life we had given up because it had cost us both too much and we'd feared it would eventually cost us each other.

Outside, I heard the squeal of a child and the admonishments of a woman, and Bjorn said, "Ingrid is here. I must escape before she sees me."

Taking up the heel of the bread I'd made yesterday, he bent down to kiss me, but before he could escape out the front, the door opened. Ingrid looked him up and down. "Your goats are much abused, Bjorn."

"The goats understand it is for the greater good of keeping my wife well serviced."

Ingrid snorted, but Bjorn only ruffled my nephew's hair as the baby crawled past, then escaped before Ingrid could respond with more words.

My friend rolled her eyes. "It is amazing you two don't starve to death, for you spend more time abed than any two people I've ever met."

"It is not always the bed." I picked up my nephew and kissed his blond hair, my brother's sweet boy wrapping his arms around my neck as I walked to the window to watch Bjorn.

Ingrid held up her hands. "I do not need the details." Her eyes flicked to the roof. "You need to fix that."

I made a soft humming sound of agreement, hugging the baby and watching Bjorn feed the horses. There was a restless energy about him that I could sense from here. Because I felt it, too, even as I absently listened to Ingrid's chatter about gossip in Selvegr.

"Freya?"

I turned to find Ingrid watching me. "Hmm?"

"Are you well?"

Making a face, I set Erik on the ground, the boy crawling immediately to the weapons chest, which he tried and failed to open. "Of course I'm well."

"I mean, are you content?"

"Yes." The word was oddly difficult to say, and I turned away from her scrutiny because I did not care to consider why that was.

Ingrid did not speak, but out of the corner of my eye, I saw her take my shield down from the hook on the wall, then remove its covering. The silver metal was bright as ever, gleaming in the early light. "It is a quiet life you live now," she remarked. "You are not meant for a quiet life, Freya. Neither is Bjorn."

"We fought for this life." My hands fisted. "Fought to live in peace. Of course we are content."

Ingrid traced a finger around the edge of my shield, watching her son trying to open the chest full of weapons and chain mail and fighting leathers, all carefully packed. "Then why don't you rid yourself of these things? Sell them for items your home needs."

"We might have need of them. Violence comes looking for even those who hide from it." Not wanting to discuss the subject anymore, I asked, "How is Taric?"

The answer was always the same, because Taric was as constant as the sun rising in the east. Born from one of the southern nations, he'd fallen in love with the mountains and fjords of Skaland. A farmer by trade, he had not a violent bone in his body and he'd stepped into the void left by my brother's death, giving Ingrid and my nephew the certainty they needed. A better man I could not have chosen for them. Geir would have approved.

"He's well. When I tell him of your roof, he is sure to come and aid Bjorn in the repair."

My eyes were on my husband, who stood in the yard staring into the distance while the chickens pecked around him.

Are you content? I silently asked him.

Am I?

Bjorn lifted his head, and a heartbeat later, I heard the pounding of galloping hooves. A rider galloped into the yard, skidding to a stop before Bjorn. Curious, I left the house. Ingrid followed after me with Erik in her arms. As I approached, I heard the rider, who was just a boy, call out, "The jarl has called all warriors to arms!"

"What has happened?" I asked.

"Raiders from the south. They're attacking villages along the coast."

My heart skipped, then raced. "Leif aims to fight them, then?"

Though I knew the blood oath that had bound me was broken, I still felt the sudden urge to reach for a weapon.

"Yes." The boy took hold of the seax belted at his waist. "He calls to arms anyone who can fight."

Bjorn's gaze flicked to me, then he shrugged. "My brother knows my answer. Unless conflict arrives on my land, I am through with fighting."

Even as he said the words, I saw fire flicker in his hand, then disappear. My breath came faster as I asked, "Is it dire?"

"Many dead. The jarl begs that you come."

"No," Bjorn muttered, even as I said, "We could at least go to Grindill and discover what has happened."

Silence stretched, then Bjorn sighed. "Perhaps you are right. We should at least have a look at what they are up against."

"And bring supplies," I added. "Raiders burn what they don't take."

He nodded. "We'll listen to what my brother has to say, then return home."

"Not more than a day or two." I turned to Ingrid. "Would you and Taric mind the animals?"

"Of course." There was a faint smile on her lips. "And see to the roof for when you return."

"It would not be more than a week," I said, Bjorn adding, "A fortnight at most, if my brother needs someone to watch over Grindill while he puts a stop to the raiders."

"It is no trouble." Ingrid jerked her chin at the boy. "Tell the jarl they'll be along, yes."

He nodded and wheeled his horse, galloping back the way he had come.

"You two shouldn't linger," Ingrid said. "I'll see to the animals."

My eyes met Bjorn's, a familiar thrill running through my veins as we started walking to our home. Inside we went to the chest, standing before it together.

"We should probably go prepared, just in case." A smile rose to my lips because Bjorn was already opening the lid, the smell of leather and steel drifting out. I swiftly changed into fighting leathers, weaving my hair into a braid before donning my mail vest, remembering how I'd sworn I'd never wear it again. My father's sword, retrieved from the river through Bjorn's efforts, was a familiar weight as I added it to my belt next to Gyda's seax, my shield still light as a feather slung over my shoulder. Like old friends from whom I'd been too long parted.

Neither of us said anything as we went back outside, though it was to find Ingrid holding the reins of both our horses, which she had saddled while my nephew terrorized the chickens. "You should hurry," she said. "Much can happen in a short time."

I gave her a wry look. "We are only going out of loyalty to Leif. We'll be back."

"The goats will be waiting with bated breath for Bjorn's dedicated care, I'm sure." She handed off the reins to us.

I mounted my mare. Walking her down the road, I settled into the familiar weight of attire I thought I'd never wear again. Bjorn rode alongside me, quiet at first, and then he said, "We didn't bring extra supplies."

"No, we didn't."

"We're not going to guard Grindill in Leif's absence, are we?"

"No." I met his gaze. "It seems I don't want a quiet life, Bjorn. I want more, even though I know that more comes with hardship." It was hard to keep my voice steady, because I felt afraid to admit it. Afraid to ask for what was burning in my heart, because it had been I who had turned my back on fighting. "But if you don't want this, we can turn around."

A slow smirk rose on my husband's face, and his axe materialized in his hand, heat wafting over me. "I go where you go, Born-in-Fire. Even if it's to the gates of Valhalla."

Blood surged in my veins, anticipation hot in my heart. Because this was what we were born to do. To risk life and limb and love to defend Skaland. If there was a call to war, we would answer it.

It was the fate we wanted. The fate we would weave together.

Digging in my heels, I drove my horse to a gallop. "I'll race you there!"

ACKNOWLEDGMENTS

A huge thank-you to my family for their support while I wrote Saga of the Unfated. I know that the late nights writing and the long days on the road are a challenge for us all, and I am so grateful for how you all held our world together while I was immersed in fantasy realms.

A huge thanks to Emily for your passion and support of this novel. I know we both worked into the midnight hours more than once to get this one to the finish line, and I appreciate your diligence and tenacity. Likewise, thank you to everyone who makes up Team Del Rey and Team Del Rey UK! The entire journey we've had together for this pair of novels has been a dream, and so much of that is because of the incredible amount of effort and enthusiasm of everyone involved.

Tamar, there are not enough words in the English language to convey how much I appreciate you as both an agent and a friend, but thank you for all your efforts on this one! Celsie, thank you for your final-hour aid in hunting down those last few typos, as well as keeping me on schedule through what has been a *very* busy year. Amy, your love for Freya and Bjorn kept me from tossing my laptop out the window more than once—thank you for everything you do for me.

Elise, I am endlessly grateful for always having you at my back, and I can't wait to do all the bookish events with you in the coming years. My ladies of NOFFA—you are the best and most supportive writers' group I could ask for, so never change!

Last, but not least, I am truly blessed to have one of the kindest and most supportive readerships out there. Having the opportunity to meet so many of you face-to-face has been an absolute dream, and I treasure every moment. I can't wait to meet even more of you as *A Curse Carved in Bone* hits shelves.

DANIELLE L. JENSEN is the #1 *New York Times* bestselling author of *A Fate Inked in Blood, A Curse Carved in Bone,* and the Bridge Kingdom, Dark Shores, and Malediction series. Her novels are published internationally in twenty-two languages. She lives in Calgary, Alberta, with her family and guinea pigs.

danielleljensen.com
TikTok: @daniellelynnjensen
Facebook.com/authordanielleljensen
Instagram: @danielleljensen